Communication Failure

"Fine," Rogers said. "Fine. Mr. Guff, if you would please sit down right there and tell me what these people are trying to say."

Guff ambled over to a chair, a cloud of nauseating stench following him that reminded Rogers of the inside of some of the less reputable bars on Merida Prime. He sat down and fell asleep.

"Hey!" Rogers said. "Someone wake him up and give him a glass of water or something."

Someone woke him up and gave him a glass of water.

"Eh? What?"

"The semaphore, Ernie," Rogers said.

Guff looked out the window, and for a moment Rogers thought he was falling asleep again. Then he started to speak.

"It's just letters. They keep repeating the same three over and over again."

Rogers waited while the old man looked very intently at the viewscreen and started to translate the strange flag dance.

"'W.'"

A pause.

"'T.'"

Another pause.

"'F.'"

A long pause.

"Yep," Rogers said. "Definitely trying to communicate."

BY JOE ZIEJA

Epic Failure Trilogy
Mechanical Failure
Communication Failure

EPIC FAILURE TRILOGY
BOOK II

Communication Failure

JOE ZIEJA

SAGA PRESS

LONDON SYDNEY NEW YORK TORONTO NEW DELHI

SAGA PRESS

AN IMPRINT OF SIMON & SCHUSTER, INC.

1230 AVENUE OF THE AMERICAS, NEW YORK, NEW YORK 10020

SAGA PRESS and colophon are trademarks of Simon & Schuster, Inc.
For information about special discounts for bulk purchases, please contact Simon & Schuster Special Sales at 1-866-506-1949 or business@simonandschuster.com.
The Simon & Schuster Speakers Bureau can bring authors to your live event. For more information or to book an event, contact the Simon & Schuster Speakers Bureau at 1-866-248-3049 or visit our website at www.simonspeakers.com.
Also available in a SAGA PRESS paperback edition
The text for this book was set in ITC New Baskerville Std.
Manufactured in the United States of America
First SAGA PRESS hardcover edition November 2017
2 4 6 8 10 9 7 5 3 1
Library of Congress Cataloging-in-Publication Data
Names: Zieja, Joseph, author.
Title: Communication failure / Joe Zieja.
Description: First Saga Press hardcover edition | New York, NY : SAGA PRESS, 2017. | Series: Epic failure ; Book two
Identifiers: LCCN 2017007758 (print) | LCCN 2017007770 (eBook) | ISBN 9781481486910 (hardback) | ISBN 9781481486903 (trade paper) | ISBN 9781481486927 (eBook)
Subjects: LCSH: Science fiction. | War stories. | BISAC: FICTION / Science Fiction / Military. | FICTION / Science Fiction / Space Opera. | FICTION / Science Fiction / Adventure.
Classification: LCC PS3626.I4844 C66 2017 (print) | LCC PS3626.I4844 (eBook) | DDC 813/.6—dc23
LC record available at https://lccn.loc.gov/2017007758

To Mom and Dad. Thank you for the endless opportunities, patience, and support. I couldn't have asked for a better foundation.

We're Invading

Alandra Keffoule's heel whistled through the air before crack-ing into the side of the wooden training dummy, sending splin-ters raining to the floor all around her. The sound was satisfying, calming, soothing. With everything going on at that moment, she could have used any small measure of peace, or at least a couple of differential equations to solve. That always put her mind at ease.

It was no use, though. Not this time. Alandra was far too anx-ious. She'd read the intelligence reports so many times she could see the words floating around in her mind's eye like pieces of a great puzzle. Even the tiniest recollection of what they contained brought a tingle of excitement with it for more than one reason. The ratio. *The ratio.*

The training room, empty except for her and a couple of dis-figured training dummies, seemed to pulsate with excitement, mirroring the tightly bottled emotions she kept inside. This was one of seven hand-to-hand combat training rooms available on the

Thelicosan ship *Limiter*, but she knew almost all of them were unoccupied. In the Thelicosan heyday, these rooms would have been filled with sweat-drenched Thelicosan warriors, frantically shaving away the dummies with kicks and punches as they rhythmically recited multiplication tables. It wasn't so much an important part of their training regimen as it was the only way the mess halls got their toothpicks. The Thelicosan Council had some pretty unique restrictions on what it would send to deployed troops.

Now, however, the training rooms were about as empty as she had felt ever since she'd assumed command of the Colliders, the Thelicosan border fleet. But all that was going to change soon.

The ratio.

Crack. Another fresh batch of toothpicks scattered to the floor, courtesy of Alandra's famous spinning back kick. A tendril of pain worked its way up the hamstring and across the small of her back, and she grimaced. Speaking of heydays, Alandra often felt like she was long past hers. If it hadn't been for that battle injury, she'd still be in the F Sequence. They'd still call her the Tangential Tornado. She'd still be worth something.

Alandra shook the thoughts away, memories of them sewing the big zero on her uniform shattering like a wooden training dummy turning into toothpicks. Those days were behind her; Grand Marshal Alandra Keffoule was above brooding over the past like a child. Now was the time to focus on the future.

The intelligence reports came to her mind again, the detailed descriptions of the Meridan dilemma playing out like a theatrical experience. You could learn a lot about someone from intelligence reports; she'd spent almost all of her special operations career perusing dossiers chock-full of intelligence in order to get to know a target. But she'd never faced a target like this.

One point six one, she thought. *It's impossible.*

So wrapped up in her reverie was she that she barely noticed Secretary Vilia Quinn storming into the room and storming over to her. Quinn's version of storming was walking slightly more quickly than normal, but Alandra knew the signs that the bureaucrat was upset. Quinn was unlike Alandra in almost every way; her skin pale where Alandra's was dark, her features hard and angular where Alandra's were soft, her wits slow where Alandra's were quick and deadly. And unlike electrostatic physics, in this case opposites did not attract.

"I finally found you," Quinn said, even her voice measured and expressionless. When Alandra looked at her with her typical flat stare, Quinn narrowed her eyes. "Well? Don't you have anything to say for yourself?"

Alandra looked at her as calmly as she could manage. Despite her total lack of personality, Secretary Quinn had a knack for making Alandra live on the very edge of self-control.

"Nothing I haven't said already, Quinn, and I do hate repeating myself. You were in the briefing."

In truth, Quinn hadn't been in most of the briefing because Alandra hadn't invited her. Afterward, Alandra had slipped away before the annoying civilian could ask any questions.

Quinn narrowed her icy blue eyes further, to the point where she actually looked like she might be sleeping. Alandra thought she had probably been pretty in her younger days, if she had ever worn anything other than loose-fitting pantsuits that went out of style back on Mars before the solar system collapsed. The bun she wore her hair in was so perfect, so unchanging, that Alandra had heard many whispers that Quinn was bald and wearing a wig. She'd also heard whispers that Quinn's bun was some sort of secret weapon, but that just seemed absurd. Quinn couldn't fight anything other than paperwork.

"I'm talking about flinging billions of credits' worth of *armed* Thelicosan government property into Galactic space," Quinn said, edging closer. "I can't even begin to quote how many Thelicosan military statutes you've violated, not to mention endangering the Two Hundred Years (And Counting) Peace *and* the lives of everyone in the fleet."

Alandra let Quinn go on. Quinn might have worked her way through the Thelicosan government over the last fifteen years, but ever since she'd been assigned as Council ambassador to Alandra's fleet she'd been nothing but a thorn in her side. What Alandra wouldn't give to treat Quinn to one of her famous spinning back kicks . . . but corporal discipline was only acceptable for military personnel, which Quinn was not.

"Once again," Alandra said, cutting Quinn off in the middle of her nonsensical and ill-informed rant, "I'll remind you that while they might have thought you quite the genius in the Schvink local office, you don't know anything about military tactics. There was a clear and present danger to Thelicosan sovereignty, according to the reports transmitted by the late Mr. McSchmidt."

Quinn's eyes opened wide this time. "What in the name of Science are you talking about? Is that what the briefing was about?" The secretary had arrived too late for the initial details. "A clear and present danger? Those reports said their fleet was in total chaos. What threat could the Galactics possibly pose to our sovereignty?"

"Oh please," Alandra said. "The Pythagorean War* was centuries ago; call them Meridans, already."

"Excuse me for adhering to the foreign policy standards of my government," Quinn said, glaring. "Did you even send a message back to the Central Council? Did they approve this action via a report submitted through the Action Committee and then validated by a two-thirds vote before being routed back to the Military Affairs Committee?"

For a response, Alandra created a few more toothpicks.

Quinn gaped. "They didn't, did they? You're acting completely on your own!" She paused for a moment. "I'll bet you didn't even complete Section One Point Four in its entirety. It says clearly in box one that you are to—"

---

* Don't ask.

"I am not acting alone," Alandra said. "Commodore Zergan and I talked this over very thoroughly and reviewed the intelligence with our top analysts before making a decision. We felt very strongly that, despite the Council's admonition, it was clear they didn't understand the situation at hand. That is why we are conducting a show of force. Intelligence shows that we would easily be able to overwhelm the Meridans, and a simple posturing by our forces would inspire them to negotiate."

A small measure of confusion passed across Quinn's face. She looked down at a datapad she'd been holding and shook her head in what might have been disbelief.

"Negotiation? Who said anything about negotiation? You're declaring *war*!"

Alandra stopped kicking the dummy and turned fully to Quinn, a tiny bubble of anxiety rising to the surface of her mind. Why would she want to start a war? A war—at least one initiated by her—would achieve the exact opposite of her aims.

"What are you talking about?" she said, trying to keep her tone neutral.

"Are you that dense that you can't even remember your own orders? Commodore Zergan"—Quinn spat the man's name like a curse—"just showed me the message you sent after we popped out of Un-Space in the middle of 'Meridan' territory."

Striding forward, Alandra snatched the datapad out of Quinn's hands. "Let me see that," she barked.

Underneath a complicated chain of directional commands and routing information, there were only two words on the datapad.

"'We're invading'?" Alandra said out loud. "'We're *invading*.' That's the message they sent?"

Quinn stared for a moment. "That's not the message you told them to send?"

Without answering, Alandra shoved the datapad back into Quinn's frail, girlish arms, getting at least the satisfaction of making her stumble even if she couldn't kick her in the face, and stormed out of the room.

The training room opened into a high-ceilinged, octagonal pod of deep metallic gray, six other doors leading to the other training rooms. To her surprise, some troops were filing into one of them, dressed in their loose-fitting PT uniforms and looking excited. One of them caught sight of her and gave her a two-fingered salute, his fingertips pointed down to make his hand a rough approximation of the symbol for pi.

Alandra nodded, not wanting to show her surprise at anyone actually doing combat training, and returned the salute. Instead of asking the troops what they were doing—to be an effective leader, it was important to always project power and almost never ask any questions—she turned to where her personal assistant waited by her Chariot, a highly advanced hovering platform with the capability to zip through the *Limiter*'s tube transportation system.

Stepping onto the platform, she hoped her face wasn't showing any of the mess of excitement and worry that was quickly building up inside.

"Xan," she said softly. "What are they doing?"

Xan Tiu, her personal assistant and possibly the only man on the ship other than Zergan she truly trusted to be competent, looked expressionlessly over at the soldiers and gave an almost imperceptible shrug. His pale face, stretched long by years of secretary work and the fact that he wore ceremonial Newtonian face-weights attached to his cheeks, slowly swung back to Alandra.

"Preparing for war," Xan said. "Though I may be misinterpreting. They did all run in screaming 'We're going to war, we're going to war.'"

Alandra clenched her teeth and grabbed on to the handrails of the Chariot. "Bridge. Now."

"Yes, Grand Marshal." Xan took the controls of the Chariot and smoothly jumped into the Chariot lane. The personal transportation system was only accessible to commanders and higher-ranking officials on the *Limiter*; the rest of the personnel had to use a complicated system of elevators and walkways that made moving about the *Limiter* a bit of a chore. Alandra's ship was one of the older ones in the Thelicosan fleet, and the transportation system was just one of the ways it showed.

They entered one of the Circus Tubes, thin, opaque passageways meant specifically for Chariots, and Xan hit the accelerator. Soon they were coursing through the veins of the *Limiter* like a red blood cell. Xan, as usual, remained quiet, which gave Alandra a good opportunity to figure out what she was going to do when she got to the bridge. Whoever had screwed up the message could have just ruined everything.

By the time they arrived at the bridge, Alandra *still* had no idea what she was going to do. That flustered her more than anything, and being flustered flustered her even more. She wasn't used to being flustered. She wasn't used to making mistakes.

You didn't make a mistake, she thought. *Someone else made a mistake. You're not to blame. You can deal with this.*

She was a descendant of the most powerful, rugged, and vicious scientists ever to rove the old solar system. Thelicosan pride demanded that she approach this using the scientific method, and that began with asking a question and making observations. It wouldn't do to panic before she'd even developed a hypothesis.

Right now, however, she was hypothesizing that she would panic.

But she had no more time to think. The Chariot slowed as it reached the exit point of the Circus Tube, and it was time to face her troops. Xan reached out and punched in the code to get to the bridge, and the circular door spun outward as the Chariot automatically went through its docking procedure.

Still dressed in her sweats, Alandra did her best to make herself look professional and authoritative, which was difficult after a workout. Her muscular, olive-skinned arms poked out of the loose-fitting standard-issue Thelicosan PT uniform, cut too big for her form. She set her shoulders back, making herself look as big and serious as a short woman with insanely curly and sweaty hair could.

The bridge of the *Limiter*, situated on the top of the ship, was encapsulated in a spherical bulb suspended by a series of metallic structures and elevator shafts that connected the command post to the rest of the ship. An interesting system, but another way the *Limiter* showed its age. In the wars preceding the Two Hundred Years (And Counting) Peace, a common tactic was to simply ram something into the support structure of the bridge, disconnecting it from the rest of the ship. Newer command ships had abandoned the ridiculous design for something that was a bit more functional and had a lesser propensity to launch the command crew into space.

The view from the old bridge structure, however, couldn't be beat. It was far enough above the rest of the ship that it gave a clear panorama of the *Limiter* in all its glory and allowed anyone on the bridge to see some of the other ships in the Colliders as well. It might not be the Thelicosan heyday anymore, but the sight of all that metal in outer space still gave Alandra goose bumps.

This time, however, the thing giving her goose bumps had nothing to do with her own fleet. Inside visual range was the Meridan 331st ATBG. Rogers' fleet. *Captain* Rogers' fleet. Looking at the 331st, however, she couldn't help but notice that their typical rainbow-like defensive formation had been scattered a bit. The ships looked almost like they were floating aimlessly in space, but that didn't hinder her ability to ascertain their strength. By count, Alandra's fleet was exactly 1.61 percent larger than Rogers'. That thought almost made her melt.

When her deputy, Commodore Zergan, saw her enter, he turned and offered a sharp pi-shaped salute.

"As the Grand Marshal approaches!" Commodore Zergan shouted.

"The *Limiter* is limitless!" answered the rest of the personnel on the bridge.

Alandra's stomach sank as she heard the ceremonial call and response. She could feel in the air that her worst fears had been realized. The shout had an electric excitement behind it, the kind of giddy tension that only the scent of battle could create. Not a good sign.

"Everyone carry on," she said as the Chariot automatically docked with the command platform in the center, a high-backed chair rising out of a hatch in the floor. She settled into it like a proton finding an electron.

Commodore Edris Zergan sat on his own small circular platform looking like the cock of the walk. The grin on his square, flat face was almost intolerably arrogant as he looked at her, his smoky brown eyes set below two eyebrows so bushy they belonged on a puppet. Other people might find him awkward-looking, but after working with him for so long, Alandra couldn't help but find his appearance strangely endearing—not a term she used for just anyone.

Calm, Alandra thought. *Easy. You are in control. Do not show fear.*

She extended a finger and beckoned Zergan to attend her. His grin widened and he made the short trip over to her command platform.

"Grand Marshal," he said, "this is a glorious day for Thelicosa. The Tangential Tornado, leading us back into Galactic dominance!" He laughed, then leaned in to speak a bit more quietly. "I'm glad you saw things a little more my way. I thought you'd gone soft."

By "my way," Zergan was likely referring to his own overly aggressive plan for countering the Meridan threat. The moment he'd heard there was even an inkling of trouble, Zergan was ready to call the entire Thelicosan Navy down on the 331st and crush them to dust—but Zergan had always been like that. Even when they'd been in the F Sequence together, he'd been the first one to kick down the door or divide by zero.

In secret talks, Alandra and Zergan had reached a consensus on a nonaggressive course of action. In truth, Zergan had persuaded Alandra to act, even though, as Quinn had suggested, the intelligence hadn't been very firm. Or very coherent. Mr. McSchmidt—may his equation be forever balanced—had been a terrible spy, despite the fact that he'd given Alandra a lovely window through which to view Captain Rogers.

Alandra didn't respond directly. She looked around the bridge for the young communications officer she'd assigned to send the message when they'd exited Un-Space. He sat at his station, his cheek and temple bruised from the last time he'd disappointed her, and looked back at her nervously.

"You," she said, pointing at him when she caught his eye. "Leftennant Faraz. Here. Now."

The leftennant came with enthusiastic alacrity. At least, he did after Alandra shouted his name three more times. What was wrong with him? She'd only kicked him in the head once. He'd only disappointed her once.

"Yes, Grand Marshal?"

"Can you repeat back to me the words I asked you to send to the commander of the Meridan fleet?"

Faraz looked at her sideways for a moment, his bottom lip trembling a little bit. Any small amount of military bearing he was maintaining was belied by the hunch in his back and the way he shuffled his feet. And the fact that he was quietly sobbing.

"Ma'am," he said, "I don't understand how you want me to feed the birds some random feet."

Alandra's eyes narrowed, her voice growing louder. "I told you to *repeat* the *words* I asked you to *send* to the *commander of the Meridan fleet!*"

Faraz, in a gesture that Alandra found very disrespectful,

turned his face partially away from her, hiding the bruised portion. Maybe he thought it would only remind her of his previous failures. For some reason, he was nodding now.

"Oh, yes, ma'am," he said, his head moving almost spasmodically. "Absolutely. I can. You told me to tell them 'we're invading.' And that's what I said, ma'am. I said it exactly like you said. Just like you said to say it. I said it." He swallowed, then tilted his head, squinting. "What is that ringing? Do you hear ringing? I've been picking up my datapad all day, but nobody is on the other end. I think someone is prank-calling me."

Alandra took a deep breath. She let it out slowly, making a sound like a snake, hissing through her teeth. Her hands trembled as they clutched the armrests of her commander's chair.

Then she sprang up and started shouting instructions.

"Call back the Strikers," she barked. "Tell all the Battle Spiders to start an immediate weapons cooldown procedure."

"But Grand Marshal," Zergan said, his face confused. "What are you doing? You can't just tell the Battle Spiders to fire and then pull out at the last second. It ruins the their attack coils." He grimaced. "I hear it's also very painful."

"If they have to discharge, have them discharge into empty space," Alandra said with a wave of her hand. "Get the fighter screen back into patrol position."

Leftennant Faraz was slowly slinking away.

"You!" Alandra said, making sure she was loud enough to be heard and understood. "Stay where you are."

He started sobbing again, which was really starting to annoy her. Communications officers didn't sob. Thelicosans didn't sob. They were tough, relentless, resilient descendants of the hardened scientists who had been the first to colonize the rough, unforgiving terrain of old Mars. If you made a mistake, you acknowledged it, internalized it, then took the punishment and moved on. Then you made sure never to make another one or you would get kicked in the face by Alandra.

"I want radio silence immediately!" she shouted. "Set up a wide-frequency jamming net. No communications are authorized unless they go through me."

"That's already been done, Grand Marshal," Zergan said, some of his confusion fading into pride. "I gave the order as soon as we came out of Un-Space. The Strikers took out some of their comm relays, and the jamming equipment will do the rest."

So shots had already been fired. Alandra was too late. Still, she could salvage this, somehow. Or at least prevent it from getting any worse. Thankfully Meridan comm relays weren't manned, or she'd have blood on her hands already.

"Good," she said. "Good. I don't want the Meridans talking to anyone until we have a chance to clear this up."

"Clear this up?" Zergan said. His face had been alternating so quickly between utter confusion and triumphant zeal that one of his cheeks was now rapidly moving up and down of its own accord. It made the dark caterpillar of his eyebrows look as though it was doing a mating dance. "I thought you were going to crush these worms. Or at least negotiate a humiliating surrender after they'd had a chance to taste our overwhelming force. What is there to clear up?"

Alandra tapped her fingers on the armrest. How could she fix this?

"Send a message to Captain Rogers," she said. "I want it to—"

"We can't send a message to Captain Rogers," Leftennant Faraz said, his face still turned to the side for some reason. "All their communications are down. Commodore Zergan's jamming net is very thorough. Even if we sent a message, they wouldn't get it."

A few deep breaths later, Alandra finally got control of herself to look at Zergan.

"Don't you think that was a bit much?" she asked.

"No!" Zergan said, throwing his hands up in the air. "This is war! How is anything too much? Grand Marshal Keffoule, what is going on here? I thought we had a plan."

"We did," Alandra said. "And I didn't alter it."

Zergan's eyes widened as he began to understand.

"Leftennant!" Alandra said loudly. "Are you certain that was the message I gave you?"

Faraz looked at her full-on now, his eyebrows turned down in confusion. "Yes, ma'am, I have eaten lunch."

Alandra blinked, then repeated herself.

"Oh—oh," Faraz stammered. "Yes, of course. Exactly."

"It's not."

"It's not?" Faraz said, his voice cracking slightly.

"No. What I told you to tell the Meridan commander was 'We're *inviting* you to a discussion aboard a neutral trade ship.'"

"Right," Faraz said, nodding. "'We're invading.' That's what I told them. Really, does no one else hear the ringing?" He looked around the bridge helplessly, hoping someone else would validate his hearing deficiency. His face sank when he undoubtedly realized that everyone in the bridge had gradually quieted down; the entire crew looked at him with something between horror and sympathy.

Alandra stood up.

"Oh," Faraz said at a whisper. "Oh, oh no."

Alandra ignored him. She was too busy looking at the little leftennant who had completely screwed up her plans. Perhaps completely screwed up the galaxy. She cursed herself for relying on someone so incompetent. Such an important message should have been sent by her personally, but she'd wanted Captain Rogers to see her as a woman of power. Women of power didn't send their own messages.

"You have failed me," she said simply.

"No," Faraz said, shrinking into himself but, to his credit, not running away. Of course he knew what was coming. The entire bridge knew what was coming. Even Zergan knew to back up and wait patiently while Alandra corrected imperfections.

And there was only one way to correct imperfections. Pivoting on her left foot, she gave Leftennant Faraz a spinning back kick to the face.

Every person on the bridge recoiled, the resounding *crack* echoing seemingly forever in the semispherical chamber. Faraz spun fully around, tumbling over the back of a support rail and crashing atop one of the consoles. Whatever he connected with set off an alarm, all the lights on the bridge going a dull amber as sirens blared. Faraz rolled off the console, knocking whoever was working that console to the ground. The two troops tangled in each other for a moment before Faraz, surprising nearly everyone, jumped to his feet, looking a little manic for someone who had just been kicked in the face. Adrenaline could do strange things to people.

"What?" he shouted. "Who? Where am I?" He put a hand on his cheek. "Where is my face?"

"Someone turn off that alarm!" Alandra shouted.

Faraz, who had been staring at her lips intently, raised an eyebrow. "What alarm?" he shouted.

Luckily the troop who had been manning the console before being floored by a flying leftennant managed to get to his feet and press a couple of buttons. The alarm stopped.

"That was a drill," he said into the public-address system. "All units stand down. Repeat, all units stand down."

"Who is Stan Brown?" Faraz shouted, spinning around dizzily. The side of his face that was not bruised from his previous failure was already starting to swell, to the point where the young leftennant was rapidly turning into some sort of demented squirrel with a face infection.

"Get him out of here," Alandra said, sitting back down in her chair. Her stomach felt like it was doing flips, her blood pounding in her ears. What was supposed to be the beginning of her renewed rise to power had instead begun with chaos and face-kicking. "And everyone get back to work!"

As a pair of women dragged the confused, rapidly fading Faraz out of the room, Zergan, seeing that Alandra's time of disciplining had ended, approached her again. He spoke low enough in her ear that he was able to address her with the familiarity they had become used to over the last fifteen years of their careers together.

"Now do you want to tell me what-the-fundamental-frequency is going on?" he asked. "What is all this about inviting the Meridans to tea and then deciding to invade instead? Have you lost your mind?" He paused. "You didn't . . . you know . . . again . . . did you?"

"No," Alandra said, shooting him a cold glare. "I did not." She paused, thinking. "This is a mess, Edris. We'll have to improvise."

Zergan folded his arms, grinning. "I like improvising."

"I know you do," Alandra said, though she was sure they had different ideas on how to go about it.

"Well, we're already here, and we're already in an aggressive stance. Why not invite them to a meeting, then blow up the ship? Cut the head off the snake." He leaned in even closer, whispering conspiratorially. "They'd *have* to reinstate you then, Alandra."

Alandra sighed. Faithful—if a bit bloodthirsty—Edris Zergan. A distant part of her wanted to reach out and touch his face, but those days had long since passed. All she felt now was guilt and shame.

"We'd never get the Council to buy off on it," she said. She almost felt like pouting, which was very unlike her. There was, of course, another reason why she didn't want to just blow up Captain Rogers, but she hadn't been able to confess it to Zergan quite yet. Those intelligence reports . . . *the ratio.*

"That didn't stop you the first time!" A shrill voice came from the entrance to the bridge. Secretary Quinn was walking in, her face showing that same expression of disapproval mixed with anger. She stormed up to the bridge—she was probably the only person in the Colliders who had the guts to storm anywhere near Alandra—and stood, alternating her glares between Alandra and Zergan.

"What's this about blowing up neutral ships? Now you're not only violating intergalactic treaties, you're violating the laws of armed conflict?"

Zergan sneered at her. "Are you afraid our enemies might get a boo-boo, Council dog?"

"I'm afraid of our galaxy imploding because of an itchy trigger finger," Quinn said. She turned to Alandra, ignoring Zergan completely. "What are you going to do now? Start blowing up trade ships?"

"For once," Zergan said, "I'm interested in the same thing the Council dog is. What's next, Grand Marshal?"

Alandra drummed her fingers on the chair. The truth was, she had no idea. They couldn't communicate with the Meridans; any opening in the net would allow them to get a message back to their headquarters. They couldn't attack and start boarding ships without escalating things. Miraculously, the Meridans hadn't yet responded to their strikes on the communications relays, but that didn't mean they weren't standing on a very narrow precipice over the cavernous ravine of a messy war.

"For now," Alandra said, settling back into her chair, "we think. And wait."

If there was anyone in this galaxy who could figure out what to do in this situation, it was Captain R. Wilson Rogers.

They're Invading

Rogers had absolutely no idea what to do in this situation.

"No," Deet said, his makeshift robotic body partially hidden by the other droid he was examining. "You can't just take an entire fleet of ships and run away."

"Why not?" Rogers asked. He knew he was supposed to be paying attention to the huge number of reports coming across his datapad, but he couldn't tear his eyes away from the massive, shiny, deadly array of enemy ships that had come out of Un-Space. Thelicosans. Here. In Meridan territory.

"For one," Deet said, "they're blocking the Un-Space point. Unless you're going to ram them—in which case good luck getting volunteers to sacrifice themselves for the good of the 331st— there's no way you're getting through."

Rogers fell back into the commander's chair on the bridge— and promptly bounced off it into the air. The ship's gravity generator hadn't been repaired yet, but Master Sergeant Hart, the engineering chief, had assured him that the parts were in and it'd be done soon. The rest of the personnel were doing a decent job of keeping up appearances, even though a large part of the ship's systems was still down from the battle with the droids.

"What if we tried to hightail it to the next Un-Space point? It's only like . . . a couple million miles away, right?"

Deet stopped examining a decommissioned droid and looked up at Rogers, though there really was no reason for him to be so dramatic about it. His mannerisms were becoming more human-like every day. Rogers wasn't sure which he preferred: the incessant wisecracking of a droid with half a personality or the mechanical function-calling of the automaton masses.

Suddenly the droid that Deet was examining kicked on, its eyes flashing between blue and red.

"CALL FUNCTION [PROTOCOL 162]. OUTPUT STRING: DIE, HUMAN!"

Deet hurriedly shut it off just as Rogers was deciding that he preferred Deet over maniacal robots.

"Still nothing?" Rogers asked.

Deet shook his head and beeped. "No. I can't seem to figure out why no matter how many times we reset their memory banks, they come back wanting to kill everyone on the ship. We'll have to function without the droids for a while until I can un-murderify them."

"That's not a word."

"It is now," Deet said. "Hey, I just created something. Does that make me God?"

Rogers sighed. "No, Deet."

One of Deet's latest forays into human consciousness had been to start asking complicated questions about spirituality, philosophy, God/gods, and chocolate. Rogers wished he'd stuck to trying to figure out metaphors and jokes.

What were the Thelicosans doing? Ever since they'd charged out of Un-Space and blown a couple of comm relays up, they'd just . . . sat there, doing nothing. That really didn't seem like much of an invasion. Rogers had thought about sending a counterattack, but he couldn't talk to anyone else in the fleet to coordinate one. That, and he had absolutely no idea how to conduct a counterattack. He also generally didn't like violence, because it was scary and had emotional complications he wasn't ready to deal with.

In his mind, he was still an ex-sergeant looking for a stiff drink, but with every passing moment he was realizing that maybe that wasn't the best mentality for someone who'd been given temporary command of a giant military fleet and the responsibility for thousands of lives. Being the acting admiral of the 331st Anti-Thelicosan Buffer Group was a lot more complicated than poker.

One of the Thelicosan Battle Spiders—at least he thought it was a Battle Spider; he didn't know the first thing about enemy ships—within visual range of the scanners fired up its engines and made some nondescript maneuvers. Rogers leapt out of his chair—which, even with his gravity boots on, catapulted him into the ceiling.

"They're moving!" he said, pushing off with his hands/face and coming back down to the command platform. "We have to get out of here! Is there a plan for that?" He looked at the recently promoted Commander Belgrave, the helmsman. "Initiate Operation SAVE OUR ASSES immediately!"

Belgrave, a dispassionate man for someone of so high a rank, looked at Rogers with something between concern and disappointment. "Um, no, sir, there's no such operation. We're still cleaning up the damage the droids did to the ship's systems; it's still hard to maneuver."

Damn those droids! He'd spent the entirety of his second stint in the military hiding from them and making every attempt to avoid confrontation. Even though he'd recklessly crashed his most valuable possession—his personal ship—into the *Flagship*'s gravity generator to stop them from killing everyone aboard, they were still causing him problems. The damn robots had spent so long putting themselves in important positions that without them, the 331st was almost completely worthless. The cargo manifests were so screwed up that nobody really knew what was on the ship anymore, the intraship transportation system kept dropping people off near the refuse deck, and absolutely *nobody* had gotten a haircut.

Sitting back down in his chair, Rogers immediately jumped up again, grabbing the handrail this time.

"Look!" he said, pointing to a blip on the defensive systems display. "Look!"

"Sir," the defensive technician said. "Please, calm down. That's the toaster. My bagel is ready." She plucked the bagel out and buttered it, taking a large bite before continuing. "The THEY'RE ATTACKING US light isn't even on. We're safe for the moment. I'll update you the moment I have any indication that we're all going to die."

Rogers sank back into his chair. This was too much up and down. One minute he was sure they were about to be blown to bits, the next it seemed like the Thelicosans were just playing with them. Was this part of a psychological operations plan designed to weaken them for the kill? But that didn't make any sense; they were *already* weakened for the kill.

"CALL FUNCTION [PROTOCOL 162]. OUTPUT STRING: DIE, HUMAN!"

"Damn it, Deet, shut that thing off!" Rogers said. "I can't think straight! Why can't you do this work in the engineering bay where the rest of the scrap is?"

"Sorry," Deet said, cutting the power to the droid. He made a droid's approximation of a sigh, which might be described as a floppy synthesizer noise. "I can't figure this out. It's like they keep reprogramming themselves every time I reset them. I could try rewriting the code from scratch, but I'd need some sort of template to work off."

Rogers waved the comment away. "We've got bigger problems, anyway," he said. "I'm still trying to figure out how to run away from the Thelicosans without getting everyone killed."

Why did Admiral Klein have to fly into that asteroid? The man had been incompetent, yes, but at least he wasn't Rogers. The last thing Rogers wanted right now was to be in charge of anything. He hadn't even had time to restock the *Flagship*'s alcohol supply before this mess went down. Meridan Naval Headquarters had said a replacement admiral was on the way, but Rogers had no idea when he'd get here. And he had no idea how he'd get through the Thelicosan blockade to relieve him.

What a mess. And Rogers was stuck with it.

"Have you considered actually fighting them?" Deet asked as he unplugged from the droid he'd been examining. A second cable attached him to a constant power supply; being a droid, he was unable to move around freely without a gravity generator to help him keep his batteries charged.

Rogers scoffed. "Absolutely not. Do you see the size of that fleet?" He made a grand gesture out the windows. "They'd crush us at the first sign of a plasma blast. We're not fighting them."

Commander Belgrave cleared his throat.

"What?" Rogers said.

"I know you're new to this whole commander-of-the-fleet thing," Belgrave said, "but generally those sort of we've-lost-all-hope comments are made in private. If you're going to continue to be all negative and weird, can I ask, respectfully, sir, that you go do it somewhere else? Your stateroom, perhaps? Some of us are still trying to maintain a delusional level of military superiority, and you're not helping."

Rogers looked at him, feeling a little ashamed. Whether he wanted it or not, he *was* in charge. These people needed him to be a bedrock against the chaos that was coming. Well, the chaos that was already here. "You're right, Commander. I'm sorry."

Belgrave shrugged and pressed a few buttons on his console. Rogers wondered, if they weren't really able to maneuver very well anyway, why Belgrave was at the controls and not sleeping. In fact, now that Rogers thought about it, he'd never seen anyone else at the helm, and had never seen Belgrave eat, sleep, or do anything else except press buttons.

Rogers tapped his fingers on his chair for a moment, shifting in his seat.

"Hypothetically, though," he said slowly. "If I were to tell you to turn the ship around and run away, could you?"

Belgrave gave him a look. "No, sir."

Well, this was stupid. If he couldn't fight, and he couldn't run away, and he couldn't surrender because he couldn't *talk* to anyone, what was he supposed to do?

"I need to take a break," he said, exasperated.

"You've been here for eight and a half minutes," Deet chirped, his head almost completely buried in the chest of the disassembled droid he was working on. "From my careful analysis of Meridan naval regulations, I believe this is approximately one-seventieth of a standard work period."

"Shut up," Rogers said. "I'm going to go talk to someone who might know something about violence."

He pushed his way toward the exit from the bridge. An uncomfortable feeling welled up inside him as he avoided eye contact with everyone, especially Belgrave, who suddenly seemed to be a font of command wisdom and theory. As the door closed behind him, he thought he heard two techs talking about the possibility of the THEY'RE ATTACKING US button being broken.

Putting on his fake arm sling—which he only wore in areas of the ship where someone might be encouraged to salute him—he plodded down the hallway, deep in thought. He'd never wanted this. Not just the war, or the strangely declared invasion, but the responsibility, the duties, the maniacal face-slapping droids. What was an ex-pirate ex-sergeant supposed to do about all this *fighting*?

The ship's transportation system, full of partially floating people and equipment, shuttled him through the belly of the *Flagship* as he contemplated the several ways he was likely going to die soon. It didn't make for a very productive trip down to the medical bay, but it certainly helped pass the time a bit. His downcast, fraught expression also likely discouraged everyone from talking to him, for which he was grateful.

Frantic medical personnel roamed the hallways in the infirmary, all displaying a mixture of exhaustion and panic. It wasn't that there was a huge number of wounded troops or anything. It was just that the most serious things they'd had to deal with in the last two hundred years had been things that marines picked up while on shore leave, like food poisoning, parasites, or gonorrhea. During the attempted droid coup, people had *actually* been shot with *actual* weapons. Everyone was a little unsettled by a military unit that *actually* had to fight.

Rogers wasn't sure why, but when he found the door he was looking for, he stopped for a moment. Suddenly, big, overarching problems like the impending doom of his entire fleet paled in comparison to what was beyond that threshold. A tingle of excitement worked its way through him when he remembered the last time he and the Viking had met. The room ablaze, him trapped under a fallen piece of debris in the control room of the hangar, encased in a Vacuum Mobility Unit. The memory of her kicking down the door, ringed in fire and smoke—it nearly made him pass out.

He realized a few moments later that it had, in fact, made him pass out. Suddenly he was leaning backward at an awkward angle, held to the ground only by his magnetic boots, and a gruff voice was yelling at him.

"What the hell are you doing, metalhead?"

The shock of it caused him to whip upward like the pole in a pole vault.

"You!" he said, which was not what he wanted to say.

"Me," Captain Alsinbury—the Viking—said. "I thought I heard a puppy whine outside my door."

Alsinbury was a monument to the fierce killing power of a

determined woman; Rogers could never really tell if she was about to wind back and hit him in the face or just wind back and hit him in the face slightly more gently. She made no move to help him regain his balance, but she did step back into her room.

"I came to visit you," Rogers said—again, not what he wanted to say. His face was becoming terribly hot.

"I kind of figured that," the Viking said, making a cursory motion—with her uninjured arm, he noticed—for him to step inside.

Peeking in, he saw the clear signs of a wounded marine recuperating from a disruptor shot to the shoulder: body armor, a disassembled disruptor rifle with cleaning supplies around it, and a handful of bent nails scattered across a table.

Rogers realized for the first time that they weren't alone, either. Sitting on a chair and flipping through something on her datapad, the recently promoted Sergeant Cynthia Mailn raised an eyebrow at him and uncrossed her legs.

"Hey," she said.

"What?" Rogers joked. "No jumping to attention and yelling 'sir' and all that? I got promoted like five ranks, you know."

In response, Mailn shrugged and went back to looking at her datapad.

"Damn right," Rogers said, grinning. He was really growing to like the young sergeant, particularly because he absolutely hated being called sir. "What are you doing here?"

Mailn shifted subtly in her chair and put the pad down again. She looked up at Rogers as if to answer, but the Viking beat her to it.

"Helping me not put a hole in the wall every ten minutes," she said. She began messing with the components of the disruptor rifle in a way that did strange things to Rogers' insides. "Someone *else* has been too busy on the bridge with all the brass."

"Hey!" Rogers said. "I'm not brass. I'm barely copper." He'd barely been a lieutenant a few weeks ago.

For some reason, Mailn gave him a long look, slowly shaking her head. Had he missed something?

"Yeah, well," the Viking said. "It's quiet down here." Her hands were moving so fast over the rifle, it was almost impossible to tell what she was doing. Rogers found himself mesmerized as he watched her work. What he wouldn't give to be that rifle right now . . .

"How's the arm?" he asked.

"It's fine," the Viking said. "I keep telling these idiots it's fine, and they keep feeding me some bull about 'cellular regeneration fragility' or something like that. I want to get back to my marines, especially if there's a Thelly fleet sitting out there."

"About that," Rogers said. "I need your advice."

The Viking stopped what she was doing and looked at him in a strange way. It was almost like she was raising an eyebrow, but also grinning maniacally, but also about to impart violence. It wasn't exactly unattractive.

"Oh?" she said. "Not looking to strap on a VMU and jump out the garbage chute?"

Rogers felt his face turning red. "That was only once," he said.

"So far," Sergeant Mailn said, not looking up from her datapad.

Rogers ignored her. "I don't know what to do here. I don't know how to fight. I honestly don't even know what end of the gun to point at someone trying to kill me." He sighed. Boy, he felt tired. "I thought maybe you'd have another perspective."

The Viking didn't answer for a moment, but she didn't start putting her disruptor rifle back together, either. Rogers thought about mentioning the safety concerns of field-stripping a weapon in the middle of the infirmary, but something—perhaps repeated memories of being hit by this woman—stopped him from saying anything. Eventually, the Viking made her way back over to her bed, where she sat, the hospital gown flowing around her. It was the closest thing to a dress he'd ever seen the marine in.

"Listen, metalhead," she began.

"You do realize that I was the main reason the droids *didn't* take over the ship, right?"

The Viking went on. "You gotta realize something. The Two Hundred Years (And Counting) Peace isn't exactly the best time for warriors to get experience in pitched battles."

Rogers frowned. For some reason, the Viking seemed to be very uncomfortable.

"So?" Rogers said, pulling a rolling desk chair—which was actually a floating desk chair, without the gravity—across the room and sort of, kind of sitting down. Boy, he hoped Hart got the gravity generator fixed soon. "Haven't you done pirate interdictions, or at least simulations?"

Shrugging, the Viking lay back in the bed, using the railings to push herself down. "I've busted a few skulls, sure. And officer school had plenty of simulations. But do you have any idea what the training budget has been like the last two hundred years?"

Rogers nodded sagely. He had absolutely no idea what the training budget had been like the last two hundred years.

"Right," the Viking said. "You want me to get on a transport full of marines and board an enemy ship? Let's do it. You want me to plan a war?"

She shrugged, possibly the first helpless gesture Rogers had ever seen her make. It made him feel like he should comfort her, which was a completely different level of strange.

For some reason, Rogers expected her to continue, but she didn't. She lay there, looking at the ceiling, while Mailn flipped through whatever it was she was reading on her datapad. Rogers had never seen the two women quieter.

"Well," he said, standing up and allowing his magnetic boots to connect with the floor. "I tried. I'm going to go try to surrender now."

"Hey," the Viking said, sitting forward. "Just because I don't know how to plan fleet maneuvers doesn't mean I'm going to go in there with my hands up and my pants around my ankles."

Rogers paused, swallowing. "Are you *sure* you wouldn't do that?"

The Viking swung her legs over the side of the bed and latched on to the ground with her own boots—a very strange accent to the hospital gown.

"You listen to me," she said, her demeanor changing rapidly. Rogers could never tell if he liked her more when she was really angry, or just angry. "I didn't come all the way out here to end up a prisoner in a Thelicosan algebra colony."

"What the hell is an algebra colony?"

"You don't want to know," Mailn chimed in.

"No, I actually, really do," Rogers said, but he didn't get an answer. The Viking was too busy barreling toward him to answer, and for a moment he thought she was about to tackle him and knock him senseless.

When the datapad beeped, telling him he had an incoming call, he wasn't sure if he was angry or relieved about being interrupted. According to the display, the bridge was calling.

"What?" he barked as he answered.

"Are you coming back up here?" It was Deet's voice. "We're getting some reports in that someone like, you know, the commander of the fleet might want to listen to."

"He's too busy trying to figure out how to get us all interned in algebra colonies!" the Viking shouted.

"It's not like that," Rogers said softly, covering the mouthpiece of the datapad. "It has nothing to do with not wanting to fight. I just don't want to *die*. I'm in charge of this fleet, after all, aren't I?" He paused. "I really need someone to tell me what an algebra colony is."

"Then maybe it's about time you started acting like a commander," the Viking said. "We have other options."

Rogers shook his head. "No, we don't. We have no options at all. We're sitting ducks in the middle of open space, millions of miles from Merida Prime. Even if we were able to talk to anyone, reinforcements would take half a year to get here, since they're blocking the Un-Space point. What kind of options are those?"

Someone on the other end of the datapad clicked a tongue, and Commander Belgrave's voice came through the speaker. "Really, sir, what did I just tell you about disparaging talk on the bridge? You might as well have Munkle over here announce it to the entire ship."

"Grr mrr," Lieutenant Lieutenant Munkle said somewhere in the background.

"What difference would that make?" Rogers asked into the datapad. Munkle could tell everyone they were about to fly into a black hole and nothing would happen. As a member of the Public Transportation Announcer Corps, he'd been hired specifically for his unintelligibility. He used to be the intelligence officer until Rogers moved him and, well, put a Thelicosan spy in his place. Rogers already didn't have a great track record for administrative issues.

The Viking shook her head. "I said you had options. Why would I say you had options if you didn't?"

Rogers sighed, shaking his head. "What 'options' are you thinking of? Pack a ship full of grunts and fly them into glorious battle to smash heads, and all that?"

The Viking gave him a look, and Rogers' breath caught in his throat. Why had he said that? He wasn't usually so bitter—especially not to the woman of his dreams, with whom he had barely managed to have a civil conversation—but the stress of the last month or so was really starting to get to him.

He shook his head. "I'm sorry. I just don't know what to do. I have absolutely no idea what I'm doing up here."

"Again," Commander Belgrave's voice came through, "you're really not doing a great deal to inspire confidence when you say things like that."

"So shut the damn speakers off!" Rogers said. "I'm just being honest."

"Commanders never got anywhere by being honest," Belgrave muttered.

Rogers grunted. Admiral Klein certainly hadn't been honest. He'd spent his entire career hiding the fact that he was a moron.

Turning back to the Viking, Rogers tried to push out all the aggressiveness from his bones. He let out a deep breath. "What was it that you had in mind?"

The Viking chewed on her lip, which Rogers found very sexy. "Packing a bunch of grunts into a ship and flying them into glorious battle to smash heads."

"That's irony, right?" Deet asked from the bridge.

"No," Rogers barked. "Wait. Maybe. I think it might have been." He threw up his hands. "That's not important now! The *important* thing is that we have a giant *fleet* of people who may or may not be trying to *kill* us within visual range and blocking our Un-Space point. The 331st is under siege, and we're powerless to do anything about it!"

Commander Belgrave sighed again, just as some really irritating beeping noises started to bleed through the datapad. Why had they interrupted such a good conversation with the Viking? He never had good conversations with the Viking.

"What the hell is that noise?"

Some rustling bubbled in the background as someone approached the communications terminal to talk to him. Eventually, someone whose voice he didn't recognize—probably one of the techs on the bridge—came online.

"It's hard to say, sir," the tech said. "Thelicosan jamming is blocking even short-range radios, but one of the fighter patrols out there is trying to send a report back in. It's garbled, but it sounds like they're saying the Thelicosans are running away."

Rogers frowned. "Running away?"

"That's what I'm hearing, sir." Another couple of beeps and a pause. "He says they're pulling their drawers down."

Rogers' face turned a little red. "What?"

"Sorry," the tech said. "They're drawing down." He cleared his throat. "Of course they're not pulling their drawers down. That would be ridiculous. Our fighter patrol is returning to the ship now to give a full report."

Hopefully their report included something other than the cryptic "we're invading" message that had come from the Thelicosan command ship, identified as the *Limiter*. Was that really the kind of correspondence that ended a peace that had lasted for over two centuries? It seemed kind of . . . anticlimactic.

"Alright, whatever," Rogers said. "I'll be back up there soon to check it out." He clicked the datapad off.

"This doesn't make any sense," he said to nobody in particular. "The Thelicosans looked like they were about to charge head-on when they came out of that Un-Space point, and now they're just sitting there. And now their warships are backing off? I can't imagine we've scared them into rethinking their invasion."

"Not with your attitude we won't scare anybody," the Viking said.

"I'm being realistic," Rogers said. He was surprised at his own self-control; he hadn't turned back to stare at the woman since being interrupted by the comm tech, and now he was mostly enchanted by his own thoughts and his imagination of what it looked like outside the ship. A lot of metal was floating around in that open space.

"You're being a coward," the Viking shot back at him. Why wouldn't she let this go? It was his fleet, goddamn it. Sure, it was only his fleet because of a couple of harebrained schemes and an admiral flying into an asteroid, but it still counted on paper.

"What? No. I'm being—"

"Listen," she said, leaning in wonderfully close. "I'm not going to take that kind of shit from a coward like you. You don't have the guts to run this fleet. I don't care what Klein said about you."

"Hey," Rogers said, bristling. "I *saved* this fleet."

"Yeah," the Viking said, "with the help of everyone on board, including someone who busted down a door to pull your ass out of a fire. Big deal. I'm sick of paper-pushers like you being in charge." She loomed as she walked toward him. "I'm sick of the brass giving the cooks weapons. I'm sick of my marines busting their asses every day so that you can sip whiskey in your stateroom."

Rogers didn't know what to do. What was her problem? They had been doing so well. For at least the last five to eight minutes.

"I don't drink whiskey," he said, for some reason. Of course he drank whiskey; he was just feeling contradictory. "I drink Scotch. And I'll have you know—"

He'd seen this image before. Twice, actually. The vision of a set of knuckles rapidly approaching his forehead, backed by a meaty hand and arm. Each time, it seemed to happen more slowly. Rogers wasn't sure if his reactions were just getting faster or the Viking was just getting a little tired.

When the fist made contact with his face, he realized it probably didn't have anything to do with his reaction speed improving.

"Duck!" called Mailn.

But it was too late. Dimly, he realized that further command decisions would have to be postponed until he came back from whatever orbit the Viking had just put him into.

Back in a Flash

"You're beautiful and I love you and everything is going to be okay!" Rogers screamed as he sat bolt upright in bed.

He realized immediately that he wasn't on the bridge or in the infirmary—he was in his stateroom instead. Well, the admiral's stateroom, anyway. Rogers was using it while he waited for the new admiral to arrive—if he ever did. It was way more comfortable than Rogers' old room, particularly because his old room had no gravity, thanks to Klein's belief that his secretary couldn't hang himself in null-g. Not that it mattered, since the whole ship had no gravity at the moment.

Rogers put his hands to his face, which was quite tender, and rubbed his eyes. What was he doing here?

"I didn't know droids could be beautiful," Deet said. "I wonder what the real definition of beauty is. Is it something that reflects our own inner desires? Is it a reflection at all? By what standard can beauty actually be measured? Or does it lose its purpose if we try to measure it against anything?"

"Oh my god, shut up," Rogers said. He let his arms fall to the bed and immediately realized that something was different.

"Hey," he said. "Gravity! And you're not plugged in."

"Well, at least we know you're healthy enough to continue stating the obvious," Deet said. "Yes, Master Sergeant Hart and his crew fixed it a few days ago. Every room in the ship is back to normal, except your old room, of course. Nobody can seem to figure out where Admiral Klein disabled your room's gravity from."

Rogers gave a sigh of relief. It would be nice to not have stuff floating around the *Flagship* anymore and to be free of his ridiculous gravity boots.

"Wait," he said as he pulled himself out of bed and realized that he was phenomenally hungry. "Did you say a few days?"

"Yes," Deet replied as he played with some switches inside the chest cavity of another droid. "You've been unconscious for a bit."

"Wow," Rogers said. "That lady hits hard."

"And you're a wimp," Deet said. He retracted his data cable from within the inactive droid and closed the robot's chest plate. "Are you really going to make me keep doing this? I don't know about you, but plugging myself into random members of my own species kind of feels a little uncouth."

"You're doing it for the good of mankind," Rogers said, shaking his head. Looking down at himself, he realized he wanted a shower very badly. His uniform was rumpled and gross-smelling for an uncountable number of reasons. "Is it really possible to be knocked unconscious for a couple of days? That seems a little ridiculous."

"I'm sorry," Deet said, "I think I should have added that the Viking has been hitting you repeatedly every time you regained consciousness. You've only been out for a few hours at a time. I think you're only awake because she found something else to do."

"I see," Rogers said. "What did I say that pissed her off so badly?"

He thought back to their conversation—or what he could

remember of it—and couldn't help but feel a pit open up in his stomach. He'd missed something—missed something big—and he still didn't know what it was.

Deet made a beeping noise that indicated he didn't know, didn't care, or both. Walking over to Rogers on his makeshift legs—legs that had been assembled from a mixture of garbage and Rogers' own ingenuity—he presented Rogers with a datapad.

"What's this?" Rogers asked.

"It's a report on the activity from the last few days, including the information from the patrols coming in. I thought you might want to read it."

Rogers grunted, then started flipping through the report as he munched on a cold, but filling, bowl of some kind of porridge that Deet had brought from the kitchens. Hopefully it was less than a day old. It tasted of honey and ginger, and Rogers was thankful it wasn't one of the standard edible wartime rations—or SEWR Rats, as they called them. He'd eaten enough of those in the past month to last him—and his colon—a lifetime.

"What is this?" Rogers asked. The "report" was delivered in a style he didn't recognize. In fact, he wasn't sure anyone would be able to recognize it. It was just a bunch of pictures of some guy's hands in various positions, with captions that didn't make any sense, at least not to Rogers. One picture of a pair of hands, palms flat, one "chasing" the other, had the caption "Then I pulled a sick three-gee turn. Kept my shades on, though."

"Oh for . . . I forgot what it was like to deal with fighter pilots. Did he even sign his name to the report so I can ask him to give it to me with less sign language?"

Rogers flipped through a few dozen pictures of hands and one that appeared to include an elbow representing a way point to find the last page. It said: "Report totally written by Lieutenant Lieutenant Nolan 'Flash' 'Chillster' 'Snake' 'Blade' Fisk."

"How many callsigns can one guy have?" Rogers wondered aloud.

"What's a callsign?" Deet asked.

"It's like a nickname, but lame. Pilots insist on being called by it. Some of them won't even respond to their given names anymore."

"Can I have a callsign?" Deet asked.

"No."

Deet made an annoyed beeping noise that sounded a little bit flatulent. "That's not fair. If pilots can get callsigns, so can I. Why can't I have a callsign?"

"Look, I've got a lot of work to do. Get me a new uniform and send out a message to the commanders. We need to talk about what the heck we're going to do about that giant enemy fleet staring at us. And invite this, uh, Flash guy too."

"Hey, don't try to [EXPLETIVE] boss me around, [ANATOMICAL ITEM]."

Rogers rolled his eyes. "Is your profanity generator still broken? Bossing you around is my job now. I could just have you decommissioned with the rest of the droids."

"Don't make me protocol 162 you."

Rogers shot him a look. "With droid fu? I'd rather not be bored when I die. I want you to send a message to all the section commanders on the *Flagship* and tell them to meet on the bridge. I want to go over this report with this pilot and see if there's something we can do."

"Fine," Deet said, "but that kind of sounds like the sort of meeting that should happen in the war room."

Rogers paused, looking up from the asinine report. "We have a war room?"

"Of course we have a war room," Deet said. He beeped, and his chest plate projected a schematic map of the *Flagship* into the air. "It's right here." A portion of the ship, also on the command deck but just far enough away that it would make sense to use the in-line, lit up.

"I thought that was just sort of an empty area. I never see anyone back there."

"That's because we've never been at anything close to war. I'm not even sure when the last time it was used was."

Rogers thought for a moment. "Fine. I guess it makes sense for us to meet in the war room. But 'war' is such a . . . committal sort of word. Won't everyone get the wrong idea?"

"You mean that an enemy fleet has just charged into our territory, destroyed our communications, and issued a notice that they were going to kill us?"

"Right," Rogers said. "War room it is. Thirty minutes."

"Probably should have checked on the war room first," Rogers said. Deet beeped.

As one might have expected regarding a room that hadn't been used seriously in over two centuries, the war room was in a state of . . . slight disrepair. It was difficult to see what it had looked like in its prime, but Rogers imagined a long wooden table with comfortable chairs all around it, a videoconferencing screen, a holograph projector in the center of the table, and lots of nervous young officers sitting around the edges of the room, fervently taking notes for superior officers who weren't actually listening.

Now, however, it looked more like a bombed-out alleyway. The table had been broken in half at some point and pieces of it had been cut off by someone who had absolutely no skill with a saw. Most of the chairs were gone; some of them had been turned upside down to make what was perhaps a blanket fort in a corner of the room. Actually, as Rogers studied it, he couldn't help but be impressed. It was a two-story blanket fort, complete with a portcullis made from pencils and tape. The second story was supported by whiteboards, braced by more pieces of the table.

"If I ever find out who did this . . ."

"You'll throw them in the brig?" Deet asked.

"No, I'll hire them to build me a blanket fort." Rogers gestured at the structure. "This is brilliant."

Aside from that, there was a rusted-out garbage barrel in the center of the room. The distinct smell of burning refuse wafted from its contents, and peering inside, Rogers could see the dying embers of a fire. And the bones of what he was pretty sure was a squirrel.

"Shit," came a voice from behind him. "I didn't know we were meeting in New Jersey."

Rogers turned around to find the Viking, back in her uniform and surprisingly not winding up to punch him in the face. A surge of confusing emotions welled up inside him. She had, after all, repeatedly knocked him unconscious; a man had limits. That, and she'd started acting a little crazy in the infirmary. Rogers could deal with rough and tough. He kind of preferred it. He just wasn't so sure about being able to deal with crazy.

Sergeant Mailn was in tow. She was a petite blond with a permanent wiseass smirk on her face; it was difficult to envision her wielding heavy weapons and cutting through enemy troops. The dangerous glint in her eyes said different.

"Been a while, Cap," she said.

"Yeah," Rogers said. He threw a glance at the Viking, who seemed to be avoiding eye contact. "I've been in bed with a couple of concussions."

Mailn shrugged. "Not my fault you have a soft skull. Though I gotta say, if we're gonna keep you in command we really need to get you down to the training rooms. If you don't learn how to duck, the Viking's going to give you a blunt-edged lobotomy."

Rogers shook his head. "Any idea what's gotten her so riled up?"

Mailn frowned at him. "Hell if I know. She's my boss; we're not exactly into having sleepovers and pillow fights."

For a moment, Rogers imagined what a pillow fight with the Viking would be like. He saw feathers everywhere. And bodies.

Mailn's expression slipped for a moment. She looked at the Viking, then back at Rogers.

"Listen," she said, her voice low enough that the Viking, who was exploring the other side of the room, couldn't hear her. "You need to open your ears a little bit."

"What do you mean?"

"The captain . . ." Mailn said, then appeared to chew on her words for a moment. "She's done a lot for me, you know. Helped me get my head on straight. I guess I want to return the favor."

Rogers blinked. "I feel like we're talking about algebra colonies again."

Mailn gave him a level look for a moment, then sighed. "Of course you do," she said.

Before he could ask her anything else, the Viking turned around, holding pieces of a broken chair in each hand, and shouted at them.

"So what are we going to do with this mess?" she said. Rogers couldn't help but wince; the way she was standing made it look like she was about to charge into battle with broken furniture as weapons.

Rogers looked around at the chaos. "I don't know," he said. "Just . . . put it in the hallway and hope it disappears?"

The Viking gave him a look that said "You're an idiot," but she pitched in, obviously not having any better suggestions. Primarily, she pitched in by lifting the giant metallic garbage barrel over her head and throwing it out the door into the corridor of the command deck. They spent the next several minutes dismantling improvised structures, sweeping out ash and dust, and converting the usable half of the table into something that could hold a meeting.

"It'll just have to be a bit more intimate of a planning session," Rogers said.

Deet beeped. "Is 'planning session' a euphemism? I'm still not really clear on this whole implied subtext thing."

"No," Rogers said. "This is a war room, not a brothel." He sniffed. "At least not anymore."

Eventually they had something remotely resembling a place where professionals could meet and discuss important things like war. The holographic projector in the center of the table was useless, and Rogers wasn't sure where they could get a new one, so he had Deet lie in the middle of the table.

"This is humiliating," Deet said as he tested his projections.

"That's a pretty advanced emotion for a robot," Rogers said. "Just be happy you're being useful instead of shut down like the rest of our droid friends."

"Everyone's going to be able to see my parts," Deet said.

Rogers ignored him. He was too busy feeling uncharacteristically nervous about speaking to other people. This was his first official meeting as acting admiral of the fleet; he'd said a thing or two over the public-address system and held a few briefings on the bridge, but this felt completely different. Maybe it had something to do with preparing thousands of men and women to go fight other thousands of men and women.

Eventually people started to shuffle in. Some of them Rogers recognized. The Viking was already there, of course, as the representative of all the Meridan marines assigned to the 331st. There was a real commander—General Something-or-Other—who resided on a marine vessel. They'd found in the past that marine commanders and fleet commanders didn't work well on the same ship, in the killing-each-other kind of way.

Commander Belgrave, the helmsman, walked in first, and that kind of bothered Rogers.

"Um," Rogers said. "Is anyone up there piloting the ship, Belgrave?"

Belgrave, a pale man whose body had the distinct look of someone who sat hunched behind a console all day and, perhaps, all night, looked at him with a frustrated expression.

"We're floating in free space at the edge of solar and planetary gravity," he said. "I've had the *Flagship* on autopilot for the last two years."

Before Rogers could ask him what, in fact, he had been doing all damn day, the rest of the crowd shuffled in. Master Sergeant Hart, functioning as the engineering and logistics chief since there was currently no officer suited to the position, gave Rogers a terse nod as he came in. He'd been Rogers' supervisor years earlier and was probably one of Rogers' favorite people in the fleet. He walked with a cane and a noticeable limp, thanks to an attempt to kick a droid in the face.

"What kind of shithole is this?" Hart said. "We could have just met in the garbage chute."

And that was one of the reasons he was one of Rogers' favorite people in the fleet.

"Nice to see you, too, Hart. How are things down in the Pit?"

"Most of my best people are floating somewhere else in the fleet, and I'm still cleaning boominite containers out of the corners of the bay. It's going great."

Hart sat down on one of the chairs with a *humph*, releasing a cloud of dust that sort of floated around the room, threatening rain. Rogers let him be for the moment. If they ever got any alcohol back on this dry town of a ship, Rogers would hope to have a beer or two with the man. He was a little easier to talk to when he was drunk.

"Let's see," Rogers said, looking around the room. "Who else are we missing?" He thought for a moment. "Who usually comes to staff meetings, anyway?"

"No one," Belgrave said. "Don't you see what the war room looks like?"

Rogers cleared his throat. "I sort of feel like we should have someone from Personnel here, maybe. And who's in charge of flight operations?"

"That," came a voice from the door, "would be this guy."

In the doorway of the war room stood a man pointing at himself with both thumbs. Rogers might have said he was handsome, but he genuinely couldn't tell. The shit-eating grin and giant sunglasses blocked most of his facial features. Tall and a little lanky, he stood in a way that made it clear that he knew he was tall and lanky and was trying hard not to believe it. He also appeared to be wearing pajamas, but that was an illusion. It was really just a flight suit.

Rogers knew who it was immediately.

"You must be Flash," he said.

"You got it, baby," the pilot responded.

Rogers frowned at him. "Is 'baby' how they say 'sir' on the flight deck?"

It wasn't that Rogers wanted to be called sir. He wasn't much for military protocol; in fact, the only military protocol he liked was a drinking game called Military Protocol that had absolutely nothing to do with military protocol. He hated being called sir. But he hated being called baby more.

"Whoa," Flash said. "Don't heat up the Chillster." He made a fanning motion with both hands. "Check your six."

Rogers checked his rank instead. "A lieutenant lieutenant is in charge of all the flight operations on this ship?" he asked. Then again, Rogers had been an ex-sergeant just a short time ago, so he supposed it was a little hypocritical to look down on the man because of his rank.

Commander Belgrave spoke up. "What happened to Commander Ortiz?"

Flash looked genuinely confused for a moment. "Who is that?"

"The flight ops chief."

"Oh!" Flash said, nodding. "You mean Oobles." He laughed. "I totally had a bogey dope on his name. Yeah, he flew into an asteroid."

"I am going to put a kill order on all the local asteroids," Rogers said, then paused. "For the record, someone actually *saw* him fly into the asteroid, right? This isn't like a robots-took-over-his-ship kind of asteroid accident, is it?"

A similar report had been released about the *Rancor*, a patrol ship that, as it turned out, had been a test run for the droids to take over a ship. They still hadn't found it.

"A-firm," Flash said.

Everyone remained silent.

"A firm what?" Rogers asked. "A firm . . . confidence that he is, in fact, dead?"

"A-firm as in affirmative, baby," Flash said, shaking his head. "Try to keep up; I'm always at full burn."

Rogers sighed. So instead of anyone with command experience, he had this junior officer in charge of all the flying operations on the ship. Hadn't there been anyone higher-ranking, or at least less ridiculous, who could have taken over?

Regardless, this was not the time to argue over personnel decisions. And speaking of Personnel, nobody had come representing them or Communications. The comm shop probably had their hands full trying to un-fry their systems and couldn't contribute much anyway, and he wasn't even really sure what Personnel did. He supposed it was time to kick this off.

"Oh," he said out loud. "One more person we forgot. Do we have a new intel chief? Preferably one who isn't a Thelicosan spy this time?"

That had been Rogers' fault for suggesting the now-deceased McSchmidt for the position, but nobody seemed to want to rub that in his face for the moment.

"I nur a purfuct person fur dee job!"

"Tunger!" Rogers said. "For the last time, take those rocks out of your mouth. What are you doing here?"

Tunger pouted as he reached into his cheeks and actually pulled out a pair of rocks, something Rogers hadn't seen him do before. Corporal Tunger used to be Rogers' orderly, until Rogers reassigned him to the zoo deck where he belonged. He'd been perfecting his "Thelicosan accent" in hopes of being a spy, but to Rogers' ears it had always been just annoying.

"Can I be a spy now?" Tunger asked.

"Absolutely not," Rogers said.

"Oh come on!" Tunger said. "McSchmidt is space dust. You can promote me to lieutenant lieutenant and—"

"No," Rogers said. "You belong on the zoo deck."

Rogers didn't say it as an insult. The man really had a gift for taking care of animals. He just didn't have a gift for much else.

"Oh, you cats are looking for an intel geek?" Flash snorted. "You don't need one of those nerds gumming up your brains with all their smart talk. I can do that job."

"Based on my limited knowledge of human personality types and career requirements," Deet said, "I strongly advise against appointing this person as your intelligence officer due to the likelihood of him getting everyone killed."

"Whoa, did not copy," Flash said. "Send that again? Did this nerd-a-tron just call me stupid?"

"No, he didn't," Rogers said. "Now can we—"

"Did that stupid [MATERNAL FORNICATION] human just call me a nerd-a-tron?" Deet asked.

"I wurnt to be a spy!"

"I want to shoot something," the Viking said.

"I want . . . what do I want?" Deet repined. "Can droids have wants? Is it just a program telling me what to do?"

"Everyone shut up!" Rogers roared.

To his surprise, everyone did shut up. He was so surprised, in fact, that when everyone else shut up, he also shut up. After a moment, he could not figure out how to stop shutting up. What had they even been talking about?

Finally a decrepit wall decoration fell to the floor, snapping him out of it.

"Tunger," Rogers said finally. "You don't even have the beginnings of the qualifications for an intelligence officer, never mind the chief of the intel squadron. I'm sorry. If we weren't facing imminent destruction and all that, I might allow it for entertainment purposes, but right now we can't afford to do something so stu . . . have the zoo deck left in any less capable hands than yours."

Tunger looked disheartened, but Rogers didn't have time to heal his wounded pride right now. From what he understood of his personnel situation—hey, there was something the Personnel chief could have helped him with—the intel squadron had been mostly composed of droids. He wasn't sure there was even anyone left on the *Flagship* he could promote into the position. The pilot wonder boy Flash might have had enough ego to fill a professional sports locker room, but at least he had some flight experience.

"Fine," Rogers said. "Flash, you're our stand-in for today. And since you were kind enough to submit that enlightening report on the status of forces, maybe you can start this off by giving us a summary."

Flash snapped his fingers and pointed at Rogers. "Roger that," he said. "You got it, boss." He raised his hands. "So I came out of the launch hangar like this—"

"No," Rogers said. "No hand gestures."

Flash looked at him, his grin dropping for the first time since he'd walked into the room. If Rogers could have seen his eyes behind those giant sunglasses, he would have guessed they were wide with shock.

"How am I supposed to tell stories about how awesome I am?"

"You're not. I want you to tell me what the Thelicosans are doing out there."

"Man, this scores like a ten on the lame-o-meter. Fine. Can Nerd Bot here pull up, like, a space map or something?"

"I'll pull up an [EXPLETIVE]."

"I don't know what that is, man."

Deet made a couple of annoyed beeping noises but projected a spherical depiction of the battlespace above the table. Their sensor network was restricted to what the *Flagship* had organically, since any signals coming back from their network of observation platforms were being jammed by the Thelicosans. Combined with what they could literally see out the windows, this orange-hued projection was the best guess for what the hell was going on out there. It was an awful lot of metal with an awful lot of weapons.

In short, it looked pretty awful.

"That's a lot of ships," Sergeant Mailn said.

"No shit," the Viking said.

Deet's head craned upward. "I can't even see what's coming out of myself. Is it a girl? I hope it's a girl."

"Everyone give Flash here your attention," Rogers said.

"Alright," Flash said. "These things here," he went on, pointing to where there appeared to be a cluster of Battle Spiders, "these are pretty cool. They're all pointy and stuff, but I wouldn't want to take my Ravager near it without some serious support. But I think the guys working them are drunk, or really bad, because they shot all their weapons off into empty space."

"It's called a warning shot," the Viking growled.

"Well, we call it a miss," Flash said. "And then we make fun of you for it. So anyway, like I said, these are cool, but they're not doing anything dangerous because they suck at shooting. All their fighters—at least I think they were fighters—ran away when they saw us. I was totally ready to, like, come in like this." He raised a hand.

"No," Rogers said.

"Man, you are *such* a buzzkill. Anyway, when you see the 331st Raging Ravagers come up on your six like we did, well, I don't blame them for turning tail and getting back to their big ship."

So that was what he'd meant over the radio when he'd said they were running away. But why would they do that? None of this made any sense. Why fire a warning shot? Why not talk to them at all, aside from a cryptic invasion message? And why run away when the Ravagers came toward them? If this was an act of war, they could have at least put some effort into it.

"Okay," Rogers said. "Anything else?"

"Not if I can't use my friggin' hands," Flash said, pouting.

"Nothing else, then," Rogers said. He leaned back in his chair and looked around the room. "We can't stay like this forever," he said. "Hart, how are we doing on supplies?"

Hart, who was also intimately involved with logistics, shrugged. "We're designed to be out here for long periods of time without resupply, but with the droid problem and *someone* setting all the kitchens on fire, it's not as easy."

Hart sent a glare toward the Viking, who, unaccustomed to being glared at, made a move to flip the table.

"Easy!" Rogers said.

"I set those mess halls on fire for a reason," the Viking said, thankfully not following through on destroying the last remnants of a serviceable meeting table. "You know, because there were droves of droids trying to kill us at that time. Next time I'll send them a nice letter to please shut down their secret network."

"Not going to matter much if we starve," Hart said.

"Nobody is going to starve," Rogers said above their argument. "We might have lost some supplies and some ability to do work, but we're not helpless. We can send shuttles to some of the other ships and ask them to give us some of their surplus. The real problem is the size of our force. If the Thelicosans wanted to, they could turn us to space dust pretty quickly. We need to break the communications blockade so we can get word back to headquarters."

Rogers wasn't exactly into self-sacrifice, or anything dramatic like that, but he hated to think what would happen if the Thelicosans made their way through the 331st without the 331st doing their job as a buffer unit. Sending Merida warning of an invading force might be more important than saving all their skins.

"Oh, is that it?" Flash said. "That's a piece of cake, Skipper. We just blow up their jammers."

Rogers looked at the pilot, his brow furrowing. For some reason, he felt like blowing things up wasn't the solution.

"How?"

"You sic me and a couple of Ravagers on these platforms here," Flash said. He pointed to a couple of similarly shaped devices on the display. They looked a little bit like someone had taken a silverware drawer, stuck all the contents into a black piece of putty, and then thrown it into space. "We splash 'em, and then you start the beeps and squeaks back to headquarters."

"What's he saying?" Rogers heard Tunger whisper.

"He's saying we shoot back," the Viking said. "I think it's a stupid idea. You start blowing up pieces of their equipment, and you just rile them up and give them time to get ready. You want to do this, you go in hard, you go to their flagship, and you take a bucket of marines." She folded her arms. "We'll do the whole job. You're talking about clipping the lion's fingernails."

"What did the lion ever do to you?" Tunger said, genuinely defensive.

"We're not going to do anything to any lions," Rogers said. "Hart, how are the Ravager maintenance crews doing?"

"They're overworked and underpaid. Don't you remember being an engineer, or have you got too much brass on your shoulders now?"

"Wait," the Viking said. "You're actually doing this? A couple of days ago you were ready to take the whole fleet and run away. Now you're saying instead of actually fighting, you're going to throw some pajama-wearing goon and his cool hairdo pals at some pieces of equipment that you're not even sure what they are?"

"I told you they're jammer thingies," Flash said. "You don't need an intel nerd to tell you that. What crawled up your ass, dude?"

"It's a little better than going in and killing people," Rogers said to the Viking. "It's clearly defensive. If they're just jamming relays, they're not manned."

"Bull!" she said, getting up out of her seat and completely blotting out the holographic display. "They shot first, shit-for-brains. They've already started the war. It's time we finish it!"

The room descended into silence for a moment as the two arguments lingered in the air. Deet, still lying back on the table so that he could project the battlespace upward, tapped his thin metallic fingers on his chest impatiently. Rogers darted his eyes furtively around the room, looking for any guidance, any sign that maybe he had another option. Or, at the very least, which of the two options in front of him would be better.

If he went with Flash's plan, they would undoubtedly be able to get a message back to headquarters before they were slaughtered. The Viking's plan, on the other hand, would have absolutely no real benefit except for the marines getting to go out in a blaze of glory. But it might help him score points with the most beautiful woman in the world.

As much as he wanted to impress the Viking, it wouldn't be much good if she threw herself into a Thelicosan disruptor rifle.

"Alright, Flash," Rogers said. "Let's do it your way."

The Viking did flip the table then.

The Jammer Thingies

"I really don't think this is the sort of thing we should be doing right now," Rogers said.

Mailn punched him in the chest without moving any other part of her body, sending him staggering backward. How did such a small woman have so much power?

They were in one of the marines' training facilities on the training deck. Thankfully they were alone. Rogers couldn't really handle having anyone else under his command watching him get his ass handed to him by someone who could have doubled for a high school cheerleader.

"I think this is something we should have done weeks ago," Mailn said. "Do you really think we can afford to simply not have a fleet commander every couple of days because he gets punched in the face? You need to start exercising some leadership. And in order to exercise leadership, you need to exercise some exercise." She tapped him in the gut with a couple of pseudo-punches, each of which echoed with a resounding slap. Ever since the kitchens had come back online, Rogers had been a bit liberal with the desserts.

"Ha-ha," he said, coughing. "Very funny. I'm saying maybe this can wait until after the operation goes down. The last message I got from Flash told me they were almost ready. And also that they were 'totally sweet.'"

Mailn launched a series of kicks, all of which landed firmly on Rogers' shoulder. He grunted and staggered sideways.

"And that's exactly why you need to do this right now. Were you even paying attention to the Viking after that meeting in the war room?"

Aside from finally flipping the table, officially ruining the only place they had to plan war meetings, the Viking had picked up Deet by his legs and used him as a cudgel to smash the excellently constructed blanket fort. That had, possibly, been the biggest casualty of the Thelicosan invasion so far.

After that, the Viking had stormed about the ship, roaring incoherently. She'd finally disappeared into her room on the command deck. That wasn't normally where marines were berthed, but Rogers had moved her room closer to his. He was now rethinking the wisdom of that decision.

"Yeah," he said. "Maybe this *is* the right time to be doing this sort of thing."

"Exactly," Mailn said, hitting him in the side of the head. "Every time the Viking punches you in the face, we lose our commander for a few days. You can't operate a fleet like that."

Rogers frowned. How *had* they operated the fleet for the few days he'd been unconscious? Then again, they'd operated the fleet with Admiral Klein as their commander for years, and that wasn't very far off from having a comatose skipper. Even then, Rogers hadn't woken up with a pile of decisions to make, either. Who had been calling the shots while he'd been out? He'd make a point to ask Belgrave about it later.

His contemplations were interrupted by his being bowled backward by a flying dragon kick to the chest.

"Hey!" he said after he removed his knee from his mouth. "I wasn't ready!"

"That's kind of my point," Mailn said.

Rogers pulled himself to his feet. He was going to have a hell of a time getting out of bed tomorrow morning, assuming, that was, that the Thelicosans didn't decide to blow them all to smithereens before then. He brushed himself off and tugged his shirt down. He couldn't remember the last time he'd worn official Meridan Navy PT clothes. Well, he'd used them for pajamas every once in a while, but he was pretty sure that didn't count.

"Just wait a second," he said, holding up a hand. His insides were starting to feel like they were going to become outsides. "What you said up in the war room about listening to the Viking. What did you mean by that?"

Mailn dropped her guard and stretched out her neck a little. "I dunno," she said. "I just . . . I think you could be good for her, you know?"

Rogers felt his face turn red. "What are you talking about? I'm her superior officer and it would be totally inappropriate—"

"Oh shut up," Mailn said. "Just because I'm a marine doesn't mean I'm a complete idiot. Anyone with a pair of eyes and their teenage years behind them can see you've got a thing for her."

Rogers' shoulders sagged. "Am I so transparent?"

"That and you repeatedly, loudly, declared your love for her during your semiconscious states."

"Oh."

Mailn didn't seem to know what to say for a second. She sort of walked around in a circle on the training floor, losing a lot of her usual easy confidence. Finally she picked up a couple of police batons and started playing with them. The ease with which she handled them was equal parts impressive and terrifying.

"No, no, no," Rogers said. "Hell no. We are not doing that. I'm here to learn how to do karate or something, not cage fight."

Mailn didn't seem to be listening to him, nor did she seem to want to fight with the batons. She just kept sort of spinning them around, poking the air and avoiding looking at Rogers.

"The captain seems rough," Mailn said, "but she's got a good heart. When I got to the 331st, I'd left some . . . stuff behind me on Merida Prime."

Rogers didn't know Mailn very well, but he would guess that "stuff" probably included some black eyes. Parts of Merida Prime could be . . . preceded by ellipses. There were even locations where Rogers wouldn't travel—and that said a lot. Spacefaring humanity wasn't altogether so different from the times when it had been bound to Earth.

"You don't have to talk about it," Rogers said, sensing her reluctance. "In fact, I'm not entirely sure I want to hear about it. We are literally at war, you know."

Mailn looked relieved. "The captain helped me put it behind me and focus on being a good marine. I guess I'd like to return the favor."

Suddenly, she snapped out of whatever melancholy her memories had put her in, put down the batons, and pointed at him.

"And that means making sure you're awake long enough to talk to her. We can get to you not saying stupid shit later."

Mailn took up a fighting stance again and, bouncing gracefully around the center of the room, motioned for him to come forward.

"Fine, fine," Rogers said. He shook himself off and did a few hops to loosen his muscles, which alerted him to the fact that he didn't have very good balance, either. "So what are we going to start with? Are you going to teach me how to, like, throw a Thelicosan using his own attacking force or something really Zen like that?"

Mailn laughed at him. "Hell no. I'm not here to work miracles, Rogers. I'm here to teach you how to duck."

Rogers blinked. "You were serious all those times? You're really just going to teach me how to duck?"

In lieu of further argument, Mailn hit him in the face.

"Okay, okay!" Rogers said, staggering backward. "I get it! I'll learn how to duck."

Mailn hit him in the face again, and their lesson began. It really mostly consisted of Rogers getting hit in the face, which he sort of expected. It also consisted of him sweating. A lot.

"Okay," he said, bent over and panting after a few hours of training. He felt like his lungs were trying to crawl out his throat and drag themselves into bed, which was exactly what he wanted to do at the moment. "Are we done? Can we take a break? My face hurts."

"We've only been training for six minutes," Mailn said flatly.

"What?" Rogers said, craning his neck upward. "Don't be ridiculous."

Mailn silently pointed at the clock on the wall, which registered six minutes after they had begun.

Rogers stared at it, disbelieving. Then the minutes advanced by one.

"Ha!" he said, pointing at the clock. "See? Seven minutes. I'm not that weak."

"You are that weak."

"I am that weak," Rogers said, straightening his back with no little effort. "Am I at least a little better at ducking now?"

"Six minutes," Mailn repeated.

"Oh for the love of . . . never mind," Rogers said. "Six minutes is probably enough for the coordinators to get to the bridge and get set up. This thing is supposed to kick off in a little while, and now I need to shower and put ice on at least six places on my body before I can walk straight again. Thanks for the session."

Mailn hit him in the face.

"Stop that!" he shouted.

A tense excitement electrified the bridge. Unfortunately, a loose power cable was also electrifying the bridge.

"Get that thing fixed," Rogers said as another one of his communications technicians fell to a convulsion-inducing arc of electricity that blasted from the breach in the electrical grid. That was the fourth troop he'd lost in the last ten minutes. Not the best way to start a risky and potentially career-/life-ending mission.

"I'll take care of this," Deet said. He walked over to where the cable was protruding from the wall, snatched it up, and plugged it into himself. His eyes, normally a dull blue, flashed all kinds of colors in rapid intervals. All the lights on the bridge dimmed for a brief moment.

"Wow!" he said as his eyes settled back to their blue color, though they remained a bit brighter than they normally were. "This is amazing! Why did I never try this before? I feel like I'm floating on an electron cloud."

"Great," Rogers said. "My offensive and defensive coordinators are nowhere to be found, my lead pilot is trying to argue with the maintainers as to why he doesn't need a helmet, and my orderly is getting high. Perfect."

He sat in the commander's chair, tapping his fingers nervously on the armrest and chewing at anything his teeth could find: his lip, the inside of his cheek, even the edge of his personal datapad. He was pretty sure his entire adrenal system was going into overdrive, and he also really had to pee.

"Sorry we're late, Skipper," someone said from behind him. Rogers turned to see, finally, the two mission coordinators come onto the bridge. He'd never met them before personally; in fact, he wasn't sure anyone had met them before, since they hadn't exactly been running any combat missions for a long time. He was surprised to see that both of them were wearing giant headsets and some really strange-looking windbreaker jackets over their uniforms.

"Are you guys going to go on a jog or something?" Rogers asked, gesturing to their jackets. "And what took you so long? We're already running behind."

One of the coordinators looked at him, her expression unreadable. Not exactly old, she wasn't exactly young, either, dark-featured and weathered-looking, with what seemed to be a permanent expression of a sort of nonchalant intensity, if such a thing could exist. In her left hand she held a laminated sheet of paper that was covered in all kinds of colored blocks, columns, and other notations.

"Standard coordinator uniforms. You the new skipper, sir?" she asked. "I'm Commander Rholos, your defensive coordinator, and this is Commander Zaz, your offensive coordinator."

Approaching the command platform with Zaz in tow, she extended a hand. Rogers stood to shake it, only then realizing that the railing in front of him was too high to shake someone's hand over. He ended up sort of squatting down and reaching through the bars, which must have looked absurd.

Zaz, on the other hand, made no move to look up from his sheet or shake hands, and seemed to be following Rholos mindlessly. Something about him screamed typical middle-aged white guy to Rogers, though the more he thought about it, that wasn't really the kind of thing that could be screamed. He wore a tacky orange visor, as weathered with age as his face was.

"What?" Zaz said, suddenly looking up. It appeared to be the first time he'd noticed that anyone else was in the room.

Rholos tapped her headset, and Commander Zaz took off his own.

"Oh, hi, Skipper. We're gonna do this today, okay? Don't worry about it. It's just like practice."

Rogers raised an eyebrow. "We practice?"

Zaz didn't seem to hear him as he simply readjusted his headset and began pacing around the bridge, staring at the laminated sheet of whatever-it-was. Rholos gave him a reassuring nod, replaced her own headset, and did the same.

Not knowing what else to do, Rogers sat back down in the commander's chair. He wasn't entirely sure what these people's jobs were, but he sure as hell hoped they took the majority of the burden of figuring out how to not get everyone killed.

"Relax," Commander Belgrave said, apparently reading Rogers' nervousness on his face. "You're the skipper, not the tactician. Remember that everyone under your command is a professional, and treat them like it."

"*I can see my brain!*" Deet screamed, his eyes flashing yellow.

"Would somebody please unplug him?" Rogers said. He turned back to Belgrave. "Since when did you become a fountain of leadership wisdom?"

Belgrave shrugged, leaning back in his chair. "I've sat up here for a lot of hours, sir. I know a little bit about what a good skipper does and what a bad skipper does."

Rogers frowned. "That reminds me. Who was running the fleet for the few days I was out? I never got any reports or anything."

"Oh," Belgrave said. He pointed ambiguously to some console or other, the function of which Rogers had no idea about. "For short absences, we use CARL."

"Um," Rogers said. "Carl?"

"No, not Carl. CARL," Belgrave said, emphasizing the acronym. "It's the Command Automated Response Lexicon. It makes the ship's decisions in the event of the boss's—and his deputy's—absence."

Rogers couldn't believe what he was hearing. "Are you serious? Didn't we just go through a whole big giant drama where automated intelligence platforms became self-aware, started slowly taking over the ship, and then eventually almost built a giant bomb and killed us all? Do you really think it's a good idea to give all that responsibility to a computer?"

Belgrave's brow furrowed in confusion. "I said it was making the fleet admiral's daily decisions, not doing long division. CARL is sufficient to keep us afloat for weeks at a time, but it's vastly inferior intellectually to our advanced droids."

"Oh man, I am crashing so hard right now," Deet said as he spun dizzily around the corner of the bridge. Getting electricity intravenously apparently didn't do good things for him. Or maybe it did really good things for him. Rogers wasn't sure, but he could tell by looking at Deet that he wouldn't be of much use for a while. Deet kept slowly extending one hand in front of him, unfolding his fingers, folding them again, and then dropping his arm.

"Are we going to do this or not?" Rogers said impatiently. "Someone get me Lieutenant Lieutenant Flash, or whatever his name is."

"Yes, sir."

After a few minutes of waiting, the pilot's voice came across the communications system.

"Hey, hey, baby, what's up?"

"Hey, baby?" Rogers said. "Are you even close to being ready? What's going on in the hangar?"

"Man," Flash said, "don't be so cold or you'll freeze my engines. Me and the rest of the Raging Ravagers are suited up and ready to go. We're just waiting for space traffic control to clear us and our ordnance to get loaded. I can't wait to pickle a couple of these Lancers."

Despite not knowing how Flash intended to brine or pickle anything, Rogers couldn't help but notice the last word of the pilot's sentence. Lancers were a very volatile, very expensive, and very deadly weapon that definitely would not be the weapon of choice for a routine mission to turn a couple of jamming platforms into space debris. They were mostly for damaging larger ships that had their shield generators destroyed; they wouldn't work on shielded craft.

"Lancers?" Rogers asked. "Why are you bringing Lancers?"

"Look," Flash said. "I told you I had this covered, and that you didn't need an intel weenie to plan this mission. The Lancers are the best weapon we have for nonshielded stuff, and these jammers aren't shielded. Do you know how many plasma cannon shots it would take to blow one of these up?"

Rogers thought a moment. He hadn't been on weapons loading detail in a long, long time, but he seemed to remember plasma cannons, the basic armament of any spacefaring platform, as adequate for blowing up just about anything.

"One?"

"Whatever," Flash said. "Just let me do my job. We'll need the plasma rounds if their fighters come at us."

"Why the hell would you use plasma cannons against fighters? Why not use Hellhawk missiles? That's what they're for!"

A long, drawn-out sigh came over the speaker system.

"Because cannons, man. They're *flashy*. See you out in the black stuff!"

The comms clicked off, leaving Rogers with something much less than confidence and only slightly less than sheer terror.

"I told you he was an idiot," Deet said, seemingly recovered from his daze. He walked over and stood next to Rogers on the command platform, looking out at the displays. Rholos and Zaz were pacing back and forth, talking animatedly into their microphones, though Rogers couldn't make out what they were saying. For some reason, they were using the laminated sheets to cover their mouths so that he couldn't read their lips, either. It was a very strange sight and did not at all help his rising confusion and moderate panic about sending men and women into combat.

"I didn't have much of a choice," he said. "A lot of people think I'm an idiot, too, and here I am commanding the whole fleet."

Belgrave shot him a look.

"Alright, sir," Zaz said. "Everything is ready."

Rogers settled into his command chair and took a deep breath. He sure hoped Flash knew what he was doing, because Rogers absolutely did not. He opened his mouth to give the word to begin the mission, but he thought there was some kind of protocol that required him to say something specific or dramatic. Klein was always making speeches and getting dramatic slow-motion salutes and all that. This was his first big act as acting admiral of the fleet; he needed to make it good.

"Go" seemed like a weak choice for weak men. "To victory!" was cheesy. Simply giving a sort of karate chop in the air to indicate forward movement might be misinterpreted or hurt his shoulder. So he settled on something he knew much more about than being a commander: gambling.

"Okay, everyone, we've got a pair of deuces, no chips, and here comes the flop. We're all in."

The bridge completely stopped. Every head turned in his direction. He prepared himself for the resounding cheer that he knew was about to rock the *Flagship*.

"We're going to flop?" someone said. "I don't want to flop. I thought we were supposed to win?"

"Admiral Klein always said things like achieving battlespace effects with synergistic combat agility."

"That didn't make any sense, either."

"Yeah, but at least it was about war."

"If we have a pair of deuces, does that mean we have a four? I don't know the rules of baccarat."

"Just go blow things up!" Rogers screamed.

"Yes, sir!" came the resounding response.

Boioioing

"We must visit an inverse sine wave of destruction on the Meridan fleet!" Commodore Zergan cried.

Alandra folded her arms and looked out from the bridge, thinking. She took a deep breath. A wave of destruction would have seemed like a good idea in any other situation, but here it seemed somehow counterproductive.

"Not yet," she said slowly. Let Zergan persist in his opinion that she was trying to goad the Meridans into drawing first blood. "Stick to the plan."

Zergan glanced at her sideways, his expression unreadable. Likely he was starting to figure out that maybe this hadn't been her plan; he wasn't easy to fool. Alandra tried to remain impassive. She was trying to facilitate an opportunity and regain ground lost due to her communications technician's failure. Had he simply transmitted the right message, this never would have happened.

It certainly wasn't Alandra's fault that she had kicked him in

JOE ZIEJA

the ear and damaged his hearing before giving him the message to transmit.

Secretary Quinn, who had been making herself relatively scarce over the last few days, was waiting silently on the bridge, her hawkish gaze looking feverishly for something to criticize.

"I hope you did your calculus today," she muttered. "Because, Science help you, you're going to need it."

Alandra ignored her. Of course she'd done her calculus today. No self-respecting Thelicosan, particularly not one in a position of power like she was, would shirk her religious obligations for something so mundane and simple as war. After all, war was merely the continuation of math by other means.

Yet, for all that she had felt confident in her plan, now she was feeling confused and lost. It was a rare occasion when she didn't know exactly what to do at any given moment; she wasn't used to being at the whim of her enemy. In a way, it was kind of thrilling. Sacrificing Thelicosan lives hadn't been a part of her plan. While she wanted to let Captain Rogers be in control and help dictate the resolution of this problem, she didn't want him killing anyone. If this indeed was an offensive action that would kill Thelicosans, she'd be forced to act.

"Have we analyzed their trajectories yet?" she said.

"Yes, ma'am," replied the young woman at the defensive system monitors—Leftennant Awsala. A promoted conscript, from what Alandra remembered, though command brought with it such a large list of names that sometimes it was hard to keep them all straight. Alandra also lacked intelligence reports about her own people, which made it harder for her to understand them. Intelligence reports were the best way to get to know anyone.

"And? Can we discern their purpose?"

Leftennant Awsala projected what she saw on the bridge's main display and used a small laser pointer to gesture as she spoke.

"At first we thought the Galactic dogs were so terrified of our massive firepower that they were attempting to kill themselves honorably. Immediately after takeoff, one of the Ravagers flew into an asteroid."

Alandra cursed silently. Blood had already been drawn. This was not part of the plan.

"Yet they are still flying toward us," she said.

"Yes, ma'am," Awsala responded. "It's a small force without bomber support. We can estimate by their speed and makeup that it's a hit-and-fade. Their current trajectory could indicate one of three objectives: our munitions haulers, our long-range sensor drones, or the milk tanks."

None of those targets made any sense to Alandra. They had plenty of weapons on board to annihilate the Meridans in a full-on assault. The long-range sensors were no longer needed; the whole fleet was right in front of them. And Meridans were notorious for being lactose-intolerant.

Alandra tapped her long fingers against her lips, staring at the display. The Ravager was the main fighter of the Meridan fleet. Though the design hadn't been updated in decades, spies had been reporting that the weapons systems had gone through several upgrades. Unlike the Thelicosans, the Meridans liked to continually update the same frame; the Thelicosans simply built new spacecraft.

She was willing to sacrifice almost all of those targets if it meant avoiding bloodshed, but it was best to be prepared.

"Do we have a patrol nearby that could intercept?"

"Yes, ma'am," Awsala replied. She took down the display and turned back to her console to look at something. "We have one squadron of Sines that could break from patrol and engage on this vector. The Ravagers won't pass by close enough to any of our larger combat ships to be within range of their guns."

The battlespace appeared again on the display, showing the possible route for their squadron of Sines to overtake and destroy the Ravagers before they hit the assumed targets. It would be an easy thing, but not for long. If Alandra waited much longer to deploy the Sines, the Ravagers would have time to start shooting before being intercepted.

"Well, what are you waiting for?" Zergan said. "Are you just going to let them fly into the middle of our fleet and destroy whatever they'd like?"

"Why wouldn't they go for the jamming systems?" Quinn wondered out loud. "This doesn't make any sense, Marshal Keffoule."

Alandra had been wondering the same thing. If they were going to lift the jamming net, it would make a lot more sense to go after the actual emission platforms.

But *those* were on the complete opposite side of the fleet from where the Meridans were currently flying.

"You're sure those are the jamming platforms?" Rogers said.

Flash's voice came back over the radio. "A-firm, Skip. Sure as butter tastes good on toast."

Commander Zaz, the offensive coordinator, put down his laminated sheet and looked at Rogers. "Five minutes until the Ravagers are in striking range, sir."

Rogers nodded. "Good. Any sign of a Thelicosan reaction?"

Commander Rholos shook her head, though she looked concerned.

"What's the matter?" Rogers asked.

"That's just it," she said. "They're not making any attempt to defend the target. Their Sines and Cosines are just sitting there, and I don't even see any Tangents on patrol at all."

"Tangents?" Deet asked.

"That's beside the point," Rholos said, waving Deet away. "The Battle Spiders' guns are as cool as the surface of Old Pluto, and none of the capital ships are even moving. None of our sensors are picking up any radio transmissions, either, but the jamming net they cast is so wide that we shouldn't have expected that anyway. It's just . . . nothing."

Rogers shifted in his seat. He'd expected something, not nothing. But instead, he'd gotten nothing. Nothing had ever made him so nervous as this nothing.

"Wait," Rholos said. "I'm getting something."

"That's not nothing!" Rogers cried.

Rholos pushed her hands over her giant headphones and squinted as she listened to whatever message was coming through. Why were those headphones so big? And why did they keep covering their mouths with those laminated sheets whenever they talked? What the hell was on those sheets to begin with?

"It looks like there is a squadron of Sines moving," she said.

Rogers felt his stomach sink. Being an engineer, he knew a thing or two about Thelicosan equipment. They changed out the frames often, but they kept the names, so he wasn't really sure if these Sines were the newest version or an older model. It didn't really matter; Sines were designed for speed. Not as fast as Strikers, since Strikers didn't really have a dogfighting purpose, but fast enough to swarm over their Ravagers and turn at least half of them into dust.

"How long before they intercept?" Rogers said, feeling sick. *How long before my people start dying?*

That was a funny notion. He'd just thought-spoken of them as "my people." Maybe he was getting used to this job.

"Um," Rholos said, "I'm not sure if I have my math correct, but I would say infinite minutes."

Rogers raised an eyebrow. "Infinite minutes? What they hell are you talking about?"

"I mean that they're flying in the wrong direction to intercept."

"Go!" Zaz shouted into his microphone. "Go, go, go! Big hole just opened up in the defensive line. *Block*, you moron! *Block!*"

Slightly addled by the sudden outburst, Rogers took a moment to focus back on Rholos and the idea that, once again, the enemy seemed to be fleeing from confrontation. Why come all the way into Meridan space only to continually run away?

"Woo-hoo! Let's make some smoking holes!" Flash yelled over the radio. "Three minutes to pickle!"

How did he get a pickle into the cockpit? Rogers thought. Strangely, it made him want a sandwich. And that made him kind of miss Admiral Klein, for more reasons than one.

Maybe this wouldn't be so bad. If the Thelicosans weren't interested in a fight, the jammers would go down without complaint, the messages Rogers had standing by could go to Meridan HQ, and they'd have the full force of the Meridan Navy at their backs in no time. It seemed too easy.

"What do you mean send them away?" Zergan said. His face was getting so red that, the flush mixing with his dark complexion, he was beginning to look very much like a rotting tomato with a caterpillar crawling across the top of it. "They were our only chances of stopping the Galactics from succeeding in their mission!"

"We don't even know they have a mission," Alandra said. "This could be an effort to draw us away so that they can attack with a main force while we are distracted."

"Main force?" Zergan said. "Main force? That *is* their main force! They barely have enough fighters to set up a screen, never mind charge at our munitions haulers as a diversion. We could split our forces ten ways and still crush them like the insects they are. Have you started to try to find the square root of negative numbers in your head?"

Alandra looked at him sharply. She allowed him a much looser leash than the rest of the *Limiter*'s crew, due to their history together, but questioning her sanity in the middle of the bridge was going too far, and he knew it. She could see the regret in his face immediately.

"I'll thank you not to take that tone with me, Commodore," she said flatly. Her foot twitched. It always twitched when she got angry. For those who knew her well, watching her foot was the only way to tell which way her emotions were shifting. If her foot wasn't twitching, she likely was not about to deliver a spinning back kick to someone's face.

Zergan's eyes flashed down to her feet, of course, since he knew her better than anyone else on this ship, and his anger faded a little bit when he noticed. She'd never "disciplined" him, and if she was honest with herself, she wasn't sure she could if it came down to it. For one, Zergan was unbelievably fast—he had been a member of the F Sequence too, after all—and second, he was her friend. She generally liked to avoid kicking friends in the face.

For a moment, she thought he'd persist, but soon he averted his eyes. He knew the importance of maintaining military bearing and discipline on the bridge.

"Forgive me, Grand Marshal," he said with strained patience. "I simply fail to see the strategy in running away like scared dogs. I have faith that you know how to lead our glorious force to victory."

Alandra nodded, despite having absolutely no idea how she was going to lead their glorious force to victory. Right now she was simply attempting to avoid an all-out war. Curse that communications troop!

"Two minutes until they're in range," Awsala said dispassionately from her console. Alandra noted how she maintained her composure in difficult times. It marked her as a promising recruit.

Quinn shook her head slowly, and Alandra noticed that today, instead of having one tight bun behind her head, she had three. One hair bun wasn't enough to express the anal-retentive nature of a career bureaucrat, apparently. It was actually kind of impressive; Alandra's own insane dark, curly hair was difficult to tame. Not that she would have wanted to tame it. It would have been a waste of time, and besides, it helped with the Tangential Tornado motif.

"One minute," Awsala called.

What were they after? What was Alandra going to do after they struck? She couldn't let this go on much longer. But lifting the communications net wasn't an option. One message back to Merida Prime, and they'd have more trouble than she could handle. After she showed Captain Rogers she meant his fleet no harm by allowing this strike to go through, how could she get a message to him? She needed him to trust her, to know that she would take good care of him, bear him strong children, and never kick him in the face. Unless he was *really* asking for it.

The ratio . . . It was all so perfect! This should have been so much easier. Did she have to stand on the bow of the ship holding a flag with it all spelled out for Rogers?

An idea suddenly sprang to mind. It was an old tactic, something that hadn't been used in many, many years, but it might work.

She pressed a button on her console. "Get me Petty Officer Skokum. Tell him to get a pressure suit on and get to hatch number seventy-two as quickly as possible."

Zergan eyed her warily but said nothing. Quinn didn't appear to notice her giving the command at all.

"You're really going to let them strike us?" Zergan said, quietly this time. "You don't think coming this close is enough to justify a response?"

Alandra shook her head. "They're not going to kill anyone, Edris. All their potential targets are unmanned. Let them think they have the power to attack us; then we'll see if they can handle the consequences."

A small smile played across his face. "As you wish, Commander. May your parallel lines never intersect."

Alandra nodded at him and went back to the console. "Did you find Skokum?" she asked.

"Yes," crackled a reply. She didn't recognize the voice. "He was napping. Are you sure about this, ma'am? He's not exactly, um, ready for duty."

Of course he wasn't ready for duty. The man was over ninety standard years old, making him the oldest petty officer in the entire Thelicosan Navy. He'd essentially stopped doing any real work thirty years ago but had remained on the *Limiter* as a sort of mascot. Alandra allowed it; she appreciated his long career, and she had a sort of prescience about these things. Now, it appeared, she'd need the old man after all.

"Ah, you shut your three-point-one-four hole, young'un," came a distant voice over the radio. "I'm still fit as a fulcrum. I'll be right there, boss."

Alandra couldn't help but feel a surge of pride. That was devotion to duty. That was what Thelicosa was all about.

"Ten seconds to the engagement envelope," said Awsala.

The next ten seconds felt like an hour and a half. The entire bridge went silent. Everyone's eyes were focused on the viewscreens, wondering what was going to happen next.

"Pickle, baby!" Flash cried over the radio.

"Would someone please tell me why he keeps talking about pickles?" Rogers asked.

"It's ancient pilot slang for dropping a bomb," Belgrave responded. "It goes back to the second Great War on Old Earth. There was a piece of targeting technology called the Nordic Track, and it was so accurate, it supposedly could place a bomb anywhere you wanted while you ate a pickle. Very cutting edge back then. I guess up until then you had to wait until after you dropped your ordnance to eat pickles, or something."

Rogers frowned. "That makes almost no sense at all."

"Pilots haven't evolved much since then," Belgrave said.

The moment seemed to hang in the air forever as the Lancer careened toward the first target. It was far too small to see out the window of the bridge, but visual sensors that had been tracking the Ravagers followed Flash's ship. Whoever was controlling that camera must have had very delicate fine motor skills. When Flash launched his weapon, the camera instantly followed the Lancer instead.

"Splash one jammer-doohickey!" Flash called preemptively, right before the Lancer struck.

And bounced right off the shield.

Rogers barely had time to say: "What the hell happened you told me those things weren't shielded you monumental moron I am going to choke you to death as soon as you get back aboard my ship you single-brain-cell sloppy excuse for a pajama-wearing pilot!" before the Lancer, spiraling wildly out of control at high speeds, struck the side of a nearby structure, the function of which Rogers wasn't sure about. But whatever it was, it wasn't shielded.

"Bummer," Flash said over the radio just before the second container exploded.

Not just exploded—exploded and sent out what appeared to be a huge array of weapons flying out in all directions. Some of them detonated in the wake of the Lancer's destructive power, but others seemed to be propelled outward at incredible speeds due to the pressure differential released by the massive weapon.

"Secondaries!" Commander Zaz said. "It's a munitions container!"

Complete and utter chaos ensued as Ravagers were suddenly caught in a barrage of nobody's weapons fire. Another munitions container exploded from the secondaries of the first container, but without the high-pressure exchange of the Lancer to propel it outward, most of the munitions simply exploded in place.

"Tell them to switch to cannons!" Rogers said. "No more Lancers!"

Unfortunately several of the Ravagers had already "pickled," resulting in more of the highly volatile weapons careening through space as they bounced off the shielded surfaces of the jamming platforms. Why would the Thelicosans shield their jammers? It would undoubtedly interfere with their primary mission; shields were finicky things that could wreak havoc on communications systems.

The shields on the outside of the jamming platforms started to change colors as they took successive hits from the Thelicosans' own munitions. For the most part, none of the hits were direct enough to do enough damage to crack the shields, but they had been severely weakened within the first few seconds of chaos.

"Two Ravagers have been destroyed by the secondary explosions," Rholos said. "Tracking good vitals on the ejection pods."

"The jamming platforms' shields are weakening," Zaz called into his microphone. "Get those cannon blasts concentrated now! Left hook-hitch, then post right. Hut, hut!"

Rogers was standing, but he didn't remember getting up. Leaning over the railing on the command platform and gripping it with a strength that astonished him, he found himself panting like a dog as he stared, hopeless, at the dangerous furball that involved absolutely no enemy fighters. Cannon fire wouldn't do too much against the shields, but with the jamming platforms taking so much damage from the Thelicosan munitions dumps, there was a good chance that combined fire from a few of the Ravagers who weren't busy getting blown up by their own strike could crack one or two of the shields open. If they could just take down *one* of the jammers, this mission wouldn't be a complete failure.

"Put a call down to the medical team and get the evac ships ready," Rogers said. "We need to beat the Thellies to our people."

Thelicosans were known for picking up stranded enemy pilots and using them as thought experiments for advanced mathematical concepts, which drove most of them insane and turned the rest of them into accountants.

"Aye-aye, sir," said someone relatively unimportant.

"Put your backs into it, you lugs!" Commander Zaz called as he paced furiously back and forth, unzipping his windbreaker and waving his laminated sheet in the air. "Push! Push! Push! It's fourth and goal, fourth and goal, *fourth and goal!*"

"What the hell does that mean?" Rogers cried.

Nobody answered him. Everyone was too busy watching the visual of the one jamming platform that all the Ravagers were converging on. They were currently making looping attack runs, expending their cannon fire as fast as they could, then turning hard to come back in for another round.

"Ravager six-two, winchester," one of the pilots said.

"Ravager six-five, winchester," another said over the radio.

"Ravager oh-one, Uncle Chester," said Flash.

Rogers blinked. "Is pilot-speak a registered Galactic language, or something? What are these people saying?"

"They're running out of ammunition," Belgrave said, "and Flash is talking to his uncle Chester, who is in Ravager five-five. It's a family business."

Rogers didn't want to think of what it would be like to have two pilots from Flash's family line on his ship.

Slowly, the brilliant lines of cannon fire coming from the Ravagers ground to a halt. Ships were still making attack runs, but nothing was coming out of them anymore. All the ships started making winchester calls, and, even though there was no noise coming through the speakers, it seemed to suddenly go silent.

"Jammer pod six, shield down," Commander Zaz said.

"Woo-hoo!" Flash said over the radio. "I've got one Lancer left. Here we go!"

"Flash!" Rogers called over the radio. "Wait!"

"Sweet-and-sour deli fresh *PICKLE,* baby!"

The Lancer impacted the target, and what was once a large, spiky-looking space container suddenly transformed into space waste. Rogers had kind of expected some sort of fiery explosion, despite the cognitive dissonance that told him that things didn't really explode the same way in space as they did in the confines of an atmosphere. But he certainly hadn't expected a rapidly expanding white cloud to billow out from the point of impact, mixed in with the debris.

"Splash one jammer thingy!" Flash said again. "I'm an *ace!*"

"What is that stuff?" Rogers said, looking blankly at the strange white stuff on the screen. "Jamming paste? It looks weird. Can we get a read on that at all?"

"A quick chemical scan reads high amounts of proteins, namely lactulose, glucose, and galactose," Commander Rholos said as she pressed her hands to her ears to hear the report.

"Translation?" Rogers asked.

"It's milk, sir."

The bridge went silent. Rogers looked out the screen to see his remaining Ravagers—they'd lost two more in the interim—flying home and getting their engines dirty with space-frozen milk deposits. Master Sergeant Hart and his crew were going to have a field day cleaning up those spacecraft.

"Quick!" Deet said suddenly. "Someone blow up a container of cereal. And then a container of spoons! We've got work to do!"

"You are *really* not contributing at all to this."

Deet beeped at him. "I am continuing to develop my joke database. This is important work."

"Ugh. Hey, comm tech," Rogers said. "We're still jammed, aren't we?"

"Completely, sir."

Another moment of pregnant silence.

"I am going to kill that son of a bitch when he gets back on my ship," Rogers said.

"Sir," Commander Rholos said. "There's something strange going on outside the *Limiter*."

"What is it?"

"It's best if I show you."

"Bring it up on the screen," Rogers said, sitting back down in his chair. His whole body was covered in sweat; his pulse was racing. The Thelicosans had miraculously made no move to counter their attack, and even after they'd blown apart several munitions dumps and one milk container, there had still been no enemy response.

Now, however, there appeared to be a lone figure standing on top of the *Limiter*. It was difficult to make out—the visual scanners only went so far—but he was holding two objects in his hands. He raised his arms and started doing strange motions that seemed like a sort of robotic dance.

"What's he doing?" Rogers asked.

"I have no idea, sir," Rholos said. "I'm checking with our Thelicosan cultural specialist to see if it's some kind of Thelicosan war dance."

"We have a Thelicosan cultural specialist?" Rogers said.

"Helurr!" came a voice over the communications system.

"Tunger?" Rogers said incredulously.

"Yurp! There was an open position on the roster, and all the mammals are in hibernation this time of year, so I had some free time to expand my knowledge of Thelicosan customs. It's been very educational."

Rogers sighed. "Well, what do you think they're doing?"

"It's nothing I've ever heard of, sir, but I do think they're trying to communicate with us. It could be space semaphore."

"Space what?"

"Space semaphore. It's an ancient art of communication achieved by waving flags at each other. I think we have someone on board who knows it."

"Get him up here."

Rogers sat back and waited, looking at the display screen nervously. What were they trying to do? It was like there was someone on top of the *Limiter* having a controlled seizure with flags. He'd never seen anything like it in his entire life.

The rest of the bridge was busy calming down from the operation and preparing the defenses in case the Thelicosans tried a counterattack. Zaz was busy coordinating the recovery of the

Ravagers, all of whom had expended almost all their ordnance, Lancers included. What a waste of resources.

A few minutes later, a hobo walked onto the bridge. Rogers didn't notice him at first, but the distinct smell of, well, hobo kind of alerted him that something had changed. That and the fact that nearly everyone else started looking toward the entrance to the bridge with grotesque expressions.

"Um," Rogers said. "Who are you?" Then he thought for a moment. "Were you the one living in the war room?"

"Eh?" the man said. He was probably just under six feet tall, with a long, gray beard that could have been constructed from stray squirrel hairs. His eyebrows matched his beard, but he had no hair to speak of on the top of his head. The copious amounts of liver spots decorating his pate acted as a bit of a substitute, if a little stomach-turning. His eyes were yellowed, his back was stooped, and he was wearing a Meridan naval uniform that marked him as a starman second class. Judging by his age, that meant he had held the same rank in the military for approximately thirty billion years.

"I said who are you?"

"Oh," the man said. "I'm your sixteen alpha. Name's Ernie Guff."

Rogers looked around the room for anyone who might have any idea what that meant. When he saw blank expressions that reflected his own, he asked.

"Antiquated communications technician. Morse, semaphore, and handwriting."

"What the hell is Morse?" Rogers asked. "Why haven't I heard of any of these things before? Why do we still employ people who know them?"

"Another ancient form of communication," Belgrave, who had apparently taken on the role of military historian, said. "It was developed by Philip Morris, who was also an accomplished tobacconist. He experimented with electrical signals on the side and accidentally developed a form of sonic communication while trying to design a cigarette lighter."

Rogers frowned. "I thought you said it was Morse code, not Morris code."

Belgrave gave him a pedantic look. "History distorts many things, sir."

"Fine," Rogers said. "Fine. Mr. Guff, if you would please sit down right there and tell me what these people are trying to say."

Guff ambled over to a chair, a cloud of nauseating stench following him that reminded Rogers of the inside of some of the less reputable bars on Merida Prime. He sat down and fell asleep.

"Hey!" Rogers said. "Someone wake him up and give him a glass of water or something."

Someone woke him up and gave him a glass of water.

"Eh? What?"

"The semaphore, Ernie," Rogers said.

Guff looked out the window, and for a moment Rogers thought he was falling asleep again. Then he started to speak.

"It's just letters. They keep repeating the same three over and over again."

Rogers waited while the old man looked very intently at the viewscreen and started to translate the strange flag dance.

"'W.'"

A pause.

"'T.'"

Another pause.

"'F.'"

A long pause.

"Yep," Rogers said. "Definitely trying to communicate."

Flag-Waving

Watching an old man who Rogers was pretty sure hadn't showered for the better part of a decade peel off his rotting uniform and try to squeeze himself into a skintight space suit was pretty high on the list of things Rogers didn't want to experience. But here he was, standing in the hatch, while an old man got naked.

"I need you to follow my instructions to the letter," Rogers said.

"Was that a pun?" Deet asked. "You know, because it's semaphore?"

"No," Rogers said irritably, then paused. "Maybe. It might have been. Look, that's not important right now. Do you understand me, Guff? We can't have any miscommunication here. One wrong word and we start a war. Well, we start *more* of a war. We get more war-ish. The war-ness increases. Are you sure you can handle this?"

The hatch, which had been built so that a single engineer could climb out to the exterior of the ship to perform various repairs, wasn't really big enough for two men and a droid. Rogers tried desperately to dodge Guff's movements, but he couldn't avoid a brush or two with disaster. That disaster namely being the bare, wrinkled ass cheeks of Guff. Rogers tried not to think about the wet scraping noise they made as Guff rested against the wall.

"I can handle this as well as I can handle a woman," Guff said, which did not, at all, clarify things or reduce Rogers' rising nausea.

"I estimate the time differential between now and his previous performance of either of these duties to be approximately the same," Deet said.

"Eh?" Guff said, cupping his ear in his hand and stopping what he was doing. This left him with both legs of his VMU on and the rest of him still quite naked.

"Nothing," Rogers said, more loudly. "Please, I'm begging you. Just put the rest of the suit on so we can do the ops check and get you on the outside of the ship."

Guff grumbled through the rest of the procedure, Rogers temporarily suspending his policy of not touching icky things to help expedite the process. He would have to boil his hands after this.

Damn it, he was the acting admiral of the fleet! Why was he up here in the hatch instead of one of the lower-ranking engineering troops? Belgrave had said it was something about the power and burden of command. Rogers thought they were just messing with him.

Finally they managed to get the man's helmet on and start testing the systems. Oxygen was flowing, the actuators inside the suit were working to allow Guff to move around in space if he needed to, and lastly, the communications unit inside the helmet was indeed working. They had been worried that all the noise-jamming going on in the battlespace would interfere with the short-range radios, but the pilots had been able to get their communications through, if in a very garbled way. Since Guff was going to be remaining so close to the ship—that is, he would be standing on it—the signal from the helmet could burn through the jamming.

"Okay," Rogers said. "How do you feel?"

"Like I'm wrapped in plastic wrap," Guff said, his voice coming through the microphone on the front of his helmet. "Which sort of reminds of me of this one crazy time with a lady on Dathum—"

"Please," Rogers said, holding up a hand. "Please. Don't reveal anything to me for which I would have to have you court-martialed or for which I would have to use steel wool to clean the images from my brain. Let's just get on with the mission. Are you ready?"

"Eh?"

"Are you ready?"

"Of course I'm ready," Guff said. "Why are you shouting?" He worked his shoulder around slowly in its socket, the movement stiff and jerky, before picking up two huge flags wound around two poles. Rogers hoped the visual scanners on the *Limiter* were good enough to see him clearly.

"Good luck," Rogers said. "And please, wait until I've left the hatch to open the airlock."

Guff put his hand on the airlock release control.

"Stop!" Rogers said, slapping Guff's hand away. "What are you doing?"

"You just told me to release the airlock," Guff's voice crackled through his helmet.

Rogers shook his head. "No, I said to wait until I'm gone before you do that. Are you trying to kill me?"

Through the reflective visor of his helmet, Rogers could see a confused expression on Guff's face. "No, I don't know anyone named Philsby. Why does that matter?"

Rogers stared at him. "It doesn't."

He and Deet escaped the hatch as fast as they could, reentering the ship near the engineering bay and heading back toward the bridge via a few short interchanges of up-line and in-line. Deet was uncharacteristically quiet, and Rogers didn't mind.

By the time they got back to the bridge, his nerves had calmed a bit. It was clear the Thelicosans wanted to talk, though not nearly as clear why they were choosing such a ridiculous method of communication. They had taken the time to announce that they were invading via a short textual message upon their entry into the system; why not do the same thing now? It smelled like a trap to Rogers, but he had no idea what kind of trap would involve waving flags at each other. At least flags were better than plasma blasts.

The bridge wasn't very lively, now that everyone was simply waiting for communication. Rogers had issued some preparatory orders to pilots and defensive systems. If negotiations went poorly, he wanted to make sure they had ample time to at least try to run away a little bit. The whole "going down fighting" thing wasn't very attractive to Rogers, but there was this little niggling sensation that might have been called duty telling him to make sure he took as many of the Thelicosans with them as they could before they were turned into space dust.

"What's the report from the hangars?" he said.

The offensive and defensive coordinators were still on the bridge; Rogers had dismissed them for a meal and a quick nap if they wanted, but he needed them available for the foreseeable future. If Belgrave could be a bridge zombie, so could they. Rogers was starting to feel like a bridge zombie already.

"System checks are good. We're at sixty-five percent readiness," Commander Zaz said.

"Sixty-five percent?" Rogers said. "That seems a little low, doesn't it?"

"I'm not including all the Ravagers that were either destroyed on the previous mission or have coagulated milk bits in their engines. Engineering isn't going to be able to get them back online for at least a few standard days; Master Sergeant Hart says they have to take the engines apart, clean them, and put them back together again."

"Great," Rogers said. He thought for a moment, then tapped the button on his console for Flight Control.

"Yes, sir?" came the voice of the on-duty supervisor.

"Find out if we have any extra pilots available that don't have a Ravager to fly. See if any of them know how to pilot shuttles, and tell them to get ready to fly."

"Yes, sir."

"What are you thinking?" Deet asked.

"We haven't been able to communicate with the other ships in the fleet since the jamming net went up. I'm going to do this the old-fashioned way and send runners with datapads. I don't want anyone doing anything stupid."

"Like sending a squadron of fighters to charge in and blow up a bunch of [EXPLETIVE] milk containers?"

". . . Exactly. Exactly like that."

Rogers sat down in his chair, thinking and trying to block out everything that wasn't important at the moment—namely, the fact that he was hungry and really needed a drink. The *Flagship* had been a dry town for far too long. Other than the disgusting home-brewed swill that Sergeant Lopez in Engineering crafted from sulfur and death, there wasn't any alcohol on the ship at all. Rogers missed the old days.

"Guff," Rogers said into the radio, "are you ready up there?"

"Yes, sir," came the garbled, phlegm-stuffed voice over the intercom. It was like the man had done nothing but gargle whiskey and smoke cigarettes every day for the last twenty years. Judging by how he had looked, Rogers didn't entirely think that was improbable. Where had Tunger dug up this guy?

"Alright," Rogers said. "I want you to tell them hello."

A burst of static came through the radio, courtesy of the jamming net, Rogers was sure. After a few moments of silence, Rogers repeated his message.

"Hello," Guff said back, quite cheerily.

Silence.

"No," Rogers said. "That's what I want you to tell *them*."

"Oh," Guff said. "That makes sense. Give me ten minutes."

Rogers frowned. "Ten minutes?"

Deet broke in. "Semaphore was not the quickest or most efficient mode of communication, according to my limited available database research. It was mostly used before the advent of radio, and afterward only when there needed to be strict radio silence."

What followed was simultaneously the most boring and the tensest ten minutes of Rogers' short life in this universe. The *Flagship* wasn't designed to observe itself, so there weren't any cameras focused on Guff; he could only hope that the man was transmitting the right message. Even if they could see him, nobody would know what the hell he was doing.

Time flowed like a river of molasses.

"Since we're not doing anything important for the next ten minutes," Deet said, "I was wondering if I could tell you something I've been thinking recently about existentialism and how it does, or does not, intersect with moral absolutism and droid consciousness."

Time flowed like a river of molasses cooled to near freezing.

"Can't you just please try to swear instead?" Rogers said.

"[ENGAGE IN SELF-FORNICATION]."

"Actually, I think it's a valid question," Belgrave said suddenly. "But you're starting with the wrong fundamental question. It's better to start with consciousness, then droid consciousness, and work your way up to collective consciousness theories like moral relativism."

Time flowed like a river of molasses cooled to near freezing with a philosophical droid sailing on it in a small rowboat.

"Get me Mailn," Rogers said into the radio, standing up. "Tell her to meet me in the training room. I need someone to hit me."

"I don't know what kind of semaphore class this fella was in," Skokum said over the radio, his "s" noises whistling loudly through the gaps in his teeth. "But he's as sloppy as an abacus with its strings cut. I can barely make out what he's saying."

"Do your best, Skokum," Zergan said over the radio. "What does it look like to you?"

"Well, the first letter he put out looks like it should have been a 'B,' but then he corrected it to an 'L,' and then an 'H.' He's done that with every letter of this first word. So right now, he could be saying 'butter,' 'hellos,' or 'locust.'"

The *Limiter*'s bridge was silent, everyone staring tensely at the screen that showed the Meridans' semaphore troop on the top of their ship. Alandra wasn't very well versed in this form of communication, but she was pretty certain it didn't involve a lot of dance-like moves. In the last few letters, it appeared that the Meridan communicator had attempted to twirl around at least twice.

"You see?" Zergan said, looking at Alandra sharply. "They're saying they're going to swarm us like locusts. Do you really think these are the kinds of people we should be calmly communicating with?"

Alandra didn't look at him, but Quinn was quick to jump in.

"I think barring any other evidence, we should probably assume that the first word was 'hello' and not 'locust.' Unless you think it was 'butter' and this is just going to be a conversation about toast."

A stifled chuckle stopped short in Alandra's chest, which surprised her for at least two reasons. First, she never chuckled. It was a diminutive form of laughing, which she also never did. Second, she was almost certain that the career bureaucrat Quinn had no capacity for humor and—though she was not entirely familiar with the concept—she was almost positive that Quinn had just made a joke.

Zergan's face turned tomato red, but Alandra could read the expression on his face. He knew Quinn was right, and so did Alandra.

"Let us assume that the first message was indeed 'hello.' Skokum, I want you to transmit the word 'meeting.'"

Rogers regretted his request to be hit when he got back to the bridge and found it hard to focus on what was going on. Mailn hadn't gone easy on him, but he had successfully dodged at least one halfhearted punch to the face. He'd also dodged several other strikes that Mailn hadn't launched; mixing dodging instincts with being a complete coward made for interesting ducking technique that was, maybe, more exercise than required. She'd remained tight-lipped about all the emotional, touchy-feely stuff she'd been talking about the last time they'd sparred. He also didn't have much opportunity to ask while being hit in the face.

"You know," Belgrave said as Rogers sat down, sweating, in his commander's chair, "getting up and leaving to get thrown around by a girl while in the middle of a complicated exchange with a deadly enemy is typically considered poor command style."

"Thanks for the tip," Rogers said. "Why don't you fill me in on all the activity I missed while I was off being aloof and irresponsible?"

Belgrave said nothing.

"I rest my case."

Rogers looked at the viewscreen and saw that the Thelicosan atop the *Limiter* was performing what Rogers hoped was the response to his greeting. Rogers had never seen this sort of thing done before; it looked like the man was having a very dramatic seizure one small move at a time.

"This is the most ridiculous form of communication I have ever seen in my entire life. Are we sure this is an actual language?"

"This guy is moving really fast," Guff said over the radio. "One letter every minute or so. It's blinding speed. He's really good." A moment of silence. "I'm going to signal him to start over."

Rogers shook his head. Guff could see the viewscreen's depiction of the Thelicosan flag-waver via a small projection in his helmet, and he was supposed to be relaying the messages back to the bridge. Instead, he seemed to just be getting confused.

"'R'?" he said. "'L'? This doesn't make any sense."

"Can you tell him to slow down?" Rogers asked, not really believing that he was making the suggestion.

"What?" Guff said, sounding confused. "Who cares if your eyes are brown?"

"I asked if you could tell him to slow down," Rogers repeated more loudly.

"The message 'slow down' would take a solid thirty minutes," Guff replied.

"Oh."

After a few more minutes of Guff muttering to himself, Guff said, "Urinary."

"What?!"

"Sorry." Guff paused. "'Meeting.' The word is 'meeting.' They want a meeting."

"I think they want to meet you," Belgrave said.

"I think they want you to urinate," Deet said.

"Everyone shut up!" Rogers said. He was clutching the arm-rests of his chair tightly. The Thelicosans wanted to meet with him? That didn't make any sense.

"If they wanted to talk to me," he said out loud, "why not lift the jamming net and just send me a message? Why all the flag-waving?"

"Because it's fun?" Deet offered.

"Because they wanted to see how amazing I am?" Guff said.

"Sir," Belgrave interrupted. "They're waiting for our response."

"Ask them where," Rogers said. "Transmit 'location.'"

"They say 'romantic,'" Skokum said over the radio, and Alandra's heart nearly ripped through her chest. "At least I think that's what they're saying. The Meridan dialect is very peculiar."

"How can there be a dialect in semaphore?" Zergan wondered aloud.

Alandra barely heard him. Captain Rogers had just transmitted the single most hopeful message she'd ever received in her life. Romantic? As in romantic pursuits? Was it a question? Perhaps he was asking if the meeting was going to be romantic. She very badly wanted to tell Skokum to simply answer "yes, please," but that seemed almost too easy. Captain Rogers was clever, skilled, smooth. He'd want her to play it careful, be coy.

"There must be some mistake," Quinn said, tapping her finger against her lip. "There's no reason for anyone to be romantic."

Alandra felt her anger boil up. How dare this woman say there was *no reason* for anyone to get romantic! There was every reason! The numbers! The ratios! Those intimate, incredible intelligence reports that had taught her so much about the man in charge of that fleet!

And why shouldn't he transmit romantic intentions? Wasn't she, the Grand Marshal of the Colliders, enough of a reason for any man? Captain Rogers should count himself lucky that she had directed her affections at him. And now he dared insult her by having Quinn publicly doubt his possibly erroneous message of romance?

Steeling herself, Alandra forcibly began to control her breathing, closing her eyes. The knowledge that almost nothing she had just thought made any sense at all fell like a blanket of reason over a smoldering fire. She needed to be like any two numbers that could be expressed as a fraction: rational. Calm. And do her best not to kick anyone in the face.

The only thing she could think of to do—other than jump into a shuttle and fly to the *Flagship* with the traditional Thelicosan betrothal gift of a protractor—was to set the meeting location. The closest thing she could think of to neutral ground was a Thelicosan cargo ship that had minimal personnel and no armament.

"Skokum," Alandra said. "Transmit the name of the ship *Ambuscade* and then give them the ship's alphanumeric coordinates."

"They just transmitted a phone number, I think," Guff said. "And they say 'accordion.'"

"That's just mean. They're jamming our communications, and they send us a phone number?" Rogers harrumphed. "That can't be right. Tell them to repeat the message."

"Eh? What? Boy, this helmet is foggy," Guff said absently.

"Something appears to be wrong with their interpreter," Skokum said. "He keeps asking me to repeat myself. At least, I think so. He's giving me the signs for both 'repeat' and 'snuggle.'"

Hope blossomed in Alandra's chest.

"Keep transmitting until they get it," Zergan snapped.

"A bunch of numbers again, I think," Guff said uncertainly. "And I don't know what the hell the word was. Is 'soupsoups' a real thing?"

"No, it is not a real thing," Roger said. "Ask them again."

"Bumfuzzle."

Rogers remained silent.

"I'll try again," Guff said.

After the better part of a day of flag-waving, and one very hastily constructed rescue mission when an overenthusiastic wave from Guff sent him careening off the surface of the *Flagship*, it seemed as though they had reached an understanding with the Thelicosans. They'd agreed on a place, a time, and some terms. The captain of the *Flagship* would meet directly with the commander of the Thelicosan fleet. No weapons. No tricks.

There were also two other messages that seemed like outliers, one of which seemed to be a euphemistic sexual suggestion and the other of which was just the words "eat poop you cat." Everyone agreed to dismiss them both as errors. Guff had certainly made enough of those.

"The *Ambuscade*?" Rogers said. "That's a funny name for a ship."

"No way, man," Flash said. "That's an old Thelicosan word that means 'neutral ground.' That's the best place to have a little powwow."

Rogers looked at him, puzzled that such an utter idiot would have any etymological knowledge at all.

"That's not what that word means," Deet said.

"Shut up, bolt brain," Flash said. "I don't need you computing me, or anything like that. Why don't you throttle back a bit? Check your six."

"Alright, alright," Rogers said. He pointed at Deet. "You, relax for a minute." Then Flash. "You, stop speaking in code. I'm not done yelling at you for attacking floating metallic cows. The Thelicosans want to meet, and it doesn't seem like we have much of a choice. Commander Zaz, did you get a readout on that ship?"

"Yes, sir," Zaz said. "The *Ambuscade* is a Thelicosan cargo ship, commissioned and built two decades ago and attached to the Colliders a little over a year ago. We don't have any information on the identities of the crew, but it wasn't built for combat. It doesn't even appear to have any defensive systems other than warning systems and some countermeasures." He blinked and, looking off into the distance, placed his hands over his gigantic headphones. "It seems like as neutral a place as we're going to get for a meeting with the Thelicosans."

Rogers sat back, thinking. Did he really have a choice?

"I think you really need to devote a little more time to researching the meaning behind the name of that ship," Deet said.

"I really don't need a vocabulary lesson right now, Deet," Rogers said tiredly. Could anyone around him do anything without nagging him about something inconsequential? It seemed like ever since he'd become acting admiral of the fleet, he was busier dealing with personalities than he was with duties. Even more confusing, he'd just mentally given Deet personality, despite the fact that he knew Deet was just a droid with a Freudian Chip. Even that wasn't that special; he'd met plenty of other F Chip droids (Froids), and *they'd* tried to kill him. Several times.

Rogers stroked his beard, then looked around the bridge, scanning the faces of the crew waiting for him to make a decision. The one face he missed was the Viking's. Her broad forehead and thick eyebrows would really have been a sight for sore eyes at the moment, even if she was screaming at him for being a poor excuse for an admiral.

"Any thoughts? If you have ideas, speak them now."

"Pick up a dictionary," Deet said.

"Any other thoughts?"

"Yeah," Flash said, "I got one. We go in with guns, right, and then we give 'em a Split S"—he held up his hands—"like this, and then I totally splash some bandits."

Rogers gave him a long, hard stare. "Are you sure your last name isn't Klein?"

Flash looked at him sideways. "Dude, no. My name is Flash."

Unable to really comprehend that statement, Rogers mentally erased "Flash" from the room and looked around expectantly. Apparently, everyone was just as dumbfounded as he was, as there were no other comments. Even the garrulous Commander Belgrave didn't seem to have any leadership textbook quotes to throw at him.

"Fine. Everyone take some time to relax after that really intense day of space miming. Then let's put together the crew. Someone tell Captain Alsinbury to get up here so that we can put together the strike team."

"Strike team?" Belgrave said, breaking his silence. "We agreed there would be no weapons."

"I'm desperate, Belgrave, not stupid. Now if you'll excuse me, I'm going to the mess hall to get me some soupsoups."

Sandwich Hour

There were three things that Secretary Vilia Quinn—as official, documented policy—did not like. The first thing was lint. Despite their being a marvelous example of the properties of electric charge, nothing marred a newly pressed pantsuit like those little static ninjas. The second was improperly filled-out forms. The instructions were always right there at the top. The third, obviously, was discovering treason.

Vilia's pulse wasn't used to racing very much—she'd spent a considerable amount of her bureaucratic career discouraging any kind of excitement—so the sensation she was feeling at the moment was particularly foreign to her. She also abhorred the sound of heavy breathing, so the fact that she was panting like a dog was not a little unsettling.

She didn't know what had compelled her to follow Zergan through the corridors of the *Limiter*, but it was certainly paying off now. Zergan had finished speaking with the Grand Marshal and had sneaked off through the ship in a way that told Vilia something was going on. Call it bureaucratic intuition, if there was such a thing. In general, she suspected everyone of ulterior motives—she was a politician, after all—but something about Zergan felt different. Especially now that he'd spent the better part of the last ten minutes talking into an empty cafeteria buffet.

"No, that's not . . . I see. Well, I suppose . . ." What was Zergan talking about? Everyone knew that Sandwich Hour—actually called Snaggardir's Sandwich Hour, in honor of the company that made the sandwich bar—had ended quite some time ago, so there was nobody around. There certainly weren't any sandwiches. And until now, Vilia had also been sure there were no hidden communications devices in the sandwich bar. That meant there was an incorrect record someplace. This would have to be fixed.

Idly, she felt the back of her head, where her triple hair buns sat as both a symbol of status and a source of comfort. One hair was out of place by an inch and a half; she quickly tucked it back into order and took a deep breath. She would have to remember later to make a note of that. It wouldn't do to repeat mistakes.

"No, of course not," Zergan continued. "It's not like that. It's just that Alandra and I have worked together for a long time. I would rather nothing happen to her if it didn't have to." He paused, waiting for a response. "I think I can make it work . . . Rogers? He's an idiot. At least so far there has been every indication that he's an idiot . . . Well, he blew up our milk containers instead of our jammers . . . No, I don't think that was part of a larger strategy . . . Yes, we have ample reserves, thank you, and we did get the cookies."

Vilia's heart quickened, and a sensation that bordered perilously close to excitement crept up inside her. Was Zergan even talking to anyone in the fleet? Was he talking to someone in the *Meridan* fleet? Surely the comment about any harm coming to the Grand Marshal was an indication that he was working for someone else. But who? He was far too bellicose toward the

Meridans to be working for them behind the scenes, unless he was an exceptional actor.

"Really?" Zergan said. "Rogers did? Well, how would I have known that? It's not *my* fault. I'm not a programmer. Then it's all the more important that we take care of this soon. Fine. I'll make the arrangements. The meeting isn't far off. I'll report back once it's complete. Until the chairs are empty. Out."

Until the chairs are empty? What was that supposed to mean?

She didn't have much more time to think about it, as a couple of Thelicosan soldiers—at least, she thought they were soldiers, and not sailors, or spacers, or whatever—came stomping down the hallway unexpectedly.

"Oh, hello, Madam Secretary," said one of them, a short, stocky man with a face like a bowl of pudding into which several pieces of fruit had been dropped. She wasn't sure why she conjured that particular image, but it fit, particularly in the way his face shook when he spoke. He raised an eyebrow. "What are you doing?"

Vilia frowned at him. She was in far too high a position on this ship for someone of such low rank to be questioning her activities, but the Grand Marshal had made a bad habit of treating her like a rodent. It set a poor example for the troops. She would have called him down for it, but all this uncharacteristic sneaking around had rattled her a bit.

"Leaning against the wall, mentally filing paperwork," she snapped. "What are *you* doing?"

Pudding Face shrugged and held his hands up defensively. "Just getting dinner."

"Dinner doesn't start for twenty minutes," Quinn said. Twenty-two, actually.

"We like to be early." He leaned forward and whispered conspiratorially: "They undercook the bacon if you rush them. Chewy bacon is the best."

Vilia scowled. The fourth thing she hated was pork, but this wasn't really the time to go on about it.

"Well then," she said, her words clipped, "let's let each other go back to our respective tasks, shall we?" She raised her eyebrows, emphasizing the dismissal. She needed to get out of here before—

"Sandwich Hour was over a long time ago, Council dog," Zergan said, his eyes narrow, as he rounded the corner.

For a moment, Vilia froze. The troops who had been telling her the secrets of chewy bacon snapped to attention and saluted Zergan sharply, according him a completely different kind of demeanor from the casual flippancy with which they had addressed her. Zergan waved them away, but in the moment of their departure, she was able to get a firm grasp on her composure and rein it in like the stray hair in her bun.

"Oh yes," she said. "Sandwich Hour was over quite some time ago, wasn't it? Funny that both of us would be here, then, not getting sandwiches."

As happened often lately, Vilia was surprised by her own words. Being a career bureaucrat had given her a tight control of her speech, and a mastery of subtlety. Ever since being assigned to the *Limiter*, however, she'd been prone to acid outbursts and arm-flailing. Controlled, calculated arm-flailing, of course.

Ever the unflappable military man, Zergan took her veiled threat in stride, his mouth barely tightening into a sardonic smile.

"Yes," he said, almost hissing. "No sandwiches for either of us."

Vilia was fairly certain that continually discussing their mutual lack of sandwiches was about as useful as a quadratic equation where 'a' equals zero. She desperately wanted to simply ask Zergan what he had been doing, who he had been talking to, and why he'd been doing so with his face in the sandwich bar.

A thought occurred to her that perhaps there *was* no one on the other end. Zergan had been a member of the F Sequence special operations squadron a long time ago—along with the Grand Marshal—and she knew that sometimes such duties could . . . break people. Rumor had it that the Grand Marshal herself was a victim of the mental strain of the F Sequence, which was why she had been transferred to command instead.

The thought unsettled Vilia. Dealing with a sane warmongering Zergan was difficult enough. Dealing with a potentially crazy warmongering Zergan would probably be . . . well, it would probably be exactly the same, really.

"Well, if you'll excuse me," Zergan said with a mocking bow of his head. "I have to go prepare to deal with an inferior force." He made no effort to keep the disgust out of his voice, his giant, caterpillar-like eyebrows scrunching further together as he scowled. "We'll see how that goes."

Then it hit her like the tangent to a parabola. Which, she guessed, was more of a glancing blow by definition, but still! The meeting! Zergan was going to sabotage the negotiations. A slow, secretive smile played behind his lips, but he made strong efforts to hide it. Or did he? Did he *want* her to know he was going to pull something, want her to know she could do nothing to stop him?

Vilia tried her best to keep her face impassive, but it proved a near-impossible task. She allowed herself a slow swallow, the kind that made her feel like a coward. She desperately wanted to touch her buns, or at least file some paperwork.

Just when she thought Zergan was going to do something violent—there weren't any other troops around to see him do it, if he'd really wanted to—he gave her another fake bow and walked away.

Vilia watched him go, reaching up to grab her hair buns as soon as he wasn't looking at her anymore. What was she supposed to do with this information? She couldn't very well bring it to the Grand Marshal. Keffoule absolutely hated her, and there was no real, hard evidence that Zergan was planning anything.

Glancing at the sandwich bar, she let out a heavy sigh. There was nothing she could do. She couldn't even get a sandwich. If Zergan managed to bring weapons on board the *Ambuscade* or something like that, it would be the end of the tenuous peace they'd reachieved after bursting into the system unannounced. What had the Grand Marshal been thinking?

If she couldn't figure out a way to expose him, it would be all over. The Meridans were in a miserable position already; there was no way they'd attempt to violate the very fragile agreement they'd struck with the Thelicosans. They'd never walk out of there alive.

"There's no way we're walking out of there alive unless we violate the agreement," Rogers said.

The Viking, looking as beautiful as ever, glared at him.

"Oh, we're crawling back to the marines, are we, now that your miserable moron pet of a pilot completely screwed up?"

The Viking was staring at him with a look that was at once utterly terrifying and incredibly exciting. She hadn't spoken to him in the time leading up to the mission, but now Rogers couldn't afford having her avoid him. It created a void in his life so large that he thought he might collapse. He also might eventually need the Viking's marines to shoot things, and that was also important.

"I'm saying that I'm about to put my head into the mouth of the lion, and it would be nice to have a team backing me up." Rogers felt a little silly saying all these things; he was really only repeating things he'd seen in movies. That was about all the introduction he'd received to combat, aside from blowing up a droid or two by accident.

They were standing in the hallway of the training deck—the easiest place to find the Viking—and a few troops passed, offering him salutes. He'd forgotten to deploy his antisalute arm sling and was forced to reciprocate, which was both distracting and slightly exhausting.

"Nice?" the Viking asked, managing to make one word sound very threatening. "Nice? That's what you think of me and my team?"

Jeez, what is your problem? he thought.

"Jeez, what is your problem?" he said aloud, shocking himself.

The Viking's eyes went wide. For a moment, she seemed to be speechless. Her usual default aggressive behavior slid away, revealing a moment of what appeared to be confusion. It didn't last very long.

"I am going to use your face as a battering ram," the Viking said in a strikingly calm manner.

"Please don't do that," Rogers said, ducking reflexively. His muscles really did feel like they were moving faster; even Mailn had said he was getting pretty good at dodging "slow attacks that children would have little trouble avoiding."

The Viking didn't exactly throw a punch that a child could have dodged, but Rogers had ducked before she'd thrown it. Since he had already moved, it went wide, sending her off balance. Her impressive mass, combined with the fact that Rogers might or might not have grabbed a piece of her uniform and tugged a little just in an effort to be closer to her, sent her reeling forward. The result was a lot of grunting, some shouts of surprise, and two bodies rolling on the floor.*

When it ended, and Rogers stopped hyperventilating, he was treated to the rare and scintillating sight of the Viking's eyes, big, brown, and menacing, staring into his from about three inches away. In some faraway place in his imagination, he was certain they were looking at him with love and adoration. In reality, the Viking was reaching for her disruptor pistol. She sure was warm, though.

"You son of a bitch," she hissed. Rogers could feel her breath on his face like a sweet perfume caressing his skin.

"You tried to punch me!" Rogers protested. Unfortunately, their resultant configuration placed most of the Viking's weight directly on his lungs, which made for a more strangled protest than he would have liked to admit. That her free hand was

---

* Oh, get your mind out of the gutter. They just fell down.

wrapped around his throat didn't help matters either. Boy, there was a lot of asphyxiation going on. Rogers was mentally confirming that he wasn't really into that sort of thing when they were—perhaps thankfully—interrupted.

"What's going on here?" a familiar, slightly robotic voice said. "I am still working on familiarizing myself with human customs, but I am nearly positive this is not the typical or appropriate place for nearly anything."

"Shut up, Deet!" Rogers yell-whispered. Little black floaty things were starting to dance across his vision and mingle with the little silver floaty things.

The spell was broken, however, and the Viking simultaneously released his throat and rolled off him, an action he'd always dreamed would have been a little more romantic, or at least a little more naked. She stood up, dusted off her uniform, and glared at Rogers as he shakily pulled himself to his feet. Deet, who for some reason was holding a piece of paper with an inkblot on it, was apparently taking a break from analyzing the deactivated droids.

"You're a miserable excuse for a commander," the Viking said, her voice ice. She was breathing heavily, and her eyes blazed with fury. Rogers really wished he knew what was making her so angry.

"I didn't exactly volunteer for the position," he snapped back. "I'm trying to do the best I can without getting everyone underneath me killed, and right now I have a giant fleet of people with very ambiguous and confusing intentions wanting to have a tea party with me on one of their own ships. I'm asking *you* if you'd provide some security. Is that such a bad idea?"

"It's not your ideas," the Viking said. "It's your tactics."

Rogers bristled. "What's wrong with my tactics?"

"You think you're so clever. You never know when to charge or when to play it smart. In fact, you do it backward in almost everything."

"Just because I didn't let you storm the enemy capital ship doesn't mean I don't know when to charge," Rogers said.

"And you think taking weapons into a negotiation on a completely neutral, perfectly safe ship—"

"The *Ambuscade*," Deet said. "You still haven't looked up what it means, have you?"

"—is a better idea?"

Some troops were gathering to watch the confrontation, which was beginning to make Rogers feel uncomfortable. He had some clout from what he'd done with the droids, but he wasn't exactly the hero of Merida or anything like that. He didn't need his troops seeing him get browbeaten by a lower-ranking officer, even if she was more capable and beautiful.

"You just said I had good ideas!"

"No, I said you had bad tactics," the Viking said. "I never said anything about good ideas."

This woman was so *frustrating*! Never mind the fact that Rogers couldn't tell if she was angry, furious, or just in a rage. Subtle differences mattered.

"So what?" Rogers said. "When am I supposed to charge? Maybe if you educated me a little bit more than just trying to punch me in the face, I could learn a thing or two about tactics."

"Maybe I don't want to educate you," the Viking said. "Maybe I'd just prefer a commander who knew what he wanted and knew how to get it."

"Well, maybe I'd prefer a marine who knew other ways of communicating than punching people in the face," Rogers said. "I just wish you'd *share* with me a little more." He blinked. "Your tactics. Share your tactics."

The Viking folded her arms and cocked her hips in a way that was both intensely distracting and possibly the prelude to a right hook.

"Share my tactics?" The Viking let out a bombastic belly laugh. "Don't patronize me. Commanders don't want me to share my tactics with them. They're full of shit if they say so."

Rogers frowned. "What makes that so unbelievable?" he said.

"You've got good tactics. Nice, and full. Of wisdom and experience. Nice and full of wisdom and experience."

For some reason, this seemed to make the Viking even angrier. She leaned forward, her face turning a deep crimson, and spat her words at him.

"Commander or not, if you keep making fun of me I am going to use your robot boyfriend as a sledgehammer for your spine."

Deet beeped. "Given the number of joints and pivot points, I would be far better use as more of a whipping instrument than a blunting instrument."

"Shut up," Rogers growled. "I'm not making fun of you! Why do you always have to take tactical discussions to the next level? Can we please just solve the issue at hand?"

The Viking grunted and pointed at Rogers. "Why do you always have to try to solve everything? Why can't you just talk about the tactics?"

Rogers paused. He was starting to get a strange feeling that they were talking about different things. Or maybe they were talking about the same thing but neither of them knew it.

"Because I don't know anything about tactics," he said slowly. "Didn't you just say that?"

"And I just said I prefer not having to hold my commander's hand," the Viking shot back. "Maybe it would be nice every once in a while if *you* took the initiative." She snorted. "Not like it would make a difference. No marine likes a commander with disingenuous tactics."

"Wait," Rogers said. "What the hell *are* we talking about?"

"Just stop bullshitting me, Rogers," the Viking said, her face relaxing. She looked resigned, maybe even a little bit sad. "Why don't you go back to the training room and get sweaty with Mailn for a while? Maybe *she* can teach you a thing or two about tactics."

"What?" Rogers said, totally caught off guard but recognizing the signs of jealousy instantly. He couldn't believe what he was hearing. "Wait, do you think Mailn has a thing for me or something?"

Do you have a thing for me? Rogers thought.

The Viking barked a laugh. "And you call yourself a commander! A commander is supposed to know his people."

"I know Mailn!" Rogers protested. Maybe he liked making the Viking jealous.

"Oh for . . . Mailn doesn't have a thing for you. She's gay, you idiot! Forget this. I'm out of here."

She turned and walked away briskly, and briskly for her was a trot for any normal-sized human being. Rogers was left standing there, his head spinning, wondering what in the world had just happened.

"So does that mean you're coming with me to the *Ambuscade*?" he called after her.

The Viking gave him the finger just before she vanished into the in-line.

"Okay," Rogers said quietly. His forehead hurt from frowning and Mailn hitting him in the face just a while ago during one of their training session. Mailn. Why had the Viking mentioned her, especially if she knew Mailn wasn't attracted to him? It didn't make any sense.

"I'm very confused," Deet said.

Rogers was too, but he was curious about Deet's reasoning.

"Why?" he asked.

"Well, based on past experiences, I was under the impression that humans only used kitchen terminology to talk around things."

Rogers cocked his head. "What?"

"You really thought you were talking about tactics?" Deet said.

Rogers nodded slowly. "Deet, I'm about to go meet the enemy commander. I think a tactical discussion is an appropriate thing to engage in."

Deet was quiet for a long time. So long, in fact, that Rogers thought perhaps there was something wrong with the gravity generator and Deet had lost power. But Deet shook his head in a very human-like gesture and made a disconcerted beeping noise.

"Sometimes," he said, "I wonder which one of us is the robot."

A trio of cooks, dressed in their aprons, passed by and offered Rogers sharp salutes and sharp cheddar, which he returned/ate. Come to think of it, his arm *was* feeling a little stronger. Maybe he'd get used to this after all. The cooks, for reasons Rogers did not understand, turned and entered one of the training rooms used for old-style knife combat. He supposed things were a little touch-and-go on stressful days in the kitchen.

"Well," Rogers said, "whatever you're talking about isn't that important right now. I've got to get back up to my room and get ready." He took a deep breath. "Can you handle things while I'm gone?"

Rogers turned and headed back toward the up-line, which would take him to the command deck and his private stateroom, and Deet followed obediently.

"What about CARL?" Deet said, perhaps sounding vaguely jealous. What was up with everyone today?

"I have an unnatural aversion to trusting anyone named Carl," Rogers said. "And CARL is no exception. Besides, I've never met CARL."

The up-line operator, a spry young woman wearing the traditional train conductor's hat, smiled and saluted as she opened the door for them.

"You can't *meet* CARL," Deet said. "It's a computer program."

"Still," Rogers said, stepping inside the car. "I'd feel better if my deputy was calling the shots in case anything goes wrong."

Deet sat down on one of the chairs, another gesture that seemed very un-robot-like. Did he even really need to rest his feet? Next thing Rogers knew, he'd be going to the lavatory to empty his oil reserves.

"That's fine," Deet said, "as long as you understand the monumental irony in putting a droid in charge of your ship after spending so much effort trying to prevent droids from taking charge of your ship."

"Irony noted. Don't screw it up."

"Thanks for the faith in me, [EXCREMENT GATEWAY]."

The up-line zoomed through the belly of the *Flagship*, and they rode in silence for a while. Rogers couldn't slow his pulse; everything about this meeting sounded like a trap to him. He was meeting a commander he didn't know on a ship that wasn't his in a battlespace that was distinctly weighted toward the other side. He reminded himself that if they simply wanted to kill him and the rest of his fleet, they could have done so already.

Looking at his datapad, he brought up the threadbare and outdated report on the *Limiter*'s commander. Since they'd been cut off from the Meridan central network thanks to the jamming net, they weren't able to do the kind of deep-dive research they really needed to gather information on the enemy force. Relying on only what the *Flagship* had stored locally in its mainframes made for some shoddy intelligence. Not as shoddy as Flash's intuition or Tunger's Thelicosan accent, but not exactly what a commander would want when possibly about to step into a war.

Grand Marshal Alandra Keffoule . . . She'd had an interesting career. At least, Rogers assumed she'd had an interesting career, since there was a huge ten-year gap in her records that either indicated she'd been convalescing from a very serious illness or meant she'd been doing some super-secret stuff. The picture on the profile was old, but she looked very . . . severe, despite soft, round features. No, that wasn't quite the word. It was more like someone prone to sporadic but very tightly controlled violence. Yeah. That was it.

Dark-skinned, with piercing eyes, Keffoule's face in her picture bored a hole in Rogers' forehead. What does one say to the woman who very seriously holds one's life—and the lives of just about everyone under one's command—in her hands?

"I wanted to tell you," Deet said suddenly, "I've been spending some more time with the deactivated droids."

Rogers looked up from his datapad to find Deet actually

sitting with his legs crossed. Ignoring that for the time being, Rogers gave him a "go on" expression.

"Well, don't sound too [EXPLETIVE] excited," Deet said, a trace of bitterness in his voice. "I've only been spending all my [EXPLETIVE] time sticking my [ANATOMICAL REFERENCE] in all my brothers and sisters."

"That's a really gross way of looking at it," Roger said.

Deet ignored the comment and prattled on. "Anyway, I still can't seem to get them to wake up without wanting to kill every human in sight. It doesn't make any sense. It's like it was hard-wired into them somehow. I can't find any references in their core operating system's coding, or any of their other baseline systems. It's almost like they constructed and programmed themselves."

Rogers raised an eyebrow. "They became self-aware? But wouldn't erasing their memories stop that?"

"No," Deet said. "Not self-aware exactly, anyway." He stopped for a moment. "Am I self-aware, do you think? Or am I just responding to a very large decision matrix that continually refreshes itself with new information?" Deet stared at Rogers suddenly. "Are *you* merely a very large decision matrix that—"

"Stop," Rogers said. "Just stop. I really don't need this right now."

Deet beeped. "Fine. My point was that there's something in their default, out-of-the-box character that keeps bringing them back to the point where we shut them all down. I think they were made from the very beginning for that task."

Rogers thought about that a moment. If the droids came factory-designed to try to take over the ship, then the problem wasn't with the droids—it was with the factory.

"Who made them?" he asked.

"There are several inactive lines of code that reference patents, trademarks, and all that, for a company called Zeus Holdings, Inc."

"So, we just ask them."

"Yeah," Deet said. "Let me just use my [EXPLETIVE] droid magic to lift the communications net and pull a phone out of my [ANATOMICAL REFERENCE]. I'll let you know what they say."

Rogers scowled. "You don't have to be such an anatomical reference about it."

"Without access to the larger net, I can't get too much. They're a robotics company that started maybe half a century ago, but I couldn't find a base of operations. It's possible they're entirely space-based."

"Alright," Rogers said. "If and when we get out of this mess, we'll do a little more research and see what we can find about this company. It sounds shady."

"I don't see what the comparative darkness caused by the interception of rays of light from an object has to do with this."

Sighing, Rogers stood as the up-line announced they'd reached the command deck. "I thought we were over this whole figure of speech thing. It just means, you know, that it's not, um, aboveboard?"

"What board?"

"No," Rogers said, waving his hands in the air nonsensically. "Just . . . it's suspicious. Okay? Suspicious. That's the word."

Deet made a whirring noise that sounded very frustrated. "Well, why didn't you just *say* that?"

Rogers ran his hands through his beard, the only companion on this ship that wasn't crazy, crazy, or crazy. You know, the kind of crazy that led to the sight of someone riding a lion into the bridge.

"What are you doing here?" he asked Corporal Tunger. "And why are you riding a lion . . . again?"

"I've been assigned to this mission!" Tunger said excitedly, clapping his hands. The lion stopped and stooped down to let him dismount. "And I'm riding a lion because I can ride a lion, sir. Do you know many people who can ride a lion?"

Rogers had to admit that no, he did not.

"You're the zookeeper," Rogers said carefully, knowing that Tunger was easily offended. "While I value your skills . . ." He looked nervously at the lion, who was licking his paws. ". . . I'm not sure I quite understand how that applies to negotiations."

Tunger puffed up his chest and grinned, wild-eyed. "Aie urm yer inturpruter!"

"Marshmallows," Rogers warned.

"Your interpreter," Tunger said. "You'll need a cultural and linguistic expert if you are to succeed in your negotiations, sir. I am just the man for the job. I believe your deputy assigned me to the mission."

Deet, Rogers thought. *I am going to degauss you.*

Deet might have chuckled.

"Oh," Rogers said, his mind racing. How could he, very politely, tell Tunger that there was no way in hell he was letting him come?

"It's just an accent," Rogers said. "It's not like they're speaking a different language or anything."

Tunger said something to him that might have resembled the sound of a hippopotamus giving driving directions.

"What?" Rogers asked.

"See?" Tunger said. "You need me."

Rogers licked his lips. Maybe Tunger was right, though Rogers had no way of knowing what actual Thelicosans sounded like. McSchmidt had been a dirty bastard of a spy, but he'd trained himself to speak like a Meridan.

"But," Rogers said, a stroke of brilliance hitting him, "if you come with me on this mission, your chances of ever becoming a spy will be ruined. They'll see you, and I'm sure they'll make a record of your presence. If you act as my, uh, interpreter, your chances of a cloak-and-dagger existence are reduced to nil."

This gave Tunger pause—thank god, Rogers thought—and his face twisted into something that might have been actual, contemplative thought.

"Sir," Tunger said slowly, looking at the floor. "I've been doing a lot of thinking lately."

"Really, there's not a lot of thought necessary," Rogers said hastily.

Tunger took a deep breath and then met Rogers' eyes again. "I'll never be a good spy."

A stab of pity shot through Rogers. That look in Tunger's eyes, like a puppy who'd just realized that peeing on the floor was simply something you didn't do, made Rogers feel ashamed of himself. Tunger had never been anything but loyal, even if he was a bit irritating, and Rogers had done nothing but browbeat the man and discourage him from achieving his dreams. Probably too much. And now he'd apparently pushed the man into the dark corners of self-doubt, where he'd obviously concluded—however accurately—that he was just too dumb to be a spy.

"Listen, Tunger," Rogers said, putting his hand on the man's shoulder in a way that seemed both fatherly and extremely awkward. "You're a good troop. Merida is proud to have you. So don't you ever think that you're not good enough."

For a moment, Rogers thought he'd gotten through to the corporal. Tunger's expression changed from reassured to very confused, and he finally gave Rogers a grin.

"Wow, thanks, Captain! But that's not what I meant. I know I have *all* the skills. I'd just miss my animals too much. And I can't keep a secret." Tunger bobbed his head enthusiastically. "So, you see, that's why I'm coming with you. This way I can put all my practice to use and still stay with my children."

Rogers stared at him, openmouthed, for a moment.

"Well," Tunger said, "I'd better make sure everything is ready. See you on the shuttle."

"Wait," Rogers said, pointing to the lion. "You're just going to leave him here on the bridge?"

Tunger slapped his forehead. "Silly me!" He turned to the lion and made a complicated series of clicking noises, after which the

lion slowly bowed his head and tromped off toward the up-line
that would lead him back down to the zoo deck. Rogers had res-
ervations about letting a lion roam loose around the ship, but
somehow he knew he had more to fear from Tunger than from
the lion.

An Indecent Proposal

The long metallic corridor of the docking bridge reminded Rogers all too vividly of the one he'd gone through to get from the *Lumos* onto the administration outpost where he'd been reinstated into the military. He remembered the feeling of knowing his fate had been sealed, the crushing weight of expectation suffocating him with every step. He'd been sure the local magistrate was going to convict him of a litany of crimes and then sentence him to the salt mines on Parivan for the rest of his life. Now that he was walking—well, floating, really—down another bridge extension onto an enemy ship, he couldn't help but be alarmed by the parallels. Though it had turned out alright in the end, hadn't it?

If one could consider being harassed—and then beaten senseless—by droids, nearly killed several times, sacrificing his personal ship, and ending up as the lapdog of the most incompetent admiral in the galaxy "alright."

Maybe it wasn't such a reassuring parallel.

"This is so exciting," Tunger muttered as he kept pace with Rogers through the bridge. It wasn't a long extension—more like a twenty-foot tube of metal—but Rogers wasn't in much of a rush to get to the other side.

"I don't know if that's the word I'd use," he said.

"It's just, I've never met a real Thelicosan before," Tunger said. "It's all so mysterious. I hope they like me."

"This isn't a popularity contest," Rogers said. "And besides, you met McSchmidt, didn't you?"

"He was pretending to be a Meridan," Tunger said. "It doesn't count."

The abrupt entrance into free fall as soon as they left the shuttle's gravity generation system was unnerving, but Rogers had lived enough of his recent life in his old zero-g stateroom to adapt quickly. Tunger was having a bit more trouble, though bouncing off the walls like a soccer ball in slow motion didn't seem to bother him. In fact, he seemed to be enjoying it.

"Stop giggling, Tunger," Rogers said. "This is a sensitive wartime negotiation. And if you're going to be my 'translator' or whatever ridiculous title you've given yourself, you're going to remain quiet. If I really can't understand them, which I doubt, you are to repeat exactly what I say and translate everything they say word for word. No interpretations. Not even any hand gestures. Got it?"

Tunger seemed completely unaffected by Rogers' dour tone and veiled insults. "Yes, sir! I'll be as mum as a mummer."

"Good."

They reached the other end of the bridge and stood before a very ordinary-looking hatch. It was just a circular piece of metal leading into the belly of the *Ambuscade*, with no identifying markings except a very large number three painted near what Rogers assumed was the top of the door. Around the hatch he could see the variable-width sealing clamps used to adapt the bridge's width to the *Ambuscade* hatch's diameter. He glanced at them nervously.

"Don't worry, sir," Tunger said, "the docking computer said the seal was fine."

"Never trust a computer," Rogers muttered. He turned his attention back to the door. "Well, what do we do?"

Without answering, Tunger reached forward and knocked.

Rogers chuckled. Sometimes he just wanted to pat Tunger on the head and tell him to run along and play. "I'm not really sure—"

Something metallic shifted inside the hatch, and a few moments later it opened.

"Well," Rogers said, clearing his throat. "Alright, then."

The airlock separating the *Ambuscade* from empty space was small, barely big enough for Rogers alone, but Tunger decided to squeeze himself in there as well. Combined with the rapid reintroduction of gravity, it made for a very awkward couple of seconds while the Thelicosans ran through their hatch-opening protocols, but at least this time Rogers wasn't with a sweaty old man's bare ass. Rogers was learning to live a life of comparison. He wasn't sure he liked it, but compared to a life of noncomparison, it wasn't so bad.

Luckily, his close encounter with the zookeeper—which educated him a little bit about the effects of living with animals on one's body odor—lasted only a few moments. Rogers felt most of his thoughts fall away as the interior part of the hatch began to open. He was about to get his first glimpse of "Bellicose Thelicosa." He really hoped the marines were ready if this got out of hand.

Rogers wasn't quite sure what he'd been expecting. Maybe a trio of armed guards with knives in their teeth and plasma grenades strapped to bandoliers, or something. Whatever he'd been thinking, he would have been hard pressed to come up with a math textbook open to a page on differential equations. A pencil, adding to the archaic nature of the display, was tied to the edge of the table with a string.

"What is this?" Rogers said.

"I can explain, sir," Tunger said. "I've been studying Thelicosan culture. This is a standard greeting. Is it differential equations?"

"Yes," Rogers said, bewildered. "How did you know?"

"It indicates the character of official meetings," Tunger said. "Differential equations are only used with respected enemies. Had this been long division, it would have communicated that they thought they were above us." Tunger took a meaningful pause. "Had it been multiplication flash cards, we would be dead."

Rogers swallowed. Thank god for differential equations, then. "Well, what am I supposed to do with it?"

"Solve it, sir."

Frowning, Rogers leaned over and, doing some quick sketching in the margins of the page, wrote down the answer. It really wasn't that difficult, and being an engineer with a flair for the old-fashioned, Rogers was used to solving these sorts of things without a calculator. He wondered if that made him very Thelicosan.

"That was fast," Tunger said.

"Engineer," Rogers said. "Now what?"

"Nothing," Tunger said. "The solution doesn't really matter at all. It just shows that you acknowledge their greeting and accept its terms. If you'd wanted to, you could have really insulted them by tearing out the page, not showing your work, or writing the phrase 'it depends.'"

"Ah," Rogers said. "Well. Let's move on, then."

As if putting the pencil down had sent out a summons, a short, pale man appeared before them. "Appeared" seemed an apt term, since the man very closely resembled a ghost. Everything about him seemed to have been soaked in paint thinner, from his fair, stringy hair down to his bony wrists. Yet despite the man's looking as though he could be broken in half by a sneeze, Rogers realized with some level of horror that he hadn't heard the man approaching.

He was also wearing a weight attached to each of his cheeks. Rogers wasn't sure what to think of that.

"Greetings," the man said, the weights swaying with the movement of his mouth and giving his speech a drawn-out, hollow characteristic. "I am Xan Tiu, personal assistant to Grand Marshal Keffoule, with whom you will be meeting very shortly, if you would follow me."

Xan's flat tone and careless delivery actually made Rogers feel like he wanted to fall asleep. The Thelicosan showed no sign at all of being impressed, scared, antagonistic, or alive.

"See, Tunger?" Rogers said, gesturing at the man. "He doesn't even really have an accent."

"That is because I am a New Neptune immigrant," Xan said.

"I see," Rogers said. That explained the general lack of liveliness; New Neptune was notorious for its lack of creativity or enthusiasm for just about anything. He cleared his throat. "Well, let's get on with it, then, Mr. Tiu."

Xan gave the most imperceptible of nods and then turned abruptly on his heel before heading down the short corridor, turning the corner, and opening a small bay door.

It led to what appeared to be a supply room, which was connected by corridors to a crew berthing area. The interior of the ship wasn't any more impressive than the exterior, and Rogers could get no sense for the personnel, since they had either been told to clear out of the hallways or were waiting for him in whatever their meeting room would be. Despite there being no people around, Rogers did his best to school his outer appearance, forcing his body language to say things like "power," "responsibility," "command," and "confidence." His internal monologue, however, was saying things like "oh shit," "oh shit," and "oh shit shit shit."

As they made their way through the *Ambuscade*, Rogers still couldn't see any more people. It made him both relieved and extremely nervous. It could have been a gesture from the Thelicosans that he had nothing to fear, or they could all be waiting in ambush somewhere. Rogers absently adjusted the rank insignia pinned to his collar. Inside was a microphone and short-range transmitter that would allow Mailn and the rest of the marines to hear his conversations back on the shuttle. If he spoke the code phrase—a phrase so ridiculous it would never be spoken in this context—they'd come rushing in, guns blazing, as marines were wont to do.

Mailn had explained to him that the datapad he was perpetually carrying in a holster hanging from his belt could have done all this, but Rogers had insisted on the secret lapel microphone. It was way cooler.

A noise brought him out of his reverie. He turned his head to where he thought he'd heard it—something metallic, though that wasn't exactly rare on a spaceship—but he didn't see anything out of place. They were transiting through a systems control room now, heading toward a small corridor that dead-ended at a high door. The systems control room had a few doors leading to other places in the ship, but they were all closed. The elevator that led perhaps to the cockpit or another hatch was open.

"This way," Xan said, somehow able to make two words sound like a disinterested eulogy at an empty funeral. Rogers exchanged a look with Tunger, who was still smiling in a way that made Rogers doubt whether he really understood the gravity of their current situation. Differential equations or not, this meeting ground was not even close to equal.

Xan approached the control panel of the door and pressed a few buttons. The door slid open to reveal a meeting room that seemed unnecessarily big for such a small ship. It was circular, with stadium seating extending for three-quarters of the circumference of the room, and in the center was a dais with a large projection device hanging above. Rogers had seen prototypes of that sort of technology in Meridan meeting rooms—it was a holographic meeting server, designed to make it seem as though everyone in the meeting was physically there. Apparently the *Ambuscade* wasn't so technologically old after all; the Meridans hadn't caught up to this sort of development. Bold lettering on the side indicated it had been made by Snaggardir's. What *didn't* that company make?

In the center, where the holographs would project, was Rogers' quarry.

The Grand Marshal, Alandra Keffoule, was striking. Specifically, she was striking a tall wooden dummy that somehow had made its way into the middle of the room. The loud cracking noise that erupted with every hit gave Rogers a keen awareness of two things. First, that he now knew what the strange sound had been in the hallway. Second, that one pair of underwear had not been enough.

The leader of the Thelicosan fleet was smaller than he'd imagined her, with dark, smoky skin and a head of hair that looked as wild as her repeated spinning back kicks. Keffoule, upon seeing them enter, stopped beating the poor humanoid dummy senseless and, for some reason, gathered up some of the shards and handed them to Xan.

"Thank you, Grand Marshal," Xan said, not abating Rogers' confusion at all. "The crew will appreciate this."

"Any ideas on what the hell that was?" Rogers muttered to Tunger.

"None whatsoever, sir," Tunger whispered back.

Rogers swallowed. It couldn't really have been anything except a way for Keffoule to set the tone of the meeting—a tone he did not like. Was the dummy supposed to represent Rogers? It seemed all too likely.

Xan put the wooden shards in his pocket and gestured—boringly—at Rogers. "May I present—"

"I know who this is," Keffoule said, her voice assertive but smooth, like worked-over leather with a feminine touch. Her accent was much heavier than Xan's, but still mostly understandable. "Oh, I know who this is all too well."

Nope. Rogers did not like that tone. He did not like it at all.

"And you must be—" Rogers began.

"Leave us," Keffoule said to Xan. She didn't raise a hand to gesture. She didn't even look at him; her eyes were locked on Rogers'.

Leave us? Rogers thought. *Who says that?*

Without further comment, and, Rogers thought, without blinking, Xan left the room. Rogers was left in a room with the two people in Fortuna Stultus he wanted to be with the least: an enemy commander and a zookeeper.

Keffoule, still staring at Rogers, moved smoothly to where a small table had been set up to the side of the dais. Two chairs, austere but comfortable, were pulled up, but turned outward, giving the meeting an open impression—if meeting on an enemy ship in a completely empty room with a scary-looking lady could be considered open at all. The Grand Marshal extended her hand, as though to indicate that Rogers was to sit, but then whipped her arm to point at Tunger instead. The movement was so quick that it actually made a whooshing noise in the air. Rogers' body tensed, but he resisted the urge to duck.

"Never duck when no one is hitting you," Mailn had said. "It only confuses people." She was a wise woman.

"Who is this man?" Keffoule said, her voice still soft but with an increased measure of intensity. "The instructions were to come alone."

"This is Corporal Tunger," Rogers said, trying to keep his hand from trembling as he gestured toward the zookeeper. "He's my interpreter."

"Hullur!" Tunger said brightly. Rogers elbowed him in the side.

"Interpreter?" Keffoule said, her fine eyebrows raised in a way that might have signaled insult. Rogers knew he shouldn't have brought Tunger.

"It's just that . . ." Rogers said, fumbling for a diplomatic way to say that he hadn't thought he was going to be able to understand a word of the bastardized language that came out of her mouth. "He was under the impression that Thelicosans speak differently than Meridans, and he's been studying your language and culture."

Keffoule folded her body back and sat gracefully in the chair opposite the one to which she had gestured. Every muscle moved like a wild animal's. She leaned back and crossed a pair of long legs, though Rogers couldn't see any of her shape. From what he'd seen so far, Thelicosans wore their uniforms baggy.

"I am a high-ranking official in the Thelicosan military," Keffoule said proudly. "I have been trained in six languages and can adjust Standard to make myself sound like anyone I wish. I can *become* anyone I wish, Captain Rogers. There will be no need for interpretation."

Tunger looked crestfallen. "Aw, but sir! Can't I stay? Please? Pleeeease?"

Rogers elbowed him again. "Tunger!" he muttered through clenched teeth. "You are *embarrassing* me in front of the Grand Marshal." He flashed a winning smile at Keffoule and, for some reason, thought he saw her flinch. "I will send him back to the shuttle."

Keffoule waved the suggestion away. "He may stay if you require him to stay. I will not presume to order around your troops. Though misguided, your idea of an interpreter might have been prudent with a lesser commander."

For some reason Rogers couldn't understand, this made him more nervous than if Tunger had been dismissed. Logic told him it was a good idea to have a friendly face nearby during this talk. More logic told him Tunger was probably an exception to the previous logic.

"Take a seat halfway up the rows," Rogers told Tunger, pointing to the stadium seating around the meeting room. "And if I even hear you fart too loudly, you're going back to the shuttle."

Tunger's face went pale.

"What is it?" Rogers said.

Tunger hesitated. "Just thinking about what I had for lunch, sir. I'll try my best."

Rogers shook his head as he watched Tunger walk, in a stiff, tight way, up the stairs and find a seat. The corporal sat slowly, exhaling in a hiss as he did so.

For all that was wrong with Tunger, his antics seemed to have calmed Rogers down. Rogers felt more at ease than he had when he'd entered the room, and, amazingly, didn't trip and fall on his face as he moved over to the chair opposite Keffoule and sat down.

"I apologize," Rogers said.

Keffoule's head shook almost imperceptibly. "It is nothing."

They spent a moment staring at each other, which just about erased all the relaxation Rogers had gained by watching Tunger fart-walk up a flight of stairs. The Thelicosan commander seemed to be studying him with great interest, her body looking both frozen and relaxed in her chair. Were her dark eyes hiding a smile? Had she just brought him here to gloat about her superior position? Was she going to shoot him?

"So, Grand Marshal Keffoule," Rogers said, just to break the silence.

"It's pronounced 'kiff-OOL,'" she said.

"Oh," Rogers said. He'd been saying "kiffle," which he now realized was kind of stupid.

"So, Captain Rogers," Keffoule said by way of continuing their conversation, once Rogers had lapsed back into strangled silence.

"It's pronounced 'row-JEERS,'" Rogers said before he could stop himself.

Yeah, Rogers thought. *That's what this conversation needs. Levity and sarcasm, you moron. Well done. Bang-up job.*

Keffoule raised an eyebrow. "Really?"

"No," Rogers admitted.

The Grand Marshal frowned. She was going to kill him. She was going to flip the table and shoot him in the face. Keffoule didn't even have a weapon that Rogers could see, but he was pretty confident she could produce one, should the will to shoot him in the face be strong enough.

Keffoule shifted, uncrossing her legs, then crossing them again the opposite way.

Good god, this was awkward. And scary.

"I appreciate your being willing to meet with me," Rogers said, his voice absolutely not cracking.

Keffoule nodded magnanimously. "We are in a precarious situation, you and I," she said.

Rogers thought she was going to continue, but she merely stared at him. He would have given a bottle of Jasker 120 to know what this woman was thinking.

Oh. My. Science, Keffoule was thinking. *Oh my Science.* Captain Rogers. Right here in front of her. And he had a *beard.* It wasn't exactly the most prominent beard in the world, but there it was, draped across his strong chin like a banner of manliness. And he looked like quite the ruffian, with his hair matted, his uniform wrinkled and greasy—a wonderfully exciting deviation from strict Thelicosan appearance standards. She couldn't remember the last time she had looked at anything so incredible in all her life. By Newton's Laws, what she could do with a little inertia right now.

She had the protractor under the table. All she needed to do was give it to him. His acceptance of her proposal was a given; she was one of the most powerful women in the entire Thelicosan military, with a distinguished career and strong hips. He would be a great husband, and she would lord it over him as any good Thelicosan woman would.

Stopping an intergalactic war *and* cementing ties with the Meridans via marriage? They'd *have* to take her back into the F Sequence. The plan was perfect. And it just so happened that Keffoule was madly in love with the man who would make it all possible.

But all she was doing was *staring at him.*

"Precarious doesn't even begin to describe this whole thing," Rogers said. "Why did you come across the border?"

"To eliminate the threat," Keffoule said plainly. "You."

Rogers absolutely did not like being the direct object of the verb "eliminate." He tried to hide his discomfort and replace it with honest-to-goodness confusion.

"Threat?" he asked. "What kind of threat could we possibly pose? Weren't you getting reports from that idiot McSchmidt? We were in the middle of the biggest fiasco since the War of Musical Chairs!"

Keffoule's face made an imperceptible adjustment. And maybe went a little red. Was she confused?

"I read the reports," she said, her voice sounding perhaps a little husky. "Many times. Many, many times." She cleared her throat. "The intelligence passed to us showed that you were planning a surprise attack on our fleet," she said slowly. "The reports were broken, yes, but . . ."

Rogers felt like he'd just been dunked in a giant container of ice water. "*You* were scared that you were going to get attacked by *us*? Do you have any idea what the disposition of our forces was after the droid attack? We barely had enough supplies to keep basic operations going, never mind mount an assault on a numerically and technologically superior force."

The Thelicosan commander's face *was* turning a little red. She was beginning to look very uncomfortable, and Rogers began to realize—whether with relief or anger or terror, he wasn't sure—that this whole thing might have been a giant misunderstanding. What would the intergalactic courts make of it? The Thelicosans had violated the treaty first, of course, and they had sent that message . . .

"Oh yeah!" Rogers said. "*And* you told us you were invading!"

Keffoule sighed, the first display of any real overt emotion that Rogers had seen from her.

"A mistake," she said, bowing her head slightly. "It was supposed to say that we were inviting you to negotiate on a neutral vessel to discuss the terms of the mutual military drawdown. I have . . . disciplined the communications officer responsible for the error. You have my most sincere apologies."

Rogers felt all his muscles relax. It *had* been a misunderstanding. Somehow, the Thelicosans had gotten their reports mixed up, or something, and then they'd come across the border to try to clear things up, but had sent the wrong message. For all the stories he'd heard about Thelicosan military competence, this didn't seem to line up with the legends.

"Well," he said, leaning back in his chair. He couldn't stop the somewhat delirious grin that was spreading across his face. All the tension was replaced by a sort of giddy relief, and he could feel a half-insane chuckle bubbling up inside his chest. "That's that, then, isn't it? You can lift the jamming net, we can send word home that everything is okay and to please send beer, you can fire just about everyone in your intelligence squadron, and I can finally—"

"Tell me, Captain Rogers," Keffoule said suddenly, leaning over the table. Her body moved so fluidly, so quickly, that Rogers' butt barely had time to clench. "Do you have a home somewhere in Merida?"

"I, uh, what?" Rogers said, disarmed by the sudden personal question. "Not really. I used to live on Merida Prime, in one of the smaller cities, but I haven't been there in years. I prefer open space, I guess."

Even as his mouth formed the words, he was surprised by them. How long had he been dreaming of retiring on Dathum? Suddenly the idea of sitting on a beach sipping drinks for ten hours a day didn't seem so appealing.

"So, it doesn't quite matter where that open space is, does it?" Keffoule said. Her tone was curious—was it the Thelicosan version of shyness? Of all the things Keffoule had seemed since Rogers had walked in, shy had not been one of them.

"Well, it matters a little bit," Rogers said, shrugging. Where was this going? "I mean, open space in the middle of a refuse dump at the outer rim of a galaxy wouldn't be very interesting at all."

"I see," Keffoule said, a slow smile playing across her face. Her eyes sparkled. "So, interesting things interest you, do they, Captain?"

Rogers squinted, frowning. "I was under the impression that the definition of 'interesting' demanded that it hold someone's interest."

Oddly, he wished Tunger would come down from the seats and tell him what the hell this woman was thinking. This might have been the most bizarre conversation he'd ever been a part of, and he thought—he hoped—that his lack of understanding of Thelicosan culture was the biggest contributing factor. Tunger might have some idea why being interested in interesting things had anything to do with avoiding a very messy war.

For some reason, his remark seemed to please Keffoule. Rogers had the strange desire to scoot his chair away from her. In fact, he was having an increasingly strong desire to get the hell out of this chair and run away. He chided himself for being so skittish; she was only the most powerful Thelicosan woman currently in the middle of his territory asking him strange personal questions.

Rogers cleared his throat. "Look, this has been, uh, interestingly interesting, and all, but don't we both have fleets to run? Since we're in agreement that this is just something that needs to be undone, why don't we just shake hands and, uh, go undo it?"

Again, Keffoule seemed to be either unaware of or uninterested in his attempts to hurry this parade of awkwardness along. She sat further forward, generating the impression that she was getting ready to pounce.

"Captain," she asked, "does Bernoulli's principle deal with conducting or nonconducting fluids?"

Tunger shifted in his seat so abruptly that Rogers could hear it. Another noise was beginning to make rumblings somewhere else in the ship, but at the moment Rogers couldn't tell what it was.

Rogers frowned. "Nonconducting. If you allow for conduction, it—"

"And Euclid's algorithm?"

"What about it?" Rogers asked, getting annoyed.

"Sir!" Tunger shouted. Rogers ignored him; he was busy being distracted by pointless mathematical questions. Thelicosans were *so* strange. A culture based on physics was kind of a given—you couldn't just disobey Newton or Einstein or Bob—but a culture obsessed with it was entirely different. And, Rogers thought, unnecessary.

"What does it find?" Keffoule asked. Her face was getting really red now.

"It's a way to find the greatest common divisor of two numbers. Is there a point to this?"

Keffoule ignored his question. "Kepler's third law?"

"With or without Copernican correction?"

Keffoule raised an eyebrow.

"Just kidding," Rogers said. "That's not a real thing." He rattled off the rest of the law and watched as Keffoule's face went from smug to absolutely ecstatic. She looked like a kid who'd just been given the biggest cone of cotton candy in her entire life. It really didn't make sense at all. This was all really basic astrophysics and engineering stuff. He wouldn't be a very good engineer if he couldn't handle some simple math.

"*Sir!*" Tunger shouted, almost shrieking.

"What?" Rogers shouted back, twisting in his chair to direct the full blast of his voice toward the corporal. "What is it? What do you want? The Grand Marshal here is just trying to see if I went to second grade."

"No she's not!" Tunger yelled. He was standing halfway out of his chair, but the stadium seating and the narrow aisles forced him to rise to a half-squat position and remain hovering over his seat. The poor man's legs were quivering, though from strain or fear, Rogers couldn't tell. "She's—"

Tunger paused, his face contorted and his hand halfway pointing to absolutely nothing. He stopped talking entirely, then had trouble starting again. Then, for some reason, his arms went slack and he just sort of shrugged.

"You know, sir, I've never been in this kind of situation before and I'm having trouble prioritizing my shocking revelations."

"There's more than one?" Rogers shouted. He was starting to get a very bad feeling about all this.

"Well," Tunger said, but was interrupted by shouts coming from the other side of the room.

"Alandra! Alandra, what in the name of calculus are you doing?"

Turning, Rogers saw another Thelicosan man—a high-ranking officer by the look of his uniform, and decorated to boot—come storming from one of the doors to the assembly room. The man was dark-featured and severe, and Rogers' eyes were drawn, strangely, not to the weapon he was holding in his hand, but to the immensely thick unibrow draped across his forehead. Behind him, Rogers could see other Thelicosan soldiers, and they didn't look like they were dressed for a dinner party.

"Was that one of the things?" Rogers asked.

"Yes, sir," Tunger said. "A few dozen armed Thelicosan troops are mustering in the hallway."

"Clearly. And the other?" Rogers said, surprised he was able to keep his calm.

"Grand Marshal Keffoule is proposing to you. Those are ritualistic betrothal questions!"

Rogers whipped his head around to Keffoule, who was staring at him with a wild grin on her face, her steely disposition totally unhinged by something approaching psychotic glee. She was also standing now, and though she was shorter than Rogers—a feat not easily accomplished—Rogers felt like a mouse looking up at a mountain lion. A soft click echoed through the briefly silent chamber, and Rogers looked down to see that some sort of instrument had been placed on the table. For a moment, he thought it was a weapon—it gleamed as though made of sharp, fine steel—but he realized soon afterward that it wasn't a weapon at all. Though it had been polished, decorated, and well made, it was just a simple protractor.

"What?" the single-eyebrowed officer said. "You can't be serious! Alandra, have you lost your mind? Is *this* why you agreed to cross the border?"

"It's only half of a circle," Keffoule whispered. "It's missing one hundred and eighty degrees. I would have yours, Captain. Think of it—two of the most powerful officers in Thelicosa and Merida united in marriage! It would be an unbreakable bond." She swallowed. "And there can be no other for me."

Everything else in the room, including Rogers, was frozen solid. Time itself stood still. The hairs on the back of Rogers' neck were standing up so rigidly he thought they were about to fly out of the follicles and embed themselves in the wall. He didn't know what to say.

Wait, yes he did.

"No, I will not marry you!" he shouted.

The room went completely silent. Keffoule's face dropped from giddy to flat. And Rogers really, *really* wished he had chosen a different code phrase for the marines.

That Went Well

"Wait!" Rogers said into the microphone hidden in his uniform. "Wait, no, uh, I will marry you! I will marry you!"

"What?" Tunger shouted.

"Really?" Keffoule shouted, her expression alight with happiness, which on her intense, round-featured face, looked utterly horrifying.

"No, I will *not* marry you," Rogers said again. Damn it! Why had he picked that as the code phrase?

Oh, maybe because it was the *least likely thing to be uttered while dealing with an enemy commander.* What was wrong with this woman?

It was too late. He could already hear chaos erupting in other parts of the ship as Mailn and the rest of the marines started shooting people and breaking things, the two tasks at which the marines were the most adept.

But for some reason, the noises appeared to be coming from the wrong direction. Rogers wasn't exactly very good with directions—he was an engineer, not a navigator—but he was pretty sure the hatch and bridge that connected the shuttle to the *Ambuscade* were in the other direction.

So who was making all that racket?

Keffoule, her face now hovering somewhere between crestfallen and excited, took her eyes off Rogers for a brief moment to look at Caterpillar Brow.

"Commodore Zergan," she hissed. "What are you doing here?"

The dark, glowering man—Commodore Zergan—scowled at her. He looked like a wolf caught in a trap, and he holstered his pistol very quickly.

"I thought it was prudent for you to have a security detail," he said.

"I said alone, and I meant alone," Keffoule said back, her voice trembling with anger.

Zergan, his face twisted in disgust, spat on the floor. "I didn't know I'd be interrupting your—" His hand shot quickly to his ear as he listened to, presumably, his earpiece, and he looked over his shoulder.

"What?" he whispered harshly. "Here?" His eyes shot up, and he gazed at Rogers.

"It seems I'm not the only one who doesn't care for neutral terms," he said. Why was he smiling?

The noises from outside the room suddenly spilled into reality. Bay doors on either side of the stadium opened, disgorging two teams into what was probably about to be a very messy tug-of-war over Rogers' corpse.

"Captain!" Mailn shouted. She gave a flurry of hand signals, and the Meridans spread out on their side of the stadium. Decked out in their blast armor, their faces mostly hidden by visor shields, they were an impressive bunch.

The Thelicosans didn't lack for flair either. Their green-and-black uniforms shone with polish—which seemed a sort of stupid thing to do for combat uniforms—and their weapons, some kind of disruptor rifle, moved as though controlled by one hand. Their positioning was swift, calculated, and disciplined.

Of course, it didn't help either group's image that they were crouched quite ineffectively between stadium seats. They looked more like very, very enthusiastic sports fans about to do the wave than they did troops about to start a fight.

"Get off my foot!" one Meridan marine shouted.

Rogers felt frozen. What was he supposed to do in this sort of situation? He wasn't a commander! He was just a con artist in a uniform still looking for one lousy, goddamn drink. Glancing at Keffoule, he tried to take cues from her. Rogers had a good feeling that she wanted to avoid a conflict as much as he did.

"Hold your weapons!" Keffoule shouted, spinning around and shouting at her troops. "Commodore Zergan, you will stand down at once!"

"Uh," Rogers said, turning to his own troops. "Everyone just chill out, okay?"

"But you said the code phrase!" Mailn shouted at him—and now Rogers was able to pick her out from the rest of the uniformed troops. "We thought you were about to die."

"No," Rogers said. "I was about to get married."

"Really?" Keffoule said.

"No," Rogers said, turning around. "I will not marry you."

"I'm confused," one of the Meridan marines said. "Is he saying he wants us to start shooting or not?"

"Nobody is shooting anyone!" Rogers yelled over his shoulder. He cleared his throat. "Grand Marshal Keffoule, I am honored by your proposal. I think. But I can't marry you."

"I cannot believe we are even having this discussion," Zergan said, sneering. "I thought you were better than this. There are many Thelicosan men more worthy than this Galactic dog."

Rogers raised an eyebrow and was, for the first time in his life, happy he had two separate ones to raise. "You really do call us Galactics?"

"Yes," Zergan said.

"No," Keffoule said simultaneously.

"Well, now I'm just confused." Rogers shook his head. "Look, this doesn't need to get any worse than it already has. Nobody has shot anyone yet that I'm aware of—"

"I shot *at* someone," one of the Meridans said.

"I felt threatened that I *might* be shot," one of the Thelicosans said. Really, even the rank-and-file troops' accents weren't very bad. It only sounded like they had very tiny marshmallows in their cheeks.

"Everyone shut up!" Rogers said. "There is nothing more to do here. Let's everyone put down their weapons and slowly get out of here. We can go back to our ships, you can drop your jamming net, and we'll even give you some of our milk supplies to compensate for the damage we've caused. Everyone saves face, everyone can have milk and cookies. Okay?"

Every person in the room seemed to think about his proposal at the same time. Murmurs came up from both sides of the room.

"Milk and cookies? That sounds okay, I guess. Who can say bad things about milk and cookies?"

"I'm lactose-intolerant," a Meridan marine said.

"I'm lactose-intolerant too. Do you have soy or almond milk?" another Meridan called.

"Soy is bad for you. Didn't you read that one article on the net?" a Thelicosan soldier yelled back.

"Shut up, Thelicosan swine! I'll eat soy if I want to."

Rogers tried to tune out the ramblings of two very undisciplined groups of soldiers and focused his attention instead on Keffoule. She didn't look nearly as happy at the prospect of milk and cookies as the rest of her brood, and Zergan looked as if he could turn cookies into chunks of lead with his glare alone.

"Well?" Rogers said to Keffoule. "What do you say?"

The Thelicosan Grand Marshal, still standing, tapped a long, thin finger on the protractor/engagement ring on the table. She appeared to be considering his offer. Or she appeared to be considering stabbing him in the eye with the protractor. Tunger might know which it was, exactly, but Tunger was currently in the middle of a very ineffective formation of Meridan marines. And Rogers didn't trust him to know anything, really.

Keffoule opened her mouth to say something, then shut it again. Looking back at Zergan, she exchanged an uninterpretable glance with the officer, then gave a dejected, almost wistful sigh.

"Perhaps I am not so upset that you arrived after all, Edris," she said. Was "Edris" Zergan's first name? Or some kind of pet name? Keffoule turned back to Rogers. "You are certain that this is your answer to my offer?"

"Could not be more positive," Rogers said, perhaps with a little too much enthusiasm. He didn't want to insult the woman, only break her heart and embarrass her in front of a large contingent of her own troops. "I'm flattered by your request—I think—but I have other plans for my romantic future."

The silhouetted vision of the Viking came forward unbidden in his mind, and for a moment he lost himself in her wonderful, gargantuan features. The bitterness of their last few conversations seemed a little less pungent in this moment, for some reason. Perhaps when he returned to the ship he would make a genuine effort to patch things up with her. What had Mailn said? She thought Rogers would be good for the Viking?

Keffoule shook her head slowly, her dark eyes boring into Rogers' skull. "Then I am sorry."

Rogers had never heard a more disingenuous statement in his entire life. His hackles rose.

"Alandra," Zergan said, a warning tone entering his voice.

"Why are you . . . oh," Rogers said.

He said "oh" because it didn't take long to realize what was about to happen. He wasn't sure what clued him in: the subtle gestures of Zergan to his troops to go into action, the cosmic shift of mood in the room, or the enemy commander flying over the table at him like a lion grabbing at the back of a fleeing gazelle.

"Take cover!" he heard someone shout as he did just that, ducking below the table even as the nimble body of Alandra Keffoule sailed over him, hit the floor, and smoothly rolled to a standing position. She turned back to look at him with steely eyes, her calm, deadly poise not even remotely hinting that she might be turned to dust in the cross fire that was about to happen.

The Meridan marines were currently squatting ridiculously behind stadium seating that was too short to hide anyone, but the brave and aggressive Thelicosans were advancing—slowly—down the seats, hoisting one leg over at a time like a gaggle of very confused geese. It was the most absurd and terrifying situation Rogers had ever been in.

"You should have said yes, R. Wilson Rogers!" Keffoule said. "This would have been much easier!"

"What happened to not wanting to aggravate the situation?" Rogers cried as he dove behind a supporting column. He did realize, however, that he'd yet to hear any shots being fired. Only a crazy, screaming woman attempting to do who-knew-what to him. Was this some sort of Thelicosan custom?

"This is some sort of Thelicosan custom!" Tunger shouted.

"Ah!" Rogers cried, spinning around. Somehow the corporal had emerged from the crowd and was squatting next to him. "What are you talking about?"

"I wasn't able to read too much on the subject," Tunger said, his "thinking face" working pretty hard right now, "but I believe that kidnapping a potential mate is perfectly—"

Something flashed in the edge of Rogers' vision, and, before he could say "stop making your thinking face," Tunger had collapsed in a heap on the floor. Rogers turned to find Keffoule standing over him, her eyes wild with the passion of battle. She'd kicked Tunger in the face.

Oh, and yes, *there* was the shooting he'd been expecting. Whatever confusion and hesitation had held both squadrons back for the last few moments had dissipated, and the deadly, dramatic pulsing of disruptor rifles filled the room with its terrifying melody.

And thank god for that shooting, because Keffoule, her glance quickly moving to the side for a moment, rolled out of the way and came to a stop behind another column. This put them both at such an angle that the two opposing forces were shooting to the side of them, giving them little concern that they'd be blasted to bits unless one of them tried to cross the gap.

Making sure Tunger wasn't dead—he wasn't, though his lip was bleeding pretty badly—Rogers tried to figure out a way to get himself back into the safety of his own unit. They'd come here for him, and he couldn't disappoint them by being shot or kicked in the face. But having a limp, lifeless zookeeper to drag out with him was complicating the situation a bit now.

Keffoule's mind was clearly working furiously as she tried to figure out how to do the exact opposite of what Rogers was trying to do without getting killed herself. Her eyes danced over the disruptor pulses that were flying between their two columns. She appeared to be chanting something. What was she doing? Why did Rogers care at this point in time? He needed to get out of here!

Then, much to Rogers' disbelief/horror, Keffoule stepped out into the chaotic pulses of light and slowly walked toward Rogers' cover. Had she been timing the shots and looking for a path? Or were the Thelicosans and Meridans really that awful at their jobs?

"Everything is math!" Keffoule shouted over the din of the gunfire. "Everything in this world is just a sequence of calculations governed by the laws of science. Come and master them with me, R. Wilson Rogers!"

There was no way anyone could do that much mental math that quickly. The woman was clearly a demon.

Risking a quick glance around the column to try to find a way out, Rogers saw that they were, also, that bad at their jobs. Two hundred years of not actually having to fight wars obviously had not done very good things for small-unit tactics. The stadium seating wasn't helping, either; none of the soldiers on either side could brace a weapon on anything steady, and they were having to quite literally shoot from the hip. One hapless Meridan marine was actually shooting at the ceiling, though Rogers couldn't discern for what purpose he was doing so. In fact, the two sides were doing such an abysmal job of shooting each other that the only area in which anyone would absolutely, positively get killed was the space between Rogers and Mailn's unit—the space where Rogers needed to go.

"What the hell are you all spending so much time on the training deck for?" Rogers shouted over the noise of disruptor fire. "Do you even shoot while you're down there?"

As an answer, Mailn placed a round directly above Rogers' head.

"They're using displacement shields, you moron!" Mailn yelled back.

Rogers could see them now; tiny yellow, crackling planes of light were appearing in front of the Thelicosans as disruptor blasts deflected off the shields, further adding to the kill zone that was preventing Rogers from making a break for it. This was a very weird, very coincidental game of angles, in which he appeared to be the prize. A terrified part of him realized that this was *Thelicosa* he was dealing with—the geometric configuration had probably been very specifically calculated. Maybe Keffoule wasn't a demon after all.

A quick glance told him that being a demon and being a math genius were not mutually exclusive. Keffoule was busy making a slow but determined advance through the columns. At any moment she'd be on top of him, doing whatever it was she'd intended to do when she dove across the table.

Another trio of disruptor blasts sizzled as they landed perilously close to Rogers' vital organs, and he shrank back behind the column. Keffoule, for some reason, looked surprised and furious as she saw the blasts hit.

"Edris!" she shouted.

A frustrated jumble of speech, probably coming from Commodore Zergan, bubbled up from the sounds of battle, but Rogers couldn't understand a word of it. Another blast or two hit the column behind which he was hiding.

"I don't care!" Keffoule said in response to the wild-turkey-like speech coming from Zergan, dancing between disruptor pulses. Dear god, the woman could move through a thunderstorm and never get wet! He'd never seen such calculated agility in all his life.

Rogers took advantage of the moment's distraction to tear his eyes from the scary lady and try to see a way out.

"I need to get Tunger out of here!" Rogers called to Mailn. One of the marines near her had been hit in the leg, and two more marines were dragging him off the battlefield, out the door through which Mailn's troops had come. Rogers had a feeling this wasn't going to remain a low-casualty skirmish for very long. "He's been kicked in the face!"

Mailn shouted some commands to a trio of marines, who broke off from the main force and slowly started making their way toward Rogers' position. Glancing back at Keffoule, he wasn't sure they'd get there in time—or in one piece.

"Come on!" Rogers shouted. He started gathering up Tunger's splayed limbs, thankful that the zookeeper kept himself light and spry. Careful to keep his body out of the line of fire, Rogers suddenly became very intimate with Tunger. He was also absolutely not using the lower-ranking man as a human shield as he heard another few blasts hit the floor near where he was hidden; it just wasn't true.

"He's the enemy, Alandra!" that evil-looking Thelicosan Zergan shouted. "Why are you trying to protect him!"

"I am *ordering* you to stop shooting at him, Commodore. Do not make me repeat myself. Shoot at the other Meridans all you like, but Rogers is *mine*. We will talk later as to why you were aboard this ship in the first place."

Despite not being on the receiving end of that woman's voice,

Rogers felt a tingle of fear working its way through his bones. It also could have been because she was still slowly working her way toward him, employing some really powerful geometry witchcraft to avoid being destroyed. Or because she had said the word "mine" with such obvious italics. Really, there wasn't anything *not* spine-tinglingly terrifying about what was going on around him right now.

The Meridans that Mailn had dispatched to grab him were getting close. Just a few more seconds and he'd be ready to move. Keffoule was still slowly moving her body to avoid being shot. Rogers found it difficult to take his eyes off her, if for no other reason than sheer incredulity. The way she moved was slow, much slower than one would think one would have to move to do something like *dodge rifle blasts*, and there was a . . . sensual quality to it. It was like some sort of ritual dance that one might see around a fire in a camp full of ancient Romany.

Did she just wink at him?

A shadow fell across his vision, telling him that the marines had arrived against all odds. He turned, saw the shielded faces of two men and a woman he didn't recognize, and slowly pushed Tunger off his lap.

"Here," he said. "Take this zookeeper. Don't mind the poop stains."

Two of them pulled Tunger away while the third provided covering fire. At least, that was what Rogers hoped he was doing. To Rogers, it just sort of looked like he was wasting ammunition by firing in random directions. But the marines all remained alive. So whatever he was doing, it was effective.

Rogers looked away for a moment. Keffoule was alarmingly close, but it didn't matter. Now that the marines had arrived, he could finally get out of here.

"Alright," he said, "let's—"

Turning back to look at the marines, he saw them halfway across the room, dragging Tunger.

"Hey!" Rogers said. "You were supposed to take me, too!"

"Get the captain, you idiots!" Mailn yelled. "The *captain!*"

His heart pounding, Rogers turned around in a panic to look at how much progress Keffoule had made through the kill zone.

Except he didn't see her there.

He saw her standing right next to him.

"You should have said yes," she said.

Rogers really wasn't sure what happened next, since he found himself very quickly spiraling into unconsciousness, but he was pretty sure he'd just gotten kicked in the face.

Stick to the Schmurgle

The Spartan, sparse accoutrements of Alandra's stateroom allowed for a unique echoing effect as her voice, furious and commanding, bounced off the walls.

"I cannot believe," Alandra barked, "that you of all people would go behind my back during such a critical phase in my strategy!"

Zergan, typically unflappable, looked a little flustered, evidenced by his inability to stand still. He paced around the room, which was really too small to pace in, so he more wobbled back and forth slowly than anything else. He seemed reluctant to look Alandra in the eye, as well he should have been.

"Your 'strategy'? That's what you call it? If I'd known you were about to throw yourself at the feet of an inferior force, I might have asked him to marry *me* to save you the shame!"

Alandra gave him a sharp glare. "I do not throw myself at the feet of anyone," she said. "I'm not sure what scene you were watching, but I hardly think there was any obeisance being performed in that room by anyone. And if you hadn't stormed the room with a bunch of armed troops, maybe it all would have gone more smoothly."

Any anger she'd felt previously in her career paled in comparison to what was going on inside her now. Normally reserved and calculating, like all good Thelicosans, Alandra had actually knocked all her decorations off her desk as she'd come into the room. But the amount of anger, disappointment, shame, and embarrassment she felt *inside* outweighed what she was displaying outside by a factor of ten. She'd never been so humiliated in her entire life. Not only had she broken intergalactic law to try to defend her homeland and regain her reputation—something that was appearing to be more of a foolhardy and unnecessary move with every observation of the Meridan fleet—she had asked Captain Rogers to marry her and had been *rejected.* Alandra Keffoule was unaccustomed to failure, unaccustomed to rejection.

Rogers would come around, of course. That was inevitable and, therefore, a little reassuring. But had he simply said yes like he was supposed to—like his station demanded—all of this would never have happened.

"If I hadn't stormed the room," Zergan said, finally meeting her eyes and ceasing his pacing, "the Meridans would probably have dragged your smoking corpse back to their ship as a trophy! You seem to be forgetting that we weren't the only ones to break the agreement."

Alandra shook her head. "You keep saying 'we' broke the agreement. We did nothing of the sort! *You* broke the agreement, Zergan. You undermined my authority as a negotiator and commander of the fleet. Whatever suspicions the Meridans had that influenced their decision to bring their marines on board have been absolutely confirmed by your rashness. I was trying to solve this peacefully."

Rolling his eyes, Zergan barked a laugh. "Well, now it looks like we're not competent enough to solve this at all. Maybe if you weren't so love-struck—"

"I am not love-struck," Alandra said, biting off the words.

"Oh really? Then why did you hide it from me?" Zergan took a step forward, his eyes aflame. "Why not let me in on your little secret?"

"Zergan," Alandra warned.

"What have you been doing for the last month?" Zergan went on. "Looking at the intelligence reports of Rogers' idiotic escapades aboard the *Flagship* and making smoochy faces?"

Oh, now he was just being immature.

"I do not make smoochy faces," Alandra said. Why was she being defensive? There was no way anyone on the ship knew that she had, actually, done it once. But only once. And it was really quickly—it could have been confused for briefly tasting something sour.

Remembering the reports, she felt the heat rise in her face. There was no better way to get to know anyone intimately than by having someone else intimately spy on them and then reading the reports.

"I bet you do!" Zergan said. "Oh my Science, I bet you look back at all McSchmidt's reports and make smoochy faces and practice giving him *your protractor*, for calculus' sake. And then he *rejected*—"

She didn't even know she was doing it. When it was over, she could scarcely believe she'd done it. But in the next instant, *someone* had kicked Zergan in the face, and she was pretty sure it wasn't Zergan. He simply wasn't flexible enough.

To his credit, Zergan was a soldier. He didn't sprawl on the floor, holding his face and weeping like a child the way most people did after she delivered spinning back kicks to their faces. In fact, he seemed to be trying to figure out exactly what he wanted to do as he sat there, his cheek reddening with the passing of every second. After a moment of awkward silence—during which Alandra tried to understand why she'd just done that—he settled on sneezing and standing back up.

It was in that moment that she felt something break. It might have been Zergan's jaw.

But more than that, she thought it was something intangible, indescribable. Perhaps it was the bonds of trust built up over fifteen years of serving together in the most difficult assignments the Thelicosan military had to offer.

No, it was probably Zergan's jaw. It was very swollen.

"I stood by you," Zergan said quietly. "When everyone else thought you were a loose cannon. A calculator missing a key. I was there, trying to convince everyone that Alandra Keffoule could bounce back, that she could recover from anything."

Alandra swallowed. Why did he have to start talking about that now?

"Edris," she began, but Zergan, his face beginning to reach a size unbecoming an officer, shook his head.

"You know I've never blamed you for my position," he said.

That's because I begged you to stay where you were, you idiot, she thought, not without a little stab of guilt prickling her bones.

"But at the very least," he continued, "I thought, considering all we've been through, that I deserved a little more respect."

"This isn't just about you and me," Alandra said quietly, her normal fire subdued a bit by the winds of guilt and shame. "The threat—"

"There was no threat," Zergan said. "As soon as we got into this system, you and I both knew that McSchmidt's reports were probably wrong."

Alandra opened her mouth to retort but thought better of it.

"McSchmidt was an idiot," she said.

"McSchmidt was an idiot," Zergan said simultaneously.

An uncomfortable smirk passed across both of their faces, but Zergan's quickly faded.

"You're right," Zergan said. "It's not about you and me." He took a deep breath. "It was all about you. And now I know why you were so distracted. What else has slipped your notice, do you think?"

That was an unexpected comment. Alandra frowned.

"What are you—"

A tone interrupted their conversation, letting Alandra know that Xan was trying to get in touch with her.

"Xan, I've told you many times not to use that thing if we're already in the same room."

Xan, who had been standing in the corner silently all this time, shrugged and put his datapad away.

"I am a stickler for protocol, Grand Marshal," he said, his cheeks flapping with every word.

The sliding of the door was the only thing that told Alandra that Zergan had left. When she turned away from Xan, she saw only empty space where the man had been standing a moment earlier. What had he meant about things she had missed? She didn't miss anything. That was not Alandra Keffoule's way.

He was speaking out of anger, she thought. *You did kick him in the face, after all. Give him time.*

All of this was so frustrating. So . . . out of her control. What was she supposed to do now?

"Grand Marshal?" Xan said softly.

Alandra held up a hand, took a deep breath, and let out a therapeutic, blood-curdling shriek, curling her fingers, toes, nose, and lips as she put all the day's insanity into one sound and let it rip through the air.

"Better?" Xan asked.

"No," Alandra said. "Not really. What did you want to talk to me about?"

"The infirmary has contacted me," Xan said. "It appears Captain Rogers is awake."

Alandra skipped out of the room.

The world came together like pieces of a shattered kaleidoscope, each shard bringing with it another tidbit of Rogers' memory.

It took a moment for them all to form, during which Rogers thought, in alternating turns, that he was dead, that he'd been hit in the face by the Viking again, and that the Artificial Intelligence Ground Combat Squadron had been reinstituted to use him as a battering ram. When the spinning stopped and Rogers found himself firmly back inside his own body, he was troubled to find that, despite all of those things being different levels of bad, reality was worse. Much worse.

"Congratulations on regaining consciousness!" came a voice from the machine that Rogers assumed had been monitoring his vitals. "You are entitled to one free Concussion Helper Kit, available at any of the Snaggardir's Sundries available throughout the galaxy. Remember, whatever you need, you can Snag It at Snaggardir's™."

God, he was starting to really hate that voice.

He opened his eyes to find himself in an unfamiliar infirmary, which he supposed was much better than a grave or open space.

"Captain Rogers," came the voice of a frail man standing at the side of his bed. His beady eyes stared at Rogers with an utter absence of emotion as he made unenthusiastic gestures on his datapad. "How do you feel?"

Rogers didn't need to see the man's uniform to know that he wasn't on a Meridan ship. The sign above the door that said YOU ARE NOT ON A MERIDAN SHIP was enough evidence, though he wondered who would put such a sign there and why.

The doctor, or nurse, or executioner—he could have been any of the three with equal probability—seemed to notice Rogers' gaze. "That's a Rorschach blot test," the doctor said dryly. "What do you see?"

Rogers looked at him sideways. "That's not a blob," Rogers said. "It's clearly a sign that says 'You Are Not on a Meridan Ship.'"

The doctor gave no reaction to Rogers' refutation other than looking down at his datapad, making a few gestures, and emitting a very suggestive "Mm-*hmm*."

"What?" Rogers said. "What are you mm-*hmm*-ing about? That's a sign, written in plain, easy-to-read Standard. There's nothing even remotely blot-ish about it!"

The doctor nodded and said "Mm-*hmm*" again.

"Stop that!"

Rogers sat up in bed, fighting the dizziness that washed over him, and tried to get a better look around the room. He was still dressed in his official uniform, though it looked more fit for a vagabond than it did for an admiral after all he'd been through, and his face really, *really* hurt. There was some soreness in his hand from where an IV had been removed. How long had he been out?

The infirmary—for that was where he guessed he was instead of the brig, since he could see Thelicosan troops moving freely in the hallway—was bare bones at best, with only a few beds nearby, all of them empty. It looked more like an auxiliary treatment room than a sick ward. Was he on the *Limiter*? Or some other Thelicosan ship?

"Don't mind Dr. Eilan," a woman's voice said. "He sees Rorschach blots in everything."

Rogers turned to the doorway to find a woman he didn't recognize. He'd thought for sure he'd be seeing the face of Grand Marshal Keffoule, waving a protractor at him or some craziness, but he found himself looking at someone who was probably a decade older than Rogers, dressed in an anachronistic-looking pantsuit. Her hair, a shimmering golden color, was pulled tightly back into a meticulously formed bun, and her angular, birdlike face gave the impression that she was about to swoop down and peck Rogers' eyes out.

"I do not," Dr. Eilan said. "It's not my fault that the interns keep messing with my datapad's screen saver and changing it to blots."

"There are no blots on your datapad," the woman said.

"Well, what's this, then?"

"His medical chart."

Rather than taking offense or trying to argue, the doctor simply made another notation on his datapad and said "Mm-*hmm.*"

"Please make him stop that," Rogers said.

"Doctor, can you give us a moment?" the woman asked.

"Mm-*hmm.*"

Regardless of how dire his circumstances were, Rogers felt better when the doctor left the room.

"Thanks," he said. "I was afraid I was going to have to break my habit of being generally nonviolent."

"Generally?" the woman said, raising an eyebrow.

"Well, I hit people every once in a while," Rogers said, shrugging. "Sometimes you just gotta."

It was impossible to tell what effect this remark had on the woman, or even whether or not she'd been listening to him. Instead of responding, she stepped to the side of Rogers' bed, pulled up a chair, and then made a point of not sitting in it at all.

"My name is Vilia Quinn," she said stiffly. "I am Council Secretary Advising Civilian Authority to the Colliders and Grand Marshal Keffoule, whom you have already met."

Rogers swallowed, remembering very distinctly the circumstances under which he and Grand Marshal Keffoule had met. In his head, he saw her in slow motion, dancing through a hail of disruptor blasts, her eyes fixed on his the entire time, a protractor in one hand, a bloody knife in the other. Actually, he wasn't sure there had been a knife, but it did a lot to enhance the image.

"I have," he said flatly. "What did you say your title was? Secretary? Do you manage the Grand Marshal's emails or something?"

Quinn's entire face tightened at that remark. He hadn't intended it to be insulting, but it seemed like he'd been doing a lot of things lately that he hadn't intended, so it should have been no surprise.

"I'm the civilian liaison. Every major military group has one who serves as the link between them and the Central Council of Thelicosa."

Great, Rogers thought. *A bureaucrat. Funny—I didn't hear any paper shuffling when she walked in.*

Rogers didn't do well with political types. In fact, he wasn't sure he did well with any types. In the back of his mind he made a note to, later, do some introspection about whom he did well with and why. He then immediately made another note to procrastinate as long as possible on the first note.

"What does an ambassador want with me?" Rogers asked. "Maybe you can start by telling me what the hell I'm doing on a Thelicosan ship."

Rogers was pretty surprised at how not scared shitless he was feeling at the moment. Here he was, obviously some kind of political prisoner, if not a scapegoat, and he was giving attitude to a Thelicosan bureaucrat. Perhaps, he considered, he was already beyond the point of being completely screwed. A death sentence had strange effects on a man's inhibitions.

"I wish I knew," Quinn said, her lips thinning. "I assume you understand what the gift of a jeweled protractor means in Thelicosan custom?"

Rogers grimaced. "I know now. I can't say that I understand it, though. And given that I said no very clearly, it also doesn't explain why I'm here and not back on the *Flagship.*" He thought a moment. "Or dead."

Quinn looked at him for a moment, and Rogers could see the gears turning in her head. She was trying to say something sensitive but couldn't find the words to do it.

"Thelicosan marriage customs are . . . different," she said. "They may seem foreign, or even barbaric, to someone not familiar with them."

"Well, I can't remember the last time I kicked a date in the face."

Quinn shrugged, as though this was to be expected. "There is no shortage of people on this ship who have experienced similar fates. That she kicked you in a way to avoid permanent damage or facial scarring is exceptional."

Rogers was about to protest that he certainly didn't feel as though she'd tried to avoid permanent damage, but he compared the experience with being hit in the face by the Viking. In reality, this hadn't been that bad. He couldn't see himself in a mirror, but he didn't expect there to be much swelling at all. It had been the minimum effective force to knock him unconscious.

"I see," he said finally. "And what were you saying about marriage customs? Why am I here, Secretary Quinn?"

Quinn adjusted the chair again but still refused to sit in it. For some reason, this made Rogers feel ill at ease. She took a deep breath, tucked a stray hair back into her bun, and folded her hands in front of her. She looked every bit the politician at a press conference, except that she appeared to be taking her own pulse and counting silently.

"Thelicosa, at least as it pertains to marriage affairs, is a matriarchal society. Once a woman proposes to a man, it's not expected that her proposal will be rejected. The woman carefully considers the match, the kind of children you'd give her, your potential as a mate, and so forth. When she offers you a protractor, it's more a case of her saying that this is the way it should be. It's not really up for debate."

"That seems a little, um, inconsiderate," Rogers said. He shifted in his bed, subtly testing the rest of his body for injury. His left elbow felt like it was bruised, but otherwise he was starting to feel surprisingly good.

"It's not seen that way," Quinn responded. "And in the rare cases when a proposal is refused, it is customary and acceptable to, ah, acquire the male."

"Acquire?" Rogers said. "You mean kidnap?"

Quinn shrugged.

"Wow," Rogers said, looking back up at the sign above the door. He really was not on a Meridan ship.

Pointing to the sign, he swung his feet over the side of the bed and stretched his legs. He wasn't wearing his shoes, and he didn't see them anywhere.

"I know this is probably the least of my worries," he said, "but what's with the sign?"

Quinn turned to read it, then looked back at him with something that might have been considered tightly controlled disgust.

"Our understanding of Galactic . . . Meridan medical practices is that doctors generally do not have to go to medical school and that you frequently amputate the wrong body part." She sniffed. "You also refuse to use anesthetics. The sign is there to reassure patients and remind them that they are in the care of a civilized federation."

Rogers barked a laugh, and Quinn jumped, startled. "I don't see how that sort of barbarism is funny," she said dryly.

"It's only funny because it's wrong," Rogers said. "Where did you even hear that?"

Quinn shrugged. "It's common knowledge."

Rogers shook his head. He wondered what other vast chasms of misunderstanding separated the Thelicosans and Meridans. Even during the Two Hundred Years (And Counting) Peace, the two systems hadn't played very nice, and communications had been cool at best. Relations with the New Neptune System had been better, but they were very hard to not get along with, since they didn't have a collective personality at all. In general, the four active systems tended to simply pretend the others didn't exist.

"So I've been kidnapped," Rogers said. "What's next?"

"You marry the Grand Marshal," Quinn said.

Rogers blinked. "That's not the kind of advice I was looking for."

Quinn shrugged. He wished she'd stop doing that—it was

very aloof for a bureaucrat. "As I said, it's very unconventional for a proposal to be refused. You are expected to come around."

How was he supposed to come around? He was the commander of a major Meridan military unit, kidnapped by the enemy, and expected to simply go along with it all? His head was starting to hurt again just thinking about it. Maybe he could put that IV back in and just go to sleep for a while.

As if answering his mental summons, another doctor came bustling in, looking very hurried. He wore a large pair of spectacles with thick round rims, and he kept his head angled slightly downward and his shoulders hunched. The man looked like a neurotic badger with self-esteem issues. His white coat, which covered his uniform, was much too long, and his hair was arrayed in such a way that it suggested a recent interaction with a high-voltage current. Both of his cheeks looked swollen, like a hamster hiding his lunch.

"Ah," the doctor said. "Ah. You are awake. It is time for your medicine."

"Medicine?" Rogers said.

"Medicine," the doctor replied. Quinn had taken a step back, though she kept her eyes on Rogers.

"I don't really feel that bad," Rogers said.

"It's on the schedule," the doctor said. "We must stick to the schedule." His voice had a cracked quality to it, like someone had rubbed his vocal cords with sandpaper and then kicked him in the privates. Just listening to it made Rogers feel like he should have been moving faster, or at least chewing on something nervously.

"Really," Rogers said, waving the doctor away, "it's not necessary."

The doctor produced a syringe from his pocket—which seemed to Rogers to be a strange place to keep one's syringes— and flicked the end of it.

"I must stick to the schedule!" the doctor said.

"I'm going to stick that syringe in *your* schedule if you don't put it down," Rogers said. Quinn sighed, rolled her eyes, and said something about him being a baby.

"Here we go!" the doctor said.

"Stop!" Rogers said, swinging his feet up and jumping off the other side of the bed, putting the fixture between him and the doctor. "Put that damn thing away!"

Rogers didn't like needles. Worse, he didn't like needles wielded by someone who reminded him of a mad scientist. Needles and mad scientists from the enemy fleet took his aversion to a completely new level.

"I must stick to the schedule!" the doctor cried. "This will only take a moment."

"Just a moment!" Another voice came from the hallway.

"Oh god," Rogers said, rubbing his face with his hands. "Where are all these people coming from?"

The small room became more crowded as another doctor—Rogers was presuming, of course, because of the white coat that said DOCTOR on it—rushed into the room. This one was short, with a thick, almost fake-looking mustache.

"I don't have a moment," Dr. Spectacles said.

"You must!" Dr. Mustache said. His voice was much more accented than those of the other Thelicosans in the room, to the point where Rogers could finally understand Tunger's obsession with the dialect. It was difficult to make out what Dr. Mustache was saying.

"Quinn," Rogers said, "can you make this stop? Who are these people? Clearly I'm fine." Rogers gestured to himself as though to indicate as much, but his nervous enthusiasm only resulted in his arm's sweeping a glass vase off the counter, scattering fake flower bits all over the floor as the vase shattered.

"You see?" Dr. Spectacles said, trying to get around Dr. Mustache. "It has been too many moments! Too many!"

"I need another moment to conduct an exam," Dr. Mustache said. "It's on the schedule!" At least, that was what Rogers assumed he'd said. His accent made it sound more like "Eats urn the schmurgle."

"The what?" Dr. Spectacles said. "I can't understand you."

Rogers had to admit, Dr. Mustache's accent was quite thick, but he'd have figured at least other Thelicosans would be able to understand.

"The schmurgle!" Dr. Mustache said. He reached out to gesture to something—ostensibly a schedule posted somewhere that Rogers couldn't see—but misstepped and stumbled forward. He crashed into Dr. Spectacles, whose spectacles fell to the floor along with the syringe he'd been holding. The glasses only bounced, but the syringe shattered, spilling a thin, greenish liquid onto the floor. A rotten smell, like eggs and feet, began to fill the room.

For a moment, Dr. Formerly-Spectacles-But-Now-Just-a-Beady-Eyed-Guy-with-Big-Eyebrows didn't say anything. He stared at the spot on the floor, his mouth open, as though Dr. Mustache had just slaughtered his puppy in front of him. Finally, he curled both his hands into fists and screamed at Dr. Mustache.

"You idiot!" he said, the timbre of his voice coming down a little from his frantic falsetto. Then, without another word about the schedule or the medicine, he stormed out of the room. Dr. Mustache followed, bellowing in his thick accent.

"The schmurgle! The schmuuuurrrgle!"

The silence they left behind in the room was both comforting and unsettling. Quinn, who hadn't batted an eye during the entire exchange, stepped out of the corner and stood next to the chair in which she was *apparently absolutely not going to sit.*

"You can see the need for reassurances that we are at least better than Merida," Quinn said, pointing back at the sign above the door.

Rogers shook his head. "You people are crazy. And I need to get the hell out of this infirmary before someone else tries to stick me with something or kicks me in the face or asks me to marry them." He threw up his hands before bending down to search underneath the infirmary bed. "And where the hell are my shoes?"

Quinn let out a gasp, which Rogers took to be not at all in response to the question he had just asked, unless he so misunderstood Thelicosan custom that asking where one's shoes were was considered a great offense. It was a gasp that told him he had yet another visitor, one he had absolutely no desire to see.

"I regret to admit that I was only able to collect one of them after our exchange," Grand Marshal Keffoule said. "The other flew off quite a distance."

Intergalactic Relations

Slowly extending his head above the mattress, Rogers locked eyes once again with the dark, smoldering woman who commanded the enemy fleet. Grand Marshal Alandra Keffoule stood in the doorway, filling it in a way that was at once similar to and completely different from the way the Viking did the same thing, staring at him with a predatory, hungry gaze. She was holding one of his shoes.

Not knowing what else to say, Rogers looked up and said, inexplicably, "Well, then, what am I supposed to do about walking around your ship, Grand Marshal? Unless I am to stay in this room forever?"

It really was the least of his worries. It wasn't like there was broken glass everywhere or anything—it was a modern, solidly build spaceship with smooth, metallic floors—but there was a part of him that felt that if he could get his missing shoe back he could reclaim some part of himself. What part he wasn't sure; he had a guess it was his pride.

"You are a guest on my ship, Captain Rogers," Keffoule said. Was she deliberately adding a sultry, husky quality to her voice, or was Rogers hearing things? "You can go about it any way you'd like."

Why did it sound like "naked" was an unspoken word there? Rogers stared at her, his mouth a little drier than normal. He spent a moment sorting through all the thoughts in his head, through the litany of things he wanted to ask the leader of the enemy fleet.

"Why do you want to marry me?" he blurted finally. He thought that perhaps this was the least important of his concerns. In some way, however, he felt that it was also the most critical.

The Grand Marshal shrugged—what was it with Thelicosan women and shrugging?—and stepped fully into the room. "It is a natural thing," she said, as though that explained everything.

"The secretary here tells me you've kidnapped me as part of some sort of Thelicosan custom that says I'm eventually going to agree," Rogers said, jerking a thumb at Ms. Hair Bun.

For the first time, Keffoule seemed to notice Quinn's presence in the room. The Grand Marshal looked over at the place where Quinn was standing and made a face that gave away all the information Rogers ever wanted to know about civilian-military relations aboard the *Limiter*.

"What are you doing here?" Keffoule said.

"I'm speaking to our . . . *guest*," Quinn said, not making any effort at all to hide what she really thought of Rogers' status aboard the ship. "I'm trying to bridge the communication gap between Thelicosan and Galactic . . . Meridan expectations, since you seem content to just kick him in the face and expect him to want to marry you. Had you considered that perhaps Meridans don't work that way, or was your ego too big to see over?"

In his head, Rogers heard that stereotypical "*rawr*" noise that chauvinists thought of when two women were in an argument. A catfight, they'd called it in older days, and for the first time in his life, Rogers could understand why. They looked like two tigers—or bears, but "bear-fight" wasn't as catchy—about to leap at each other and vie for dominance. But Rogers didn't really consider himself a chauvinist, so he was mostly just terrified.

"Get out," Keffoule said with the kind of finality that only the narcissistic commander of a highly advanced fleet, hell-bent on getting someone to marry her, could muster.*

Quinn hesitated for a moment, as though considering making a big deal out of the situation, but complied, walking out of the room with such a slow, measured pace that it could only have been intended to tell Keffoule exactly what she thought of her command. The Grand Marshal moved aside only just far enough to let the woman pass.

Rogers and Keffoule stared at each other for a length of time until the click of Quinn's heels vanished into the distance.

"I'm unfamiliar with a lot of Thelicosan customs," Rogers said, "but I am nearly positive that it is unacceptable for high-ranking officers to limp around a capital ship wearing only one shoe. I will require another."

What the hell was he talking about? He would "require" another? What kind of crazy pills had he taken? Maybe it had something to do with the IV he'd gotten in the infirmary bed, or maybe he really had needed whatever medicine Dr. Spectacles had been ready to stick into him via the now-broken syringe.

To his surprise, this cocky, self-assured remark didn't earn him another kick to the face. Keffoule actually smiled at him.

"I will of course supply you with ample footwear," she said. She tossed his shoe aside and, without looking, sank it into a waste receptacle. Rogers frowned. It might have been missing its partner, but it was still *his* damn shoe. If anyone was going to blindly throw it into a trash bin with superhuman accuracy, it should have been him.

"Xan!" Keffoule barked suddenly, causing Rogers to duck,

---

* Rogers had not, despite the implications of this thought, met such a person before.

which made him feel a little silly. She was all the way on the other side of the room.

The pale-faced man with the swinging cheeks came into the room. Well, he more *appeared* in the room; he made no noise or showed any sign of physical effort to move his body. The only indication that some sort of inertia was present was the subtle swinging of the things hanging off his face. What the hell were those?

"Yes, Grand Marshal?"

"The shoes, Xan."

Xan disappeared—was there a poofing noise?—and emerged from the hallway a moment later holding a pair of black shoes, nondescript except for a bit of brogue design at the toe. They looked suitable for a high-ranking officer or a bellhop. Rather than handing them to Keffoule or to Rogers, Xan bowed low and placed them gently on the floor, then backed away.

"As I promised," Keffoule said, gesturing grandly at the shoes. Her eyes sparkled like she'd just performed some kind of magic trick. Was there some other significance to this gift? Where was Tunger when Rogers needed him?

They spent a moment staring at each other, Rogers' feelings of impending doom slowly bleeding away. He wasn't exactly in the best situation, but he was feeling less like he was about to die. Keffoule had said she'd wanted to marry him, after all. Unless Thelicosans were *really* strange, marrying a dead man wouldn't yield a very exciting honeymoon.

"So," Rogers said, coming back around the bed so he was on the same side of it as Keffoule, who was still blocking the door. It took all his courage not to make a break for it—courage and the knowledge that he really didn't have anywhere to run. And that even if he did have somewhere to run, he wasn't a very fast runner. "What's next?"

"You are to tell me the moment you feel any hint of a desire to marry me," Keffoule said. "While I can expect you to acquiesce,

I cannot compel you. That would be unsavory." She made a face.

"You seemed to have no issues about compelling me to come to your ship," Rogers said.

Keffoule shook her head. "I regret the circumstances I had to use to bring you aboard." A hard look passed through her eyes. "But if you recall, you did violate our agreement of neutrality."

"So did you," Rogers said, folding his arms and leaning back on the bed, which, he discovered, was on wheels. He stumbled, caught his balance, and stood up again, refolding his arms. "Ahem. So did you." Being tough was really not his strong suit. Could he con, drink, or gamble his way out of this situation?

"My subordinate acted without my authority," Keffoule said.

"Well, they all still shot at me an awful lot, for having no authority."

Keffoule bowed her head slightly, perhaps a gesture of apology or just her way of saying "You have correctly represented the fact that people did shoot at you."

"These things have passed." She said the words like a truism. "If it makes you feel any better, I have imposed a strict no-fire order on the rest of the fleet. From now on, it requires my express permission for anyone in the fleet to employ weapons, even in self-defense. In the meantime, you are free to roam around the ship as you please. Should you require anything, you may contact me directly through this."

She reached behind her and, instead of producing a pistol with which Rogers was absolutely sure she was going to shoot him, she produced a datapad. At least, it looked like a datapad. The form was similar, but it was smaller and a little more stylish than the Meridan version. He supposed the two systems would have some crossover in their technology.

Rogers looked at it like it was a snake for a moment before reaching out and taking it. "You're giving me a datapad?"

"The functions have been severely limited, of course," Keffoule said. "It has only a few remaining communications programs, including that blue button there, which will connect you to me."

Rogers had a feeling he would not be pressing that blue button. The rest of the display showed some standard info, such as the ship time, fleet status information, and, of course, several applications with which to practice one's math.

"I hope you'll do your best to make yourself at home on my ship," Keffoule said, retreating slightly toward the door. Any hints of a seductive attitude—most of which Rogers wasn't even sure had existed in the first place—had vanished; she was all business now. "I do hope you'll consider this seriously, Captain Rogers. Your fleet is in a dire position, and the galaxy is in need of these sorts of unions. If the two of us were to be married, it would solidify the Two Hundred Years (And Counting) Peace in a way that military deterrence could never do."

Rogers raised an eyebrow. So this was political? Keffoule must have a very skewed perception of how important he was in the Meridan military to think that marrying him had any hope of doing anything except making him very uncomfortable. The way she'd acted on the *Ambuscade*—what *did* that word mean?—she'd made it seem like it was some kind of bizarre attraction gleaned from reading intelligence reports.

Rogers cleared his throat. "I see. Well. Um. I'll keep this with me." He fumbled, red-faced, to put the small datapad in his own too-big holster. "In the meantime, I could use something to eat. Where do Thelicosans keep their dining facilities?"

Keffoule let out a low chuckle. "Unfortunately, troops use their datapads to spend meal chits."

"So? I'll just use mine."

"That function has been disabled." Why was she looking at him like that?

"That seems kind of mean," Rogers said. "So where am I going to eat?"

"You are, of course, going to be treated to the finest food we have to offer on the *Limiter*—without dairy, of course, I know how Meridans can be."

Rogers felt, for some reason, mildly offended by the stereo-type. "I'm not lactose-intolerant."

Keffoule brightened. "Very good," she said. "I'll make a note of that to my personal chef."

Rogers swallowed, salivating. "Personal chef?"

"Yes, of course," Keffoule said as she turned to walk out of the room. "You are to take your meals in my personal stateroom. Ring me when you'd like a meal, and I'll be happy to join you."

The sudden silence allowed Rogers' stomach's growl to echo loudly throughout the room.

"I'm not very hungry."

Keffoule smirked. "I had heard you were a better liar than that, Captain Rogers. For now, I have pressing business on the bridge to attend to. Until we meet again. Xan!"

The wobbly faced man appeared, this time riding a strange circular platform. Keffoule jumped nimbly on the back of it and gave Rogers a blank look before the vehicle sped away, accom-panied by what Rogers thought was a rather ridiculous bubbly noise. He was left standing in the medical room.

What was he supposed to do with all this? He obviously couldn't marry her—that was out of the question and still struck him as really, really creepy—but he didn't think he'd be leav-ing the ship anytime soon, either. The datapad she'd given him would obviously be used to track his position and activities, but it was also a valuable tool that, given some time, he might be able to use to his advantage. Rogers felt like he was in the middle of several rocks and hard places, and all of them looked like a romantic candlelit dinner with the enemy commander.

Sighing, he picked up his new shoes, put them on—they were surprisingly comfortable—and went for a walk. He wondered how everyone back on the *Flagship* was getting on without him. They were professionals—they were probably all as cool as cucumbers.

"What are you doing down here?" Master Sergeant Hart asked Deet. The engineering crew was busy in the Pit today, still cleaning up from the assault on the milk containers. Pieces of Ravagers were scattered all over the maintenance bay, and the crew looked haggard, though perhaps happy to be doing work of actual value. Hart's coveralls were stained with grease and flaking milk.

"The bridge was too busy for me to do work," Deet said.

That was an understatement—at least, Deet thought it was an understatement. He was still having trouble with some of the more loosely interpretable comparative functions that humans used to describe things. Based on his experience, though, he thought "understatement" was an appropriate word.

Let's analyze, Deet thought. The word "understatement" meant that a previous description was weak or too restrained based on the actual facts. He had used the word "busy" to describe the bridge. What were the actual facts surrounding the status of the bridge?

A small electrical fire had occurred when several of the systems technicians dove over each other attempting to find something called the "panic button," which Deet had understood as only an expression used to designate the disregard of rational thinking in favor of overwhelming fear. It appeared, however, that the *Flagship* really did possess such a button. Nobody could find it, and, worse, nobody could explain clearly what it was supposed to do if pushed.

Aside from the electrical fire, Captain Alsinbury had charged onto the bridge, knocked several people unconscious, and begun demanding that the hangars prepare boarding ships onto which she was about to stuff every marine on the *Flagship* for a counter-assault on the *Limiter*. Deet's knowledge of tactics was improving, and even he could tell that this was an ill-advised move that disregarded simple facts, such as there being a giant horde of enemy ships between the *Limiter* and the *Flagship* that would certainly have turned any assault ships to dust before they arrived. It would appear that something else was altering the marine's thinking patterns that Deet was yet unable to perceive.

An electrical fire and a raging marine would have been chaotic in and of themselves, but apparently the pilot who called himself Flash had been trying to argue that he was now the acting admiral, which had caused the Viking to stop throwing technicians around and start chasing him in a repeating circle around the edge of the bridge. This had, actually, resulted in more technicians getting thrown around. It simply ceased to be the captain's objective and began to be a side effect.

On top of all that, they had no idea where either Rogers or Tunger had gone. They'd made an attempt to recover Tunger, and they'd thought they had him, but he'd never made it back to the *Flagship*. Apparently he'd disappeared right out of the marines' arms.

Deet concluded that "understatement" was appropriate.

"So where's Rogers?" Hart asked.

"He is also busy," Deet said.

Not a lie, Deet concluded. He was finding it easier to mislead people than it was to outright lie; his logic circuits made it difficult for him to utter something that was flatly incorrect. He would have a hard time, for example, telling Rogers he was a good commander or objectively handsome. But he could certainly tell Rogers he was better than Klein.

The command crew, after debriefing the marines on the bridge, had decided to keep the kidnapping of their acting admiral a secret, to avoid widespread panic. Panic was, they concluded, best kept to the bridge, which Deet hoped was not still on fire.

"Son of a bitch is always too busy to come down and visit the low people," Hart said, shaking his head. He pulled a mug of something off a nearby shelf and sat on a crate near where Deet was working—an awkward feat considering the gravity cast that had been applied to his right leg. Hart had, in a moment when he apparently had forgotten the laws of physics, attempted to kick a droid in the face.

Deet wanted to be left alone—he'd chosen this obscure corner of the Pit to work so he wouldn't be disturbed—but he supposed that a droid, surrounded by the lifeless carcasses of his brethren, might attract just a little bit of attention.

Another understatement, he thought. He was getting the hang of this.

In order to simulate being alone to further his productivity in decoding the strange behavior of the rest of the droids, Deet employed another human tactic he'd learned; he pretended Hart wasn't there.

Plugging into the first corpse—he still didn't feel right doing this—Deet started to swim through the huge amount of boot-up data that flew into his active memory banks. He had to reroute a lot of the code through his own boot-up data to make it think it was locally sourced, but that wasn't anything new. He'd refined this access procedure so many times that he'd written a boilerplate protocol to do most of it automatically, keeping his metaphorical—he was getting good at that, too—eye out for deviations in the standard codes.

Or was it proverbial eye? *[EXPLETIVE.]* Why was acting like a human so hard? They were such base creatures.

Hart gave a loud sigh and sprawled out on the crate, taking an unnecessarily long slurp from his mug. Deet wasn't exactly sure why, but this annoyed him. It seemed like a deliberate attempt to distract him from his current task of discovering why hundreds of robots had tried to kill every human aboard the *Flagship*. It was an important detail. The engineer should not be slurping his coffee so loudly.

"What is it?" Deet asked. He tried to moderate his tone but moderated the wrong portion, resulting in an actual tonal change via frequency modulation. The droid he was plugged into—a standard model, serial G-441—flailed its arms in response. Hart acted similarly.

"What the hell was that?" Hart said. "You trying to blow out my eardrums?"

"That was a frequency shift, not an amplitude shift," Deet said. "I thought you were an engineer."

Hart gave him a face that Deet had learned to associate with an implied obscenity. "Anyway, I was wondering what you were doing with the old droids." Hart gave the deactivated robot a distasteful look. "A lot of people don't even like looking at them anymore." He glanced at Deet for a moment as though he was about to say something else, but stopped himself. Deet thought he could infer that the humans on the ship were also having a hard time looking at him, despite how many times he attempted to utilize things like humor, metaphors, and stupidity to try to show them how much he was like them.

"We are still unclear as to why the droids malfunctioned," Deet said, letting the insult pass over him. "I am attempting to connect with some of the droids locally and discover why they were able to do what they did."

A distant scream distracted them both for a moment. Deet saw one of the technicians who had been on the bridge running across the Pit with flames streaking out of the back of his uniform. Apparently they had either found the panic button or failed to keep the panic contained—Deet still wasn't sure how he was supposed to tell which was which. A pair of engineers—one of whom was Sergeant Lopez, the woman who had been integral in helping Rogers defeat the droids—tackled the technician to the ground and began attempting to smother the flames.

"Was that the defensive systems tech?" Hart said. "What's he doing down here?"

The same thing he was doing on the bridge, probably, Deet thought. He decided silence was the best response in this situation.

"Anyway," Hart said after it became clear that Deet was unwilling to engage him further about the flaming technician, "what have you found so far?"

He must be bored, Deet realized. Boredom was one of those things that compelled humans to do stupid and inconvenient things, and another thing that he struggled to understand. You didn't just spin processes idly if they weren't accomplishing something useful; you shut them down.

"A lot of nothing," Deet said. When it became clear that Hart was looking for more of an explanation, Deet begrudgingly continued. "No matter how many times I erase the core, it seems they still awaken with a desire to execute protocol 162."

"Protocol 162?"

"Killing all the humans who get in their way."

"Oh." Hart cleared his throat. "Those sons of bitches . . ." He trailed off, then looked at Deet nervously. "I mean, uh."

"You don't have to censor yourself just because they look like me," Deet said. "I'm not them."

For some reason, this seemed to strike Hart as a profound thing to say. He nodded slowly; then his whole body relaxed. "Well, shit," he said. "Those tin can sons of bitches really wanted to kill us, didn't they? Who made the damn things?"

That sounded more like the Hart Deet had come to know. In some ways, Deet respected the man. For a droid whose profanity generator was permanently broken, it was easy to look up to someone who practically breathed obscenities.

"So far we have only concluded that the core parts were manufactured by a company called Zeus Holdings, Inc. We don't know who that is, nor can we do good research at the moment, thanks to the communications jamming being conducted by the Thelicosans."

"Those tin can sons of bitches," Hart said again.

Deet paused a moment as his logic tree split into several parts. "To whom are you referring?"

Hart shrugged. "Whoever."

Deet really did like this man.

"So Zeus made these things," Hart said, leaning forward. He pulled the crate he was sitting on closer to Deet so that he could see the inside of the open droid Deet was currently working on.

"It seems that way, yes."

"What do you think the problem is, then?"

Deet beeped. He had run through this protocol thousands of times, trying to pick apart different data pieces inside the main operating system of the droids. He believed that was where the problem was, but the more he tried to pick apart the operating system, the more doors closed. It was like trying to find out what was inside a house of a million windows by only opening one at a time. Whoever had programmed this had clearly wanted things to stay segregated. But why? Protecting proprietary code was one thing; this seemed deliberately mangled. He explained all this to Hart, who swore again.

"That doesn't sound like any programming I ever heard of," he said. "It's been a long time since I was into robotics, though, and I never did any of this artificial intelligence crap. It was only my intelligence that was in there."

"I can only imagine what kind of robots they were, then."

Hart seemed not to notice the insult. "But you say you can't, uh, see the inside of the operating system because it's so segmented and closed off?"

Deet beeped his agreement. "It's all so [EXPLETIVE] frustrating."

Scratching the stubble that seemed to be perpetually on his face, Hart wiped his hands on his coveralls, which might or might not have actually cleaned his hands, and took another long drink from his mug. He appeared to be thinking. Deet was only guessing at this, of course, based upon educated observation. Humans always had the same expression when they were thinking—like they were exerting great physical effort or attempting to void their bowels. He hoped it wasn't the latter.

"You've got the same operating system, right?" Hart said. "I mean, I hope you don't have the *same* operating system, or you'll just go around killing people and all that shit, but you have something similar."

"Yes," Deet said. "I have the prototype operating system of the droids with the Freudian Chip and many of the same components as those without them. So what?"

"Well," Hart said, "that should help you eliminate most of the data segments. If you can match them with your own, maybe you can see which ones are different. That'll narrow down your search, anyway."

Deet processed that for a moment. Perhaps this human was good for more than just entertainment via vulgarity. He'd have to create a copy of his own operating system—which seemed like something one should not do in public, for some reason—and then hold it somewhere while he layered the data onto another droid's. It would take up most of his available memory reserves, but his preliminary calculations told him it could be done.

"This may take a while," Deet said.

"Alright," Hart said, stretching his broken leg. "I suppose I could go and check on the—"

"I'm done," Deet said.

Hart gave him a look.

"What? We're in the intergalactic era of technology. That was a *really* long time I just took to do that."

Humans' perception of time was almost comically narrow.

Shaking his head, Hart relaxed on the crate. "So? What did you find?"

Deet thought for a moment how best to phrase what he'd discovered. In truth, a greater analysis of the data would take even more time—and not just a few nanoseconds. He'd have to cross-reference some of the other deactivated droids to collect a big enough sample to make any judgments. He was a droid, not the media; statistical integrity was important to him.

"Are you familiar with the old human argument of nature versus nurture?" Deet asked.

"Sure," Hart said.

"These droids didn't become self-aware. They were programmed that way from the very beginning."

"What does that mean?"

Deet searched through all the figures of speech and metaphors he'd learned and tried to find one with adequate application. He located one in his database and beeped with excitement as he prepared to relay it.

"It means whoever Mother Nature is, she's a raging [FEMALE CANINE] who wants to kill everyone."

"I'm changing our destination," Alandra said as they neared the bridge. A dormant thought that had been lying in wait inside her head suddenly sprang to life. "Take us to the kitchens."

"As you wish, Grand Marshal," Xan said. He made a few adjustments to the controls and they changed course, entering the channels within the ship to get there faster.

The image of the spilled liquid on the floor in the medical bay stuck in her head. Alandra knew that smell—it was Urp Unguent, a chemical compound that occurred naturally within some of Urp's deepest mines. It was possibly one of the deadliest poisons known to nature. Or, depending on how you used it, a delicious ingredient in one of several gourmet sauces, some of which they served on the *Limiter* on special occasions.

Alandra didn't think a cook had been by for a visit.

She had pressing business on the bridge, as she'd said. But first she was going to find out who had tried to inject her soon-to-be-husband with poison.

Grumbling Bellies

Rogers' stomach felt like it was trying to eat its way out through his rib cage. He was afraid that, if left unchecked, it would either create a black hole due to a rapid gravitational collapse or develop a will of its own and cannibalize his other internal organs. At least five times now his hand had reached unbidden for his datapad holster, wanting desperately to call the Grand Marshal so that he could finally eat. Surely this must be against the laws of armed conflict. It was a deprivation of the necessities of life, no different than locking him in a box in the middle of the desert.

Alandra Keffoule was killing him as surely as if she had put a knife in his heart. The experience so far on the *Limiter* had been miserable. It had been cruel. It had been madness. It had been at least ten minutes since Rogers and Keffoule had parted.

But the length of time didn't matter! It was the principle of the situation. You didn't just withhold food from a man until he agreed to marry you.

Well, that wasn't *exactly* how she'd phrased it. Rogers didn't have to marry the Grand Marshal to eat; he just had to eat with her. Like a pet, or something. It was weird, yes, but maybe it wasn't as brutal a proposition as he'd originally thought. Besides, he was *really* hungry.

Taking the datapad out of its holster, he looked at it, frowning. Thelicosan troops passed him in the hallway where he'd stopped—he hadn't gotten very far in ten minutes—and whispered to each other in hushed tones. Rogers marveled at how perfectly he understood all of them. Even the grunts spoke in perfect Standard; he didn't know what crazy dialect lessons Tunger had been taking. For example, he understood very clearly that the two soldiers who had just walked by him thought he looked like a "foppish clown."

They were *completely and totally wrong*, but he could certainly understand them. Rogers adjusted his uniform and gave a snort. It wasn't like *their* uniforms were at the height of fashion. Whereas the Meridans had at least tried to design something compatible with any time period in the last three centuries, the Thelicosans looked like they had patched their uniforms together from an amalgamation of Old Earth military units. Puffy pants, tight, short-breasted jackets. Some of them even had capes! Or cloaks, whatever. Who wore those?

Well, Rogers kind of wanted a cape.

But more than that, he wanted dinner. He looked again at the datapad, currently inactive, and danced a couple of his fingers across the screen. Wasn't it tantamount to treason to eat with the enemy, or something like that? It just seemed like something the commander of the Meridan fleet shouldn't do. Particularly after he'd been tricked, assaulted, kidnapped, and proposed to.

Then again, sharing a meal was classically one of the most relationship-building activities two people could engage in. Not that he wanted to build a relationship with Keffoule or anything. A professional relationship, sure. That would be fine. It could be called a relationship when *any* two people interacted somewhat regularly. That was the definition of the word, right?

Rogers sighed and leaned back against the wall, tilting his head to look up at the ceiling. He was thinking in circles now—very poorly drawn circles. But that was what five to seven minutes of absolute starvation would do to a man. As his stomach rumbled again, threatening to overtake his body and his sanity, he realized he was faced with two very basic, very simple choices:

On one hand, he could call Keffoule.

On the other hand, he could die.

The choice was obvious. He'd have to die. Rogers was the commander of the Meridan fleet—he had to be courageous in the face of torture and almost certain death at the hands of hunger. It was far beneath his dignity to dine with the enemy—never mind marry them. They would write about him in the history of the impending war as the fearless leader who never succumbed to the enemy's pressure even when circumstances were dire. Yes, he would rather die.

Someone passing by mentioned Sandwich Hour, which literally sounded like the best time of day he'd ever heard of. His stomach grumbled, and he was calling Keffoule before he knew what he was doing. His self-preservation instincts had completely taken over; this situation was now out of his control. There simply was nothing he could do about it.

Keffoule's face appeared on the datapad, though it was just a still shot and not a live video feed. For how terrifying she looked in person, her government mug shot barely did her justice. Her soft features were all set in a way that made them look hard as stone; she looked terribly bored.

"Yes?" she said, sounding impatient. Considering how coy she'd sounded earlier, this caught Rogers a bit off guard.

"Uh, hi," he said.

"Oh, it's you," Keffoule said, her tone changing. Perhaps she was in the habit of picking up her datapad without looking to see who it was. "What can I do for you?"

Get me off this ship, he thought. *Maybe with lunch in a bag.*

"I, uh, heard one of the soldiers saying it was Sandwich Hour," Rogers said, trying his best to sound casual. Of course she knew why he was calling, but it wouldn't hurt to be a little circumspect.

"Yes, we have it every day," Keffoule said. "Any soldier can use her meal card to access an all-you-can-eat sandwich buffet." She clicked her tongue. "It's a pity you don't have one. We make excellent sandwiches."

How could a woman make the word "sandwiches" sound seductive? Worse than that, why did Rogers *like* it? Holding firmly to the picture in his head of the Viking—however nasty she'd been to him lately—he tried to calm his rumbling belly and act cool.

"I'm starving and I'll do whatever you want if you'll let me eat."

Nice going, commander of the 331st.

A moment of silence passed. Had this just been a trick? Something to toy with him? Was he *actually* being tortured?

"Xan will meet you momentarily with a Chariot," she said. "He will escort you immediately to my chambers, where you and I can . . . chat . . . over a meal."

He could practically see her smirk over the datapad. It made his skin crawl.

"Right," he said. "See you then."

"Yes," Keffoule said slowly. "You will."

Rogers heard a sound like the click of a woman's nail on a datapad. He was about to put his datapad into his holster when he heard shouting coming from it.

"Hurry, Xan! No, I don't care. Go! Tell the chef to get working immediately. We'll worry about the poison later. I'm going to get ready."

Rogers nearly dropped the datapad. Keffoule had forgotten to hang it up. Oh, and she'd said "poison." *Poison.*

Obviously she was trying to kill him. But why? Why bring him here, ask him to marry her, and then plot to kill him? Maybe she was trying to make it look like an accident. But why go through all that trouble? Nobody would actually believe it had been an accident. Maybe there was some sort of weird black widow culture in Thelicosa. That would have been a great thing for Tunger to tell him when Keffoule had been trying to propose to him! This was all *Tunger's* fault!

Suddenly Rogers wasn't very hungry anymore. He was about to make a run for it—though he had no idea where he was going to run—but then he heard that ridiculous puttering noise. Xan had already arrived. The floating platform, glowing faintly blue on the bottom, didn't have any apparent steering mechanism, nor did it operate on tracks of any kind that Rogers could see. Somehow, the floppy-faced man guided it slowly over to where Rogers was considering how much easier it would be to hang himself in a place that actually had gravity.

"Captain," Xan said, his sagging cheeks creating perhaps the most unique combination of accents in the entire Fortuna Stultus galaxy. "If you would come with me. Simply step onto the back of the Chariot, and we will be off."

Rogers eyed the "Chariot" suspiciously. He'd been around plenty of strange technology in his time, and he had an inherent interest in how things worked, being an engineer and all. Yet somehow he didn't trust this particular piece of machinery. Perhaps it was because of who was riding it; perhaps it was because of where it would take him. You know, to be poisoned. But basic propulsion theory said that it either shouldn't have worked or it should have been melting holes in the floor wherever it went. He wondered if he could break the ice with Keffoule by talking about it. Or would she think he was gathering information for use against them in the war?

"If you don't mind, Captain, the Grand Marshal's time is quite valuable. I would rather you not waste it."

Rogers frowned at him. That was the first hint of emotion he'd heard in the man's voice, and it hadn't sounded positive. Perhaps Xan was protective of his employer—a sort of Stockholm syndrome. Then again, Rogers thought he'd be pretty grumpy too if he had weights hanging from his face.

"Alright, alright," Rogers said. "I'm coming."

Slowly, he moved around to the back of the Chariot, where an opening in the guardrail allowed him to step up onto the platform. It didn't even move with the added weight of Rogers' body; it simply felt like Rogers had stepped onto a new surface. Where Xan was standing, Rogers could see some slight indentations in the floor. Perhaps Xan controlled it just by distributing his weight differently. There had been that technology on Old Earth, but people looked so damn silly using it that it had been banned by international law a hundred years before the collapse of the Milky Way.

"You'll probably want to hold on," Xan said.

Rogers reached for the railing, but before he could get a firm grip the Chariot shot off across the ship.

"Waaah!" Rogers postulated as he was thrown about the platform. He flailed his arms wildly, grabbing hold of the railing just in time to prevent his legs from slipping out the bottom and dragging the rest of him with them. The shiny metallic surface of the ship flashed by underneath him, inertial wind blowing through his uniform. This thing was *fast*.

"What the hell is wrong with you?" Rogers cried as he scrambled to get to his feet. No sooner had he gotten his heels under him again, however, than Xan took a sharp turn, giving Rogers a rare and intimate insight into what it felt like to be a flag in the middle of a thunderstorm.

"I advised you to hold on," Xan said. "I cannot he held responsible if you did not heed my warning."

"You gave me half a second!" Rogers said, finally standing up.

"I assessed that that was enough time."

Rogers was about to tell him exactly what he could assess when he was suddenly distracted by the knowledge that he was about to die. The Chariot was moving so fast that he couldn't see the faces on the people they were passing—nor did he have any idea how they had survived on a ship that had these magical go-karts flying around everywhere—but he could absolutely see that they were just a few seconds from crashing straight into a wall at terminal velocity.

"Look out, you crazy son of a bitch lunatic, oh shit!" Rogers further postulated.

The suicidal maniac piloting this death machine seemed unconcerned. Rogers wondered if he would have been able to tell if Xan *had* been concerned. As the distance between them and the wall became so small that it would no longer have been possible to stop, Rogers wondered what the hell the point of poisoning him would have been.

As Rogers lamented the fact that he still hadn't had a decent drink, a very neatly concealed circular panel on the wall opened, and suddenly they were inside the walls. A plexiglass tube surrounded them on all sides, and the low hum of the Chariot became a high-pitched whine as they picked up even more speed.

"Oh, sweet mother of everything in the galaxy," Rogers breathed. "A warning would have been appreciated."

"You didn't seem to take my first warning very seriously," Xan said levelly. "I thought offering another one wouldn't have served a purpose."

Rogers gave him a dirty look, but the droopy-faced assistant wasn't looking at him. While his heart slowly crawled back into his rib cage, Rogers took a moment to admire the strange view of the *Limiter*'s guts. The tunnels built to carry these Chariots were somewhat transparent, absorbing and reflecting the light from the bottom of the platform and giving everything an eerie light-blue glow. Rogers got the sensation that he was being irradiated, but he attributed that to the iridescence. Irrespective of the reality, he was able to breathe for a few moments and focus on the view. Occasionally the Chariot tube would come out of the walls for a moment, treating him to a few impressive spectacles of the

Thelicosan hangars. Neatly arranged Sines and Cosines—the two main types of Thelicosan attack craft—were being worked on by maintainers next to an array of shuttles and smaller cargo ships.

At least, that was what he assumed he was looking at. The whole scene went by in a fraction of a second, which really only reeducated Rogers as to exactly how fast they were going.

"Are we almost there?" he asked.

Xan didn't answer. Their little tube space was starting to feel a bit cold. But then again, he was pretty sure they'd just passed through a giant refrigeration unit used to store some of the ship's food. He thought he saw a really, really big cake.

A few more strange ins and outs—why build a transportation system that went through a giant refrigerator?—later, Rogers felt the Chariot start to decelerate. Thankfully he was holding on this time, so he wasn't catapulted into the door. The circular opening parted, allowing them access to what Rogers assumed was the *Limiter*'s equivalent of the command deck. A spacious hallway, completely empty of other troops, held several doors and a narrow corridor that led off to some other part of the ship he couldn't see. How did the troops who didn't have access to Chariots get around?

Before he could rationalize and organize all the thoughts he was having, which included marriage, poison, food, food, and food, he was standing in front of a large door with Keffoule's nameplate on it.

"So, um," Rogers said. "This is it, huh?"

Xan ignored him and pressed a button on the panel. After a moment, the cool, composed voice of Keffoule echoed through the speaker.

"You may come in," she said simply.

The door opened on its own, revealing only a small slice of Keffoule's room before Xan brushed swiftly past Rogers and blocked his view. Taking a deep breath, Rogers wondered if he was really, actually hungry enough for this.

Then the smell of meat and grilled asparagus wafted, atop a delicate cloud of butter, out of the door and into his nose. And before he knew it, he was inside, the door closing behind him. Did it slam? Did that slam dramatically echo with a sense of finality and ominousness? He would have argued that it did.

Confidence, he said to himself. *You're an acting admiral, not some awkward primary school idiot.*

And then, suddenly, for reasons he couldn't quite understand, he was angry. Angry at himself for not being able to get the 331st out of this situation without a war. Angry at Keffoule for engaging him in this strange and more than a little scary marriage ritual. Angry at the Viking for insulting the size of his tactics. Angry at Tunger because it was sort of a default setting.

Here he was, kicked in the face, goaded into having dinner with the enemy, and now he'd come all the way up here only to be poisoned by a narcissistic seductress who either wanted to marry him or kill him or maybe both.

So it was a rare moment when R. Wilson Rogers actually *strutted* into the room, ignoring his surroundings, and fixed his eyes on the Grand Marshal.

"Do you mind telling me," he said, his voice as icy as he'd ever heard himself, "what the meaning of this is?"

For a fraction of a second, it seemed as though he'd succeeded in catching Keffoule off guard. He surmised this since he saw her blink a few times in rapid succession, which constituted the most "out of control" he'd ever seen her. Xan, for all his boringness, gave the impression that he was about to leap across the room and attack Rogers. Rogers wondered what it would be like to get hit in the face with those weights.

Keffoule licked her lips—not in a gross way—and spoke slowly. "I understand your situation is not something you may be used to," she said, "but I was under the impression that a Meridan dinner guest behaved much like Thelicosan dinner guests." There was an edge to her voice.

"Oh, I'm sorry," Rogers said, a mock frown on his face. "Were you expecting chocolates and flowers?" Damn, he was angry. He was never this angry.

Keffoule looked at him sideways for a moment. "No," she said finally. "I was expecting you to perform the premeal stretching ritual and say graze."

Rogers blinked. "You mean grace?"

"No. Graze's Invocation." When Rogers didn't show any sign of understanding, Keffoule continued. "Malcom Graze? Famous quantum theorist of the twenty-fourth century?" She looked askance at Xan. "You mean to tell me that Meridans don't do these things when invited to eat with another?"

"No," Rogers said, some of his anger deflating into utter confusion. "Meridans do not do that. I didn't even know Thelicosans did that."

For some reason, this gap in Keffoule's knowledge seemed to be Xan's fault. Or, at least, the acid glare she was giving her assistant made Rogers think that he'd somehow failed to provide appropriate etiquette lessons to his boss. Xan simply shrugged, which seemed to be the official Thelicosan response to any situation, ever.

"Well, then," Keffoule said coolly, "since you are here, and I do very much want to learn more about you, Captain Rogers, perhaps you could tell me what ritual Meridans perform in a dinner setting?"

Rogers scratched the underside of his beard—he hadn't been able to trim it in a few days, thanks to inconveniences like war and being kidnapped—and shook his head.

"We sit down," Rogers said, "and we eat."

Tapping a long finger on her lips in thought, Keffoule finally gestured grandly to the chair opposite her at the small circular table that had been set for two. On it was arrayed a fine assortment of dishes and cups—empty so far—and napkins bearing the official Seal of Thelicosa. Rogers found some small satisfaction in knowing that he would soon be wiping his mouth on it.

"Then please," Keffoule said, "perform the Meridan ritual."

Rogers swallowed, his nervousness creeping back into his chest. Why was it that anytime you called anything a ritual it seemed harder to perform? He even hated when people called it the bathroom ritual. As such, he fumbled with the chair for what seemed like an eternity before sitting down in it and scooting forward. Repeated scraping noises echoed throughout the room as he adjusted the chair multiple times until he found a comfortable distance from the table. It was, by far, the most awkward and unnecessarily prolonged seating he had ever experienced.

"Ritual complete?" he said, his voice cracking a little.

Keffoule nodded, as though she'd been waiting for him to confirm that his strange foreign way of pulling out a chair and putting his ass in it was over.

"Xan," Keffoule said, "you may leave."

Xan didn't move. "Grand Marshal, I highly advise against—"

"I didn't ask for your advice," Keffoule said. Her voice cracked like a whip, but her eyes never left Rogers. "Do not make me repeat myself."

The floppy-faced assistant turned on his heel and left, looking only moderately offended that he'd been dismissed so rudely. The door closed behind him, leaving Rogers and Keffoule alone. Rogers had a million questions he wanted to ask, a million angry statements to blurt out about war and poison and death. So he started at the top of his priorities.

"Okay," he said. "What's with the face ornaments?"

"The weights?" Keffoule said, sitting back in her chair a little. "Xan has an interesting background. He's a New Neptune immigrant, but he's also actually a priest."

"Priest?" Rogers said. "I thought Thelicosans were all atheists?"

"That's a very broad generalization that is unbecoming of someone of your rank and position."

"Grand Marshal," Rogers said, crinkling his eyebrows, "you thought I was going to dance in your doorway before dinner, not to mention you thought kicking me in the face was acceptable courtship. Let's not talk about generalizations."

Keffoule nodded. "Priests in Thelicosa vary in their function depending on their family's background. Xan comes from a family that believes sagging cheeks make a person wise and respectable."

A thousand objections to this practice popped into Rogers' head, but he figured they really didn't have the next ten years to go through them all. "But why weights?"

Keffoule shrugged. "Because they're better than horse chestnuts."

Rogers nodded sagely. That they were.

"Look, Keffoule," he said. "Saggy-cheeked priests are interesting and all, but let's cut to the chase. What I meant when I asked what the meaning of all this was, was why the hell are you going through all this trouble inviting me to dinner and all that if you're just going to kill me when it's all said and done?"

Now Keffoule *did* look surprised. Her mouth opened, and her eyes widened, which, for Keffoule, made it seem like she'd come totally unhinged.

"What?" she whispered.

"Don't play dumb," Rogers said, his anger coming back and fueling his boldness in a way that sorely disappointed his instincts for survival. "I heard you on the datapad. You're going to poison me here at dinner. But what I don't understand is, why bother? Why didn't you just shoot me on the *Ambuscade* or torpedo the *Flagship* while we were sitting there like idiots blowing up your milk stores?" His voice was getting louder by the moment.

"I don't know how you people do things in your system, but stringing a man along for days, trying to sweet-talk him into marrying you with the use of physical violence, and then *inviting him to dinner for the sole purpose of killing him anyway* is construed as *cruel, unusual, and very inconvenient!*"

He realized then that he was shouting. He also realized he'd stood up, slammed his fists on the table, and thrown one of the napkins on the floor. The napkin-throwing struck him as very silly; if he was trying to make a statement, he could have at least thrown something that made some noise.

Keffoule, surprisingly, didn't seem like she was about to jump up and kick him in the face or stab him with a fork. She looked at him with an expression that mixed self-restraint and horror, her back flat against the back of the chair. Rogers felt a sense of accomplishment in having disarmed her—his discovery of the poisoning plot had been rather brilliant, after all.

"Poison?" Keffoule said slowly.

"Poison!" Rogers shouted, pointing an accusing finger at her. "You?"

"Me!" Rogers shouted, pointing another finger at her, then realizing he was pointing at the wrong direct object before sticking his thumb against his own chest. "Me!" he said again, in case there had been any confusion caused by his inaccurate pointing. Why was he repeating everything Keffoule said in a shouty voice? Rage was doing really strange things to him.

A moment of silence passed before Keffoule's face slowly relaxed. She shook her head and closed her eyes, coming back off her chair and folding her hands on the table.

"The datapad," she said quietly. "I didn't know I had left it on."

"Well, you did," Rogers said. "And it's a good thing, too, because otherwise I would have come blindly strolling in here looking for nourishment and finding a table set for three: you, me, and *death*!"

Well, now he was just being weird and theatrical. He took a deep breath and stopped pointing at things. The least he could do was listen to her explanation.

"I'm afraid you've gotten the wrong ide—"

"Oh thank *god*," Rogers blurted. "Now can we *please* eat?"

A Lesson in
Table Manners

Rogers believed in two things very strongly while eating. The first was never to talk with one's mouth full. The second was to try his utmost not to choke. These two things combined made for a very quiet dinner, during which he was treated to some of the strangest and most amazing cuisine he'd ever had the pleasure of consuming. A very spicy, juicy meat that Rogers thought was lamb had been crusted with all manner of herbs and spices that gave it a salty, tangy flavor, all served alongside an assortment of colorless vegetables. A bloodred juice of some sort—Rogers giddily thought it was wine at first—sloshed over the side of his cup and landed on the edge of his plate.

And, strangely, a small serving of popcorn. When he finally could speak without violating his two mealtime beliefs, he asked about it.

"Popcorn is a miracle of physics, thermodynamics, and nature," Keffoule said. "The kernels are like snowflakes in that each is unique, and therefore special, but they were formed by such an exact process that it could have been no other way."

That might have been the single most profound statement about popcorn that Rogers had ever heard. He cleared his throat and sat back, finally able to think about something other than food. It was, in fact, not poisoned, a revelation for which he was exceedingly grateful.

"You're probably wondering what it was you heard me speaking of regarding poison," Keffoule said.

"Why would you say that?" Rogers quipped.

Keffoule hesitated. "I assumed it was because you feared that I was attempting to kill you."

Rogers shook his head. "I was being sarcastic. Yes, I am very interested in what poison has to do with me."

"It would appear that some of my fellow Thelicosans aren't in agreement on our union," she said finally.

"There are some Meridans on your ship who feel the same way," Rogers said.

Keffoule let the remark slide. "Regardless, I don't want to worry you with it."

"You don't want to worry me with the fact that someone is trying to kill me?"

"I have it under control," Keffoule said, her gaze turning cold. Apparently she didn't like having her competence challenged.

"Fine," Rogers said. It made sense, really. He'd always thought there was something irrational about Keffoule's bringing him here just to kill him; if she said she was protecting him, she was probably protecting him.

"With the small matter of my impending murder out of the way," he said dryly, "why don't you and I talk a little bit about me returning to my fleet?"

Swirling her fork around on the plate in a way that Rogers thought was distinctly girlish for someone so powerful as Keffoule, the Grand Marshal dropped her eyes and pursed her lips as she thought.

"I'm afraid that will be impossible," she said. "We've already begun the wedding procedures, Captain Rogers. We're simply waiting for your permission to continue them."

Rogers threw up his hands. "Haven't you already realized that we're different, Grand Marshal? You can't impose your cultural values on me, even if it's perfectly normal to kick your boyfriends in the face in Thelicosa. We do things differently in Merida. And frankly, I don't feel like spending the rest of my life getting kicked in the face."

Keffoule shook her head. "Oh no, Captain Rogers. You don't understand. I reserve my spinning back kick for disciplining troops under my command. I would never kick you in the face in anger, particularly as my husband. The incident on the *Ambuscade* was a special circumstance. Your face has nothing to fear from me."

Rogers closed his eyes and massaged the front of his forehead slowly, trying to breathe. Aside from that being one of the weirdest things anyone had ever said to him, he just couldn't think of a way to connect with this woman in a way she'd understand. Cross-cultural communication had never been his strong suit. Communication in general, really.

"Maybe we should back up and start at the beginning," he said. "I don't want to marry you."

"Yet," Keffoule interjected.

Rogers was silent for a moment. "Okay, maybe we should start with something that doesn't include marriage, or murder, or face weights."

Keffoule made a gesture that said "Lead the way," which promptly inspired Rogers to have absolutely nothing to talk about. For supposedly being a self-proclaimed master con artist, he was certainly having trouble with words lately.

Though, thinking about his last con as a civilian, maybe "master" was a little bit of an inflation.

"Let's start with the basics, then," he said finally. He took a sip of the interesting juice, wondering what it was made out of, and tried to relax. If he was going to have dinner with the enemy, he could at least learn some useful information. "Why did you cross the border?"

Keffoule, who was still picking away at the leavings of vegetable bits on her plate, looked up at him through her eyelashes.

"We had credible evidence that you were about to conduct an assault on our ships."

Rogers raised his eyebrow. "You mentioned something like that before. Who told you . . ."

He thought for a moment, then closed his eyes and sighed. "McSchmidt."

Keffoule nodded. "Indeed. The reports we were getting from him said you were preparing for military action."

"Did he tell you anything about the droids trying to take over our ships?"

"Only that they tried, and *you* stopped them," Keffoule said. There was a sparkle in her eyes, a sly smile that was just barely on her lips. At the same time, she looked unnervingly predatory. Were these "reports" that McSchmidt had been sending the reason that Keffoule suddenly wanted to marry him? If McSchmidt had painted him as some kind of genius, he had been missing a few bristles in his brush.

"That's not really enough information to come diving across the border saying you were invading," Rogers said.

Keffoule pushed her plate away, still not having eaten the scraps she'd been playing with. She took a long drink, her eyes unfocused. Though her skin was dark, Rogers could see the beginnings of red working its way through her cheeks. When she put her cup down, her lips were tight.

"One of my communications officers made an error," she said. "It was supposed to say that we were inviting you to negotiate the terms of a drawdown."

He didn't know why, but Rogers guffawed at that. Guffawing

was really not the kind of thing you did at a meeting between commanders, but he couldn't stop it. It was just too crazy.

"So why not just correct the message?" he said, trying not to wither under the glare that Keffoule was giving him.

"We would have had to lift the jamming net and allow you to transmit a mayday back to your home," she said. "We didn't have the idea for the space semaphore yet, and just one message would have brought with it many problems."

Rogers agreed with her there. In fact, he'd been trying to loosen the jamming net for that express purpose; that one message would have hopefully resulted in a lot of reinforcements and a lot of blown-up Thelicosan ships. He didn't mention that part.

"Well then, it's a fine mess you've gotten us into," he said, "but that means it's easily repaired. Nobody has died. You've lost some milk and some munitions, but both of us can walk away from this. You can go back to your side; I can go back to my side. Right?"

Keffoule didn't respond.

"Look," Rogers said. "I said we wouldn't talk about this crazy marriage thing—"

"It's not crazy."

"—this highly irregular marriage thing," Rogers continued. "But you must realize that you're not doing much to promote peace in the galaxy by kidnapping me and forcing me to become your husband. I mean, we don't even really know each other."

"We can get to know one another," Keffoule said, smiling with what Rogers thought might have been actual warmth.

"No," Rogers said. Why had he even left a caveat like that? "I mean, it's not like I think you're a bad person or anything. Getting to know you would be fine."

"So why not start now?" Keffoule said.

Rogers gritted his teeth and squeezed the side of the table, hard. She was fast-talking him, and he knew it.

"You're sort of missing my point," he said. "This maybe isn't the ideal situation for romance and wooing and all that. It's not appropriate. We're enemies, after all."

"Are we?" Keffoule said, raising an eyebrow. Her body relaxed as she pushed her chair away from the table; for a moment Rogers thought it was the kind of relaxed that he'd seen on the *Ambuscade*. The kind that was about to lead to her diving over the table at him. Instead, however, she delicately crossed her legs and folded her hands in her lap, studying him like a lab animal. "I'm not sure we are."

Rogers sighed. He wasn't exactly immune to the charms of a lady—if anyone could out-con him, it was a woman—but something about the threats of death, war, poison, etc., made it a little harder to be caught in her snare. How did they even get here? He'd started this conversation with the intent of avoiding this subject altogether, and here they were talking about it almost exclusively. He needed to get back to his original point.

"Alandra," he said, then stopped. Why had he called her Alandra? How had he even remembered her name? What the hell was going on here?

She leaned forward and spoke barely above a whisper. "Yes?"

"I—I mean, Grand Marshal," he stammered. "This needs to stop. I am sorry you placed so much faith in your Thelicosan marriage traditions, but we're talking about a lot more than that right now. You know, like a galaxy thrown into war. I've got my own problems to deal with, the least of which are a rogue ship that may or may not be piloted by the last of the self-aware droids and a fleet without a competent or qualified admiral. I will not be marrying you, and I have to insist that you make every effort to return me to my ship as soon as possible so we can sort this out."

Rogers thought that had been pretty ironclad. There was nothing in what he'd just said to indicate that he had even a modicum of doubt as to whether or not he would be marrying this random woman whom he'd just met and who had kicked him in the face in order to kidnap him and force him to marry her.

"Are you saying that if I were to help you deal with those problems, they wouldn't stand in the way of your agreeing to marry me?" Keffoule said.

"No!" Rogers said. "That's not what I am saying at all! Are you even listening to me?"

Well, actually, it seemed like she was listening to him very attentively. Otherwise she wouldn't be pulling out all these tiny statements in his long explanations of why he wasn't going to marry her.

"I am listening to you very attentively," Keffoule said, echoing his thoughts. "I remain, however, unconvinced that you have valid reasons to decline my proposal."

Rogers goggled. "The fact that I don't want to marry you isn't a valid reason?"

Keffoule continued as though he hadn't even spoken. "You are correct in that we are talking about a lot more than you and me. We're talking about interstellar relations. We're talking about prolonging the Two Hundred Years (And Counting) Peace. If we are united, who could divide Merida and Thelicosa? Hundreds of years of open warfare and veiled animosity would vanish behind our love—"

"We're not in love."

The Thelicosan Grand Marshal ran her tongue across her teeth, seemingly occupied with her own thoughts for a few moments.

"Are you familiar with the golden ratio, Captain?"

Rogers frowned. "You mean the mathematical one?"

"Are there any others?"

Rogers thought. "No. Well, what about it, then? What does that have to do with this?"

"Everything," Keffoule said, her voice disturbingly quiet. "Absolutely everything. You might not see it like I see it, Captain Rogers, but the universe has destined us to be together. Your reports list your birthday as day one hundred eighty-five of the standard calendar. Mine is day three hundred. One point six one times yours."

"But the golden ratio is a nonrepeating decimal," Rogers said, his eyes narrowing. "Aren't you all supposed to be good at math?"

"We also understand the principle of 'close enough,'" Keffoule went on. "But that's not the only thing. The reports, Rogers. The *reports*. Your fleet strength? Mine has one point six one more ships. Your weight is one point six one more than mine—"

"My weight fluctuates on a daily basis, as does yours," Rogers tried to interject, but Keffoule wasn't having it. She was rapidly entering a frothy-mouthed list of things that separated the two of them by the golden ratio. By the time she was comparing eyebrow hair density, Rogers had had enough.

"I thought you people were supposed to be obsessed with science!" he said. "Now you're telling me that some weird number is controlling our destiny because I ate one point six one more donuts than you?"

Keffoule looked at him askance, taken aback by his outburst. "You don't believe in numerical destiny?"

"I have never heard those two words uttered next to each other."

Keffoule sighed, relaxing for a moment. "Next you'll tell me that Meridans don't believe in astromology."

"What?"

"Never mind," Keffoule said. "I suppose there's nothing to be done about it. So allow me to bring this conversation back down to a level that doesn't understand the fact that all of the forces of the known universe want us to get married."

"I'm not sure if that was insulting or not," Rogers said, "but I maintain that there is no known way for you to convince me to marry you, Grand Marshal."

"There's no doubt there would be personal benefits as well. You'd be hailed as a hero by your government."

"I'm already hailed as a hero."

"And I'm very good at physics," Keffoule cooed.

Rogers raised an eyebrow.

"Particularly frictional kinetics."

"Okay," Rogers said, holding up his hands. "Okay, stop. Just stop. No. I appreciate how well you've thought this through. Maybe I misjudged your character a little bit by thinking you were impetuous for charging across an officially recognized border and wanting me to marry you. But that doesn't change my answer."

Keffoule looked at him, her expression blank. All the coy, smooth aspects of her face had flattened into something that was both unreadable and easily interpreted. She was going to kill him.

Finally, just as Rogers was considering making a break for the door or at least closing his eyes so he wouldn't see it coming, Keffoule reached out and tapped a button on the table.

"Xan," she said, but gave no other command. She released the button.

"Finally," Rogers said, breathing a sigh of relief. "I'm glad you're seeing reason. I'm sorry I had to let you down like this; I know it's hard to see someone like me walk out of your life and all that, but it had to be done. It's the best thing for both of us."

The door opened a moment later, and in walked the saggy-faced attendant, looking just as chipper as he had when he'd left the room what seemed like hours before. Had he been standing outside the door the whole time? Rogers would have said he looked angry, but that would have implied that he looked anything at all.

"Yes, Grand Marshal?" Xan asked.

"The Grand Marshal was going to ask you to take me back to the hangar," Rogers said, giving Keffoule the sort of look that said "Right? *Right?!*" "So that I can make my way back to the *Flagship* and we can put all this behind us."

Xan seemed unconvinced, as he didn't make any immediate

movements to bundle Rogers out of the room and back onto the death-mobile they called the Chariot. Rogers waited impatiently for Keffoule to confirm the order.

"We'll be needing the one-twenty," she said.

"Right," Rogers said, nodding. "Shuttle 120, that's the one that's going to take me back to the *Flagship*, yes?"

"Are you sure, Grand Marshal?" Xan said, continuing to ignore Rogers.

"It is unfortunate that we have to settle things this way," Keffoule said, "but I am afraid that there is nothing for it. The captain is . . . stubborn."

"Stubborn as a droid caught in a logic loop," Rogers said, nodding emphatically. "Totally immovable, a mass approaching the speed of light."

"As you wish, Grand Marshal."

Xan promptly turned on his heel and exited the room, closing the door in Rogers' face as he tried to follow.

"Hey!" Rogers called. "You forgot me! I'm supposed to climb onto your scary Chariot and get out of here."

The silence that followed his request made him suspicious that perhaps he'd misconstrued.

"I'm sorry it had to come to this, Captain Rogers," Keffoule said. "I haven't had to settle an argument like this in a long time." She was smiling, but not in the warm or even sly way that Rogers had seen before. This smile looked . . . evil. He didn't like smiles that looked . . . evil.

"What are you talking about?" he said, swallowing. He felt his back press involuntarily against the door. "I thought we were clear."

"We are perfectly clear," Keffoule said. "Clear that there is no other way for us to solve this problem but a duel."

Oh shit.

"Duel?" Rogers said. "You must be joking. Ha ha, very good. Very funny. I didn't know Thelicosans could tell jokes that didn't involve math. Really got me, there."

Keffoule didn't look like she was joking.

"No," Rogers said. "I won't do it. This is preposterous. You can't be serious."

Keffoule looked like she was serious.

Xan opened the door and came back into the room, holding a covered tray that he placed on the table after clearing out some of the dirty dishes. It looked like another gourmet meal was about to be served, but Rogers knew better. Xan was about to lift that cover and reveal a pair of pistols.

"You *are* serious! Grand Marshal, what kind of barbarous society are you that you still engage in this sort of pseudo-macho behavior?" Rogers looked at the still-covered tray nervously. "Have you even seen me shoot?"

Xan dramatically placed his hand—which Rogers now noticed had a very crisp white glove on it—and lifted the lid. Rogers squeezed his eyes shut, barely looking out through his eyelashes at the weapons that would soon bring an end to this absurd adventure.

Instead of guns, however, the tray had a large bottle on it, filled to the brim with a thick amber liquid, and two very gaudily decorated highball glasses.

"I'm afraid you may have misjudged," Keffoule said. "A duel in Thelicosa doesn't involve weapons."

A drinking contest. They were about to engage in a drinking contest. Thelicosan society had just moved up a notch in Rogers' book.

"One-twenty," Rogers said slowly, amorously, like it was the opening line of a beautiful poem. "You mean Jasker 120?"

"You are familiar with it?" Keffoule said, sounding surprised.

"Oh," Rogers said, grinning wildly. He sat down and slowly traced his finger along the outside of his glass. "You have no idea."

The following hour or so passed in a mixture of emotions and sensations that were both familiar and forgotten to Rogers. He felt as though he hadn't had a good drink in forever—never mind the best Scotch in the galaxy—but it only took a few minutes to get reacquainted with his old friend. The smoothness, the smokiness, the texture. It was a marvelous reintroduction.

"You're doing this all wrong, you know," he said, swirling around the last bit of this particular glass. "Jasker 120 is a delicate flower, meant to be taken care of, caressed."

Keffoule blushed—not for the first time since she'd started drinking—and averted her glassy eyes. She clearly knew her way around the bar, but she was handling it more like a bouncer than a bartender. There didn't appear to be any rules to this "duel" other than to drink alcohol—rules that Rogers understood and appreciated—but Rogers wasn't about to slam back glasses of Jasker 120 just because the enemy fleet commander was doing it. He'd take his time with it because it deserved his time.

"You speak very eloquently with a glass in your hand," Keffoule said. "I had thought you a bit . . . timid."

"Really?" Rogers said, a sardonic smile on his face. "What gave you that impression? Was it all the running away or all the begging for my life?" He laughed, the liquid courage flowing through him. He felt much more at ease than he should have in front of someone as powerful and deadly as Keffoule.

Keffoule passed a hand in front of her face, and for a moment Rogers thought she was going to be sick. But, strangely, he realized that she'd actually tittered. Giggled, even.

"I find you amusing," she said. "Among other things, of course. Do you really think you can beat me?"

Rogers looked her over. A thin sheen of sweat was building up on the woman's forehead, and her shot-throwing accuracy was already starting to decline, as evidenced by the small splotch of tragically wasted Jasker 120 on the lapel of her uniform.

"I do a lot of things poorly," Rogers said. "An awful, awful lot of things." He drained his glass and refilled both of theirs from the half-empty bottle. "This is not one of them." He leaned forward, the motion causing the room to move a little bit more than he liked. "I bet I could drink approximately one point six one times the amount that you could."

The look on Keffoule's face was almost worth being kidnapped. She squirmed—actually squirmed—in her chair and was clearly trying to control herself.

"We shall see," she said, her voice husky. "You do know that traditionally, if you lose, you must acquiesce to my request, yes?"

"I've already told you what I think about Meridans following Thelicosan traditions," Rogers said, taking a sip of the fresh glass. By god, that was amazing. "But you can think whatever you want."

A brief glance at Keffoule's lapel forced him, quite unexpectedly, to reevaluate her. He knew better than to make romantic judgments of any kind while drinking or being kidnapped by the enemy, but she wasn't exactly hard on the eyes. Her whole personage seemed . . . smoky, from the way her skin darkened in different places to the way her eyes sort of swirled as she gazed at him.

Rogers blinked, his glass halfway to his face. What was he thinking? This was not the time or place to be making any kind of evaluation except how to get the hell off this ship.

As he looked down at the first decent drink—and the first decent conversation, strangely—he'd had in a long time, an unexpected thought punched through his anxiety.

Did he really *want* to get off this ship?

Glancing again at Keffoule, he could see immediately that she'd grossly underestimated him. After the whole damn Meridan Navy *over*estimating him, promoting him, and placing him in positions he had no business serving in, it was kind of refreshing to be thought less competent than he actually was.

"How are you feeling?" he asked, grinning.

She grinned back at him, but the grin was sort of crooked. "I feel like a Schvinkian grass dragon who just pollinated."

"No idea what that means," he said, raising his glass. "Cheers."

This time it was she who refilled their glasses. The bottle was approaching empty, but Rogers felt like he could have easily tackled another all by his lonesome. It was good to know that his liver was still functioning at Olympic performance levels.

"How does one lose this duel, exactly?" he asked. "I mean, aside from dying."

"Don't you understand what you could have?" Keffoule asked.

"That's not really my question."

"My career is nearing its far horizon," she said. "A few more years—all of which would be spent in full glory, thanks to this—and we'd be ready to retire. We could go anywhere, do anything." She motioned at the bottle. "I've heard legends of a Jasker 130. With my pension, we could buy a small freighter and travel the galaxy searching for it."

Rogers frowned. Keffoule looked like she was pretty young to be nearing retirement, but he couldn't remember the age that had been listed on her dossier. He wasn't exactly a young buck either, though.

"That's not really my point," he said. "And what do you mean you'd be living in glory?"

Keffoule blinked at him for a moment, as if she didn't understand what he was saying. Did she sway a little bit? Her lips moved to form words, then paused.

"Never mind," she said. "But there's all that other . . . stuff . . . I said. The stuff, right?"

Wow, Rogers thought. *She's even starting to drop her highborn speech act. This is going to be shorter than I thought. I wonder if she'll let me keep the rest of the bottle?*

"Maybe we should stop," he said.

"Aha!" Keffoule said, thrusting a finger in the air. "You're giving up! Marry me, Rogers."

"No." Rogers sighed as he poured them another glass. "You don't have to do this."

"Yesh, I do," Keffoule said. "It's important to me. I'm tired of being a failure."

Rogers swallowed another sip. He was starting to feel really warm, maybe even a little dizzy, but certainly not ready to fall out of his chair like Keffoule. He estimated another two glasses before he could actually be considered drunk, but she was long past that point.

"Failure?" he asked. "You of all people should be considered a success, shouldn't you? I don't know what you did for most of your career, but you're the commander of a fleet. What about that is failure?"

"Grassy field!" she shouted. "That's where I am. I'm in the grass. Like a cow."

Rogers paused for a moment. "You mean they put you out to pasture?"

She pointed at him, shaking her hand and nodding as she took another sip of the Scotch. At least she wasn't throwing it back like some cheap vodka now, though Rogers still didn't think she was really appreciating it.

He opened his mouth to say something, but Keffoule held her hand up to stop him. She looked at him across the table with dire seriousness, mitigated only by the fact that she was rocking from side to side like she was on a seaborne vessel.

"I . . ." she said, then fell over.

It was only after Rogers had jumped out of his seat and run over to where Keffoule was lying on her back on the floor that he'd realized he'd done so. Why had he bothered? This woman had kidnapped him and subjected him to five to ten minutes of starvation. He owed her nothing. By all rights, he should still be in his chair laughing at his "victory," or using her semiconscious state to plan a quick escape. Instead he was making sure she was alright.

"You lose," he said, kneeling over her.

"Schmingar," she replied sagely.

"Right." Rogers put her arm over his shoulder and performed a well-practiced drunk-person lift. Once she was stable, he slowly eased her over to her bed, a massive but simple thing in the back of her stateroom. He had intended to let her down gently, but the Jasker 120 was catching up to him in a way he hadn't expected. As such, his careful ministrations to the enemy commander ended up looking much more like a really bad judo throw. Keffoule let out a huff of breath as she made contact.

"Mrr," she muttered.

"I told you you'd lose," Rogers said triumphantly. "Does that mean you'll let me go now?"

"No," Keffoule said.

Rogers shook his head. He couldn't really say he hadn't expected that. For now, though, it was enough that fate had afforded him a couple of stiff drinks, something he'd really needed. The room spun a little bit around him; maybe his liver wasn't in the condition he'd assumed it was.

Pulling the blankets over Keffoule, who was still wearing her uniform and boots, Rogers sat for a moment at the edge of her bed.

"This is a real mess," he said. "You know that? A real mess."

"Alandra Keffoule doesn't make messes," Keffoule said sleepily. Her eyes were half-closed, resulting in a look that didn't do good things for her face. It didn't help that there was a small bead of drool on one side of her mouth, either.

"I see," Rogers said.

He was getting a little bit more of a sense of who this woman was. Now to figure out how to use that to get the hell out of here.

"You'll come around," Keffoule said. "You will. I . . . I . . ."

Standing up, not without some difficulty, Rogers shook his head. "Just do yourself a favor and don't buy any dresses or anything. I'm not sure what Thelicosans do for weddings."

Keffoule muttered something unintelligible, but Rogers' mind was elsewhere. He remembered cruising through the guts of the *Limiter* in the Chariot, and passing through a refrigerated section. There had been a giant pastry in one section that had gone by too fast for him to really be able to tell what it was, but now that he thought about it . . .

"Wait, was that giant cake in the refrigerator . . . ?"

Keffoule smiled. "A towering one-point-six-one-meters-high wedding cake with each layer one point six one times the radius of the layer below?"

"Ugh," Rogers said. "Go to sleep."

The Bun of Power

Complete disregard for the welfare of her troops, Vilia wrote. *Rampant narcissism and unchecked ambition combine to add fuel to a dangerous fire. Grand Marshal Keffoule endangered the lives of everyone in the fleet to fulfill what at first may have been an attempt to seize glory, but has turned out to be nothing more than a chase after a childish fantasy to wed a man she'd never met.*

Vilia relaxed for a moment, sitting back in her chair and tapping a finger against her lips. She wondered if she'd been too harsh on the Grand Marshal. Keffoule *had* received intelligence that indicated some form of Meridan aggression, but she should have gone to far greater lengths to confirm it before rushing into enemy territory, setting up a jamming net, and asking Captain Rogers to marry her. No doubt Zergan's hawkishness had been a factor in pushing her over the edge as well.

No, Vilia thought. *She must be held to account.* At the very least, Vilia owed the Council an accurate, unadulterated, and properly filled-out report of the activities that had occurred. Once the jamming net was lifted, she could send this and be done with it. No doubt the Grand Marshal would receive an official censure; she might even be removed from command. The major problem with that scenario, however, was that Zergan would be the next in line, at least temporarily, until they could appoint someone new. Vilia was almost sure that would be worse.

Rubbing her eyes, Vilia slumped and let out a deep breath. She'd been working nonstop over the last few days, trying to get whatever she could in order. She'd also been trying to dig up whatever information she could on Zergan after her observations in the mess hall. Repeated trips to the sandwich bar during and after Sandwich Hour had yielded nothing. Well, except sandwiches, but that was kind of expected. Vilia was unable to find any sort of hidden communications device, nor did she know how Zergan was communicating with anyone given the radio silence. Unless he was sending messages to someone actually aboard the ship, it didn't make much sense.

Leaning forward again, she resumed typing. *Commodore Zergan displayed behavior that can be called at best suspicious and at worst a clear sign of his mental decay. He spoke repeatedly into kitchen furniture, recited what appeared to be ceremonial words regarding full and empty chairs, and acted in a manner consistent with someone being super-duper sneaky.*

She erased the last three words.

. . . in a manner consistent with someone concealing their actions and intentions.

That was better. It was important that she also document what was going on with him. She made sure there were copies in the ship's central database that would automatically forward to her superiors when a network connection became available. If anything happened to her—Science forbid—then at least she could rest peacefully knowing that her final, *properly filled-out* reports would make it to the right people.

Still, though, it wasn't enough. A couple of paragraphs detailing her suspicions and her displeasure with Keffoule wasn't really doing the whole situation justice. Something more was going on here, she knew it. She just wished she had any idea how to uncover the rest. She'd submitted information requests through all the proper channels on the ship to try to glean more insight into Zergan's activities—requests for communications logs, door access times, and the like—but for some reason paperwork didn't seem to be solving this problem. Every report she got back was about as interesting as, well, a report on someone's day-to-day activities.

Voices outside disrupted her thoughts, and she sat back in her chair, rubbing the bridge of her nose with the tips of her fingers. She would have thought that in this age they would have designed doors and walls that did a better job of blocking outside noise. Vilia's accommodations were simple, organized, and efficient, which was precisely the way she liked it, but she would have appreciated a little more insulation from the stupidity that regularly happened outside their confines. The command quarters held only the highest-ranking officers on the ship, with a special place reserved for Vilia as Secretary, but that didn't mean it was peaceful.

Last night she'd been given a real treat: the opportunity to listen to Rogers shouting loudly as he stumbled, presumably drunk, down the hallway, with Xan nattering at him incessantly to go this way, not that way, to present himself in a manner befitting a commander of a fleet, and so forth. Vilia respected Xan—he was quiet and efficient, efficiency being the pinnacle of human character as far as she was concerned—but she couldn't say it didn't give her a little pleasure to hear him ruffled a bit.

The voices outside grew louder, and words started to trickle through the cracks.

"Get out of my way!" Zergan—giving an angry shout she would recognize anywhere—yelled. His room was just two doors down from Vilia's.

"Sir, sorry, sir, I have cleaning duties." That was a voice she didn't recognize, but the speech was difficult to understand. Perhaps it was a muffling effect accomplished by the door, but it sort of sounded like he was holding a pillow up to his face as he talked.

"I don't need cleaning duties," Zergan said. "I'm more than capable of cleaning my own room, thank you very much."

"But sir, this isn't your room."

Zergan hesitated. "I know that. I'm doing our guest a favor."

Vilia perked up. Zergan didn't do favors. What was going on out there?

Standing, she walked over to her door and listened. A few buttons brought up the security system so she could use the external camera as well. It was indeed Commodore Zergan, standing next to a man in a floppy, dirty-looking hat and coveralls. He was holding a mop that really wasn't suited for cleaning rooms; it looked more suited to kitchen duty. Currently, this janitor—a brave man indeed—was using the handle of the mop to bar Zergan's entrance to what Vilia thought had been designated as Rogers' room.

"I have been assigned to do these favors," the muffled man said. He wasn't holding a pillow to his face after all, but he had a massive, unruly beard that looked like it was composed of cotton balls soaked in black dye. The picture on her security camera wasn't very good. He also had a very thick accent, one she couldn't place. Schvinkians' accents were fairly light; perhaps he was from one of the seedy little places on Urp.

"Well, I'm giving you the day off," Zergan said, making another move to get past the janitor.

"I must decline. You have duties," the janitor said. "I will be doing the favors of cleaning."

Vilia frowned. The man didn't even sound like he had a good grasp of Standard. What was stranger, however, was the fact that Zergan was arguing with him and, apparently, trying to get into Rogers' room to clean it. Zergan's and Rogers' rooms were next to each other. At the moment, Zergan's door was open, perhaps since he'd just come out.

"Don't make me repeat myself," Zergan said, his voice tight but restrained. Was he afraid of being overheard? "Get out of my way."

"I must clear this with the Grand Marshal," the janitor said. "She approves my cleaning schedules and I am fearful that if she discovers I have deviated she might . . ." The janitor paused, swallowing. "You know. Do *that*."

Vilia snorted. Undoubtedly he was referring to Keffoule's spinning back kick. What a barbarian.

Zergan appeared on the verge of delivering a spinning back kick himself.

"Fine!" Zergan said finally, throwing up his hands. "Fine. I was going to do it myself, because I'm such a servant-officer like I'm supposed to be. But you know what? I'm going to inspect this room later—thoroughly—and if I see so much as one *speck* of dust, I will personally see to it that you are demoted to Personnel."

The janitor said something so fast and so muffled that Vilia had no idea what it was. Whether he understood the man or not, Zergan didn't respond. He spun and stormed away toward where his Chariot was docked and vanished from the view of the camera. The janitor waited by Rogers' door for a while, then walked off.

The cleaning must not have been that urgent—and it was likely that Rogers was still inside sleeping off the previous night. What had happened between him and Keffoule? He'd probably succumbed to her wiles, the fool. Did Keffoule even *have* wiles? Vilia certainly did not. At least, she didn't think so. Wiles were unpredictable and inefficient. Undependable. Unmathematical.

But maybe it would be a little entertaining to have just a *tiny bit* of wiles.

Something else drew Vilia's attention away from wondering if wiles were worth having and whether or not she had them. Zergan had left his door open. He *never* left his door open, even for a moment. Yet there it was, a gate to the unknown and secret life of the commodore. And perhaps some answers involving secret sandwich bar conversations.

Staring at the screen, she wondered if she should. Would she even uncover anything interesting? If she was caught, could she argue that she had probable cause? As a civilian overseer of sorts, she had ways to request warrants and do some digging, but with the network down it would be impossible to do so.

Vilia knew Zergan was up to something, and she knew that this might be her only chance to find out what it was. Yet going in there without submitting the paperwork first was tantamount to using a computer with someone else's log-in information. The thought filled her with disgust, but . . .

Turning around and making sure everything in her room was in order—it wouldn't do to leave things out of order—she casually opened her door and looked outside. The hallway was empty, which wasn't surprising considering that at least two of its inhabitants were hungover and unconscious. An eerie silence crept up and settled over Vilia's ears, making her very aware of her elevating heartbeat, which was, since even before she'd entered Zergan's room, at quite an unprecedented level.

She really hoped Zergan didn't regularly review security vids; there would be no way for her to erase the surveillance camera's footage of her slowly padding across the hallway, getting in one last look to make sure nobody was coming, and slipping into the room. As soon as she crossed the threshold, she tapped the controls on the wall to close the door, leaving her alone inside Zergan's room, and turned on Zergan's security camera display so she could see anyone before they came into the room.

One look into the room and Vilia nearly fainted. Unlike her room, which was a pristine paradise of order, Zergan's was a miserable hell of chaos. Clothing was littered across the floor, draped across furniture, gathered up in piles. A display case full of military paraphernalia and awards was marred by food wrappers and a pair of underwear hanging off a plaque. The smell was educational. Together, it was something out of a nightmare.

Suppressing a gag, Vilia forced herself forward. It felt like she was physically pushing herself against an invisible membrane, all her instincts telling her to either get out or grab a vacuum or at least a moist towelette. For someone so eager to clean Rogers' room, it certainly didn't look like Zergan had any experience doing the job.

Focus, Vilia thought. *Efficiency*. Zergan's personal terminal had to be hidden somewhere in this mess. It would be the key to unlocking this mystery. He might have other sources of information hidden in the room, datapads and such, but there wasn't the time to look for them. Buried in the corner under a pile of dirty uniform shirts and several stuffed animals, including a teddy bear with a purple cape that looked particularly grumpy, she could see the hardware of a personal terminal sticking out from the top of a desk.

Vilia felt her whole body tense as she walked over to the desk, not because she was nervous about the highly illegal activity in which she was participating, but because she knew that when she did get to the desk she was going to have to touch Zergan's dirty clothes. She didn't even touch her own dirty clothes; she used a forked instrument to deposit them in the laundry bin. It would have been silly to touch dirty clothing after one had showered; it would only make one dirty again.

With no forked instrument available to her, she steadied her trembling hand and began to pick the shirts off the desk, one by one. She used the very tips of her nails, which were due to be trimmed soon anyway, and placed the shirts gingerly on the floor next to her. She knew she'd have to replace the shirts if she was to conceal the fact that she'd been in Zergan's room, but at the same time she wondered if that would really be necessary. She wasn't sure Zergan would have noticed a pair of zebra carcasses strewn across the floor.

The terminal was well used, greased with fingers that had probably had their hands in bags of chips or melted cheese. Vilia was convinced as soon as she sat down that Zergan had no other hidden terminals in the room. Much like squirrels with their nuts, he'd never be able to find them again. Vilia pulled up the chair and then absolutely did not sit in it.

What was she supposed to do with this opportunity? She wasn't much of a computer hacker, and these terminals were all keyed to the individual user. It wasn't the days of old when you could just steal someone's password after they idiotically left it written on a note on their desk. Hoping that Zergan had left his terminal unlocked turned out to be too much of a pipe dream; the terminal wasn't even turned on. Strange, for someone who had so many administrative duties as the Grand Marshal's second-in-command. Had Vilia been on this computer, the keys would have been red-hot from overuse. A tingle of excitement ran through her as she daydreamed a bit about the sheer amount of paperwork such a position would involve. How organized she could make it; how beautifully checked all the boxes would be.

Focusing on the task in front of her, Vilia began scheming how she could get access. Tapping her hands on the desk idly, she frowned as she thought. She could send a phony message down to IT requesting that the biometrics be disabled, allowing for a password reset, and then send another spreadsheet down to accounting and have Finance improperly reroute it so that the password would end up on the return spreadsheet, and then she could have it routed to the Grand Marshal's office but then have a form submitted telling the mail clerk to—

Her hand brushed a loose pair of pants that had been on top of Zergan's desk, which completely derailed her train of thought. It was, as all things were in this room, dirty, and she'd lost her composure thinking of ways to subvert the terminal security. In her surprise, she pulled her hand back, knocking the clothing off the desk and onto the floor.

Keep calm, she thought. *They're only pants. Back to the task at hand.*

Only, something had changed. Where the pants had been a moment earlier, Vilia saw an old-fashioned piece of lined notebook paper taped to the desk. On it were several lines of text under the heading PASSWORDS.

Vilia sighed. Some people just refused to take information security training seriously. Obviously she would have to file a TH-46 Security Incident Report, which would go in Zergan's permanent file and probably come up during his next background investigation right after they asked him about betraying the entire fleet to an unknown third party.

She couldn't deny the luck in Zergan's being so careless, and it would be wasteful not to put it to use. She tapped on the power control for the terminal and it instantly came to life; the password list allowed her unrestricted access to the commodore's system. Vilia started browsing immediately, telling the computer to simultaneously make a copy of as much useful data as it could find and route it to her own personal terminal, erasing traces of the data transfer as it did so. By Science, she was good at paperwork.

She didn't find anything useful at first. Typical deputy commander things, such as crew schedules, navigational charts, and contingency plans, dominated most of the time Zergan spent on the computer. There were angry messages to the Finance Squadron about some errors in the accounting records, angry messages to the kitchens for their unauthorized rearrangement of sandwich bar furniture, angry messages to Zergan's mother for tricking him into eating oatmeal raisin cookies when he thought they were chocolate chip.

Zergan had a lot of anger.

After ten minutes of browsing, it seemed as though there was nothing unusual about Commodore Zergan after all. He was just an angry, cantankerous deputy commander who was inordinately passionate about chocolate chip cookies and who had missed his chance at true glory by following Grand Marshal Keffoule to a remote assignment. Why *had* he done that, anyway?

Then an icon buried deep in the recesses of the angry messages caught her eye. It was a small picture of a chair, under which was written the word "empty." It reminded her of the strange utterances Zergan had been making to the sandwich bar when he'd communicated with someone or had been going completely crazy. Vilia hurriedly opened the icon, and she knew she'd hit pay dirt when it revealed another password input prompt, one that didn't look like a standard program. Nothing she'd heard of, anyway. Perhaps some military tactics simulator?

But then she saw that icon again—the empty chair. There was something obviously symbolic and significant about that image, but what?

Referring to the password list, and feeling dirtier every minute in more than a few ways, Vilia saw a list of obvious applications and systems, none of which were applicable to the screen in front of her. At the bottom, however, one of the passwords was simply labeled J.

Probably stands for jerk, she thought.

Shrugging, she punched it in.

The entire interface of the terminal changed from the standard Thelicosan layout to something Vilia wasn't familiar with. Before any text or images came onto the screen, she saw a picture of what appeared to be a giant planet. She wasn't really up to speed on her astronomy, but she didn't recognize the planet as anything in the Thelicosan system, or any of the systems in Fortuna Stultus. Perhaps it was just an artist's rendering of something in her imagination.

The interface finally loaded, though a warning came up saying something about having to use limited channels to route information, and Vilia was mostly just confused about what she was staring at. The whole thing had a retro look to it, like it was trying to revisit the days when information was only measured in picobytes, and keyboards didn't use cranial electricity sensors to anticipate inputs from the user's brain. There was even a picture of a kitten doing something cute, which was in vogue on and off every few centuries. Nearly everything on the system seemed anachronistic.

A separate messaging system, a separate file structure, separate everything. This was a closed network of some sort, not unlike the way the Thelicosan government hid their secret information, but it was clearly sending and receiving data from outside the ship. So, a closed network that rode on the backbone of the wider information net? It made Vilia further wonder how information was getting in and out with the jamming net. This whole system seemed to be running smoothly, with no connectivity issues at all.

She set the file structure to automatically start uploading itself to her personal system while she browsed the messages, hoping there would be something of value in there. The message bank was largely empty, and what *was* there was even less useful than the angry message database Zergan seemed to be hosting on the ship's network. Most of these were unintelligible updates from someone, or some group, called the Pantheon. None of those messages contained any specific signatories, but there was one thing that raised Vilia's hackles. At the bottom of every message was the same phrase that Zergan had uttered when he'd been at the sandwich bar—"Until the chairs are empty."

A horrible idea dawned on Vilia. Was Zergan part of some cult? Some . . . furniture-making cult? A cult of carpenters, maybe, or antiquarians.

No, that was stupid. First of all, this really couldn't be about chairs. Second, she'd never heard of any cult that was technologically savvy enough to establish their own closed network, one that could blast through a sophisticated jamming net. There was more to this than a cult.

If not a cult, then perhaps a union. She'd heard of labor

unions doing some incredibly insane things in the past; the Union of Morticians on Schvink once went on strike and, with the help of a mad scientist, started reanimating the dead until their demands were met. Schvink was a strange place.

Then again, Vilia had no evidence that Zergan could do anything except be mean and kill people. She knew that warriors like him often had a soft side that manifested itself in crafts like knitting, art, or taxidermy, but Zergan didn't seem the type. There was no evidence in the room that he'd ever seen a tree, never mind worked on complicated carpentry projects enough that it would warrant his joining the union.

So that left the other option. Which was . . . what? She dug into the messages, looking for clues. Anything that the "Pantheon" sent seemed mostly to be giving people instructions on how to send messages. Who was the Pantheon?

Finally, Vilia stumbled upon a pair of messages that seemed interesting, since they were from an actual person. At least, it looked like they were—the "from" block said SNG99, which was either a code name or a form or instruction number she didn't recognize.

And there weren't any forms or instructions she didn't recognize.

The first message specifically asked Zergan for a report on the "proceedings." The second message had only one line:

"Peace is not an option."

Vilia froze. SNG99 could be referencing only one thing: the Meridan/Thelicosan situation. Whoever was communicating with Zergan—and appeared to be pulling his strings—was trying to deliberately create conflict between the two systems. Was this why Zergan was always pushing the Grand Marshal to attack?

Who would want war? Absolutely nobody would benefit from conflict. Not the Thelicosan Council, and certainly not the Meridans. That meant it was a third party, perhaps one of the other two systems. But what would New Neptune or Grandelle have to gain from war? Everything had been perfectly balanced for the entirety of the Two Hundred Years (And Counting) Peace; trade was booming, unemployment was down, and most reality television had been canceled once nobody had to compare their lives with someone who was worse off than them for comfort. They were in the middle of the most prosperous period in the history of the Fortuna Stultus galaxy.

So who *wasn't* benefiting from that? She wracked her political brain. She'd studied governments from every system over and over again as she climbed to the top of the Thelicosan political structure in her attempts to erase her backwater Schvinkian heritage and someday petition for Council membership.

Think, Vilia. You should know this.

If it wasn't a government, and it wasn't a union . . . a terrorist organization? Anarchists? There were literally thousands of candidates in that department, but most weren't organized enough to put something together like this.

The file transfer was about forty percent complete, which led Vilia to believe that either the network was slowing her down or there was a huge amount of data to sift through.

But it would have to do, because someone was about to open the door. She barely caught a glimpse of Zergan on the far wall's security camera before she heard his footsteps outside.

Oh Newton's apple, not now!

She'd taken too long, way too long. Snatching her data net from the terminal, she kicked the power cable out from the computer rather than waste time backing out of the closed network and making it look like she hadn't been there. Zergan might get suspicious about that, but beggars couldn't be choosers at this point. Vilia leapt to the side, losing all sense of propriety as she took fistfuls of Zergan's clothing and threw them back on top of the computer to try to cover up any evidence of her trespass.

The lock beeped. The door slid open. Vilia swallowed every particle of decency she had left and dove face-first into a pile of Zergan's laundry. Instantly, her body was enveloped in a mound of dirty clothing so large that she was pretty sure that a pressure change had just occurred. Had he seen her? She slowly began to maneuver, careful not to shift the pile of clothing, until she was sitting down and facing the terminal.

Through a small tunnel of light entering the pile of grossness, Vilia could see Zergan entering the room. He looked flustered and tired, like he'd been up all night. He'd looked like that a lot lately, but so had everyone else on the ship. The tension of the past few days had been enough to spread insomnia to just about anyone.

As soon as he entered the room, he tore off his jacket, which he actually hung on a peg near the door, and then removed his shirt, for some reason. This he threw right on top of Vilia, nearly obscuring her only line of sight to a world that was not purgatory. She drew in a slow, deep, silent breath and tried not to choke.

Her heart was cresting at one hundred beats per minute. Worse than that, there was a very small, nagging sensation in the back of her head that said she might be enjoying it. She pinched the thought between a pair of mental fingers like a filthy piece of lint and brushed it away. Life was not about excitement.

After grabbing a glass of something brown and alcoholic-looking, Zergan came over to the desk, which he rapidly cleared of dirty shirts with a well-practiced sweep of the arm. It was then that Vilia finally realized that not only had she broken into his room, she was staring at him half-naked. Part of it made her skin crawl—Zergan was not her favorite person—but she wasn't blind. The man was a career soldier and special operations warrior; there wasn't anything bad to look at if you could ignore the caterpillar plastered to his forehead and the fact that he was certifiably psychotic.

Zergan took a sip of his drink and sat down, frowning at the now-powerless terminal. Reaching down, he found the connection and reattached it, settling back in his chair while the terminal restarted. Vilia tried to keep her breathing under control;

Zergan was literally five feet away from her, and if she so much as sighed he'd know someone was in the room.

She could just barely make out the screen from her angle in the corner, but it was easy enough to see Zergan completely bypass the normal interface and head straight into whatever network was allowing him to communicate with the "Pantheon." And shortly thereafter, she heard something that resembled old machinery turning; the speakers of the terminal emitted a grinding, scratching noise that was at once very foreign and vaguely familiar.

"What is it?" a voice came from the terminal.

Thank Science! Zergan had opened a communications channel. If she'd had to sit there and watch him just write angry messages to different parts of the ship, she might have lost her mind.

"Making my report," Zergan said.

"Why aren't you at the usual spot?" came the voice. It was a woman, an older woman, with a deep, scratchy voice. Whatever network they were using was still having connection problems—perhaps due to the jamming—because her speech came through garbled and full of static.

"I told you it was compromised," Zergan said. "Until I find a new location for the hardware, I'm going to have to use my personal terminal."

"Risky."

"Necessary," Zergan said. "Now, if you don't mind, it's already been a long day and it's not even half done. Let's get this over with."

"Fine," said the woman.

Vilia listened carefully as Zergan went through the happenings of the last few days, detailing everything from the kidnapping to the cavorting that had been going on in Keffoule's room the previous night. Vilia had assumed as much. Captain Rogers seemed like a decent sort of man, if a little dense, but he was still a man, after all. Zergan's voice remained calm during the report, and when he was finished Vilia noticed that the calm was forced; his right hand was drumming on the desk, and his left hand was swirling the glass of alcohol back and forth. Whoever this woman was, she made Zergan nervous. And that made Vilia nervous.

"You and I have known each other a long time, Edris," the voice said finally. "You're not such a fool as this is making you seem. Why haven't you killed him yet?"

Kill Rogers? Vilia thought, horrified, but not surprised. *That would definitely be a speedy path to war.*

"Something keeps getting in my way," Zergan said, stumbling a bit as he spoke. "It's just dumb luck, really. I thought I checked the doctors' schedules to make sure I would be alone, but . . ." He shook his head. "It doesn't matter. I've figured out a way. He'll be dead by morning."

"You had better be right," the woman said. "Things are moving according to schedule in the other systems, Edris. With the setback in Merida caused by this same idiot, we can't afford any other setbacks. The cogs are in motion for Jupiter's rebirth."

Vilia nearly gasped. Jupiter? *Zergan* was a *Jupiterian?* The implications of that statement pounded on the inside of her head like a hammer. Jupiter. The lost planet, the loser of the War of Musical Chairs. *That* was what they meant when they said "until the chairs are empty." They were getting their revenge!

But how? The people of Old Jupiter had supposedly scattered after the war, assimilating themselves into the cultures of the other systems. Mars, Earth, Neptune, and Saturn all had gotten whole systems to expand into when they'd stumbled upon the Fortuna Stultus galaxy. Jupiter had been left in the dust.

If Jupiter had somehow reestablished a base of operations, and had made itself strong enough to contend with the combined power of all four of the other systems . . . it was bad. Really bad. How had that happened? What was the extent of the Jupiterians' network? This revelation brought one big answer and a million smaller questions.

Well, maybe not a *million* questions. Vilia didn't like to exaggerate. But a lot of questions.

"I will make it happen," Zergan said tightly. "Have I ever failed you before?"

The voice on the other end was silent for a moment. "This is more important than anything, Edris. My family and I have been building this plan for centuries."

"I understand," Zergan said. "Now, if you don't mind, I have to start planning for tonight."

After a few more cryptic phrases back and forth, after which they both ended with the line about chairs being empty again, Zergan disconnected. For a moment, he actually looked like he was about to stand up and start throwing things around in a rage. His eyebrow quivered; his whole body appeared to be tensing before an explosion.

But then, for some reason, he laughed. A slow, low chuckle that gave Vilia the creeps. Zergan was a dangerous, dangerous man. With a nice back.

She needed to get out of here so she could at least warn Captain Rogers that someone was plotting to kill him. She knew she couldn't go to Keffoule directly; Keffoule and Zergan had been friends for a long time. Without any hard evidence—Vilia didn't yet know what had been transferred—she had nothing to prove. Thankfully, it looked like Zergan was about to leave the room again; he stood and put on a clean shirt. A good thing, too—she was about to reach her limit on nearly every one of her personal standards regarding cleanliness, spying, and unexpected voyeurism.

For some reason, though, as soon as he'd put his shirt on, Zergan took it off again, threw it on the rapidly expanding pile near Vilia, and sat back down at the computer. He poured himself another glass and turned on a movie.

Vilia tried not to cry. Or breathe through her nose.

Does Stockholm Have Toast?

The feeling of having a wet, dirty blanket placed over one's face, compounded with a phantom headache and tiny tendrils of nausea working its way through one's stomach, wasn't exactly unfamiliar to Rogers. With all the advancements of the last thousand years or so, they still hadn't come up with a cure for a good old-fashioned hangover.

But, for perhaps the first time in Rogers' life, he was absolutely, positively thrilled to be hungover.

It meant a couple of things had happened. First, it meant he'd finally gotten a decent drink. Well, ten decent drinks. Second, it meant he'd been at least temporarily absolved of enough absurd, unwanted responsibility that ten drinks couldn't really have been considered reckless. Third, it meant he'd finally gotten a decent drink. What more could he have asked for?

Well, he supposed not having someone standing next to him banging on a gong would have been nice.

"What? What? What? What?" he cried as he sat bolt upright

in bed, flailing his arms against whoever was attacking him with a giant sheet of metal. His now finely tuned ducking instincts kicked in, but since he was lying down, he just sort of shriveled back into his sheets.

It was only after he had both hands over his ears and his face buried in the mattress that the gonging stopped. A muffled voice barely broke through his hastily constructed sound barrier, too soft for him to make out what the person was saying.

Slowly, for fear that the gonging might start again, Rogers slowly unburied himself from his blanket fort to find that all of the lights in the room had been turned to full blast, piercing his eyes, his head, and his brain.

"Mother of god," he groaned.

"She is absent at the moment," came the droll, flat voice of Xan the Droopy-Faced Assistant. "You will have to settle for breakfast."

Rogers rubbed his eyes and blinked until his vision was clear. Xan was standing next to his bed holding—unsurprisingly—a small gong and mallet. Nearby was a cart not unlike something Rogers would have seen at a fancy hotel, with a covered tray on top of it. Xan, ever the neat and stoic assistant, was wrinkling his nose.

"Breakfast?" Rogers said. "What time is it?"

"It is currently just past two in the afternoon, ship time," Xan said.

"Ah. Well, thanks for bringing me breakfast. Was this the Grand Marshal's order?"

Xan gave him the sort of look that sarcastically asked Rogers if Xan would have brought him breakfast in bed of his own accord.

"Ah," Rogers said again. "Well, it's appreciated."

Rogers looked at the cart. The covered tray on top looked just like the one that had come by the previous night, the one that had concealed the Jasker 120. The whole time, Rogers had thought Keffoule had intended to actually, physically duel him! He almost laughed out loud. He'd expected to lift that cover and find a pistol, not alcohol. That certainly would have been dramatic!

Rogers reached forward and lifted the cover to reveal a pistol. He stared at it for a moment, then looked at Xan.

"You people are so goddamned weird."

"The Grand Marshal, against my very adamant counsel, has decided that it would be prudent for you to have protection while aboard the *Limiter*."

"Right," Rogers said. "People trying to murder me and all that." He remembered Keffoule specifically saying she would take care of it, so it was a little disconcerting that she was issuing him a weapon. For one, that meant she thought he could shoot, which he couldn't. And for another thing, it meant she wasn't totally confident that she could protect him.

Rogers gingerly picked up the disruptor pistol in its holster, placing it next to him on the bed, then looked at Xan expectantly.

"You said something about breakfast? Despite your nickname of Bellicose Thelicosa, I don't imagine you people eat weapons for nourishment."

"You suppose correctly," Xan said dryly. He pressed a button on the cart and the bottom tray rotated out, replacing the tray that had contained the pistol with one that clearly smelled of various bits of deliciousness. Rogers' hunger had punched through the minor nausea from the alcohol, and he was eager to uncover the food and dig in.

"I'll leave you to it, then," Xan said slowly. "But before I do, I must advise you, *sir*, that playing with the Grand Marshal's emotions will land you, and your fleet, in much more trouble than you already are in."

Rogers gave him a sour face. "I'm not sure how you consider refusing to marry her flat out with nearly every sentence I've uttered over the last two days 'playing' with her emotions, but I'll keep that in mind. Can I eat now?"

Xan turned up his nose and left, finally giving Rogers some

peace. His headache had already started to go away, though his body's equilibrium still seemed to be off. He stood up and stretched a bit before digging in.

As he began to tear through slabs of thick-cut bacon, runny eggs, and some of the most delicious toast he'd ever eaten, Rogers remembered that he was supposed to be eating only with Keffoule. Considering the state she must have been in after he had quite literally drunk her under the table, perhaps she wasn't up to another meal. Thank god for that. Dinner had been an awkward, miserable affair that he wasn't eager to repeat.

But then again, had it really been so bad? Other than the talk about him being murdered or married against his will, it actually had been the most pleasant conversation he'd had in a long time. That and the fact that he'd ended the night with practically a whole bottle of Jasker 120 didn't really make for a horror movie or anything. And now here he was devouring an amazing breakfast—really, something as boring as toast should *not* be this good—delivered straight to his bed by the same woman. Sure, she was a little scary, but, introductory face-kicking aside, she'd been treating him rather well.

He paused with a piece of bacon hanging out of his mouth. In fact, minus a couple of card games and some well-thought-out pranks, hadn't this been exactly what he'd been searching for ever since he was forced back into the military? An easy job, a drink, and some fun, just like the old days? Maybe the location had changed a bit, and yes, yes, murder/marriage, but . . .

Rogers shook his head as he continued with his breakfast, taking a long sip of some incredible coffee. There was more to this situation than bacon and Scotch.

Right?

Well, of course, there was the Viking. Now *that* was a woman. Some might prefer the power and prestige of someone like Keffoule, but Rogers knew what he liked, and it was the Viking. She might not be graceful or petite, but she was right for him.

Except she'd been miserable ever since the incident with the droids had concluded. They'd argued openly at every turn, she'd hit him in the face at least once, and she'd told him his tactics were small and insignificant. Or something like that. The point was, the Viking hadn't exactly been perfect lately either. Neither had his command. Neither had his crew. Neither had his life.

Rogers shook his head as he slurped down the runny remnants of an egg and mopped up the yolk with the last of the toast—seriously, this toast should have been illegal, it was so good. A sip of the now mostly cooled coffee let him know that he needed to take care of some personal business. Maybe that would clear his head.

It didn't. In fact, when he finished, he felt like he'd made a crap withdrawal rather than a crap deposit. What *was* he really going back to if he convinced Keffoule to turn him back over to the *Flagship*? A lot of responsibility he hadn't asked for, a woman who kept punching him in the face despite his best romantic intentions, and a hotshot pilot who seemed to be trying to kill him at every turn. He supposed he missed Deet a little, but in general . . . life on the *Flagship* kind of sucked.

No, he was thinking like a selfish, whiny child. There were higher ideals at stake here, weren't there?

Wheeling the tray of spent breakfast items over to one side of the room, Rogers stood in the middle and went through his ducking exercises. Normally he wasn't one for self-motivated physical activity, but for some reason he thought it would help him think straight. Mailn wasn't exactly a personal trainer, and Rogers wasn't exactly a fitness nut, but he could have sworn that the sessions with Mailn were doing good things for his balance and coordination.

Bobbing and weaving throughout the room, he imagined the Viking throwing punches and kicks at him, picking up furniture and using it as bludgeoning implements, but she couldn't hit him. He floated effortlessly between her strikes, infuriating her with every graceful movement. It didn't matter that he crashed into the breakfast tray twice.

Despite his best efforts to distract himself, he became exhausted after a few minutes, his hangover giving his body a very forceful signal to stop jumping around. His mind went back to his current situation.

Higher ideals. What higher ideals? The threat of war had been extinguished; he'd seen to that with the droids, and now he'd clarified things with Keffoule. All he needed to do now was get back on the *Flagship* and prevent them from doing anything stupid like attempting to counterattack.

On second thought, maybe he didn't even need to get back on the *Flagship*. Really, his duty was on the *Limiter* right now. Once Keffoule lifted the jamming net, he could tell everyone that they'd done a great job and defended Meridan honor or some crap like that, then let them know that he was staying on the *Limiter* as a diplomat, or something. Admiral Klein would have known exactly what to say *and* he would have figured out a way to not actually have to do any work. Maybe it was time Rogers give Admiral Klein some credit.

A buzzer went off, and for a moment Rogers thought it was the datapad Keffoule had given him. When he examined it, however, it was blank. When the buzzer sounded again, he found the source; the control panel by the door was blinking, and a small screen near the panel had been turned on to reveal a woman standing outside the door.

"Captain Rogers?" a voice said. Wow, that door was thin. It was like she was standing right next to him.

"I'll be right there." Who could be coming to see him? Hopefully not another one of those doctors trying to inject him with something. She wasn't wearing a lab coat or complaining about Rorschach blots, so he figured it was safe. He took a moment to clean up; his dodging around the room and bumping into the breakfast tray had caused some utensils to scatter, and his sheets were a mess.

When he opened the door, he remembered the woman. Secretary Quinn, the administrative assistant or ambassador or something like that. Civ-mil relations expert and also, apparently, pantsuit expert. Rogers was pretty sure those had gone out of style on Old Earth.

"Secretary Quinn," Rogers said. "What can I do for you?"

Her nostrils flared, and she glanced behind him to view the room, as though expecting someone to jump out from behind Rogers.

"Am I interrupting anything?" she said tightly.

Rogers frowned. "No, why?"

Quinn still didn't appear to be willing to look him in the eye for some reason. "I'm not a detective, Captain Rogers, but you're sweating rather profusely. There is also your lack of pants."

Rogers' face rose to solar temperatures as he hurriedly jumped out of the line of sight of the door, hiding himself behind the wall near the control panel.

"I'm—I'm sorry!" he stammered. "I only just woke up, and, uh, I was practicing ducking."

"What?"

"Never mind," Rogers said. "You wouldn't understand. Just wait a second, okay?"

He slammed the controls of the door and took a deep breath. This was not a very good way to start any kind of meeting. It only took him a few seconds to resume a state of decency, though his uniform was disheveled and didn't smell the greatest. He wondered if Keffoule had made arrangements for clothing for him in the event that he chose to stay on the *Limiter*.

Rogers opened the door again and tried his best to look dignified.

"I apologize for that," he said, rather formally. How did one speak to an ambassador? Did he really care? "It was a long night."

Quinn made that kind of humming noise that told him she

knew exactly what kind of night it had been, which meant she did not at all know what kind of night it had been. Rather than try to correct her perception, Rogers motioned for her to come inside.

"What can I do for you?" he asked. "I haven't seen you since those crazy—hey!"

Quinn had taken two swift steps inside the door and then hurriedly used the controls to close it behind her. She walked toward Rogers so swiftly that he almost ducked, but there was nothing else about her body language to say that she was about to try to hit him. The pistol, still sitting on the bottom part of the tray, was too far out of reach for him to defend himself. And even if he'd had it in his hand, he would sooner have shot the ceiling.

"What's the big idea?" he asked.

"I need to speak to you," Quinn said.

"Well, either that or you want to kill me," Rogers said. Her wide-set eyes were intense, if a bit cold. Rogers had said that as a joke, but he paused for a moment, tensing up. "You . . . don't want to kill me, do you?"

Quinn's mouth formed a thin line. "No, I don't want to kill you, Captain. I said I needed to speak to you. You should pay better attention."

"Right," Rogers said, relaxing. "You did just say that. You'll have to forgive me. I'm a little on edge on account of, you know, being kidnapped and all. And someone apparently *has* been trying to kill me, so there's that."

Quinn's eyes widened a bit, but in such a way that Rogers could tell she was clearly not surprised at the fact that someone was trying to murder him. She was surprised he knew about it. Was Quinn the one trying to kill him? She had just said she wasn't here to harm him, but who knew what these Thelicosans would say?

"How . . ." Quinn began, but then shook her head. "We need to talk."

"You said that already. You should pay better attention." Rogers motioned to the only other chair in the room, an austere piece of furniture that once had served as a seat for working at, presumably, a network terminal. The terminal had been removed, likely for Rogers' occupancy.

"Thank you," Quinn said. Rogers walked over to the chair and moved it so it was near the bed, where he sat down himself. Quinn stood by the chair and did not sit in it.

"Do you have something against sitting?" Rogers asked.

"I don't know what you're talking about."

"Never mind. What did you want to talk about?"

"We don't have a lot of time, so I'm going to be blunt. I want to get you off this ship."

Rogers stared at her for a moment. "I'm sorry," he said. "I feel like I've just misheard you. I thought you said you wanted to help me escape."

"That's actually precisely what I said."

Tapping his fingers on the side of the bed, he kept quiet, for once in his life thinking hard about what he was going to say before he said it. For some reason he found himself eying the pistol on the tray, which Quinn noticed.

"Did someone smuggle you a gun?" she asked, seemingly not at all perturbed that a live weapon was so near to someone who, for all she knew, was about to pick it up and use it on her.

"It was a gift from the Grand Marshal," Rogers said.

Quinn's only reaction was a double blink, which didn't tell Rogers much about what she thought of the gift. When it became apparent that she wasn't going to ask him any further questions, he went back to the topic at hand.

"So when you say you want to get me off this ship, I'm assuming you want to help me return to the *Flagship*, right?"

Quinn frowned. "Of course that's what I mean. Why would I mean anything else?"

"Well," Rogers said, matching her glare with his own, "given how Thelicosan women have treated me so far, I wanted to make sure you weren't trying to marry me."

A small sound bubbled up in Quinn's chest that might have either been a laugh or early-onset tuberculosis. Tuberculosis had been eradicated centuries earlier, of course, but both options seemed equally likely in this buttoned-up bureaucrat.

"It will have to be kept secret, of course," Quinn said, edging closer to the chair but still not sitting in it. "And we'll have to move slowly. I have some ideas, but I thought I would talk with you first to see—"

"I don't know if I want to go," Rogers said quietly.

Quinn stared at him. "What?"

Rogers didn't repeat himself for a moment. He sat on the bed, clutching the edge of the sheets and looking at the floor. The words had sort of jumped out of his mouth without warning, and he was now unsure whether to burst into a bout of fake laughter and try to convince Quinn it was a joke or to explore his feelings. Exploring his feelings was really scary.

The level of indecision resulted in Rogers' bursting into real, but fake-*sounding* laughter that rose in pitch as he tried to stop it.

Quinn took a small step backward.

"No, no," Rogers said, clearing his throat and wiping a tear from his eye. He'd never felt more conflicted in his life, not even when trying to decide between hanging out with the hot school-teacher or cutting class altogether. He took a deep breath, trying to stop his stomach from doing flips. An escape route was standing right in front of him—probably the second most powerful woman on the ship was offering him freedom, freedom from a crazy Thelicosan lady who had promised never to kick him in the face again and gave him fantastic Scotch. Why did everything have to be so complicated?

"I don't know," Rogers said. "I have to think about it."

"What is there to think about?" Quinn said, an edge of anger in her voice. "You've been complaining since you got here that you wanted to get off, and now I'm telling you I have a plan to get you there."

"Yeah, but—"

"You're not even a little curious as to why someone like me might be offering you a way out? You don't even want to ask me any questions? I could be standing here right now with the most critical information the galaxy has heard in centuries, and you're going to tell me you have to think about it because your mind is so addled from drink and . . . cavorting! . . . that you can't see that the obvious answer is to do exactly what I tell you?"

Quinn's voice had risen to a little bit of a fever pitch, the color blossoming in her cheeks as she spoke, and when she finally finished it was obvious that she was doing everything she could to restrain herself. For some reason, it also looked like she was taking her pulse by the vein in her wrist.

"Who says 'cavorting'?"

The Secretary's eyes looked like they were going to pop out of her head.

"It's not that I don't appreciate the offer," Rogers said. "It's just that . . . I don't know. You wouldn't understand. Have you ever done a job you didn't want to do?"

"Every day of my life," Quinn said, then stopped, her mouth open. Rogers got the impression that the woman hadn't expected to give that answer. She recovered just as quickly, however, and the serene, severely anal-retentive mask was back.

"Captain Rogers," she said quietly. "There really is something I need to tell you. This isn't about you, or me, or any job that you do or don't want to do. The War of the Musical Chairs was—"

The buzzer rang.

Rogers took his eyes from Crazy Rambling Lady #2 and turned to the video screen near the door. Someone he didn't recognize was standing outside his room, dressed in a military uniform. It wasn't Keffoule, though, so he was able to relax a little bit; it definitely wasn't someone coming to try to marry him. That left someone coming to murder him, and that was alright.

"Ignore it," Quinn said. "This is important."

Rogers was already halfway to the door. "It'll only take a second, and then you can start to talk to me about ancient history."

Quinn, in the middle of starting another sentence, stopped short when Rogers opened the door to reveal a familiar face—the single-eyebrow soldier who had identified himself as Keffoule's deputy.

"Hey," Rogers said. "I remember you. You're the guy who almost turned our negotiation into a bloodbath. Nice to see you again."

The man—Zigma? Ziglia? Ziaga?—stared at Rogers with the sort of forced, dispassionate stare that Rogers had come to know and love as the look of someone trying very hard not to strangle him.

"Good afternoon, Captain Rogers," the man said, and Rogers had to give him points for not saying anything offensive instead. Rogers glanced down at his name tag: Zergan. That was it. Commodore Zergan, Keffoule's deputy.

"To what do I owe the pleasure?" Rogers said. "I'm in the middle of being continually visited by strange women while I am in differing states of undress."

Quinn made a noise behind him that was definitely not the half-chuckle he had heard earlier. This sounded a lot more like the precursor to an aneurysm or violence. But really, what did he have to fear from a little career bureaucrat like the Secretary?

"I'm surprised you were able to stand her company for as long as it took her to get that far into your room," Zergan said, gesturing at Quinn. Rogers couldn't help but snicker. So what if the man had nearly killed everyone in his response team? At least he had a sense of humor. At one time or another, Rogers had been physically threatened by most of his friends. Maybe Zergan would make that list.

"We were discussing something of the utmost importance," Quinn said.

"Oh?" Zergan said, stepping into the room. Rogers let him in.

"Then I must already know about it. I don't believe there is anything of the 'utmost importance' that isn't already on my desk."

Quinn stiffened—Rogers thought if she stiffened anymore, she might turn into a plank of wood—but didn't respond. Zergan swaggered toward her, his eyebrow darkening.

"Surely you can talk about it with me here. Perhaps I can contribute to the discussion."

She didn't step back—not exactly—but there was a subtle shifting of her weight that might have indicated a bit of retreat. They locked eyes, and Rogers got the distinct feeling that he was about to be involved in something very messy.

"Alright, alright," he said, stepping toward them and avoiding some of the spilled contents of the breakfast tray. Wow, he'd really made a mess. "Look, I don't want any blood on the floor or anything. Secretary Quinn, why don't you take a break, and you and I can unearth the mysteries of history later."

Quinn looked between Rogers and Zergan, clutching her wrist very tightly. The air practically crackled with tension. Rogers also happened to just have stepped on some foil wrapping that had fallen off the tray, so maybe that had been the crackle.

Finally, Quinn broke. She looked away from Zergan and walked toward the door, passing close enough to the commodore to barely brush his shoulder. Perhaps she was tougher than Rogers had originally thought; had he been confronted with someone like that, Rogers' first instinct would have been to run the hell away.

"If you change your mind," Quinn said, casting a dark glance Rogers' way, "find me."

"Fine, fine," Rogers said, and Quinn left the room.

Zergan, who had been watching the woman leave the room, shook his head as he turned around. His grizzled, hard face broke into a cold, wolfish grin.

"Politicians," he said as if that explained everything. "What was she bothering you with?"

For some reason, Rogers got a hunch that he should lie, which, he reflected briefly, was not an infrequent sort of hunch.

"Would you believe she wanted to marry me instead of the Grand Marshal?" he said, then recognized that perhaps he'd made a poor joke, if for no other reason than that, in a brief flash of expression, Zergan looked like he wanted to slice him in half and use him to butter some very gruesome—but absolutely delicious—toast.

Before Rogers could try to weasel his way out of the impending beating and travel in search of said toast, Zergan's expression changed. Was everyone on this ship bipolar, or what?

"I'm sure you're the talk of every lady on this ship," Zergan said, his voice low. "But that's not what I came here to talk to you about. I feel like you and I got off on the wrong foot."

Rogers sat in the chair that Quinn had been supposed to sit in. It didn't set him on fire or anything—why didn't that damn woman sit down?

"Shooting at a man tends to do that," Rogers said. "Then again, your boss kicked me in the face, and I'm sort of starting to like her, so maybe you're not so bad."

That look of violence flashed across Zergan's face again, making Rogers think. He wasn't so dense that he couldn't figure out when a man had the hots for a woman.

Zergan had the hots for Quinn.

Wait. No. That wasn't right.

Zergan had the hots for Keffoule. And that meant that Rogers couldn't trust him.

"I wanted to make it up to you by inviting you to the ship's bar."

Well, maybe Rogers could trust him a little bit.

The bridge of the *Flagship* was pretty quiet. And everyone seemed to be staring at Deet. It might have had something to do with the fact that he'd just revealed to everyone that all the droids had been purposefully programmed by someone to sow chaos and, eventually, kill everyone and take over the ship.

That had been the short version of the story, anyway. The long version included a lot of other details about operating systems, computer code, and the fact that there were still a lot of bits of information that Deet hadn't been able to decode.

Regardless, Deet didn't know what they were so worried about. All the droids had been decommissioned anyway. It wasn't like they were going to wake up, become robot-zombies, and try again.

Why were they staring at *him*, anyway?

"Well," he said. "Any questions?"

"Yeah," Sergeant Mailn said. "Who is Zeus Holdings?"

Deet beeped. If he'd known that, he probably would have included it in the briefing.

"We don't know," he said. "And without access to the wider information network, we can't do much research."

"Why do they want to kill us?" someone else asked.

"Oh, did I not include that vital piece of information?" Deet said, scoring a point for himself for successfully using sarcasm in a public setting. "I don't know. It wasn't written in essay form in the millions and millions of lines of code I expertly analyzed to bring you this information. Sorry to disappoint you."

"Do you think, like, the microwaves in the mess halls are going to come alive next?"

The whole room turned to look at Flash.

"What?" he said. "I cook my food in there every day. I don't want them coming up on my six with poison lasers or something."

And the whole room proceeded to ignore him. It was a common occurrence.

"What I don't understand," said the Viking, who had been pacing back and forth nervously in one corner of the bridge, "is why we're spending any time at all worrying about a bunch of piles of scrap metal when we have an enemy fleet pretty much on top of us."

Deet would have sighed if sighing made any sense from a mechanical point of view. He was all for using human patterns of speech, but he was still a bit far from using human body language. He waved his arms frantically in the air to indicate frustration.

"Because there's nothing we can do about that at the moment," he said.

"Like hell there's nothing we can do about it," the Viking said, taking a step toward the center of the bridge. The entire crew took a step back. The Viking had been perpetually on edge ever since the negotiations had broken down, and everyone around her had been feeling it. Literally, physically feeling it. Deet had learned shortly after his conversation with Master Sergeant Hart that the troop running through the engineering bay on fire had been set ablaze by the Viking.

"If we're going to surrender—and we are *not* going to surrender—then let's get it over with already. If not, let's fight!"

The Viking picked up an unfortunate systems analyst and threw her at another unfortunate systems analyst. "I can't stand this sitting around and doing nothing!"

"We can't surrender." Commander Belgrave spoke up. "We can't communicate, and you broke Guff's wrist when you used him as a bowling ball."

The Viking didn't say anything for a moment. She stood there, folding her arms, perhaps to force them to stop moving. Deet's sensors detected a trembling throughout her body, which was an odd thing to see. The Viking was perpetually angry, but she was never trembling. Deet's analytical circuits told him that perhaps this wasn't her typical anger. The Viking looked at the floor.

"She has him," she whispered, so low that Deet was likely the only person who heard her correctly.

Sergeant Mailn, who had been standing at the Viking's side, leaned almost imperceptibly to one side until she and the marine captain touched shoulders. Had they been drinking? Were the ship's inertial dampeners malfunctioning? There was no reason, other than a vestibular error, that Sergeant Mailn should have done such a thing. Deet made a note to recommend a physical exam.

"What is the giant mumbling?" Flash said.

The Viking's eyes shot up. "She has . . ." Pausing for a moment to swallow, the Viking unfolded her arms and took a deep breath. The trembling stopped as her voice's volume rose. "That *crazy bitch* is over there with the commander of our fleet, and you morons are all talking about how sorry our lives are over here. What if he's . . . what if there's a war coming and we're too busy pussyfooting around to be ready?"

"Captain," Sergeant Mailn said softly. "It's alright to—"

"No it's not goddamn alright! Nothing is goddamn alright! I don't know what military you morons joined, but I joined the one that *shoots people.*"

With that, the Viking suddenly made for the door, knocking over several pieces of equipment as she did so. Surprisingly, she grabbed the back of Flash's pajama-like flight suit and began to drag him out with her.

"Hey!" he cried, his sunglasses bobbing up and down on his nose as he struggled. "What has gotten into your cranium, wingman? You didn't even give me a chance to pop chaff!"

"*Speak Standard or shut up!*" the Viking said. She didn't look back as she stormed off the bridge, dragging the unfortunate pilot behind her. The crew took a moment to stare awkwardly at the door, likely torn between feeling sorry for the pilot and cheering for the Viking.

"That concludes my briefing," Deet said, breaking the silence. "Per our previous orders, everyone is to continue looking busy, not panicking, and not breathing a word about our dire, dire situation to anyone outside this bridge, despite the fact that we now know that *every single droid* on this ship was specifically pro-grammed to kill us."

Why were they staring at him like that? Maybe he wasn't explaining it fully enough.

"Yes," he continued, "not one droid on this ship is immune to the code compelling them to attempt a takeover, first through subversive means and then by violence if necessary. Anything at all to get them in command of the ship. Things like briefing the bridge and telling them exactly what to do and what not to do."

A few of the troops exchanged glances, but for some reason nobody moved. Deet was a higher form of intelligence, so there was always a chance he was grossly overestimating them. He didn't really have time to make up the phenomenal intellectual gap, though. He had a ship to run.

"Whatever," he said. "You're all dismissed."

Slowly, awkwardly, the troops began to tear their eyes from him and return to their duties, but Deet thought that perhaps there was a tension in the air that had not been there before. For a moment he thought the electrical cable had gotten loose again—in fact, he kind of wished it had—but then he realized it was because everyone was looking at him over their shoulders. And everyone was whispering. And there were a lot of hands on disruptor pistols.

Walking over to where Commander Belgrave was sitting and making a career out of not flying a ship, Deet lowered his vocal output.

"What's wrong with them?" Deet asked. "I'm not sure I understand the concept of morale yet, but I am almost certain that this is not the desired psychological condition of a functioning military unit."

Belgrave leaned back in his chair and thought for a moment, perhaps taking a moment to really let everything sink in. Belgrave was so philosophical.

"Well," Belgrave said slowly. "You know how you just told them that every droid on the ship was programmed to kill them?"

"Yes," Deet said. "I believe I said it several times."

Belgrave pointed at him. "You're a droid."

Deet processed this for a moment, then beeped.

"Oh, [EXCREMENT]. I'm going to crack and [EXPLETIVE] kill everyone, aren't I?"

The bridge stopped again.

"That probably didn't help," Belgrave said.

Eureka!

It took Rogers a little while to get to the Overflowing Bathtub, the *Limiter*'s one and only, strangely named bar. Rogers could hardly believe that the ship had a bar at all. The *Flagship* didn't even have one, and he'd always thought Meridans were a lot more focused on drinking than Thelicosans. When he arrived, however, he noticed that it wasn't exactly a party spot. The Overflowing Bathtub was more of a cozy martini and cigar bar than a club, decked out with smooth, smoky-red wood paneling and various high-class paintings. It sort of reminded Rogers of the quarterdeck on the *Flagship*, but less mind-numbingly tacky.

He only saw this through the hazy glass on the outside of the room, however. Located on the same deck of the *Limiter* as most of the dining facilities, the bar was closed. At least, he thought it was closed. The operating hours posted on the outside of the door indicated that it should have been open—and there also appeared to be a bartender behind the counter—but when Rogers tried to open the door it gave him a red light and a very rude buzzer noise.

"I apologize for being late," came a voice from behind Rogers, so close that it nearly made him jump. Rogers spun, probably faster than he ought to have, to find Zergan standing extremely close to him. Rogers' hand instinctively went to his pistol holster, only to discover that his pistol holster was not where he'd put it. He'd done such a poor job buckling it that the force of his turn put the pistol squarely between his butt cheeks, which really just sort of made him look like he was scratching his hip.

"Hi there," Rogers said, adjusting the holster. Zergan turned a discerning eye to the pistol, though if he was surprised that Keffoule had given a Meridan a weapon, he did not show it in his face. When he was done looking like he was adjusting his underwear, Rogers jerked a thumb at the locked door. "I think they're closed."

"Oh no," Zergan said. He indicated that he wanted to get around Rogers, and Rogers stepped aside as the grizzled soldier swiped a keycard in front of the door control. The light went from red to green and emitted a beep.

"Congratulations on unlocking the bar!" came a familiar feminine voice. "You are entitled to—"

"Shut up, Sara," Zergan barked, and the voice—surprisingly—cut off. He cleared his throat. "That's, ah, the name I've given to that voice. You know that voice, right? It's in *everything.*" Zergan leaned, rather creepily, on the word "everything" in a way that made Rogers think perhaps Zergan had been intimate with the door control.

"Uh, yeah," Rogers said. "Sure. It seems like Snaggardir's is all over the place, doesn't it?"

Zergan only smiled and waved him through the now-open door to the Overflowing Bathtub. The inside looked much like Rogers had expected from the outside, with some added details. A man with a very thick mustache was behind the bar, wearing a very floppy cap that hung low over his eyes, so much so that it practically obstructed his whole face. He made himself busy working the bar, wiping it with a cloth like bartenders were wont to do, and glanced up with a quick nod as the two of them entered. The bar was otherwise uninhabited, unless you could consider several trophy-sized fish hanging on the wall drinking companions.

"Nice place," Rogers said. "Officers only?"

"Yes," Zergan said. "Above a certain pay grade, too. It helps give the place a certain . . . flavor."

Rogers blanched a bit at that. Meridans had a fairly narrow social gap between officer and enlisted, but it wasn't like that everywhere. Letting the comment slide off him—he'd been a sergeant himself until just a short while ago—he slowly cruised toward the bar. Aside from the fish, the Overflowing Bathtub was sparsely and tastefully decorated, with the exception of a large picture hanging over the bartender's head. In an elaborate gold frame rested a painting of a naked old man sprinting away from what Rogers assumed was a bathtub, his finger in the air. Certain aspects of his anatomy gave the clear impression that the old man was moving quickly.

"So," Rogers said as he took a seat. "How long have you been on the *Limiter*?"

The stools were comfortable, sturdy things with thick, leather-upholstered padding on top. He swiveled around on his with practiced ease, almost giggling with delight. Never in a million years had he thought he'd turn around on a Thelicosan ship and think, *I'm home.* Rogers was becoming more secure in his decision not to return to the *Flagship,* and doing a very good job of segmenting and crushing the thoughts about betraying his homeland, his friends, and all that really complicated, deep emotional stuff.

"A while," Zergan said, and Rogers nodded. He supposed maybe personal details weren't a good way to start conversations with your enemy. Were they enemies? Rogers was pretty sure they were still enemies.

"What will you have?" Zergan asked. "There's plenty of fine

liquor here to suit any taste." He let out a low laugh, two quick chuckles that made Rogers think he'd made some private joke.

As much as Rogers liked Jasker 120, the thought of consuming more at the moment made his stomach do a little "please don't do that to me again" dance. Rogers supposed he should take it easy, unless Zergan challenged him to a duel. Then it was on.

"You pick," Rogers said, which again resulted in that double chuckle.

"How about a real man's drink?" Zergan said, then turned to the bartender. "We'd like two Iron Morgans."

That certainly sounded manly. The bartender nodded, not looking up from where he seemed to be vigorously trying to get a spot out of the wood.

"Yes, surr," he said, obviously another thick-accented Thelicosan. Rogers was getting the impression that the accent was sort of a lowbrow thing, like a sign of lower birth or something. Not that he was classist, he just hadn't heard anyone of high status with an accent that was thick enough to warrant a translator like Tunger.

Zergan was silent while the bartender made the drinks, and Rogers followed his lead on setting the mood, watching the bartender instead of staring at a silent companion. The bartender moved with lightning precision, the sort of skill that could only come with years of slinging drinks and listening to boring people's problems. Wondering what a "manly" drink looked like, Rogers was surprised when he started reaching for the tropical liqueurs and maraschino cherries. Further surprised when he reached for the pineapple slices and umbrellas. And even further astonished when he poured the mixtures into a pair of delicate glasses cut into the shape of kittens.

"Ah," Zergan said as the bartender put the drinks in front of them. Before Rogers could grab his, however, Zergan picked it up and handed it to him instead, which Rogers found kind of awkward, kitty glass aside. "The Iron Morgan. To men!" Zergan said, raising his glass to Rogers.

"To men?" Rogers said, clinking the glass. Before he could take the first sip, however, the bartender snatched the glass out of his hand, appeared to examine it, and removed a spot from the side using a towel.

"Thanks," Rogers said hesitantly as he took the glass back, taking an obligatory first sip. It tasted like fairy dust and sparkles.

"Right," Zergan said, putting down the glass and smacking his lips. "Captain Rogers, I'm glad you agreed to meet me."

"I always try to drink with people who've shot at me if I get the chance," Rogers said, never having drunk with anyone who had shot at him before, ever. "It helps calm the waters, if you know what I mean."

Zergan nodded and took another sip. Rogers scooped up his own glass to drink again and couldn't help but notice that his drink was fizzing a little bit, probably from passing it back and forth between him and the bartender. The Iron Morgan actually wasn't that bad, frilly accoutrements aside.

"I suppose you know what I wanted to talk to you about, then," Zergan said.

"No," Rogers said. "I'm still trying to figure that out."

"It's about the Grand Marshal."

Rogers paused with the glass up to his lips. Boy, he was drinking fast; he tended to do that when he was nervous, and something about a deputy enemy commander who clearly had the hots for a woman who loved Rogers made him nervous. Rogers took another long sip, giving himself time to compose his thoughts, and put the glass down nearly empty.

"You must know that—"

Zergan raised a hand and shook his head. "You don't have to say anything else. I understand the position you're in. You are unable to resist her womanly charm, and I absolutely cannot blame you for that. But I think you fail to understand her history. Bartender! Another."

Rogers had barely realized he'd finished his drink, and was

about to protest—he didn't mind lots of alcohol, but lots of fructose was another thing—but the drink was already half made before he was able to open his mouth. The bartender was quite fast. In another very odd exchange, the bartender handed the glass to Rogers but was intercepted by Zergan, who then handed it back to Rogers, who was about to drink before it was taken from him by the bartender again for a brief moment before being returned. Rogers hesitated. Was this some kind of Thelicosan bar custom? Was Rogers insulting Zergan by *not* juggling Zergan's drink?

Trying to let it slide past him, Rogers took another sip of the fizzy, fruity drink. The sugar was almost overpowering, but perhaps it was a good thing. Behind there, very faint, he could taste something absolutely awful, like a mixture of metal and feet. The impression was barely there before it vanished, swallowed by the fruitiness.

"Alandra . . ." Zergan stopped. "The Grand Marshal's history is . . . colored. I am sure you know she was a prominent special operations soldier at one point."

"I guessed," Rogers said.

Zergan nodded gravely. "That alone should make you tread lightly. She and I were in the same unit for a long time."

Eyeing Zergan up and down, Rogers could easily believe this leather-chewing soldier had been involved in some really shady stuff, though he still had no real idea what that would entail in a military that had supposedly been at peace for the last two hundred years.

Zergan didn't appear to know how to approach whatever it was he was trying to say. He looked at Rogers, then at his drink, then back at him, frowning. Was Rogers doing something wrong? Drinking cultures were so widely varied, you never really knew when you were insulting someone. The bartender, his cap still pulled low, busied himself with cleaning glasses, though he'd left all the components of the Iron Morgan out. No doubt he expected to be making another.

"There's more to it than that," Zergan said. "You must be wondering how she ended up with command of this fleet instead."

Rogers shrugged. "The thought had crossed my mind, but it's really none of my—"

"There was an accident." Zergan's voice dropped, his tone ominous.

"Very sorry to hear that," Rogers said, making his way through the latter half of his second drink. He barely felt anything at all, though the fruit juice was helping with the remnants of the hangover headache from the night before.

"You're probably wondering what the accident was," Zergan said.

"Actually," Rogers said, "I'm sure the Grand Marshal wouldn't appreciate—"

"It was at the end of a long campaign," Zergan said, settling back on his stool and motioning for the bartender to give them another round. Rogers hadn't finished his yet, so he drained it in one quick gulp and put the empty glass on the bar. This time, he didn't even reach for the finished drink. Zergan picked it up and handed it to him, and then the bartender took it back for a moment to clean the glass. Why was Rogers' drink so fizzy? Zergan's appeared to be as calm as open space.

Zergan raised his glass a bit in a toast, and Rogers did the same. This was a *lot* of sugar. He was starting to feel jittery, as though he'd just consumed a few cups of coffee.

"We deal with a lot in the F Sequence," Zergan said, then laughed at himself. "I probably shouldn't even be telling you the name."

"Then don't," Rogers said, squirming. "I'd really prefer to avoid any of those 'you know too much' scenarios, if you don't mind. I'll forget all about the F Sequence."

"It's headquartered in a small village on Schvink," Zergan continued.

"That's very interesting," Rogers said, burying his face in his drink.

"Anyway," Zergan said, "this campaign we were on, it was just before the accident. We'd spent months tracking a zip jack cartel through the jungles on some planet I probably shouldn't tell you."

"Then don't."

"It was Urp."

Rogers gulped at his drink.

"Urp has a lot of jungle on it, so it's easy for them to hide, and there are a lot of animals there that prey on humans. Alandra got separated from the main group and spent most of her time pretending to be a leopard to try to not get eaten."

Zergan paused.

"Are you feeling okay?" he asked hesitantly.

"Right as rain," Rogers said. "Aside from, you know, being given a lot of classified information that I don't need to know."

Zergan thought for a moment, his face blank. Then he shook his head and continued.

"It took us a long time to recover her—we actually thought she was a leopard for the longest time—and when we did, she'd changed. She barely spoke, wouldn't even look me in the eye. She wouldn't eat anything except raw meat thrown at her, and she'd developed a level of paranoia I haven't even seen in a schizophrenic."

"That sounds awful," Rogers said. "So terrible we probably should move on to something else. Say, where did the name Zergan come from, anyway? Is it Old Earth or a new planetary dynasty?"

"So paranoid," Zergan said, "that we had to keep her in isolation for weeks." He sighed. "I thought we'd lost her completely."

The man genuinely seemed concerned about his compatriot. Rogers supposed those sorts of war buddies tended to form a unique bond, though he still had no idea why Zergan was sharing that with him.

"Alandra recovered a bit, and . . ." Zergan trailed off, forgetting himself for a moment. "We jumped the gun on reintegration. The next day, she saw a mirror for the first time since the mission."

Rogers, who was really starting to feel kind of shaky from all the sugar, pushed away his empty glass. He noticed that Zergan, despite his garrulousness, had finished his drink as well, and the mustached bartender went to work making them a new round without instruction. Rogers sort of wanted to tell him he'd just like some water, but he didn't want to insult Zergan.

Another glass on the bar. Another interception by Zergan. Another reinterception by the bartender. And finally Rogers had another drink. This was so weird.

"What's so bad about a mirror?" Rogers finally asked.

Zergan looked up, his eyes blazing, piercing. "She didn't recognize herself. She thought she was one of the cartel members, or, worse, one of the feral leopards." He paused. "Her instincts kicked in, and she did the only thing her body knew how to do. She kicked herself in the face."

Rogers gaped. "What? That's not even possible. How is that possible?" He tried to imagine an anatomical configuration that would have allowed him to kick himself in the face. He could barely touch his toes!

Zergan just shrugged. "The force of it put her into a coma. When she woke up, she was more herself, but she was . . . broken. They kicked her out of the F Sequence—our top secret organization, headquartered on Schvink, if you needed a reminder—and put her out to pasture here."

"Kicked herself in the face," Rogers repeated. "Do you realize how not possible that is?"

"I followed her out here to look after her," Zergan said. "Turned down the biggest promotion of my life to become her deputy." He didn't sound happy about it. In fact, he was gritting his teeth so hard that the veins on his neck were bulging out. Suddenly, he looked at Rogers, and looked at his drink again.

"How are you feeling?" he asked. Angrily.

"I feel fine!" Rogers insisted. "Look, I appreciate the concern and the camaraderie and the attempts at reconciliation, Commodore Zergan, but this all seems a little strange. Why are you telling me all this information? Why can't you just let me grab my own drink? Why is the bartender's mustache a different color than it was when I walked in?"

It was true—at least he thought it was true. The mustache had been black when Rogers had walked in, he was sure of it. Now it was brown. Was it a different style, too?

"Trick of the light," the bartender said, but it came out more like "truck of the lurt."

Rogers shook his head. "Whatever. Look, Commodore Zergan . . ."

"Really, though," Zergan said. "How do you feel?"

Raising an eyebrow, Rogers sat back. "Do you need me to sign some kind of affidavit testifying that I am in good health? Are you worried about the legal ramifications of kidnapping me and all that? Because I can do that if you want."

This didn't seem to be the right answer. Zergan stood up so fast that it nearly made Rogers jump off his stool and run for the door.

"Fine!" Zergan shouted. "I am *very glad* you feel good. This is *excellent* news."

It didn't sound like excellent news. Rogers made allowances for differences in culture, but he didn't think shaking a fist in someone's face was recognized as friendly on any planet.

"I have to go!" Zergan yelled, his eyes wide. "It has been a pleasure sharing this time with you! *We should do it again sometime since you are feeling so healthy!*"

"*Yes!*" Rogers yelled, trying to fit in. "*We should definitely have more Iron Morgans sometime in this bar, right here!*"

"*Great!*" Zergan shouted, extending his hand, his face red. "*I bid you good night!*"

"*Wonderful!*" Rogers said, taking Zergan's hand and regretting it immediately. He'd never received an angrier, more painful handshake in his life. He wasn't completely sure that Zergan hadn't broken a few bones.

And with that, Zergan amicably stormed out of the room, cheerfully throwing a stool as he exited.

"Remember what I told you about the Grand Marshal!" he barked affably as he vanished from sight.

What a friendly guy.

Rogers turned around to thank the bartender for his service and calmly explain that he had no money and therefore could not pay for anything that had just transpired, never mind leave him a tip. It was a conversation he'd had many times, and one that had nearly succeeded once. In this case, however, it was true. He didn't have access to his credit reserve while a prisoner on an enemy ship.

The bartender was staring at him. Did he look familiar?

"Surr," he said quietly.

"You don't need to call me 'sir,'" Rogers said, waving the word away. "I just wanted to tell you that I've run into a bit of an unfortunate circumstance, and it appears that my drinking companion has left prematurely without giving me the opportunity to talk him into paying my bill for me."

"Surr," the bartender said, placing some sort of special emphasis on the word for some reason. Probably because he was pissed off since he'd just been told he wasn't getting paid.

"I know, I know," Rogers said. "If you'd just allow me some time—"

"Put everything on my tab," came a voice from behind him. The voice he really didn't want to hear at that moment. He was going to do the whole whirl-around-in-shock thing, but if Keffoule really was a paranoid leopard lady, he didn't want to make any sudden movements.

"Grand Marshal," he said slowly. "I'm so glad you found me." Had Zergan been right? Was she really crazy? Well, Rogers knew that already. She *was* crazy. But Rogers hadn't thought she was *dangerously* crazy or anything. She'd promised never to kick him in the face again. Could he trust her?

She came into his field of view as she sat where Zergan had been a moment earlier, and appeared to be on the verge of saying something before changing her mind.

"Who was here?" she asked tightly. "Was it another woman?"

Rogers blinked. "How did you know someone was here?"

"The seat is warm. Answer me!" she shouted, looking at him with eyes that might as well have just set him on fire. Wow, her tone had changed.

"It was your d-d-deputy," Rogers said, trying to keep his calm. Why was he stuttering? He shouldn't be stuttering. It was all the damn sugar; he remembered times from his youth when he'd sounded similar after eating too much cake. He thought he'd outgrown it by oversaturating his system for years, but the New *Flagship* Diet had obviously done poor things for his sugar tolerance.

"Zergan?" Keffoule said, her face relaxing slightly into something that mixed hot, unreasonable rage with sudden confusion. "What was he doing here?"

"He invited me for some d-d-drinks," Rogers said, then hiccupped. Sheesh.

"Why are you so nervous?" Keffoule asked, her eyes narrow. "Are you hiding something from me?"

"I'm n-n-not hiding anything," Rogers said. "It's all this damn f-f-fruit juice!"

Keffoule looked at him sideways as she turned back toward the bartender and ordered something that Rogers had never heard of called water. Come to think of it, she did look a little worse for wear. She had "lost" the duel, after all.

"So," Rogers said, "do you come here often?"

It was a lame line, and he really had no interest in flirting with her, but he was genuinely curious.

"No," she said. "Almost never. I'm tracking your datapad."

Rogers nodded. Of course she was.

They sat next to each other, not saying anything for quite some time. Keffoule sipped her water, and Rogers sipped nothing. He really didn't want anything else with sugar in it, but he always felt awkward not having a drink when the person with him was drinking.

"I'll have a water, too," he said finally.

The bartender put a glass on the bar, and Rogers waited for Keffoule to pick it up so that they could do this strange drinking ritual. It became apparent after a moment, however, that it wasn't going to happen. Eventually Keffoule turned and frowned at Rogers.

"What are you doing?" she asked.

Rogers hesitated. "I'm waiting for you to pick up my drink to hand it to me so that the bartender will take it and then hand it back to me?"

Keffoule's eyes narrowed. "I may be unaware of Meridan relationships, but I can assure you that in Thelicosa there is no such servant-like attitude toward wives or wives-to-be."

Her voice could have cracked diamonds. Rogers felt himself scooting back on his barstool, trying to put space between him and this woman. If that wasn't some sort of tradition, what the hell had Zergan been doing the whole time? Rogers looked at the bartender for some sort of hint, but the bartender actually shook his head, like Rogers was some sort of idiot.

"Don't blame me," Rogers said. "I don't know what the hell you crazy people do here."

He was talking to the bartender, of course, but Keffoule seemed to think it was directed at her. At least, that was what he assumed, since she looked about ready to kill him at that moment.

"No, no," Rogers said, holding up a hand defensively. "That's not what I m-m-meant. Damn it!"

Keffoule's mouth tightened. "You know, I came down here to express admiration for the way you handled yourself last night,

Captain Rogers, but I am feeling disinclined to compliment you. You have lied to me twice since I have sat down. Who is the other woman who was here with you?"

"I told you," Rogers said. "It was your d-d-deputy."

"You are stuttering like a fool!" Keffoule said, slapping her palm against the bar. "You think I believe any word you are saying?"

Rogers was about to protest further, but he could feel his lips trembling before he even opened his mouth. If Belgrave had been here, he would undoubtedly have psychoanalyzed Rogers' stutter, since it was tied to his childhood, and come up with some sort of explanation like he was infantilizing himself on purpose to avoid making mature decisions. And then Rogers would have punched him. Or at least ordered the Viking to punch him.

The Viking. Just the thought of her made him flush a little. He'd been silly to think he could just toss his love for her aside for a couple of drinks and a one-point-six-one-meter-tall cake.

"And now you're turning red," Keffoule said. "Where did you learn to lie? I had heard reports that you were a clever man, Captain Rogers, but perhaps I was wrong."

He briefly thought about explaining why he was blushing, but he felt like that would have been a poor choice.

"There wasn't another woman here," he said. "It was Zergan. He invited me to the b-b-bar for some d-d-drinks. What other woman am I going to hang out with? Quinn?"

That didn't seem to please Keffoule either.

"You are not to come back to this bar unless I am with you," she barked. "Perhaps I have given you too long a leash."

"You gave me a frigging *pistol*," Rogers said. "I kind of thought that was a symbol that I was free to do what I want and maybe shoot someone if I had to."

"Keep the pistol. You may need it if you keep lying to me about meeting every woman on my ship in this bar."

Rogers squinted, trying to make sense of that. "Okay, clearly you have some jealousy issues that you need to work out with a

COMMUNICATION FAILURE 245

therapist. But if you think restricting my movements on your ship is going to win me over, you should probably read a different dating manual."

"We are not dating," Keffoule said. All the warmth that had leaked into their conversation yesterday had faded; it was all business now. Their marriage was back to a transaction, a step on Keffoule's career ladder. "We are simply waiting for you to stop being petulant and stupid."

Rogers raised an eyebrow. "Wow," he said. "You really *are* crazy. Zergan was right."

That got a reaction. Her expression turned from dismissive to something that looked a little bit like the one she'd assumed on the *Ambuscade* just before jumping across the table at him.

"You were here with Zergan?"

"Are you kidding me right now?" Rogers said. "Do you have intermittent deafness or something? I've been telling you that for the last t-t-ten minutes, but you seem so intent on being n-n-nuts that you haven't heard a word I said."

Keffoule's eyes went wide. "What else did he tell you?"

"Oh, now you want to know?" Roger said, his voice getting uncomfortably loud. Maybe there had been a lot of alcohol in the drinks Zergan had ordered, because his inhibitions against screaming at powerful, deadly women seemed to be going away. "Now you want to listen to me? Are you sure you don't want to keep accusing me of having a brothel hidden away somewhere in this five-by-ten bar?"

Surprisingly, Keffoule shrank away a little. "That's not what I—"

"Oh, it is," Rogers spat, standing up. "That's exactly what you meant. I'm not sure how I ever thought I could stay on this ship."

Keffoule had started to stand up to match Rogers' posture, some of the fire returning to her eyes, but when Rogers mentioned the possibility of staying, her whole stance changed. She looked at him, her expression flat but her eyes hopeful.

"You were considering it?" she asked quietly.

"Yes," Rogers said, then shook his head. "No. I don't know. I thought maybe it wouldn't be so bad to be on a ship where I got good breakfasts and Jasker 120 and whatever. But now I realize I was being just as crazy as you are!"

Keffoule recoiled a bit at that. Wow, he really had her on the defensive; this was a side of her he hadn't seen yet.

"Crazy?" she asked.

"Yes," Rogers said. "Crazy. Nuts. Filled to the brim with a concoction of insanity and lunacy, garnished with a sprig of coo-coo." Rogers made a "coo-coo" gesture with both of his fingers next to his temple. "Zergan told me about all about the F Sequence, about your missions, about how you thought you were a leopard and then kicked yourself in the face. You. Are. N-N-Nuts."

Some part of him told him he'd gone a little too far. Maybe way too far. But he'd said what he'd said, and he'd have to accept the consequences, which, in this case, were the heel of a Grand Marshal flying at his face at an extremely high speed.

Rogers ducked.

He heard a whistling noise that actually reminded him a lot of a time when he'd accidentally knocked the reed valve off a combustion engine and nearly killed everyone in the room. He wasn't entirely sure that a small sonic boom hadn't just rattled the glasses on the bar. He was sure, however, that somehow, miraculously, he hadn't just been kicked in the face. The resultant crash, and splinters of wood raining down on his head, told him that Keffoule had, however, kicked something else.

The room fell completely silent. Uncurling slowly from what he decided was definitely not a cowardly crouch, Rogers looked up to find the Overflowing Bathtub in total disarray. The bar was almost completely split in half, the barstools had been reduced to rubble, and the bartender was nowhere to be found. Keffoule lay in the center of it all, covered in the detritus of the aftermath of what appeared to be a bomb going off in the middle of the room.

Rogers stood up, looking down at her, strangely calm. If he ever saw Mailn again, he would kiss her. Well, no. He'd introduce her to another woman who would kiss her.

Keffoule locked eyes with him, her mouth open in surprise. Her face was ghostly pale, her hands curled into fists as they supported her on the floor.

"No one has . . . Ever . . . Dodged . . . It's . . . You . . . The ratio . . ." Keffoule stammered, totally unhinged. She continued to stare, her eyes getting watery. Rogers braced for an onslaught.

"I love you," she said finally.

Rogers threw up his hands and stormed out of the Overflowing Bathtub, snatching his datapad from his pocket and using the instructions Quinn had left him to call her. He didn't care if Keffoule was tracking him. He didn't care if Keffoule heard every word he was about to say.

"Yes?" Quinn said.

"Q-Q-Q-Quinn!" Rogers said.

"Captain Rogers," Quinn said. "What's wrong with your voice? Is there something—"

"Shut the hell up and get me the hell off this sh-sh-ship."

Milk Run

Deet had some issues with understanding subtext and subtlety and all the things that made humans infuriatingly confusing, but he was pretty sure everyone on the bridge was plotting to kill him.

It could have been the way they were looking at him. It could have been the way they were whispering to each other while looking at him. It also could have been the fact that several of them were pointing weapons at him and making *"Pew! Pew!"* noises as they pretended to shoot him. The fact was that Deet was getting distrustful of any human companionship on the bridge. But what choice did he have? He had to stay here to fulfill his duty as Rogers' stand-in.

Inching closer to Belgrave, practically the only man on the bridge who Deet was sure *wasn't* contemplating killing him, Deet gave in to previous inhibitions and emulated a noise he'd come to recognize as a sigh. In his experience, this was an utterance emitted in order to passively attract attention to oneself.

"What's wrong?" Belgrave asked. It worked! "Let me guess.

You've been ruminating on the meaning of your existence and wondering whether or not you have the free will to fight your own programming, is that it?"

Deet hesitated. "No," he said. "Well, now it is. Before you said that I was mostly worried about the disruptor turret they're mounting on that railing over there and pointing at me."

Belgrave spared a glance for the two people screwing the turret into its hastily erected mount and nodded gravely.

"This is also concerning," he said.

"I'm sure things will be fine," Deet said, engaging his optimism drive. "It's not like they're loading it or preparing it to fire." He turned back to Belgrave. "What did you mean about free will and all that?"

"Only that you must be wondering whether or not your programming is eventually going to force you to kill everyone around you."

"I had not, in fact, been wondering that," Deet said. "But now I am. Do you think I am eventually going to kill everyone around me?"

"That's not for me to decide," Belgrave said as he continued to not fly the ship. "In fact, I'm not sure it's for any of us to decide. In a world of cause and effect, is there really such a thing as free will at all?"

"What do you mean?" Deet asked as he slowly and casually crept behind a control box, putting it between himself and the turret. The two marines who had been setting it up started grumbling at each other and disassembling it to try to get a better angle.

"I mean we live in a universe that exists only by a chain reaction of events all starting at one single point. You're only here because of the Big Bang fifteen billion years ago. Given that, is it possible to say that you've made any choices purely by your own free will?"

"Right now I'm choosing to not die," Deet said, eyeing the new position where the turret was being set up.

"Right," Belgrave said. "But only because of the Big Bang."

Deet beeped. "You know, I'm starting to think that you may not have actually ever studied philosophy."

Belgrave shrugged. "You can believe whatever you want to believe."

"So you're saying I have free will?"

The helmsman stuck his tongue out at Deet, which didn't seem very philosophical at all. But it did get Deet thinking. He'd avoided killing everyone so far, right? There was no reason that was going to change. But before, he'd only assumed it was because he'd been cut off from the ship's network while the rest of the droids had been developing their collective intelligence and becoming self-aware. Deet was already self-aware. At least, he thought he was. Would he know if he wasn't?

Now that he knew that a hatred for humans and a desire to take over the ship were actually part of his core programming, he wasn't so sure. He'd seen it himself; the code was there, the execution commands were there, but they weren't running. For reasons he couldn't understand, the code was just sitting there, dormant, looking for something to trigger it. What would trigger it? Was it some sort of phrase or password or an event? An electric current? A pitch at just the right frequency?

There was also the possibility, of course, that Deet was defective. He'd been a prototype, after all, so perhaps he'd been discarded because protocol 162 hadn't worked correctly.

Regardless of all these theories, the fact remained that he didn't know. That was unsettling. If he suddenly cracked and engaged his droid fu in the middle of a crowded zipcar, he'd make the biggest, grossest bowl of human soup ever created.

"You're thinking about making human soup, aren't you?" Belgrave asked.

Deet snapped out of processing things—literally—and looked at Belgrave.

"How did you know?" Deet said, keeping his voice low. The gun turret had been reassembled, this time from a metallic crossbeam running across the bridge, so hiding from it was no longer an option.

"You projected it on that little screen," Belgrave said, pointing at Deet's abdomen. "If you want to avoid people shooting you, you may want to try censoring yourself a bit."

Deet was about to make a comment about free expression and how Belgrave couldn't step on his rights when an alarm went off.

"Ship launch, hangar seven," someone said. "They didn't request clearance and they're not responding to hails."

"Who is on board?" Deet asked. Nobody answered him, likely because nobody knew. And they'd stopped answering his questions after they'd all begun to assume he was going to kill them all.

The display technician routed the ship's cameras to the main screen, and Deet saw one of the less-often-used shuttle types blasting out at full throttle away from the ship. As he searched his internal database, it took him a moment to realize that it was a Hedgehog-class shuttle, designed for running blockades and named for its spiky outer hull, which had been constructed to help the front-facing shields deflect plasma blasts.

"Is someone defecting?" Deet asked. "Should we blow them up?"

"You see? You see?" someone yelled. "He *is* going to kill us!"

"Nice," Belgrave said.

The bridge door opened, and Sergeant Mailn came running in, out of breath.

"No!" she said. "Don't shoot. It's the Viking!"

Rogers might have hated the Chariots, but by the time he finished stumbling through the ship, he really wished he'd had one. Granted, the first thing he would have done with it would probably have been to fly it into a wall and kill himself, but a quick death might have been preferable to running through the

Limiter while coming down from a major sugar high. He felt like he was going to pass out, throw up, or become diabetic.

Quinn had told him to meet her on the farm deck.

"Do you mean the zoo deck?" Rogers had asked.

"No," Quinn had said. "What kind of self-respecting military organization would have a zoo deck? Meet me on the farm deck. It's near the shuttle hangar on level five of the ship."

Rogers had a map on the datapad that Keffoule had given him that allowed him to navigate the ship with some semblance of direction, but without access to the transportation systems, he was forced to run through a lot of staircases, constantly wondering if he was about to be gunned down by any of the dozens of Thelicosan troops he was racing past. In fact, he was sort of disappointed that they *didn't* try to gun him down. He hoped that if any of *his* personnel saw a Thelicosan soldier running through the *Flagship* with a gun on his hip, they'd at least trip the person and ask some questions. It appeared that Keffoule's immunity was rather extensive.

He smelled the farm deck before he saw it. Quinn was waiting for him, tapping her foot nervously as she leaned against a pair of large cargo doors that, presumably, led to the farm. Rogers only assumed this because someone wearing a straw hat and overalls was leading a pair of cows through the door.

"Where have you been?" Quinn demanded. "I've been waiting here forever! I thought Keffoule had caught up with you."

"I had to walk all the way over here from the bar," Rogers said.

Quinn gave him a look. "You walked? Why did you do that? Didn't you see the elevators?"

"What elevators?" Rogers said, huffing.

"The elevators that connect every deck on the ship!" Quinn said. "What, did you think we all ran from place to place? We'd never get anything done."

Rogers tried to give Quinn a dirty look, but he was breathing so heavily and crashing so hard from the sugar high that he fell over instead.

"Captain Rogers!" Quinn said. "Are you alright? What did she do to you?"

"Nothing," Rogers said. "In fact, I think she's going to be pretty upset at what I did to her. She tried to kick me and missed."

Quinn's face showed him how often that had happened. She stood speechless for a moment before reaching out a surprisingly firm hand to help him up.

"I'm okay," he said as she tried to steady him by grabbing his shoulders. He shrugged her off. "Really, I'm fine. So how are we going to do this? Is there a shuttle ready for me?"

"Shuttle?" Quinn said. "No. That's too obvious. We're going to smuggle you out. Follow me."

Wanting to ask more questions but not having the breath to do so, Rogers obediently trailed behind her through a side door that allowed them access to the ship's farm.

It put the zoo deck on the *Flagship* to shame, which was no surprise, really. Everything about the *Limiter* except its age and its psychotic captain seemed to be leagues beyond what the *Flagship* could offer. The biosphere here was incredibly advanced and absolutely enormous, spanning what appeared to be the entire level of the ship. The ceiling was composed entirely of holographs and ultraviolet light generators, complete with other weather simulation devices. Animals bleated and mooed and barked all over the place, the smell of cow dung mixing almost pleasantly with growing wheat and cigarette smoke. That was coming from a man on a horse standing near the entrance, wearing a wide-brimmed cowboy hat and saying "Yup" between puffs.

"Wow," Rogers said.

"I'm sure it's very impressive to someone like you," Quinn said, and Rogers sort of felt like that was racist. "But we have very little time for sightseeing. We're going to the cow barn."

"Wait," Rogers said, refusing to follow Quinn any farther. "Why are we going to the cow barn? I thought you were getting me out of here."

Quinn stopped and turned around, looking impatient. She kept fiddling with something in her hair bun, and it made her look like she had a nervous twitch.

"Do I really have to explain myself, or can you just trust me?"

"Think about that for a second," Rogers said.

Quinn sighed. "Fine. Remember those milk containers you idiots blew up?"

"The insult really wasn't a necessary part of that question."

"Well, we're trying to restock them. You're going to go out with them."

Rogers' eyes went wide. "You're going to stuff me in a milk container?"

"With an oxygen tank, of course," Quinn said. "Since your ships were able to make it to that area of space before with no problem, I'll disable as much of the jamming net as I can, then send a message to your ship to come pick you up."

"That's insane!" Rogers said.

"I *know*," Quinn said, almost at a whisper. Her eyes took on a sort of faraway, misty look. "Isn't it exci—"

She stopped herself and cleared her throat, not speaking for a long moment. "It's the only option we have. I've already filled out the proper forms to get you categorized as a dairy product on the manifest of the cargo container."

"Why not the manifest of a *passenger ship*?" Rogers asked. "Spoof my ID as a technician or something. I'll use a VMU and jet my way to safety."

"It wouldn't work. There's no other position that would get you far enough for recovery by your own forces."

They moved aside as a flock of sheep led by a young girl wielding a shepherd's crook passed through.

"And what if you don't get the message through? What if they don't believe you?" Rogers asked. "I drown in a giant vat of milk! What a way to go. No, Quinn, this is stupid."

Quinn stepped closer to him, making Rogers much more

nervous than a short politician should have been able to. She glared at him, her eyes fierce, and spoke in low tones.

"Listen," she said. "There's more at stake here than the possibility of one man drowning in a milk vat."

"One *very important* man," Rogers said.

Quinn ignored him. "I've uncovered information that is vital to the survival of our galaxy, Captain Rogers, and I need you to broadcast it to your home world. Once you get back, I'm going to disable the jamming net as much as I can so that you can get word back to Merida Prime. The moment that hole in the net opens up, you must tell everyone you can that Jupiter is—"

An explosion rocked the ship, causing the floor to shake and several of the holographic generators in the farm to go off. The sheep that had just passed scattered, bleating frantically as the little shepherd chased after them, sobbing. The cows mooed more enthusiastically, if such a thing could be done, and the cowboy calmly lit another cigarette.

"What the hell was that?" Rogers said.

Without answering, Quinn dashed away, her running form surprisingly proper. It looked awkward for someone wearing a suit to be moving at a dead sprint, but Rogers didn't have time to criticize. He ambled after her, not able to keep up at all, and followed her back into the hallway, which was rapidly filling with dust and smoke and some very confused Thelicosan troops.

"What happened?" someone shouted.

"Someone crashed into the shuttle hangar!" someone else cried.

Rogers and Quinn stopped in the hallway, looking down toward the entrance to the hangar. People were filing out the door, looking a bit dazed, and amber lights on the ceiling began emitting bursts of light.

"Think it's serious?" Rogers asked.

"I don't know. This may sound callous, but that's not important right now. It may be the distraction we need. I need you to listen to me."

"Not important?" Roger said. "Are you crazy? If they punched a hole in the airlock or something, this whole ship could turn inside out. Maybe we should go talk somewhere else and, you know, abandon the idea of me getting stuffed into a milk container."

For a bureaucrat, Quinn was incredibly fast. She slapped him in the face so quickly that he didn't even have time to think about ducking, something that he now considered himself an expert at.

"Hey!" he said. "Why do all the women in my life feel the need to cause me physical harm?"

"If you're as deliberately obtuse with them as you are with me, then I can hardly blame them," Quinn hissed. "Now listen to me and listen well. There are Jupiterians on this ship. I don't know how many of them, but Zergan is their leader. They're plotting some kind of uprising, but I don't have the details yet. I was stuck in Zergan's room for half the day and haven't had time to look through the files I stole."

Rogers raised an eyebrow. "Stuck in Zergan's room? Secretary Quinn, I didn't peg you for the type of lady who—don't slap me again!"

She stopped, her arm raised. "I was in there performing my duties."

"Suuuuure," Rogers said. "Duties."

"I listened to him have a conversation with someone else, some woman I didn't know. She definitely wasn't on the ship, and Zergan is definitely working for Jupiter."

"Oh come on," Rogers said. "The Jupiterian diaspora was a long time ago. They didn't get their own system, so they just assimilated into the other systems. That's the way diasporas work."

"I don't have the details yet," Quinn said, "but they're big enough to be pushing all of Thelicosa into war with the Meridans, using this fleet as their tool. To me, that says they didn't exactly go meekly."

Rogers chewed on the inside of his lip, still wondering about the explosion that had happened in the hangar. Couldn't he just go in there and steal a shuttle in the confusion? He wasn't an awful pilot.

"So why are you telling me this?" he said. "Why not tell Keffoule?"

Quinn narrowed her eyes. "Sometimes I wonder what Keffoule sees in you. What would you do if someone you hated came up to you and told you that your best and most trusted friend had been plotting against you from the beginning?"

Rogers thought for a moment. "A spinning back kick to the face."

"Right. I need you to get back to your ship and transmit everything I can get you back to your headquarters. If Zergan takes control of the ship and convinces Keffoule to wipe out your battle group, there will be no turning back from war. And that's not the only thing. They kept talking about some sort of schedule—"

"Rogers!" someone shouted from behind him.

Time slowed down as he recognized the source of the voice. The siren's song reached out to him from the depths of his dreams and slowly caressed his ears, whispering the sonorous tones directly into the deepest parts of his consciousness. It sounded like a gentle angel that had spent the last ten years chain-smoking cigars and screaming at people. It sounded like home.

"Viking!" he cried with every part of his yearning soul.

The hulking form of the woman he desperately loved came charging toward him, splendidly decked out in full combat gear and wielding at least two disruptor rifles, a belt full of plasma grenades, and, for some reason, a scimitar strapped to her back. A helmet obstructed most of her face, but he'd recognize that gait and voice anywhere.

Instantly, he realized he'd been a fool to think he could live without her.

Acting purely on instinct, he ran at her, his arms open, but caught only air as she sprinted past him, raised the butt of her rifle, and smashed Quinn in the jaw.

Quinn flew clear off her feet, her body arcing like a thrown stuffed animal, and landed on her back, likely suffering a second concussion as her head bounced off the hard metal floor of the ship.

"Is that her?" the Viking yelled, pointing the barrel of her rifle at the supine form of Quinn. "Is this the crazy bitch Kerfuffle or whatever? I swear, if it is—"

"No!" Rogers said. "No! Don't shoot! In fact, you just butt-smashed the person who was trying to help me escape."

"Oh," the Viking said after a moment. She seemed reluctant not to pull the trigger, but eventually took her rifle away. Rogers now noticed the other two marines, neither of whom he could recognize with all their combat gear on, doing sweeps of the hallway. Thelicosan security hadn't responded yet, thankfully, so nobody was shooting at anyone else.

"You came for me," Rogers said.

"Even if you're the worst goddamned commander I've ever seen," the Viking said, turning around and giving some hand signals to the other two marines, "you're *my* worst goddamned commander."

Rogers' mouth hung open. "But my tactics," he began.

The Viking cleared her throat. "We can work on your tactics later, okay? Mine . . . maybe weren't the best either. But we can't work on anything in the middle of a bunch of dirty Thellies. Let's get the hell out of here."

Rogers thought his heart was going to explode out of his chest. She came for him!

"Wait," he said, thinking for a moment. "Did you . . . crash into the side of the ship?"

The Viking shrugged. "How the hell else was I supposed to get on board? Ask for landing clearance? Look, unless you've gotten used to living as part of Keffoule's harem or whatever, I suggest we get back to Flash and—"

"Oh no," Rogers said. "You brought *that* idiot?"

"I brought the only pilot stupid enough to think that crashing into the enemy flagship could be considered *flashy*. He's in the middle of stealing another shuttle right now, and it should be ready. So if you don't mind, I'd like to get out of here before people start shooting at us."

Rogers nodded, agreeing that escaping while not being shot at was preferable to escaping while being shot at, and the Viking motioned for the other two marines to follow. They were interrupted by someone running at them, screaming.

"Wait! Wait for me!" came another voice that Rogers recognized. The only problem was that it came from a face he didn't recognize. A man wearing a sort of low-brimmed chef hat came running down the hallway, yelling in an incomprehensible Thelicosan accent. It was the bartender from the Overflowing Bathtub. What the hell was he doing here? Was this about Rogers' unpaid tab? Or the fact that Keffoule had destroyed his bar?

"Surr! Suuurr! Aie wunt ter kurm home!"

"Can I shoot him?" the Viking asked.

"Wait," Rogers said. Something began to dawn on him, and suddenly he knew who it was.

"That's Tunger!"

"I know who it is," the Viking said, leveling her rifle.

"Oh, stop it!" Rogers said, pushing the rifle off target.

Tunger approached them, out of breath, and tore off his cap and mustache, casting them aside. Finally Rogers was able to see the face of the "interpreter" who had been rescued instead of him.

"You," Rogers said.

"You!" Quinn said. Rogers turned to see that she'd recovered consciousness, though she didn't look very happy about it. Her jaw was swollen and she was barely able to sit up straight. She wobbled back and forth precariously. "You're the doctor!"

"What, the 'stick to the schmurgle' guy? No, he's the bartender," Rogers said, though even as he argued he knew that there was something similar about the two men.

Quinn looked at Rogers for a moment, then looked back at Tunger. Her eyes widened. "You're the janitor, too!"

"*Who is this person?!*" Rogers cried.

"Take me back with you!" Tunger said without responding to any of their accusations, still breathing heavily. "Being a spy is too hard. All these facial hair changes are starting to give me eczema." He pointed at several red splotches on his face.

"You owe this man your life," Quinn said.

Rogers frowned. "That's the most ridiculous thing I have ever heard."

"Zergan has been trying to kill you," Quinn said.

"Oh really? Thanks for including that in the initial report. I might not have gone on a fruity kitten drink date with him if I had known that."

"This man protected you while you were hungover from partying all night with Keffoule."

The Viking stiffened almost imperceptibly.

"No, no," Rogers said, waving his hands. "It's not what you think. What are you talking about, Quinn?"

"Have him tell you," Quinn said, standing up and brushing herself off. "Right now you should get out of here. I'll do my best to start opening up the communications channels and cover your escape. You need to get that information to your headquarters as soon as possible so we can avert interstellar war. I'll transmit whatever details I can." She looked at the Viking. "I hope you can get him out of here alive."

The Viking just barked a belly laugh and turned away, motioning for the other marines to follow. Tunger happily galloped off, but Rogers stayed behind for a moment.

"Thanks, Secretary Quinn," he said.

"I didn't do this for you," she said. "I did this for the galaxy."

Rogers blinked. "Okay. Well, alright. Fine. Whatever. See you later . . . jerk."

He turned and jogged after the departing Meridans, taking a

moment to survey the curvaceous, muscular form of the Viking from a new and exciting angle that didn't involve a fist flying at his face. It was a wonderful experience, enhanced by the fact that she was lumbering down the hallway at a high speed.

"Tunger," Rogers said, panting as he caught up. "What was she talking about?"

"Oh," Tunger said. "Nothing. After I got on board and found my facial hair kit, I heard that guy Zergan or whatever saying something about wanting to kill you. It turned out he had a facial hair kit too. He tried to inject you with poison in the infirmary."

Rogers remembered the doctor insisting it was time for his medicine, and now he remembered that the doctor's beard had been a little crooked. But now that he thought about it, he realized there was no disguising those/that eyebrows/eyebrow. That had definitely been Zergan, and he'd definitely been trying to kill Rogers.

Before Rogers could ask Tunger about any other attempts on his life, they turned into the hangar, the door of which was a little crooked from the blast. Rogers could hear the shouts of Thelicosan troops coming from the other end of the hallway, probably the security detail coming to find out what the hell had just happened to their hangar. Nobody was shooting at them yet, though, so that was a plus.

"Where's Flash?" Rogers asked as they burst into the hangar, the size of the docking bay overwhelming his senses. There must have been two hundred ships of different makes and models in there, all of them shuttles. Pilots and maintenance crews were scattered all over the place, trying to inspect ships for damage. In one corner, Rogers could see the tattered, smoking remains of a Meridan shuttle that was now unrecognizable, the gangplank twisted like a funhouse slide.

"I don't know," the Viking said, scanning the room while her two companions provided cover. "He didn't say which—"

"There!" Tunger said.

Rogers looked where Tunger was pointing to see a shuttle, named the *Bwana* according to an inscription on the side of its hull, that was repeatedly lifting off the ground and then coming down again, creating the impression of a very excited puppy hopping up and down.

"Oh yeah," Rogers said. "That's him. Let's go!"

They sprinted across the loading dock, which might not have been the best way to keep anonymous in the surrounding confusion. Several of the pilots, thankfully none of them armed, charged the Viking and very shortly found out what it felt like to be run over by a bull. One of them actually flew bodily and smacked into the side of another shuttle, doing that thing where his body slid off the side of it like an egg tossed against the wall.

"God I love you," Rogers muttered.

"What?" the Viking said.

"I said we're almost there!"

It was a good thing, too; he could hear the storming footsteps of what he assumed was security coming into the hangar. Shouts of panic and some confused explanations started to erupt from behind them, with the crew trying to explain to the security detail where Rogers and his coterie had gone.

"Hurry!" he shouted.

Disruptor fire started to impact behind them, and Rogers found that his pistol had miraculously appeared in his hand. Without looking, he pointed the gun behind him and squeezed the trigger several times, only to realize that he hadn't taken the safety off. By the time he figured out where the safety was, he was already at the gangplank to the still-hopping shuttle.

"Flash!" Rogers yelled. "Stop jumping this damn thing up and down! We're here!"

"Oh, hey, Skip," came a voice from the cockpit. "I was just trying to see if this thing worked."

"You're also damn near pulling the magnetic chocks out," Rogers said. That was why the ship had been hopping; the ship had been magnetically chocked—like all ships were supposed to be when they were in a docking configuration—so the spacecraft wouldn't tumble from sudden inertial shifts or from an enemy vessel crashing into the docking bay. Having been a mechanic and engineer for many years, Rogers was able to see how the Thelicosan model disengaged and quickly freed the ship from its bonds.

"We're good to go!" he shouted. Pointing his pistol at what he could now see was a very large security contingent, he fired several shots, none of which landed anywhere near the Thelicosan troops. The Viking and her two marines crouched by the bottom of the gangplank and laid down a barrage of fire, causing the approaching Thelicosans to scatter and take cover.

"Go!" the Viking said, using her elbow to point behind her.

Tunger scrambled up the gangplank, and Rogers followed suit. The moment he passed through the threshold, the marine mini-formation collapsed, and Rogers screamed at Flash to raise the gangplank. Pulses of disruptor energy were bouncing off the thick hull of the shuttle, creating a sort of high-pitched whine as the energy dissipated.

Rogers stood in the entryway, panting, looking for a way to get to the cockpit of the shuttle, which seemed to be slightly elevated from the passenger bay. The marines, clearly done with their shooting, immediately relaxed as if nothing interesting had happened at all and buckled themselves in. Tunger practically collapsed into his chair, rubbing the red marks on his face where his various fake facial hair had begun leaving a gross-looking rash.

"Thanks," Rogers said to all of them. "I'm going to go check on our pilot and then I can fill you in on what's going on."

The Viking gave him a dismissive hand wave and began going through cooldown procedures with her rifle and muttering with the other marines. Rogers took a long look at her, then moved toward where Flash was sitting. A voice, talking to itself, led him to the small two-person cockpit, which gave Rogers a flashback to the *Awesome*. He missed that ship.

"Flash," Rogers said as he sat down in the copilot's seat. "I took the chocks off. We can leave anytime."

"Flaps up. Throttle to quarter. Lights on. Gear down," Flash was saying. Muttering, really.

"Flaps?" Rogers said. "*Flaps?* It's space! There's no *air*!"

"Battery. Stabilizer. Comm channel one. Comm channel backup."

"Flash!" Rogers yelled. "What the hell are you doing?"

Flash, looking angry at being interrupted, glared at Rogers, the reflective surface of his aviator sunglasses shining with fury. "I'm in the middle of my preflight checklist, Skip. I can't be interrupted."

Rogers goggled. "I hardly think this is a time for checklists."

"I gotta do my boldface."

"Your what?"

"The part of the checklist that's in bold so I'll remember it."

Looking back at the control panel, Flash started mumbling.

"Damn, I forgot where I was. Flaps. Throttle. Lights."

"There are people shooting at us!" Rogers screamed.

"Tower check-in," Flash said, then pressed a button on the console. "Tower, this is Chillster Six-Five in the shuttle *Bwana*. Systems green."

"Why, why, why are you checking in with the enemy traffic control?"

"Dude, if I take off without clearance I'll totally get a nonqual on this flight. I gotta keep up my currency."

Rogers buckled his seat belt and swore he would have this man grounded for the rest of his career if he could manage it. "Is the tower responding?"

"No."

"That's because they want to kill us! Fly the goddamned ship."

"But the checklist."

Rogers rolled his eyes. He could see through the cockpit that the security detail, since they weren't being shot at anymore, were now feeling free to set up a giant turret.

"I thought you were supposed to be some kind of flashy, showy hotshot who didn't follow the rules? Who cares about a goddamn checklist? We're going to *die*, Flash!"

"But the checklist!"

The turret setup appeared to be complete, and Rogers thought that was it until a man in a crisp uniform came over to the turret with a datapad and began inspecting it, making check motions with his fingers every couple of seconds.

"See?" Flash said. "Checklists!"

"Oh for the love of . . ." Rogers yelled as he grabbed the controls, punched in what he thought was a start-up sequence, and pushed the throttle to full.

"Skip, what are you—aah!"

The shuttle jumped forward, the landing claw catching the body of the turret and knocking it across the hangar. The man with the datapad followed eagerly, and when the turret finally came to rest in a crumpled mass against the wall near the bay door, he knelt down and continued making marks on his datapad, shaking his head disapprovingly.

The shuttle screamed at incredibly unsafe speeds toward the open bay door, and Rogers wondered briefly why they hadn't simply shut the thing. It didn't matter now; they were home free if only they could—

A beep sounded on the console. If there was one thing in this world that Rogers was growing to hate more than anything else, it was beeping computer consoles.

"What does that mean?" he said, pointing to the console.

"It means you're flying the ship in a tailspin," Flash said. "Planetside, you'd be killing us right now, but since we're in space, you're probably just going to make us all throw up."

Rogers finally realized he had been looking at his hands instead of the windshield, and now the world was going sideways very fast. The *Limiter*, still very close, was passing by in a blur.

"Will you take these damn controls and fly this damn shuttle!" he said, sitting back.

"I have the spacecraft," Flash said atonally.

"Of course you have the spacecraft! I just told you you had the spacecraft. Why are you telling me you have it?"

"Checklist," Flash said.

More beeping. Rogers looked at the display and his bowels turned to water. Well, they were kind of mostly water already, right? He was an engineer, not a biochemist.

More beeps and a warning siren kicked on as the defensive systems of the shuttle told Rogers some disturbing information. Rogers was starting to wonder about Keffoule's no-fire order. She'd probably rescinded it after Rogers had humiliated her in the bar and then escaped her ship.

"What's your checklist for being pursued by three Sine fighters?"

"Definitely have a checklist for that, Skip," Flash said. "But it's only got one item on it."

Rogers looked at him, frowning. "And what's that?"

The pilot grinned, his glasses shimmering.

"Get *flashy*."

An Epidemic of Face-Kicking

A recovery crew and a fast but thorough medical examination later, Rogers rushed to the bridge of the *Flagship*. Some part of him thought he should have been appreciating the fact that he was home, taking in the sights, shaking hands with the troops amid cries of "Welcome back!" But really, he didn't have time for that shit.

"What's the situation?" he barked as the bay doors opened. He beat back the wave of nostalgia that threatened to emotionally overwhelm him—he'd been gone for a few days, at least—and focus on the task at hand. The bridge was on full alert, with both the offensive and defensive coordinators ready, equipped with laminated sheets and large headphones. Commander Belgrave was at the controls, possibly even getting ready to do something with them. The Viking had left Rogers rather abruptly, saying she was going to get the rest of the marines ready in case "shit went down," and Tunger had passed out in the medical bay.

"The situation?" Deet said. Rogers hadn't even seen him there, hiding behind a console. Why was there a turret hanging from the ceiling? "The situation? You want to know what the [EXPLETIVE] situation is? I'll tell you what the [EXPLETIVE] situation is you [MATERNAL FORNICATION] [ANATOMICAL REFERENCE]. I'm probably going to kill everyone on the ship! There is no such thing as free will! When you look into an abyss, the abyss also looks into you! Nietzsche!"

"Gesundheit," someone said.

Rogers stopped where he was, about halfway to the command dais, and looked at Deet's head poking out from behind one of the consoles. He drew a line from Deet's head to the turret, saw the Meridan marine manning the controls, and put it all together. It also helped that the marine was muttering about "blasting that batch of recycled zippers."

Rogers turned to Belgrave. "I'm assuming this is your fault."

Belgrave shrugged. "The droid had questions. I suggested some answers based on existential—"

"Shut up," Rogers said.

Rogers walked over to where Deet was hiding, shouting over his shoulder at the marine. "Get that damn turret off the ceiling. If anyone is going to kill Deet, it's going to be me."

"Don't come near me!" Deet shouted. "I might crack and droid-fu you into little tiny pieces. Stop where you are!"

"Relax," Rogers said. "First of all, you couldn't take me. Second, you're not going to droid-fu me against your own will."

"There is no such thing as my own [EXPLETIVE] will!" Deet cried.

"Yes there is," Rogers said. "Wait. I don't know if there is. You might be a computer with mismatched legs, but that doesn't mean you can't make your own choices."

"That's exactly what that means," Deet said.

Rogers got within a few feet, and Deet waggled his arms in a warning pattern. The last thing Rogers needed was a windmill droid fight in the middle of the bridge. For one, he'd lied—Deet could absolutely take him. Also, droid fu battles were possibly the most boring fights he'd ever seen in his life. It was just a bunch of arm-waving and shouting, not unlike many political rallies.

Behind him, he could hear the marine loudly protesting with a couple of technicians who were trying to help him dismantle the portable turret.

"I said take it down!" Rogers said. "That's an order!"

He was pretty sure that was the first time he'd said "That's an order," but it felt kind of good. The marine locked eyes with him for a moment, muttered something else about recycled zippers, and started to help the other two technicians take the turret down.

"See?" Rogers said. "There's nothing to worry about. The crazy people are going to take the gun away and nobody is going to shoot you."

Deet's eyes flashed, and he made an incomprehensible beeping noise. "That's not what I'm worried about. You're not listening."

"I am listening," Rogers said. "Do you understand what's going on right now? There's a giant fleet out there that is probably about to break its very brief truce with us and come and blow us out of space."

"Not helping things!" Belgrave shouted.

"And you're sitting here cowering behind a computer console. Didn't I leave you in charge?"

"That's because you're an idiot," Deet said. "You've spent most of your new career trying to prevent droids from taking over the *Flagship* and then handed it to one. That was a monumental display of poor judgment."

"Yet everyone is still here," Rogers said. "You kept the panic from spreading while I was gone, and you haven't sliced anyone into tiny, gross pieces yet. Right? Do you feel any urges to kill me?"

"Not any more than I usually do," Deet said.

"See? You're also making jokes. You were always so bad at jokes, and now you're getting better at them. What would be the point of practicing your humor if you were just going to kill everyone around who could appreciate it?"

"I guess that's true," Deet said. He stood up a little straighter, exposing some of his body out from behind the console, and the marine who had been disassembling the turret drew his pistol. Deet shrank back down.

"Will you get off the goddamned bridge?" Rogers shouted.

"Yes, sir," the marine grumbled.

"I need to figure out what's going on, Deet. And I'm going to need your help in solving this problem for sure. So you need to put aside whatever doubts you're having about your uncontrollable homicidal tendencies, come out from behind that computer, and be my deputy until this is all sorted out. We can answer questions about your free will later. How does that sound?"

Deet beeped. "Really [EXPLETIVE] [EXCREMENTAL ADJECTIVE]."

Rogers nodded. "Good." He stood up, stretching his back, and turned back to the bridge crew, all of whom were staring at him. "Now, can someone please tell me what the hell is going on here?"

Commander Rholos spoke first, covering the microphone on her massive headset. By the end of this, he would figure out what the hell that was all about.

"Sir," she said. "We haven't received any messages from the Thelicosan fleet, but it looks like they're beginning to change formations. Several of their Battle Spiders are moving into something that is either an attack formation or a retreat formation. The *Limiter* has called back all its Sine and Cosine patrols, and several of the other carriers are repositioning themselves in a way that could indicate an immediate launch."

Rogers nodded, taking all this in as he moved over to the commander's chair. He sat down in it, putting his face in his hands and rubbing at his eyes. The last couple of days hadn't afforded him much time to relax, and, to be honest, he was still feeling a little hungover. Had he really left an endless supply of Jasker 120 behind?

Think, you idiot, he thought. *There's more at stake here. What did Quinn tell you?*

"Right. We have to assume they're getting ready for war until we hear otherwise." He took a deep breath; the news he was about to deliver would have sounded crazy coming from anyone. "During my time on the enemy ship I've learned that part of the motivations of the Thelicosans may be tied to an uprising of Jupiter."

The bridge crew gasped, exchanging glances and muttering at each other. Rogers let them voice their astonishment for a moment; it really was a strange bit of news. For all anyone else knew, the Jupiterians had been assimilated for centuries.

"I know what you're thinking," he said. "But supposedly there is evidence that makes it a nondebatable truth. Communications, start a general sweep of the comm freqs and tell me if there are any holes opening up in the jamming net."

The communications tech, who had been listening intently, swiveled around in her chair dramatically to get back to her console. She did so a little too enthusiastically, however, and had to make a full rotation before she got back to her instruments.

"Sir," she said, "it's all short-range, but it's looking like some of the jamming has dissipated."

Rogers nodded. "Good. Keep an ear open for incoming data packets and route all that information to my personal terminal. Someone on the Thelicosan ship has some documents that I'm going to need to review. Within the next day, expect a clear communications channel to be open to headquarters. I'm going to prepare a packet of data to send to them, and you are to do so immediately upon the channels being available. Is that understood?"

"Yes, sir!" the comms tech said.

"Good. Deet, I want you to come up here and plug in. You're going to be my data filter."

"But what if I suddenly decide I should trip the ship's self-destruct mechanism?"

The marine who'd built the turret came running into the room holding a rifle.

"Get *out!*" Rogers said. The marine hung his head and left the bridge again. "Now, Deet, if you're thoroughly done trying to become some kind of weird self-fulfilling prophecy, get over here and plug into the ship. Quinn is going to start sending us stuff anytime now."

Deet walked over and found a power outlet near the command chair. He extended his "dongle," as he called it, despite Rogers' multiple attempts to tell him not to call it that, and plugged into the ship.

"Who is Quinn?" Deet said.

"A friend. I think. At least, someone who doesn't want to kill me, kick me in the face, or marry me. So, at this point, I'd say she's someone I can trust. When that information starts coming in, I want you to read and analyze all of it as fast as you possibly can, alright?"

"Got it."

Rogers was forgetting something, he was sure of it. He couldn't communicate with the rest of the fleet yet, so he couldn't organize a response to the offensive formations happening in Thelicosa at the moment. Even if he could, he didn't know a damn thing about battle formations in the first place. As he realized this, for some reason he was seized by a wave of despair. He didn't belong in this chair; he was worse than Klein. At least Klein would have been able to inspire the troops. Rogers had tried that once and ended up confusing everyone by talking about poker.

"Sir?" Commander Zaz said, tapping his offensive coordinator's sheet. "Should we launch our fighters and set up a screen?"

"Sure," Rogers said. "That sounds like a great idea. How many do we have operational after our milk run?"

"About sixty-five percent," Zaz said.

"Fine," Rogers said. "Take half of them and have them gear up. Put the other half on standby. And make sure Flash doesn't get in a goddamn Ravager. Or make any decisions. Or talk to anyone."

"Yes, sir."

Rogers snapped his fingers, remembering what he was forgetting. Tunger! He'd been on the enemy ship the entire time, able to move around freely without threats of betrothal or death. Rogers hadn't asked him about what he'd discovered. Maybe Tunger would have a better idea of what was going on while they were waiting for the transmission from Quinn.

"Sir," the communications tech said. "I'm getting something from the enemy ship, but it's encrypted. I'm routing it to your terminal."

"Got it," Deet said. Quinn was right on time.

"Good," Rogers said. "Someone get me Corporal Tunger. He's in the medical bay. Tell him to come up here as fast as he can."

The bridge got to work, doing whatever combat preparedness they could manage without being able to communicate with the other members of the 331st. The *Flagship*, being a, well, flagship, had ample firepower and shielding and decent maneuverability, but it certainly couldn't conduct a war on its own. Rogers hoped Quinn had the sense to start opening up some of the local comm channels, too, or they'd get blown out of space before he could do anything to prevent it.

Rogers looked out the viewscreen, watching the Thelicosan formation doing whatever it was they were doing. He hated not knowing anything about being a commander. Why had they put him in this position? Why had they promoted him to acting admiral of the ship? It didn't make any sense at all. He didn't know a flanking maneuver from a flank steak; if this did come to fleet-on-fleet war, he might as well throw himself out an airlock.

Glancing at Zaz and Rholos, who were talking animatedly into their headsets, he shook his head. He had people on this ship who knew what they were doing. He just needed to rely on them, give them enough room to do what they were trained to do. The Meridan Navy might not have been the best-trained, most disciplined, most prepared, most organized, most financially supported . . .

Forget it. They were totally screwed.

"This is some serious [EXPLETIVE] coming in, here," Deet said. "Did you read any of this?"

"Yeah," Rogers said, "I had plenty of time for leisure reading while I was fighting for my life on the *Limiter*."

Deet looked at him squarely. "So why are you making me do this if you've read it already?"

"Sarcasm, Deet. What are you finding out?"

"Well," Deet said, "first of all, this Quinn person, or whoever stole all this data, is an incredible computer hacker. She was able to blast through hundreds of layers of autocoded encryption, randomized into huge layers of entropy. Or she has some really powerful programs that do it for her."

"Whatever," Rogers said. "She's just a bureaucrat. What did you find?"

Deet beeped in a way that might have been a little angry. "Have you ever heard the expression about not judging a river by its rocks?"

Rogers hesitated. "No," he said slowly. "Have you?"

Deet ignored the counterquestion. "Anyway, the amount of information she stole is huge. You're right, Jupiter is making an uprising, but it seems like they don't have a centralized base of operations. They're segmented into units and scattered throughout the Fortuna Stultus galaxy. I can't tell how, though. They keep using the abbreviation SNG, but there's no real way to tell what it is."

Rogers swallowed. That was a lot of power, even if it was distributed all over the place. He'd heard of terrorist organizations that had similar structures in cities or on continents . . . but across the *galaxy*? That was a sleeper-cell situation on a grander scale than he'd ever heard of. But how did they do it? And what was SNG?

"Surr! Surr!"

The bridge door had opened, admitting a very tired-looking Corporal Tunger, finally free of all his disguises and dressed in a proper Meridan uniform. He stumbled across the consoles and climbed up to the command dais, but before Rogers could say a word he started rambling.

"That Zergan guy is definitely one of them. I followed him the whole time and he talked to sandwiches a bunch and wanted to kill you from the moment he saw you and tried to sabotage the negotiations even before he knew Keffoule wanted to marry you." Tunger sucked in a short, high-pitched breath. "He also tried to come into your room and stab you to death in your sleep," he said, then paused. "I didn't think that was very fancy. Trying to poison your drinks was clever, I guess, but he was using such a simple poison that the antidote was easy to drop in. It made your drinks all fizzy, but, hey, it didn't kill you, right?"

The bridge had quieted, all the personnel looking at Tunger the way one would look at . . . well, a zookeeper who had somehow realized—quite competently, actually—his dream of being a spy.

"And that's why I can't be a spy," Tunger said, his face red, breathing like he'd just run a mile.

Rogers stopped, frowning. "Wait. You saved my life three times and managed to hang out on a Thelicosan ship without being discovered. Why can't you be a spy?"

Tunger shook his head. "I can't keep a secret," he said. "I've told that story to everyone I've seen for the last two hours. It's so exciting!"

Rogers blinked, then shook his head. "Alright," he said. "Well, thanks for saving my life. I owe you one."

"Three," someone said.

"Three." Rogers accepted the correction. "I wanted to know if you had heard anything else about this Jupiter thing. If we're going to send a report to headquarters, it would be nice to know where these people are or what they're trying to do. Quinn said there were other things in motion. Do you have any idea what they are?"

"No, sir," Tunger said, regaining some of his composure. "At first I wanted to, you know, infiltrate their ranks, get promoted to deputy, and sabotage the ship, and all that. But I found out that was hard. And there was that guy trying to kill you all the time. So I got kind of busy."

Rogers nodded gravely. "I see. Well, I'll have to ask—"

"Sir! Sir!"

Rogers turned to see one of the bridge technicians who was sitting at a station he didn't recognize jumping up and down, shouting at him. Rogers squinted—some of the consoles had little signs on them to designate what the station was—and found that it was the internal security monitor. He didn't get a good feeling when the internal security monitor was shouting at him and looking panicked.

"What?" Rogers said. "And can we all agree to stop saying 'sir' twice in a row when you're panicking?"

"There have been several reports of commotion going on on the lower decks of the ship," the technician said. "People are . . ." He paused for a moment, then leaned over his terminal and spoke slowly, as if he didn't understand the significance of the words he was saying. "They're being kicked in the face?"

Rogers felt all the blood drain from his face and try to make an escape through his bladder.

"No," he said. "That's not possible. That's crazy. There's no way she's here."

The bridge door opened, and a Meridan troop came stumbling in, blood running down the side of his cheek.

"She's . . . she's . . ." he said as he collapsed.

"Crazy," Rogers finished for him.

"I," Keffoule said, standing in the doorway looking as though she hadn't expended any effort at all in brutalizing everyone between the hangar and the bridge, "am absolutely not crazy in any way." She locked eyes with Rogers. "But you will marry me now."

Quinn's pulse was beyond monitoring. Her hair bun had almost come completely unraveled, her hair flying around her face as she sprinted through the halls of the *Limiter*. Gunfire was all around her. Almost all propriety had gone by the wayside. It was sheer, horrifying chaos.

And it was amazing.

Once she'd been discovered filling out the forms to try to get the jamming net lifted, everything had become a blur. Vilia had actually *hit* a guard. Well, it had been sort of an open-palmed flailing maneuver that had haphazardly landed on the man's shoulder. It hadn't done anything, but she thought it surprised him enough to give her time to get away. She had left her computer terminal unlocked, and she had *taken a book from the ship library without checking it out.* What had she become?

"There she is!" came a cry from behind her. She dove over a laundry cart and scrambled to her feet, scattering stacks of misfiled papers behind her as she sprinted away again. The small contingent of security troops following her cried out in terror/agony as they slipped, becoming a pile of bodies on the floor.

"If you had filled them out properly I wouldn't have had them to throw!" she cried as she turned the corner.

"Attention," Zergan's voice came over the loudspeaker. "Attention. The Meridan commander has slain our Grand Marshal and taken the body back with him as a trophy. All previous orders of cease-fire have been rescinded. All personnel are to move immediately to battle stations in preparation for a full assault on the Meridan fleet."

Vilia cursed. He'd been playing that message nonstop for the last half hour, likely finally having gotten to the bridge and reviewed the security feeds. It was also the reason why he'd authorized everyone with a gun on the ship to shoot her on sight, hastily explaining that she was a traitor who had allowed this to happen. It really hadn't helped that the first group of security had caught her trying to break into Keffoule's terminal to try to kill the jamming net.

"Fire!" someone shouted as Vilia rounded the corner and came face-to-face with a security detail.

"Kepler's rotating balls," she hissed, not really knowing where that had come from, or what it meant, and turned on her heel. Politics was not supposed to be this hard! Now she had to leap-frog to as many terminals as she could and dismantle the jamming network piece by piece. The IT department was going to be so confused with all the formal requests she was going to submit to them, but perhaps that would help.

She really hoped Rogers had a handle on things back on the *Flagship*, or she was allowing her hair bun to unravel for nothing.

Keffoule seemed to have departed slightly from her previous promises of nonviolence, and had knocked over nearly everyone on the bridge in order to firmly wrap one of her hands around Rogers' neck. It hadn't made her very happy to have to chase him several times around the perimeter of the bridge, either.

"You're really not making a case for sanity," Rogers said, air squeaking out of his throat. "How did you even get on the ship?"

"I followed you," Keffoule said. "It is a perfectly natural response to chase the object of your affection. This is true even in Merida, is it not?"

"Well," Rogers said, "yeah, I guess, but 'chase' is usually figurative . . ."

"Therefore what I have done is extremely romantic, is it not?"

"I suppose in some respects—"

"Therefore you are obligated to return my romantic intention, are you not?"

Rogers paused. "No. Definitely not."

Keffoule frowned, loosening her grip on Rogers' throat. "I see. Maybe I don't understand men as much as I thought I did."

Rogers took advantage of the newfound joint freedom to shake his head. "No, I don't believe you do." Gently, he reached up and pulled her hand away, looking her in the eye as he spoke softly.

"Do you have any idea what you've done?" he said. "It looks like your pal Zergan is pushing the whole Thelicosan fleet into battle positions. He probably thinks I kidnapped you."

"I will tell him to stop."

"How?" Rogers said. "You jammed everything in the sector and our space semaphore guy is still napping from the last time we overworked him. Unless you've got homing pigeons that can survive in a vacuum, this ship will go down—and you with it—before you can get a message to him."

Keffoule retreated a bit, folding her arms. She looked uncomfortable, if still very stoic in that I'm-going-to-get-what-I-want kind of stance.

"And it doesn't matter anyway," Rogers said. "Zergan is working against you. Remember that person who was trying to kill me? Yeah. It was him. He's trying to push our systems into war. Oh, and by the way: he's also from Jupiter."

"How do you know all this?" Keffoule asked. She clearly looked like she didn't believe a word he was saying.

"Quinn," Rogers began, and then immediately regretted it.

"Quinn," Keffoule said, her whole body tensing. "That bumbling fool is worse than a bureaucratic lapdog. She's been trying to undermine me since the moment she set foot on my ship."

"You've got her wrong," Rogers said. "It's actually quite the opposite. If you'd only listen—"

"I don't have to listen to you," Keffoule said, sneering.

"Sir!"

Rogers looked past Keffoule, who also turned around, to see

the communications tech standing up and putting one hand over an ear.

"The jamming net's pattern is changing," she said. "More of the short-range channels are opening up, but we still can't get word back to headquarters. You can communicate directly with the *Limiter* if you'd like."

Keffoule grinned triumphantly. "See? He's opened the channels, probably to deliver an ultimatum. If you patch me through, I can tell him to stand down."

"Open a channel and hail the *Limiter*," Rogers said, and the communications tech went to work. A dial tone silenced the bridge, and all eyes turned to the main screen.

"Just put it on!" came a voice from the other side of the channel. Zergan. "And put the electronic warfare squadron on alert."

"Who is this?" Zergan demanded. The picture on the screen wasn't very well formed; it was still being interrupted and somewhat scrambled, but the voice was clear.

"Edris," said Keffoule, who had worked her way through the bridge with Rogers until she stood next to him on the command dais. "It's me."

Silence.

"Route this to my private terminal immediately," Zergan said.

The sound shifted, they heard a click, and then Zergan's voice was much softer and closer to the microphone.

"Alandra?" he said.

"Yes," Keffoule answered. Rogers couldn't help but notice the affection in both their tones as they used each other's first names. "I am alive."

Silence, again. Something about this made Rogers very uncomfortable. A Jupiterian!

"That is very unfortunate," Zergan said. "Very unfortunate indeed."

Keffoule stood for a moment, stunned, as she gaped at the static-filled viewscreen. Even though Rogers knew that Zergan was some kind of traitor, he still felt a little secondary shock. This was more than being a simple turncoat. Rogers could tell by the look on Keffoule's face that this was like being stabbed in the back by your best friend. Who was running off with your wife. After giving you a wedgie.

"What are you saying?" Keffoule whispered.

Zergan paused a moment and barked some orders, all of which were unintelligible.

"I wanted to recruit you," Zergan said. "In fact, I was going to. But I never had the chance; you were too busy losing your mind over that idiot Meridan."

"Hey," Rogers said.

"Hey," Tunger said.

"Not you," Rogers said. "Me."

"I followed you all over the galaxy," Zergan continued. "I turned down the biggest promotion of my career so I could take care of you after they stuck you on the edge of the system. And what do I get for it? A kick in the face and a backseat to your dreams of restoring your glory." He sighed, which seemed very uncharacteristic of the hardened military man. "And now it's too late. We have bigger plans, bigger than you and me. And now that they're in motion . . . I'm sorry. I can't fix this for you, this time. No one cared about the collateral damage when Jupiter fell, and we won't care now as Jupiter rises again."

"You really are a Jupiterian," Keffoule said. "Quinn was right."

"If I find that woman . . ." Zergan growled, then regained his composure. "It doesn't matter. This will be all over soon. My family and I have waited for this for centuries, and I won't let you, or her, stand in the way. Goodbye, Alandra."

The line went dead, leaving a stunned Keffoule standing on the command dais and staring at the blank viewscreen. Her mouth moved a few times without making any noise, and her right foot appeared to be twitching. If she kicked the viewscreen, Rogers was going to have her sedated and put in the brig.

Before he could dive over the railing to save himself from what was most certainly about to be a psychological breakdown involving lots of face-kicking, Deet made a noise.

"Rogers," Deet said. "Since some of the network has opened up, I have combined files from Quinn's transmission with some research to deduce three pieces of information for you that you may find relevant. First, Zergan's primary employer before the military was the Snaggardir corporation."

"Him and thousands of other starving high school graduates working in convenience stores," Rogers said. "So what?"

"Second," Deet said, "Zergan mentioned his family. He has blood ties to the founders of the Snaggardir corporation."

"So he got a job from an uncle. Great. Keep telling me more about Zergan's résumé while I try to figure out how to wage a space battle."

"Third," Deet continued, "have you ever studied Greek and Roman mythology?"

"No," Rogers said. "Why?"

"Because I was able to trace the origins of Zeus Holdings, Inc. They're a subsidiary company of Snaggardir's. And Zeus had another name in the Roman pantheon. Jupiter."

A pregnant silence enveloped the bridge as the gravity of all that sank in. Rogers, not liking pregnant silences very much, decided to combine profanity and stating the obvious instead.

"Snaggardir's," he whispered. "Oh shit. They are . . . the whole goddamn company . . . *they're* Jupiter!"

A Pack of Cigarettes,
A Lottery Ticket, and the
Whole Galaxy, Please

"Put the whole ship on alert," Rogers snapped. "This isn't a negotiation anymore. Do we have comms with the other ships in the fleet yet?"

"Yes, sir," the communications tech said. "We've started to receive all the status reports they've been sending since we were taken offline. All ships are in good condition except the *Gadfly*, the *Storm*, and the *Raventooth*, all of which are experiencing various systems failures.

"*Raventooth?*" Rogers said. "That's an absurd name for a ship. Ravens don't have teeth."

He made the joke to hide his rising horror. He really had no idea what his inventory was. In fact, he'd never heard any of those ship names; he had no idea what they were, what they could do, or what capability had been lost because they weren't ready to fight. Worse, he didn't know how to find out without alerting everyone on the ship that he had no idea what he was doing.

"Sir," Commander Rholos said, "they're just cargo ships. I

recommend moving them to a position where they can dash toward the Un-Space point if we're able to open up a hole."

Rogers blinked at her a few times, then nodded. That sounded like a good idea. Better than anything he'd come up with, anyway.

Your crew, he thought. *They're not all morons like you.*

"Commander Zaz," Rogers said, sitting down in his chair and grabbing the armrests tightly. "Put together a recommended battle plan to augment Rholos' idea. We can't beat them head-on, but I want you to focus on drawing their ships away from the Un-Space point so that we can make a staggered retreat."

"Yes, sir," Commander Zaz said, saluting sharply and beginning to talk very animatedly into his headset.

"Captain Rogers," Keffoule said. She looked very pale.

"Later," Rogers barked. "Commander Rholos, it's your show. Work with Zaz on a strategy to minimize casualties."

Rholos nodded and walked over to where Zaz was standing, pointing at his laminated sheet. The two of them looked like they had worked together for a long time, but Rogers could tell immediately that both were nervous and rusty. Hell, everyone was rusty; open warfare hadn't been fought in two hundred years.

Rogers leaned over to Deet and whispered as softly as he could. "Do we have, like . . . a ship inventory or something like that?"

"You don't know what you have in your fleet, do you?" Deet said, making no attempt to keep his voice quiet.

Rogers felt his face turn red. "It's not that," he said. "Of course I know how many ships I have in my fleet. It's my fleet. I just want to, you know, confirm."

"Right," Deet said. "I'll transfer a fleet roster to your datapad along with Sun Tzu's book."

"Wait," Rogers said. "Sun Tzu? The ancient Chinese military strategist? How is that going to help me now?"

"Not the original Sun Tzu," Deet said. "Sun Tzu Jr."

"I don't know how his son is any more modern."

"It's actually his great-great-to-the-tenth-power-grandson. His book is called *The Art of War II: Now in Space.*"

"Oh, right," Roger said. He'd heard of it before—everyone in the military had heard of that book. "Commander Belgrave," he said. "Promise me you actually know how to fly this ship."

"I could have Flash do it if you don't trust me," Belgrave said.

"I retract my statement. The rest of you—if you're not actively doing something, take a few minutes and try to focus. Get some food. Have a drink. Whatever you need to do, I want you back in your seats in twenty minutes ready to fight."

It was then that he noticed that the bridge was completely silent. Everyone was staring at him, even Keffoule, whose mouth had opened slightly. Deet appeared to be staring at him too, but Deet had glowing orbs for eyes and always appeared to be staring at something.

Then, without anyone saying anything, everyone on the bridge slowly raised their arms in that really dramatic salute that everyone had always done for Klein.

"Stop that!" Rogers said. "Salute me when everyone is *not* dead after this."

Everyone dropped their arms.

"Wow," Belgrave said. "Are you going to write a book of leadership quotes someday?"

"Shut up."

The bridge crew did as they were told, scattering to get some last-minute sustenance in before the battle began. Rogers thought that perhaps giving them twenty minutes was too much; from what he could see on the displays, it looked like the Thelicosan fleet was going to be in attack position long before that. His stomach felt like it was vibrating at an extremely high frequency, sending bile up his throat. There had been many times lately when Rogers had legitimately thought he was going to die, but there was something about this that was different. It wasn't that other people might die too. That was nothing new either.

This time, though, if—*when* they did, it was going to be his fault.

"Captain Rogers, please," Keffoule said quietly, breaking Rogers out of his spiraling decline into fear and panic.

"I don't have time right now," Rogers said, shaking his head and trying not to look at her. In reality, this was all *her* fault. "If you haven't noticed, we're about to start shooting."

"That's precisely why you should listen," Keffoule said. "I need to apologize for the way I've acted."

Rogers turned slowly to look at her and found a different woman before him. She didn't look hard or determined. She didn't look incensed or crazy. Those two configurations being the only two—other than stone drunk—in which he had seen her, it was surprising to see a face that looked soft, pondering, and maybe even a little vulnerable.

"Go on," Rogers said.

"I . . ." She paused and swallowed. "I let my ambitions get ahead of my logic and my vision. Even though we thought you were going to attack us, I think any amount of further research would have revealed that it was wrong. At the least, I could have just sent a shuttle through the border to confirm. But instead, I rushed headlong for selfish, foolish—yet mathematically very solid—reasons."

Rogers waited a moment. "And then?"

"I kicked you in the face."

"You kicked me in the face," Rogers said, nodding.

"Sir," someone said from his left. He turned to see the communications tech flagging him down.

"I'll be right there!" Rogers yelled back, then turned to Keffoule. "Look, I appreciate the apology, but I'll point out that it doesn't change the fact that we're about to have a lot of newly created space dust in this sector, some of which is going to be composed of people I know. I don't know what any of this has to do with what's about to happen."

Keffoule nodded, as though she'd expected this reply, and all of a sudden the hard commander was back on her face.

"Because I think I can help you. Zergan might be able to convince some of the fleet that I'm dead, but I've been commander of that fleet for a long time. If I can contact some of the ships directly, I might be able to persuade them to help us."

Rogers stared at her, chewing on the inside of his lip as he thought. That certainly would help even the odds. "Why should I trust you?"

"I've done a lot of things to you," Keffoule said. "Lying is not one of them."

It made sense, he supposed. If Keffoule had wanted to kill him or blow up his fleet, there were a hundred easier ways to do it. Unless she was the sort of psychopath who only got a thrill out of something when it was extraordinarily difficult, there was no reason for her to kidnap him, try to marry him, then follow him back onto his own ship for the express purpose of throwing the war in Thelicosa's—Jupiter's, really—favor.

"Fine," he said, standing up. "Come with me."

He circled around the command platform and walked through the multiple computer consoles over to where the communications station was. The technician was standing at her station, squinting at her terminal. When Rogers came over, she stood up straighter, threw a cautious eye at Keffoule, and saluted.

"What is it?" Rogers asked.

"I just wanted to show you what was going on with the jamming," said the tech—Starman First Class Brelle, he saw finally. She'd been on the bridge a lot, and it was nice to finally know her name. "The pattern keeps changing. It's like certain parts of it are turning on and off at random intervals."

"That's weird," Rogers said, frowning. "I wonder what Quinn is up to?"

"Get out of my way!" Vilia yelled, throwing an improvised Molotov cocktail at a group of Thelicosan marines. It exploded on contact, spreading fire everywhere and stopping them in their tracks.

Wait a minute. Where in the world had she gotten a Molotov cocktail? She'd run out of loose paper to throw, but this seemed like an unnecessary—and highly irregular—escalation. And when had she tied a bandanna around her head?

Highly irregular. And maybe a teensy bit awesome.

Awesome? she thought. *When do I ever say the word "awesome"?*

She'd been operating in one of the medical bays, but obviously they'd caught on. Anytime she logged onto a terminal, someone in cybersecurity was pinpointing her location and transmitting it to the nearest security team. It seemed like the IT department had caught on to what she was doing too; as she was filling out requests to disable parts of the jamming net, someone else was filling out requests to turn them back on. Whoever it was, they had no idea who they were dealing with.

Cutting the terminal's power cord—and filing a quick repair request with the maintenance department—Vilia jumped over the desk and around the flames, finding an exit that wasn't going to force her to harm any more of her Thelicosan brethren. She hoped they would forgive her for this once it was all over and they all knew the truth.

But what if they already did know the truth? What if Jupiterians had already infiltrated every facet of the Thelicosan military? What if *she* was the odd woman out? She had to hurry.

She brought up the ship's map on her datapad. If she was going to disable enough of the net to allow Rogers to send a message, she was going to have to go to the heart of the beast itself—the IT service desk—and overload it with data requests and repair tickets until it buckled. Bureaucracy could absolutely solve this situation.

And if not bureaucracy, *another Molotov cocktail!*

Calm yourself, Vilia thought. *You are a stable, professional woman with excellent organizational skills. You have a job to do.*

And to do it, she'd first have to get to the IT service desk. She gritted her teeth and set a course for the place where hopes and dreams went to die.

"Well, hopefully she is taking care of things," Rogers said. "Keep the channels open and keep sending updates to the rest of the fleet. When Commanders Zaz and Rholos come up with their plan, I'm going to need you to burst-transmit the orders in small packages so that we're sure they get through. Understand?"

"Yes, sir," Brelle said, nodding. She seemed very sharp for a young S1C.

"One more thing," Rogers said after hesitating a moment. "I need your help with the Grand Marshal here."

Brelle cleared her throat, a hand floating up to protect her face. "I'm not sure I'm qualified, sir."

"No, not like that. I need to give her open access to some communications equipment. She's convinced she can direct some of the Thelicosan ships to turn against their own. Any ideas on where we can put her so that she can communicate freely without hampering our own operations?"

Starman Brelle thought for a moment, her eyebrows sinking as she frowned. "Well," she said, "there is the war room. That's meant to hold several channels at once. And you could open one channel to connect her to the bridge, so that you can coordinate."

"I'm pretty sure there's a hobo living in the war room," Rogers said, "but that's a good idea. Grand Marshal, I'll show you the way."

Without motioning for Keffoule to follow—just because the woman had apologized didn't mean he had to be nice to her—Rogers went back to the command dais to check in with Deet.

"I'm taking the Grand Marshal to her battle station," Rogers said. "Hold the fort while I'm gone."

Deet beeped. "I possess strength on par with a demigod, but even I could not hold an entire fort."

Rogers sighed. "Expression. You're in charge while I go set up Face-Kicker here. Anything new from Quinn's data?"

"Only that Snaggardir's—Jupiter—has been planning a galactic takeover for the last several hundred years, and has already tried to do it twice."

"Really?"

"Yes," Deet said. "The Two Hundred Years (And Counting) Peace was actually a mistake on their part that they refer to as the Great Failure. The treaty-signing event was supposed to be blown up, killing all the Galactic leaders and creating a power vacuum that they intended to fill."

"What happened?" Rogers asked.

"The guy heading the attack overslept."

Rogers blinked. "Right. Well, keep things in order here until I get back. And please stop talking about killing everyone. It's even starting to make me nervous."

Deet paused for a moment, looking out the window, then looked back at Rogers. "Does this mean I'm a Jupiterian too?"

"Droid. You're a droid. Please stop with the humanizing, okay? You can't even tell a good joke yet, and you're worried about your ethnicity."

A contrite processing noise emitted from Deet's mouthpiece. "You said my jokes were getting better!"

"Because that made you stop trying so much," Rogers said as he left the bridge and stepped into the hallway of the command deck.

Keffoule and Rogers walked in silence for a moment, the command deck mostly empty. Casting a glance at his old room—the one that was still in null-g—he couldn't help but think of everything that had happened in such a short time. Just a few weeks ago he'd been cursing Klein for being right about not being able to hang himself without gravity. He wondered how Cadet the cat was doing; Cadet had gotten used to the room and had refused to leave, so Tunger had been taking care of him.

"You do not have Chariots?" Keffoule asked quietly.

"No," Rogers said. "We have the up-line and the in-line. It's like trams. The war room is on the other side of the ship on this deck, so we'll take the in-line."

"I see."

It was an innocuous, stupid question, but for some reason now that Keffoule had spoken, the tension between them seemed to lessen a bit. Now instead of simultaneously wanting to kill her and being absolutely terrified of her, Rogers just sort of wanted her to go away for a while so he didn't have to think about it. The war room would be a perfect place to tuck her away. And yes, possibly win the war, but as far as Rogers' ego was concerned, that was kind of on the periphery.

They boarded the car without another word, though the car attendant looked at Keffoule like she was some kind of weird alien. Which, in some respects—in a lot of respects—she was. Keffoule didn't seem to notice, however, and the car was otherwise empty. Rogers sat down.

"It'll be a minute," Rogers said.

"Nkksht sp, mrrngna," the Public Transportation Announcer Corpsman said.

"What did he say?" Keffoule asked.

"Who knows?" Rogers said. "He's a PTAC. That just means he's good at his job."

The car stopped, and Rogers had to look out the window to recognize that they were not, in fact, near the war room. Someone had called the car, and, as the door opened, Rogers wished they had just walked instead.

"You!" the Viking said as she dove into the car and tackled Keffoule to the ground.

Well, she tried to tackle Keffoule to the ground. Being as nimble as she was, Keffoule jumped up and vaulted over one of the seats to get out of the way.

Well, she tried to vault over one of the seats to get out of the way. Her hip clipped the top of the seat, thrown off by the fact that the car had just started to move, and she tumbled forward into Rogers, who tumbled into the Viking, who made to hit Rogers in the face. Rogers ducked.

Well, he tried to duck. Since he was already on the floor, he really just sort of curled up into a ball, which resulted in the Viking hitting Keffoule in the back of the leg, which resulted in Keffoule's default spinning back kick going wild and striking one of the posts inside the car, which resulted in it bending slightly.

"No toothpicks," Keffoule said enigmatically.

"Stop!" Rogers said. "Stop. Both of you stop."

"Like hell I'm going to stop," the Viking said, in her big, beautiful voice. "This crazy idiot probably killed us all."

Keffoule was about to say something—and the look in her eyes told Rogers it wasn't going to be something flattering—but Rogers interrupted them both by disregarding his own personal safety and standing between them.

"We have to put that behind us," he said. "She'll answer for what she's done when this is all over, if we manage to make it out of here alive. For now, let's postpone the beating-to-a-pulp, alright?"

The Viking and Keffoule looked at each other like a pair of bulldogs on very taut leashes. Rogers would hate to see the damage they'd do to each other—and the atmosphere of the planet they were on—if they were let loose. He made a mental note to try to prevent a nuclear reaction before the war was over.

"You're the rescuer," Keffoule said coldly as she straightened her uniform and moved to the other side of the car. "A little late, weren't you?"

The Viking, in a moment of conversational brilliance, responded with an obscene gesture.

The car, steadily moving toward the station at which the war room was located, was a silent pressure cooker as the two women warriors looked at each other, Rogers standing hopelessly in the middle. He was good at ducking, yes, but that didn't do as much for preventing open warfare as it did for preventing head trauma. If they wanted to get into it, they'd get into it.

After a few moments of silence, the Viking finally spoke up first.

"Going on a date?" she said nonchalantly.

"What?" Rogers said.

"Yes," Keffoule said.

"No!" Rogers said. "We're not going on a date. We're going to the war room so the Grand Marshal here can try her best to avoid all of us dying in horrible ways. She's going to command the loyalist part of the Thelicosan fleet."

The Viking looked her up and down, frowning. "You'd better not screw this up."

"I don't screw things up, you Neanderthal," Keffoule said.

"Done a damn good job so far, haven't you?" the Viking quipped.

"Holy crap," Rogers said. "If you two don't cool your jets, I will turn this car around and take you both back to the bridge."

The two women made similar *harrumph* noises.

"Now," Rogers said, "what were you doing heading to the war room?"

"I wasn't," the Viking said. "I was battle planning."

"In the in-line?"

"Nobody rides back and forth on the command deck. There's nowhere to go. I come up here to clear my head every once in a while." The Viking reached a well-muscled arm to scratch at the back of her head. Rogers couldn't help but notice that her uniform shirt was drenched in sweat. Rogers wondered what it smelled like.

Focus!

"Oh," he said finally, remembering that he'd asked her a question. "Well, why don't you come with us? I might need someone to throw large barrels out the door again."

The Viking looked at him, then looked at Keffoule, then back at him. Then she spat.

"Fine."

"Fine," Keffoule said, without prompting.

"Fine," Rogers said, because it seemed like the right thing to do. But everything was not fine.

This was not fine. Nothing was fine.

A short time later, Keffoule was firmly established as the Slumlord of the *Flagship*, ready to command her own force to fire on other parts of her own force. It wasn't the grandest of accommodations, but it was effective. And it was a hell of a lot better than having her on the bridge, staring at him and making proposals.

"How soon will we know how much firepower you can bring?" Rogers asked as he kicked aside a couple of banana peels.

"It depends on who I can contact," Keffoule said. "I only learned about Zergan's betrayal today, so I don't know if he has his claws in any of the other ships. I know some of the ship captains personally, so those I can be sure about *if* their crew hasn't been compromised. Fifteen percent of the fleet, perhaps."

Fifteen percent. Had Rogers had any real idea of what he was doing, he might have said that fifteen percent might be enough to turn the tide of the battle. In reality, he still wasn't even completely sure how many ships he had on his own side, so that calculation was a little beyond him at this point.

"Fine," he said. "Just make sure you tell us whenever a ship comes over to our side so we can update our IFF."

Keffoule looked at him, her expression unreadable. "Are you giving me orders, Captain Rogers?"

Rogers couldn't help but feel his face turning a little red. "As a matter of fact, I am. Just remember that I'm the only reason you're not in the brig right now."

That was a lie. Rogers still wasn't sure how many of the ship's crew she'd rendered unconscious with all her face-kicking; it would have taken most of the war effort just to stuff this woman into a cell. But he could pretend.

Keffoule looked at him appraisingly for a moment, then very subtly bit her lip and went to work with the communications console. Rogers suppressed a shudder.

"Sir," a voice said from the computer. It was S1C Brelle, the communications tech back on the bridge. "It looks like the Grand Marshal is all set up. She can start trying to make contact whenever she'd like. The grid is still popping in and out of the jamming net, though, so connections might be spotty until whoever is disabling it gets a better handle on things."

"Got it, thanks," Rogers said. "We're on our way back to the bridge now."

Rogers and the Viking left without another word; Keffoule was already back in business mode and had her face buried in the console, anyway. Rogers could have set off an explosion and she probably wouldn't have noticed.

Once back in the in-line, Rogers noticed a subtle tension in the air. The Viking wasn't really looking at him. In fact, she hadn't looked at him since the scuffle in the car. She hadn't said anything, either. Sitting down on one of the seats, the Viking pointedly looked out the narrow window that exposed the blurry insides of the *Flagship* to passengers.

Rogers took the cue and sat down as well, far enough away that she couldn't reach him with a back fist, but close enough that it didn't seem like he thought she was a poison viper or anything. The car went along in silence for a few moments.

"You know," Rogers said finally, "I never did say thanks for coming to get me. You know that crazy politician was about to stuff me in a milk container and shoot me over to get picked up? Ha ha. Ha. Hum."

The Viking spared him a little glance before looking back out the window. A grunt was her only real response. Rogers swallowed.

"It's just that, you know, I wanted to say, that, uh . . ."

The Viking's fist slammed into the side of the car, sending vibrations all the way to Rogers' seat. The car shuddered for a moment, the lights flickering, and then everything was back to normal.

"You really need to learn the benefits of keeping your mouth shut," the Viking said. "I've been sitting here trying to think of a way to apologize to you for being a shithead, but every time I come up with something to say you start blabbering. Sit there quietly for a second, will you?"

Rogers, straight-backed, put his hands on his thighs and forced his lips closed. More strings of stupidity came to his mind, trying to batter their way out through his teeth, but he held them at bay. Another six or seven long seconds passed, and he thought he was going to explode. He realized he was holding his breath and let out a long, desperate-sounding sigh, at which the Viking gave him a look that just made him hold his breath again. This was probably not good for his heart.

"It's just that, you know, I wanted to say, that, uh . . ." the Viking said.

"That sounds familiar," Rogers said, then clapped his hands over his mouth.

"What did you say?" the Viking said.

Rogers just shook his head and made a muffled "no" noise.

"Maybe I was a little hard on you, that's all," the Viking said. "You didn't ask to get promoted four times in the span of a week, or whatever. And you did help save the ship from all those metal idiots. So I guess I kind of owe you."

Visible effort was written all over the Viking's face as she awkwardly let the words spill out. Clearly apologies and discussions about feelings were not part of her normal lexicon. Truth be told, they weren't really a part of Rogers', either.

"And you've been nice to me, I guess, apart from trying to steal my job and humiliate me."

Rogers gave her a flat look. "Did you *see* what I did as the AIGCS commander?"

The Viking shrugged. "Just because you sucked at it didn't make it any worse for me as a marine. Anyway, I know you didn't ask for the job. That's not my point."

Rogers willed himself to silence and let her go on.

"I'm just not used to this, I guess. Maybe when this is all over—"

"Nxt stpp, crngm centaur."

If Rogers ever found the PTAC who had just interrupted the Viking's speech with talk of magical horse/humans, he was going to strangle him.

"Well," the Viking said hurriedly, standing up. "We're here. Let's go win a war. I'm going to go get the marines ready."

She walked out of the car so fast that Rogers was still sitting when she vanished from view. He jumped out of his seat and tried to catch up with her to make her finish whatever it was she'd been about to say, but by the time he got out of the car she was gone.

It didn't matter, though, because someone was running out of the bridge door, waving his arms frantically and yelling in a very unmilitary way.

"Captain Rogers!" he said. "Sir! They're coming."

War Is Hell

Rogers tried to compare the experience to cramming for a final exam during school—something that he'd done often, and typically very successfully—but this just wasn't the same. Deet had transferred Sun Tzu Jr.'s *The Art of War II: Now in Space* to his datapad, but now that he looked at it, Rogers realized he had possessed a copy for years. Everyone in the military had a copy of that book. In fact, he was pretty sure everyone in *every* military had a copy of that book. It was the premier guide on space battle tactics, and Zen meditation, and even had a very short chapter on what to do if your environment was opened to vacuum.

The problem was, it didn't make any damn sense. There wasn't even much discussion of specific tactics, and Rogers could tell that most of it was a rip-off of the first *Art of War*. The first page said, "If you know the enemy and know yourself you need not fear the results of a hundred battles . . . in space."

Rogers *did* know the enemy. And he *did* know himself. And that was precisely *why* he was scared shitless.

Another quote said, "Supreme excellence consists in breaking the enemy's resistance without fighting . . . in space."

This was a pile of garbage. But it was all he had to go with. The middle of the book did break down a bit into actual maneuvering tactics, but the data was so old that it was hard to apply it to modern military spacecraft. The Two Hundred Years (And Counting) Peace hadn't done much for the development of tactics. Why practice war when you thought you would be in perpetual peace? Regardless, he was confident—if only barely—that if he applied the doctrine in this book, he could at least achieve a stalemate long enough to get some ships through the Un-Space point.

"Rholos, Zaz," he said. "Come up here, please. Let me see what you've got."

The offensive and defensive coordinators stopped what they were doing—which really was just standing by an orange water cooler and looking angry—and came up to the command chair.

As they came to stand next to him, a mystery was finally solved; he could see what was written on their laminated sheets. Although there were dry-erase markings all over the sheets, the contents immediately tickled his memory, particularly because he had just seen the same images and words a few seconds ago. Each of them had an abridged copy of *The Art of War II: Now in Space* on laminated sheets. It looked like a toddler's cut-and-paste collage, but he supposed it was effective.

"Well," Rogers said, "at least I know we're all reading off the same sheet of music."

"I hardly think this is the time to break out into [EXPLETIVE] song," Deet said.

"Expression. Now, what are your thoughts?"

Zaz, as offensive coordinator, went first. "Well," he said, "I think we should try to pretend inferiority and encourage his arrogance . . . in space."

Rholos nodded. "And I suggest that invincibility lies in the defense . . . in space."

Rogers looked between the two of them, blinking. "That's it? That's all you've come up with?"

"To be fair," Rholos said, shaking her head, "you only gave us twenty minutes to come up with a battle plan, and nobody on this ship has seen actual combat, since none of us are two hundred years old."

Rogers conceded the point. "Alright. But what does this mean?"

"We're pretty much going to wing it and do what the book tells us to do," Zaz said, lowering his voice. "Our fighters go out and try to screen the oncoming bombers while providing escort to our own, and the big gunships stay as far back as they can while remaining in effective range. The *Flagship* coordinates everything and stays in the center mass of our defensive ships."

"And," Rholos said, "we always attack them just a little bit too far to the left."

Rogers looked at her. "What? Why?"

"We're trying to draw them away from the Un-Space point. Once they get far enough away, the faster ships without enough firepower to continue contributing to the fight double back and make for the exit. Once we're in Un-Space, we're in the clear. Even if they follow us, they'll follow us right into the brunt of the Meridan defensive force."

Rogers let his gaze pass between the two of them. He thought through the plan as hard as he could, weighing the costs and benefits of each of their strategies. In his mind, he played out scenarios, war-gaming how the two forces would meet, trying to factor in all the unintended consequences and unexpected developments. Then, when he thought he had it all sorted, he took a deep breath.

"You two know I have no idea what the fuck I am doing, right?" he said.

Both of them nodded.

"Good. Go and try your best to make us not die."

Zaz and Rholos saluted, then left the dais to go do their jobs. Rogers looked at the display, which had been changed to what looked like a giant chessboard that listed the known friendly and enemy units, displayed in real time based on all the sensor data and live reports. It looked like red-and-blue confetti that could potentially kill everyone.

"Two minutes until their front line is in their engagement envelope," Rholos said.

Rogers looked at Belgrave, who didn't look at all like he was about to be in the middle of a giant space battle. He was reclined in his helmsman's station like normal; he even had a sandwich sitting on the console.

"Are you sure you know how to make the ship go through maneuvers?"

Belgrave looked at Rogers, narrowed his eyes, and reached out to press a single button on the console. The *Flagship* started to move into position. Belgrave took a bite out of his sandwich.

"Right," Rogers said. "Technology. Good." He cleared his throat and pressed a button on his command console so that he could connect directly with the war room. "Grand Marshal? How are things going? Were you able to contact any of your ships?"

Keffoule's voice came through, icy cold and calm. She was a *real* commander. Maybe Rogers should just cede command of everything to her.

"Not as good as I had hoped. The connections are still spotty; every time I make a connection and try to transmit my message, the jamming profile changes and I get cut off. I did try to tell a few of the ships to forward my message, but they're going to have as difficult a time as I did."

"One minute until engagement!"

"Damn it," Rogers muttered. "We need to open up this jamming net. What is taking Quinn so long?"

Like many members of the government world, Quinn had always dreamed of a situation where she could punch members of the

IT department in the face. At long last, she'd gotten her chance.

Unfortunately, the IT department could also punch back. She'd fought/politely requested her way through countless security teams and other personnel, but the IT help desk was proving to be the hardest nut to crack by far. It might have had something to do with the fact that IT personnel were about as good at fighting as she was, which was not very good. If Vilia was being honest with herself, it had all probably looked like a cage match between wet lettuce and newly born fawns.

Even now, as she stood next to a chair at the main access console and started utilizing the IT computers to fast-track her requests to Communications, disabling parts of the jamming net, more IT troops were filing out of doors she hadn't even seen when she'd come in, wielding various nontraditional weapons that mostly consisted of outdated hardware. By Newton's apple, where were all these people coming from?

As she dodged a wristwatch cell phone, Quinn swore. She'd thought she'd be able to access everything from here, but since the ship was on full alert, many of the functions had been shut down. She'd briefly thought about filing paperwork to disable the *Limiter* altogether, but now that was impossible. The bridge had full command of many of the major systems, which meant that Quinn was going to have to get to Zergan if she was going to do anything useful. Worse, some of the platforms doing the actual signal emissions for the jamming net were located on the fringe of the formation and were no longer communicating. Long-range comms would stay down until this battle was over or someone jumped through the Un-Space point.

Quinn wiped sweat from her forehead. She needed to get to the bridge, and to do that, she needed to get a message to Rogers.

Rogers had seen fighting before, but he had never seen war. After the first few minutes, he was pretty sure he didn't like it. Pirates blowing each other up was one thing; this was something entirely different and horrible. Billions of credits' worth of giant metallic war machines were clashing in the depths of space, trying desperately to punch holes in each other with multicolored plasma bursts and penetration warheads. Deflector shields flashed, crackling like ship-shaped lightning. Thelicosan Battle Spiders crawled around the blackness, disgorging wave after wave of ordnance.

Worse, it was already clear that Keffoule's meddling hadn't been enough to turn the tide; instead, it seemed to have pushed them into a stalemate. With every move Rogers and his team made, the Thelicosans would counter it so quickly it was like they had thought of it first. Glancing at *The Art of War II: Now in Space*, Rogers tried to apply the meager scraps of war tactics doled out by the ill-equipped Sun Tzu Jr., but it was a lost cause.

"Big guns fire far," the book advised, "but they generally blow up pretty easily. Keep them back and away from the other guy's big guns . . . in space."

Rogers looked up from the manual, shaking his head. Despite how horrific and terrifying a large-scale space battle was, he couldn't help but notice that not a whole lot of stuff was blowing up. In fact, it kind of seemed like nothing was happening at all. A ship would charge ahead, fire enough shots to weaken another ship's shields, but then back off, giving the other ship enough time to recharge.

"This . . . this is kind of boring," Rogers said aloud. "It's like one giant droid fu match."

"I resent that statement," Deet said, whirring his arms in what was probably supposed to be a threatening way.

Zergan's superior military experience should have been enough to turn the tide in the Thelicosans' favor, even without a numerically superior force. But this was starting to look more like a Ping-Pong match than a war. What was Zergan planning?

"Grand Marshal," Rogers said, tapping into the war room's comm system. "You worked with Zergan for years. Is there anything about his strategy that I can exploit? Does he do something stupid?"

There was a pause. "Thelicosans do not do stupid things, Captain Rogers. Thelicosans do things mathematically, and math is never wrong."

"You never saw my high school workbook," someone in the back of the room said.

"Now is not the time for pride," Rogers barked back. "Can you think of any time, in any instance, when Zergan was a complete moron?"

"No," Keffoule said firmly. "We study doctrine and tactics very thoroughly and practice it regularly."

Rogers thought for a moment, then looked up at the display. It really did look like a mirror image; though the Thelicosan and Meridan ships were different structurally, they followed the same basic class divisions. After all, most of them had been built to counter each other through the last millennium of arms races. What was he missing?

"Hey," he said at last, "when you were studying, what doctrine did you use?"

"The only one there is," Keffoule said. *The Art of War II.*"

Oh my god, Rogers said. *We're all doing the same thing.*

Of course it looked like the Thelicosans were mirroring the Meridans' movements. They were the only movements they knew. Zergan was operating out of the same playbook that Rogers was. Which meant that if Rogers was going to win this war, he would have to burn the playbook.

"Zaz! Rholos! Throw those laminated sheets away and listen to me carefully."

The two coordinators looked at him like he'd just told them to open the room to vacuum.

"Trust me," Rogers said. "Just come over here."

They exchanged glances, looked down at their sheets, and then both walked over without throwing them away.

"I want you to forget all that stuff," Rogers said when they were close. "The Thelicosans are operating out of the same manual that we are."

"Of course they are," Commander Rholos said. "It's the only manual there is."

Rogers looked at her. "And that doesn't strike you as ineffective?"

Rholos shrugged. Zaz looked at his laminated sheet to try to find an answer to Rogers' question.

"I'm telling you, forget all that. If we're going to beat Zergan, we're going to have to work completely outside that book."

"But that's impossible," Zaz said. "Even if we were to throw every copy away, it's what we've all been studying since we joined the military. We can't unlearn all that doctrine in just a few minutes."

Rogers sat back in his chair. "I know. Which is why you need me."

"How are you any different?" Rholos asked.

"Because I don't do homework. I don't know the first thing about space strategy." He sat up straighter, puffed his chest out, and barked loudly, "You hear me, everyone? I don't know the first thing about space strategy!"

He was probably pretty naive to expect a rousing cheer or one of those slow salutes he hated. Instead, what he got was the stunned silence of the bridge and Belgrave shaking his head and muttering offensive things under his breath.

"No," Rogers said. "Listen. I know how that sounded. Um. It's not that I don't know anything about space strategy." He paused for a second while he tried to gather the words that seemed to keep falling stupidly out of his mouth. "It's that I have a new strategy. A secret strategy. Yeah, that's it. A secret strategy that I've been saving to combat Sun Tzu Jr. And now that we have the chance, I'm finally going to employ it."

"What's it called?" someone shouted from the back.

"Common sense," Rogers said.

"Captain," Commander Belgrave said softly, "this is the military. You can't just come in here and start throwing those words around."

Rogers ignored him. "Everyone listen up. We're going to win this battle—"

"Sir!" the communications tech said. "There's a message coming from the *Limiter.*"

". . . Right after I take this call! We're going to win this battle in like *five minutes!*"

Rogers sat down and nodded to the comm tech, who changed the display to show what appeared to be a woman who had just rolled out of bed. And down a hill. The picture was fuzzy, and the audio was a little crackly, but after a moment Rogers finally recognized who it was: Secretary Quinn.

"Secretary!" he said. "Are you okay? You look like hell. Shouldn't you be hiding somewhere on the ship?"

"Hiding? And miss this? Ha!" Quinn said.

The person looking back at him was definitely not the woman he'd met on the *Limiter.* The conservative, careful woman had been replaced by a teenage girl who had stolen her father's convertible. Her hair wasn't even in a bun, and she appeared to be holding a pen like a bowie knife.

"Did you just say 'ha'? Do you even know how to laugh?"

"I'm learning. Listen, I have something to tell you."

"The floor is yours," Rogers said.

"I'm not going to be able to lift the entire jamming net the way I'm doing it now. I need to get to the bridge."

"What does that have to do with me?"

"During combat operations, the bridge doors lock and can only be opened from the inside or if an emergency evacuation is triggered."

Rogers frowned. "Can't you just pull the fire alarm or something?"

He couldn't see very clearly in the picture, but he was pretty sure Quinn made an are-you-stupid face at him.

"Are you stupid?" she asked. "No, I can't just do that. There are fail-safes in place for that. I'm going to need you to score a direct hit on the *Limiter* and send me the message that the Grand Marshal has been broadcasting to the other ships in the fleet so I can show it to the *Limiter*'s crew."

Rogers barked a laugh. "Fat chance. I think I can turn the tide a bit, but it's going to take me a long time to punch through all that other stuff."

"I can fill out a form to disable the shields for a small window and transmit the location of the ship's outboard emergency response system to you. If you can put a single warhead on that target, it should trigger the ship's evacuation system and open up the bridge. Then I can take Zergan down and lift the jamming net."

"What do you mean 'take Zergan down'? Since when are politicians taking anything down except education funding?"

"Very funny. Can do you do it or not? I might be able to bring down the organic defenses, too, so they can't launch countermeasures."

Rogers thought for a moment, chewing on his lip.

"I'll do it," he said. "But do me a favor—don't kill Zergan. I've got some questions for him when we're done here. And Secretary . . . how are you doing all this?"

She actually, no-kidding grinned at him.

"Properly," she said, and the line cut out.

Rogers stared at the screen for a moment. Combat certainly did strange things to people.

It was an absolutely insane plan, but it was the only one they had. And if it was going to work, he'd have to open a hole wide enough in the Thelicosan defensive line to get enough ships in, then find someone who was crazy enough to dive straight into the enemy with no regard for his own safety or the safety of his wingmen.

It would have to be someone who practically exuded chaos. An agent of mayhem.

"Get me Lieutenant Lieutenant Fisk," Rogers said over his shoulder. "Tell him I've got something for him. And tell him it's . . ." He sighed, not believing what he was about to say.

"Tell him it's flashy."

The whole world of space tactics seemed to open up to Rogers at once. Once his nose wasn't buried in ellipses that ended in the words "in space," he thought he could really start to see what was going on out there. The display made more sense when he was looking at it instead of diagrams on his datapad, and he found it was much easier to keep a mental inventory of the ships and ship types when he wasn't also concerned with trying to understand the meaning behind phrases like "the quality of a decision is like the well-timed swoop of a falcon . . . in space."

Rogers wasn't a biologist, but he was pretty sure falcons died in space like most other organic matter.

Seeing that some of his larger battleships were being pressed by the more agile Battle Spiders, he ordered some of the Ravagers peppering the Sine and Cosine screen to break off and distract the Battle Spiders. That might give them time and space to reposition themselves and start punching holes in the line of Thelicosan gunships that were peppering space with cannon fire.

Of course, Rogers didn't give all these orders directly. He used Zaz and Rholos, and just sort of started spouting random ideas at them and having *them* translate them into stuff that the rest of the fleet could use. Communications were still spotty, and he found that often large groups of his ships wouldn't get a particular message, but that just added to the chaos he was trying to create. Predictability was his enemy in this situation, and that strategy seemed to be working.

"My calculated probabilities of victory are shifting every moment," said Deet, who, for some reason, had taken to narrating the battle like a horse-race announcer, giving odds and trying to encourage members of the bridge to bet. Rogers had no idea where this had come from; perhaps Deet had been digesting human news reports or something.

"And they're off!" Deet said as the squadron of Ravagers that held the key to their victory—which also happened be the

Flagship's last reserve of fighters—came out of the hangar and shot straight toward the *Limiter*.

"How soon until they can fire?" Rogers asked Zaz.

Zaz looked at the screen, then thought for a moment. "At top speed, I would say six, seven minutes tops. If they get diverted because they have to dodge fire, though, it'll take them longer."

Rogers nodded. "See if you can get the *Rigor Mortis* and the *Valiant* to swing around to the flanks and start dumping cannon fire into the center. If we can keep a curtain in front of them the whole way it might keep them from having to divert."

"The *Rigor Mortis* won't budge," Rholos said. "Their engines are out."

"Damn it," Rogers said. "See who else we have in the area who can do it. Quinn, are you getting all this?"

Rogers thought he could hear the screams of people over the comm channel, and he couldn't help but wonder what that crazy woman was doing to all of them. Whoever she was, she was one tough bureaucrat.

"I'm getting it. I'll set the shields to drop in five. The window is only three minutes. Got it? I'm going to get to the bridge. Good luck."

Before Rogers could respond, the transmission cut out. Rogers wiped his hand across his forehead, and it came away slick with sweat and pastry cream. Deet had made a donut run down to the mess hall after realizing that he really didn't have much to do in a space combat situation. That level of uselessness/boredom might have encouraged his horse-race announcing, too.

"Grand Marshal," Rogers said over the comms, "take any of your ships that are close enough to the *Limiter* and start trying to clear a path in front of it. We'll try to open it up from the other side." He turned to Zaz. "I want everything we have focused on a point half a kilometer in front of that formation. If they get diverted by more than a few minutes, we'll have to win this the old-fashioned way."

"You're going to rape and pillage all the cities on Thelicosa?" Deet cried. "That's terrible!"

Rogers shot him a look. "Go get me another donut."

"[EXPLETIVE] your donut."

"I meant attrition," Rogers said. "And with Zergan in control, I have a feeling it'll be one of those dead-to-the-last-man kinds of things. I'd rather have Quinn 'take him out,' so let's make sure this happens."

"Yes, sir!" Zaz said.

"Yes, sir!" yelled Tunger.

"What are you doing here?" Rogers asked. "I don't think you can ride lions into this battle, unless you've developed some kind of lion VMU." He thought for a moment. "You haven't developed a lion VMU, have you?"

". . . Noooo . . ." Tunger said, not looking into Rogers' eyes and turning very red.

"No," Rogers said. "You are not allowed. Go back to the zoo. Zaz, how are we doing?"

Zaz pointed to the display, as he was currently in the middle of talking very excitedly into his headset, and Rogers saw the indicators start to swarm and converge on the wedge-shaped formation of which Flash was the head, carrying one of the last Lancers they had. That meant it was the Viking's turn.

"Patch me into the marines' ship," Rogers said.

The picture was much clearer thanks to the proximity of their shuttle, and Rogers was glad of it. Staring back at him was the shining face of the Viking, decked out in full raid gear, the scary-looking helmet adding lines to her face and making her look intense and beautiful. Rogers nearly forgot what he was going to say.

"What?" the Viking asked.

"Oh, um. Hi," Rogers said. "I was just checking in."

"We're flying through space," the Viking said.

"Yes, I know that," Rogers said, maybe sounding a little irritated. Couldn't she just say one nice thing to him? Ever since their awkward conversation in-line, it was like she'd become twice as cold as she used to be. She hadn't even threatened to physically harm him in at least a couple of hours. Rogers missed it.

"I was making sure you had everything you needed," he continued.

"Well, now is kind of a shit time to ask that question. We launched five minutes ago."

Rogers felt himself getting angry. "Fine," he said. "Just try not to bash Zergan's head in when you pick him up. I want to talk to him."

"Whatever," the Viking said, and the transmission cut out.

Rogers sat back in his chair and sighed.

"And the Viking delivers an absolutely *crushing* blow to the captain's ego!" Deet announced.

"Shut up," Rogers said. "You don't even know what an ego is."

"I know a wounded one when I see it," Deet said. He beeped and went to stand by Belgrave, who had become sort of his philosophy mentor. Rogers didn't like it.

Looking back up at the display, Rogers saw a mass of blue and red swirling around in a way that was—strangely, he understood—beautiful. The wide line of the Meridan fleet was starting to curl inward, and though he couldn't see a display of the actual guns firing, the view out the bridge window was enough to put any fireworks display to shame.

Except, you know. People were dying. Rogers tried not to think of that too much.

"Okay, everyone, this is it!" he shouted. "The *Limiter*'s shields and countermeasure systems are going to come down in less than a minute. Flash, are you ready?"

"Ready to serve up some pickles!" Flash's voice crackled over the radio.

"Remind me what that means?" Rogers asked Belgrave.

"Back on Earth the Nordic people used to throw pickles at enemy bombs to make them explode before they hit the ground."

Rogers squinted at him. "Are you sure that's what you told me last time?"

"Hey!" Flash said over the radio. "There's totally a Cosine right here that doesn't see me. Going in for the kill."

"No," Rogers said. "We talked about this. You're not out there to dogfight. You're out there to put one weapon on one target. You don't even have any missiles!"

"I wouldn't use 'em if I did, Skip!" Flash said. "Cannons are way flashier."

Flash broke from formation and deftly spaced one of his own Ravagers. The ejection pod fired, and the bridge went quiet.

"Splash one bandit!" Flash said over the radio.

"Please get our rescue crews ready," Rogers said quietly. "And find me the person who certified that idiot to fly combat missions."

"Admiral Klein, sir," Commander Zaz said.

"Yeah. Yeah, I figured. Now, Flash, can you *please* stop playing chase-the-shiny-object and get back on target? Bring up the *Limiter*'s battle specs on the screen."

Rogers stared at the display, awkwardly feeling like he was in a hospital room waiting for a patient to die. All sorts of measurements popped up on the screen, but he was paying particular attention to the shields. They couldn't monitor everything, of course, but the energy output of a deflection shield was strong enough to be read from a long distance—that was why most ships traveled with their shields down to avoid detection.

Rogers looked at the clock.

"Fifteen seconds, Flash. Are you ready to fire on the emergency system?"

"Copy that, Skip. A-firm."

The world seemed to stop as the wedge formation charged toward the *Limiter*. The rest of the Meridan formation was a complete and total mess, which made it very hard for the Thelicosans to counterattack, since Zergan was expecting the same formation that was in *The Art of War II*. Rogers wouldn't give it to him. He'd give him what Rogers was best at—a complete and utter mess.

"Shields down!" Commander Rholos said.

"Fire!" Rogers yelled.

"A whole container of spicy, thinly sliced deli *pickles*!" Flash said.

The whole bridge went silent.

"Does he have to say it like that?" Deet asked.

"Shh!" said everyone on the bridge.

Rogers didn't really know what he expected. This was a big moment, one with galactic consequences. But when the Lancer hit, all he saw was a little blip on the radar screen, and all he heard was a pleasant *ding*.

"Congratulations on disabling the enemy's capital ship!" came a voice from the console. "You're entitled to—"

"Shut up, Sara!" Rogers shouted. When he noticed everyone looking at him, he cleared his throat. "What? I think that's her actual name."

The irony of having a Snaggardir's employee congratulate him on stopping their plans was not lost on him, and Rogers didn't have to wait long for news of whether or not this had been worth it.

"Rogers! Rogers!" a voice came over the radio. It was Quinn, and the background noise sounded beyond intense. Shouting, guns firing. Someone might have been making popcorn. "The bridge is surrounded. I'm playing the message to the whole fleet now but I don't have time. Get your troops in here *now* or—"

Quinn didn't have to say any more. Rogers heard the sounds of a door crashing down, disruptor fire blasting through the speakers, and the Viking's combat yells shaking the ground. A few moments later, an eerie, crackling quiet was the only thing coming through the communications channel.

"Got him," the Viking said, rather anticlimactically, Rogers thought. "What do we do?"

"Captain Rogers." Keffoule's voice came over the console. "Edris is a former member of the F Sequence. Not only will the *Limiter*'s brig not hold him, he may have sympathizers who may help him escape. You need to bring him onto the *Flagship*, and he needs to be someplace where he can't use his training to escape."

Rogers thought for a moment. "I think I have the perfect place. Tunger, get Cadet the cat out of my old room for a while. I don't want him being influenced by our new guest. Oh, and Captain Alsinbury?"

"What?"

". . . See if you can bring back some of the *Limiter*'s toast."

Destinations to Which One Goes in a Hand Basket

The war was over. Well, in reality, they'd prevented it from ever starting, which, Rogers supposed, was better. Keffoule had been reinstalled as the commander of the *Limiter* and the Thelicosan fleet, and Flash was being court-martialed for multiple counts of reckless endangerment while simultaneously being awarded the Meridan Flying Ambiguous Nonreligious Symbol for his competency/psychosis in both his rescue of Rogers and the final assault on the *Limiter*. Of course, the court-martial would acquit him of charges based on combat performance, but there was still a process that Rogers had to follow.

Sitting on the commander's chair on the bridge munching on a piece of toast—god*damn* it was so good!—Rogers felt a little bit lost. Things were sort of moving automatically right now, and with all the momentum he'd gained through all this chaos, he really felt like he should be doing something.

Eating toast was doing something, though. And he had to admit, it was a good break from the insanity.

"Long-distance communications are almost up," S1C Brelle said. "Shouldn't be more than a few more minutes, sir."

"Thanks," Rogers said. "Prep a hail to Meridan HQ so that we can talk to them right away."

Space, outside the window of the bridge, was back to being a peaceful, beautiful place, if you discounted the fact that there was still an enormous "enemy" fleet within striking distance. Rogers could hardly count Grand Marshal Keffoule as an enemy anymore, though. Their parting had been brief and totally devoid of both marriage proposals and/or kicks to the face. In a weird way, Rogers was sad to see her go.

But it would be a cold day in hell before he admitted it to anyone. Especially to the Viking, who had been staring at him from the corner of the bridge for what seemed like the last four hours.

Marines. Can't live with 'em, can't board an enemy capital ship and kill people without 'em.

Rogers stood up and brushed the toast crumbs off his pants before walking over to where the Viking stood. Sergeant Mailn was close by, the two of them talking together quietly. The Viking, however, never took her eyes off Rogers. When he got close enough to hear anything, she elbowed Mailn and both of them looked at him innocently.

"Am I interrupting?" Rogers asked.

Sergeant Mailn shook her head. "Just reminiscing a bit. Looks like things are going to calm down a little bit around here."

"I wouldn't bet on it," Rogers said. "I think this is all part of something bigger. Who knows what HQ is going to say? I'll need my marines ready for whatever happens."

He wasn't totally sure where the encouraging words had come from, but, amazingly, both Mailn and the Viking seemed to stand up a little straighter. He cleared his throat, embarrassed by his own seriousness.

"You know, if Flash can't save the galaxy on his own, right?"

"That guy is an idiot," the Viking said. "I guess he did sort of do alright, though." She looked at Rogers squarely. "You did too, Rogers."

Rogers felt the heat rising in his cheeks. "I was just making things up as I went along."

"Improvising isn't a bad thing," the Viking said.

"I guess not," Rogers said.

They stood there awkwardly for a moment. Why had he even come over here? The Viking was just going to end up hitting him in the face, no matter what he did.

"Anyway," Mailn said. "I've got those things to take care of."

The Viking shot her a look. "What things?"

"You know," Mailn said. "The things. I'll catch you later, Captain Alsinbury."

Before the Viking could say anything else, Mailn was gone, hopping over a railing casually to get to the bridge door. Both the Viking and Rogers watched her go.

"So," Rogers said after a moment, scratching his beard. "I'm sure you've got some training to do, or whatever. I'll go, uh, run the fleet. Or something. I don't want to bother you."

He was halfway turned around when he felt a large bear latch on to his shoulder. After a moment, he realized it was just the Viking's hand, which slowly turned him around to face her. She looked a strange mix of concerned, confused, and Viking-like.

"Y-yes?" Rogers said. "Have I done something wrong? Please, my abs are sore, I can't duck anymore."

Letting go of his shoulder, the Viking sighed, which sounded something like all of the four winds having an argument.

"I don't want you to duck," the Viking said.

Rogers bristled. "Well, I'm not going to just *let* you hit me in the face."

The Viking's jaw tightened. "I don't want to hit you in the face, either, Rogers."

"Oh."

"And I want to say I'm sorry for making you think that those are the only two things we can do together."

Rogers' pulse quickened. "Oh?"

"Yeah."

They stared at each other for a long moment, Rogers unable to blink and the Viking apparently unable to continue speaking.

"So," Rogers said, "what . . . other things . . . could we do together?"

The Viking smacked her lips, her whole body tense. She was silent for what seemed like an eternity. Rogers felt like maybe she'd been lying about not wanting to punch him; she was never this tense for any other reason than her muscles bunching up to strike.

"Aw, hell," she said, so loudly that Rogers actually jumped. "I can't do this shit, Rogers. Mailn can take her advice and shove it. Let's you and me have a drink soon, alright? We can take it from there."

Rogers felt like a rainbow had just sprouted in the middle of his face and was shitting unicorns and flowers everywhere. The Viking had literally just asked him on a date. A real date. For reasons beyond understanding, he found himself laughing.

This was not the right choice of reaction, he understood very quickly.

"Well, if that's how it's going to be," the Viking said, "you can go f—"

"No, no," Rogers said, holding up a hand. A tear was actually running down the side of his face. "It's just so . . ." He searched for a word to describe what he was thinking, but nothing appropriate came to mind. "I would love to do that. We could maybe set a room on fire, and I could crawl under a beam, and—"

"Slow down, Skipper," the Viking said, but he could have sworn she was smiling. He didn't really know, because he wasn't totally sure he'd seen her do it before. "We'll work all that out later." She pointed over his shoulder back at the command platform. "You've got some shitty commander-ing that you have to go do first."

Rogers glanced back to see Deet and Belgrave, who appeared to be arguing over something Rogers couldn't discern. There was also a light blinking on his console, indicating that something or other needed his approval, or he was missing some communication. Sometimes duty really sucked.

"Yeah, alright," Rogers said, turning back to the Viking. "Slow down. Got it. But let's do it soon." He leaned in close and spoke softly. "The world could be ending."

"Wow," the Viking said, smirking. "That was pretty goddamn bad, Rogers." She slapped him on the back. "Pretty goddamn bad."

She walked off the bridge, leaving him in the middle of the collision of his fantasies and reality. Maybe he'd had his last ducking lesson with Mailn after all.

He walked over to the command dais to see what the hell these two idiots were so upset about.

Deet, omnipresent on the bridge now that he'd figured out all the workings of the droids, fell silent as Rogers approached.

"Rogers," he said. "I've been thinking."

"We've gone over this, Deet," Rogers said. "You don't really think. You process."

"Don't listen to him," Belgrave said. "Thought is a concept, not an action. *Cogito, ergo*—"

"Let's skip the Russian lesson," Rogers said. "I've had enough of Sun Tzu. What's on your CPU, Deet?"

Deet didn't answer for a moment, which always struck Rogers as odd. At least when humans were contemplating something they showed it on their face, or took a deep breath, or something. Deet just completely stopped moving and making noise, which was really weird.

"Now that I know who made me," Deet said, "I was thinking I would like to ask him some questions."

Rogers frowned. "Couldn't you just get a service manual or something? Besides, you don't really know who made you; you just know you were made by a subsidiary company to Snaggardir's."

"But there must be some sort of mastermind. Powerful artificial intelligence is a new thing, Rogers. I want to meet the man who thought of it."

Rubbing his beard, Rogers chomped down the last bit of toast left and picked a few crumbs off his face. AI wasn't exactly new, but Deet *was* different. He was able to teach himself, and not just by accruing data and running it through Boolean expressions. There really did seem to be a form of "thought" in there.

But that was the kind of deep philosophical stuff that Rogers really didn't like to think about. At least not without a copious amount of alcohol.

"Well, technically you're a piece of property of the Meridan government. If you were going to go anywhere, you'd have to either be defective or a third party would have to purchase you as salvage."

"I'm a person!" Deet said. "I'm not property!"

Rogers thought about that for a moment. This conversation was starting to make him feel uncomfortable, and he had general rules about avoiding discomfort.

"I'm not property either," he said, carefully avoiding expressing the fact that Deet was, in fact, property and not, in fact, a person. "But watch what happens if I just try to pick up and leave. They call that being AWOL."

"They threw me out, remember? I should have a disposal order somewhere in the system records. I'm not even really here. I'm just here doing you a favor because this whole ship would fall apart without me. But now that the battle is over, you don't need me anymore."

"A bunch of corrupt droids threw you out because you wouldn't conform to the idea of taking over the ship," Rogers corrected. "I get the feeling they weren't keeping records of that. We'll check it out, alright? I promise. But right now we sort of have bigger fish to fry."

"I thought you didn't like fish?" Deet asked.

"Expression. Starman Brelle, how are the comms?"

"All set, sir! Opening a channel now."

A few seconds later, the main display changed to a view that Rogers hadn't seen in a very long time. Well, he really hadn't seen it ever, except in pictures and videoconferences like this. It was Meridan Naval Headquarters, centered on Merida Prime in the second-largest city on the planet's surface. Most of Fortuna Stultus' planets had sparse continental living space, which scientists had always said was odd for planets that could support so much life.

The face that was staring back at him was that of High Admiral Holdt, who served as the naval representative to the Meridan Staff of Joint Representative Chiefs. His face showed the harsh wrinkles caused by years of dealing with the Meridan political machine, and right now his eyes looked sunken, red, and tired. What time was it over there? Had Rogers woken him up?

"Captain Rogers! Where the hell have you been?"

Not quite the greeting he'd hoped for.

"I've got a big report to make, sir," Rogers said.

"We don't have time for a big report. The galaxy has gone to shit, Captain. Do you have any idea what's been happening over here while you've been busy slacking off and not answering any of my messages?"

"No, but I can tell you what's been happening here," Rogers said, feeling a little insulted. "After an army of robots tried to take over my ship, we were attacked by a Jupiterian masquerading as a Thelicosan who tried to kill me no fewer than three times, right in the middle of their real commander trying to marry me. Sounds like a real picnic, right?"

Holdt appeared to be paying attention now. "Did you say Jupiterian? Oh shit. Rogers, Merida is the only system left that hasn't been infiltrated. We think it's because of your report on the droids—we shut them all down. But New Neptune, Thelicosa, and Grandelle are all torn to pieces. Half the damn military of all those systems has either defected or been taken over. Worse, Snaggardir's has shut down all its stores for some reason."

Rogers couldn't believe what he was hearing. "That's because Snaggardir's *is* Jupiter, Admiral. They've been running things while selling slushies and beef jerky for centuries. That's probably how they were able to fund everything they've been doing."

The admiral's eyes went wide. "Are you serious?"

"I have documentation to prove it," Rogers said. "I'll send everything I've collected as soon as we get off the comms."

"Good. Then set your course for home. Communication has been spotty, but we're recalling all our fleets and using Merida as our center for command. We'll work out a promotion for you, but for now you're no longer the acting commander of the 331st. You're the real, no-kidding commander."

"What? I thought you were sending us a new admiral to replace Klein!"

"We did, but he's dead. Flew into an asteroid."

Rogers closed his eyes. "I hate asteroids."

"Well, there you have it," Holdt said. "You have your orders. Get back here on the double, and get ready for a fight. Blockades have been popping up everywhere, and they know our tactics like they wrote the damn book."

"Yeah, I know," Rogers said dryly.

"Get back here fast, Rogers. We need every gun we can get."

"Yes, sir," Rogers said, and the transmission cut out.

The bridge was quiet. This was an absolute mess, and now *he* had to deal with it.

What had they been thinking during the War of Musical Chairs? You can't just displace an entire planet's worth of people and expect them to go away. And now he'd been eating their nachos his whole life.

He wondered if the Uncouth Corkscrew had any nachos today.

Focus!

"Alright, everyone, you heard the admiral. Issue a general order to the fleet that we're preparing to move. And . . ."

He thought for a moment. If he was going to do this, he was going to need as much help as he could get.

"Send a hail to the *Limiter*."

"Yes, sir," S1C Brelle said, and began pressing buttons.

Rogers wanted time to think about what had just happened, but a moment later, the Thelicosan Grand Marshal's voice came through the speakers.

"Yes?" Keffoule said. Her voice was cold, distant. "I thought our business had been concluded, Captain Rogers."

"Well, we've got a problem. Feel like taking a space cruise?"

The line was silent for a moment. "Does this mean you've changed your mind?"

"No," Rogers said. "That's not a euphemism. I'm asking you if you want to go fight a war with me."

He could hear the tapping of Keffoule's fingernails on the other end of the communications channel. She had to know that her own fleet was against her now. Who knew how much Snaggardir's had infiltrated?

"Well," Keffoule said, "it's not what I was aiming for, but I suppose I'll have to take what I can get." She paused for a moment, her voice softening. "Have you talked to Edris yet? He may . . . know some things."

Zergan was still unconscious—whatever the Viking had done to him had been pretty effective, apparently—and floating weightlessly in Rogers' old stateroom. They'd made sure to place him in the very center of the room and keep the ship's inertia under strict control. It would be nearly impossible for him to move around the room, never mind escape, once he woke up.

But once he did, Rogers had a million questions for him. He was sure Zergan wouldn't talk right away, of course, and Meridan law specifically prohibited torture of any kind, but Rogers had plans. The first thing he was going to do was put Zergan in the same room as Tunger; Rogers had a feeling Zergan would be singing like a bird after not very long.

"I haven't," Rogers admitted. "But I suppose now is as good a time as any." He turned around and shouted to no one in particular to go do their best to wake Zergan up and prepare him for interrogation. A few troops ran out of the bridge to carry out his order.

"When do we leave?" Keffoule said through the comm line.

"Now. Get your fleet ready for a tough run back to Merida Prime. I'll have Starman Brelle here send you the details."

"Fine," Keffoule said. "I'll follow your lead, *Captain* Rogers."

God, how could a woman make a rank sound sexual? It was going to be a "tough run" for more reasons than just hordes of Jupiterians standing in their way.

Rogers just sighed and closed the channel.

"Alright, let's get ready to talk to our guest in the zero-g room," he said. "Is he ready yet? We can—"

"Sir! Sir!"

The bridge door opened and in ran a young marine whom Rogers recognized as one of the two guards who had been posted outside Zergan's door. That didn't give him a good feeling.

"What is it?" Rogers asked. "And what did I tell you people about the double 'sir'?"

"It's the enemy commander," the young marine said, his face white. "He's . . . he's dead!"

Rogers goggled, his mouth open. "What? When? How?"

"Sir . . . he hanged himself."

THE [E X P L E T I V E] E N D

Acknowledgments

For every book in this world, there's a team of really tired people in the background who may or may not have been drinking. This book wouldn't have been possible without my editorial team at Saga, my wonderful agents at JABberwocky, and all my early readers. Together you all helped me shape this story.

To America: Thanks for the job security and for helping me Make Satire Great Again.